The Pirates of the Sea of Cortés

A novel

by

Maurice Azurdia

Maurice Azurdia

The Pirates of the Sea of Cortés

Maurice Azurdia is a retired airline pilot, adventurer and novelist. He is the author of e-a Novel and The Fourth Stripe.

BOOKS BY MAURICE AZURDIA

The Pirates of The Sea of Cortés

e-A Novel

The Fourth Stripe

The Pirates of the Sea of Cortés

Maurice Azurdia

First Cyber Rose Design LLC Paperback Edition
DECEMBER 2020

Copyright ©2020 by Maurice Azurdia.

All Rights Reserved. Published in the United States of America by Cyber Rose Design LLC, Phoenix, Arizona.

The Cataloging-in-Publication Data is on file at Library of Congress.

ISBN: 978-0-9981342-7-7

For my daughters Leslie and Adrienne.
I am proud of you.

Mar de Cortés Foreboding

Oh, Mar de Cortés your wealth and beauty is legend
Such sweet temptation thou dost proffer me
Your altruism might almost satisfy my constant need
If I were not human born to live and breathe
I take more than my fill yet you provide without question
Like two lovers we lie together in sweet embrace
Please be careful my darling as you sate my hunger
For one day my greed will be your undoing

John Murray

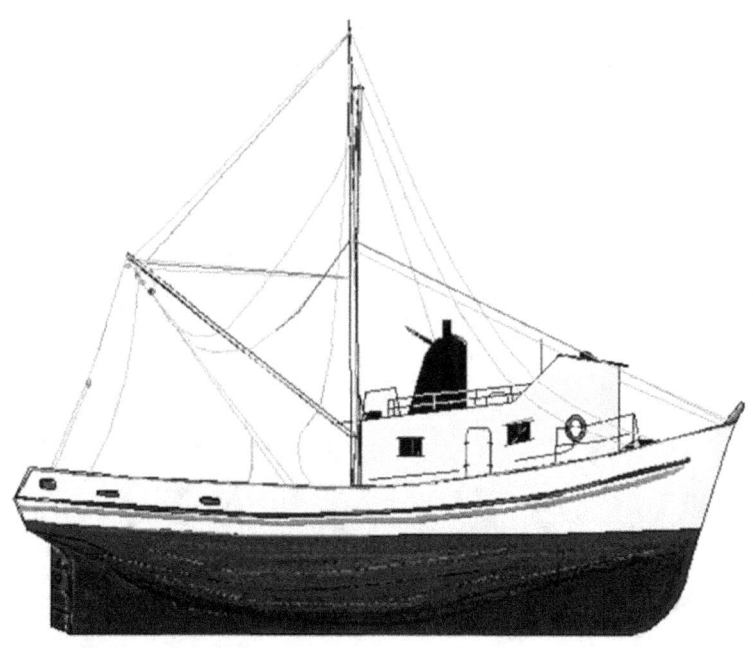

Trawl'er (-ê), n. A person or craft that fishes or dredges by trawling.

Trawl'ing v. To fish or catch with a large bag net dragged at the bottom in seafishing.

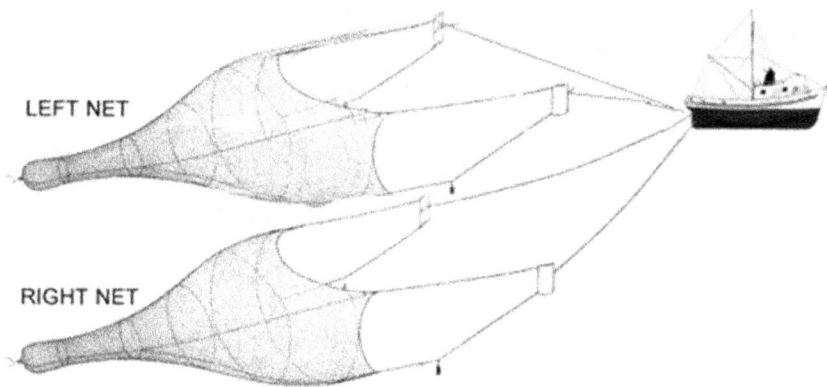

LEFT NET

RIGHT NET

Shrimp trawler with two nets

1

Somewhere in the Sea of Cortés, Mexico.

Capitán Ernesto Molinar glanced at the screen of the 7-inch color Garmin Global Positioning System mounted in front of him. The GPS showed their position nearly twenty miles south of Kino Bay.

Two hours, tops.

He had the 540-horsepower Caterpillar engine on his shrimp boat wide open, although his trawler was not built for speed. It was built to drag heavy nets along the floor of the sea while capturing shrimp, and the best it could give him was ten knots balls-to-the-wall. Ten knots would have to do.

Fifty-three-year-old *Capitán* Molinar had been up all night and was tired, he and his crew of six had been fishing from sunset to dawn. These first few days of the season were so important, the days which could make or break a fishing operation. Despite the light haze enveloping his brain due to being drunk from fatigue, Molinar couldn't help but smile. God had been generous to them the previous two nights. They had at least three tons of magnificent Blue shrimp onboard, a very good start to the shrimping season. Over sixty crates of beautiful export-quality frozen shrimp in his cargo hold.

After fishing all night, the shrimp boat and her crew would normally drop anchor and the sailors would all hit their bunks for some well-deserved sleep. Shrimp in the Sea of Cortés was only caught at night, so the three-hundred plus shrimp trawlers fishing the Sea could be found at anchor during the daylight hours, all along the east side of the peninsula of Baja California.

Capitán Molinar could've just dropped anchor out at sea around the area where they'd been fishing during the night, but had he chosen to remain in the area, it would have presented two distinct disadvantages. In the first place, it would pinpoint to the other shrimp boats fishing in the area the precise location of good fishing grounds, and shrimp boat captains were not in the habit of giving away the location of a good catch to other captains. In the second place, shrimp boat captains routinely helped themselves to some of the product they caught and sold it furtively to black market buyers, using the cash proceeds to supplement their incomes and purchase prostitutes, liquor and drugs for themselves and their crews.

No better place to peddle some of the product than Kino Bay. So, that's where they were headed.

"How much longer till we arrive, Cap?" Lalo, the first mate, was sitting on the rear window sill of the small wheelhouse aboard the *Concepción*. The temperature in the small wooden bridge was already well above one hundred degrees at seven in the morning.

"About two hours," *Capitán* Molinar responded. His mouth was dry and he wasn't much in the mood for talking.

The outline of the east coast of the Sea of Cortés was clearly visible in the distance, to starboard, as the *Concepción* steamed northbound. The Sonoran Desert around those parts was more of a pinkish lunar landscape than a green tropical one, though the prevalent high ambient temperatures were more reminiscing of the planet Mars.

"Miguel's cooking breakfast for the guys. He made *chilaquiles*, scrambled eggs and black beans. Want me to bring you some?" The first mate didn't have any duties to perform at that time, other than sit behind the Skipper providing a second pair of eyes to scan the sea.

"Naw, thanks. No breakfast. Did he make any coffee?"

"Yea, want some?"

"Bring me some coffee."

The first mate disappeared down a small door in the back of the bridge. The air smelled strongly of salt and diesel fumes.

The men would be fed and rested by the time they arrived at Kino Bay.

Kino Bay, a small town in Mexico, on the east side of the Sea of Cortés, was named after Father Eusebio Kino, a Jesuit priest who explored that area of

Mexico during the 17th Century. The town had no harbor or port facilities, and all fishing activities were conducted right off the beaches south of town. The shrimp boats at anchor several hundred yards from shore used the small skiffs they carried to unload shrimp and take the sailors into town for women, tequila, pulque and mescal.

Lalo, the first mate reappeared on the bridge, handing his captain an enameled blue metal cup with very black, very hot coffee.

"Thank you," *Capitán* Molinar grunted. The aroma of the hot coffee penetrated the mental fog induced by fatigue and the old sailor smiled, sipping the aromatic brew carefully, so as not to scald his lips or tongue. At fifty-three, *Capitán* Molinar held a coveted position in that area of the world.

He was a shrimp boat captain.

Although the fishing season wasn't going to last all year, he'd make enough money during the three months he was allowed to fish to live very well the rest of the year. And with over three tons of top-quality Blue shrimp in the hold only five days into the season, it was looking to be a very good season, indeed.

The old-timer scanned the sea ahead with the practiced eye of the mariner. The grizzled sailor didn't just sweep his gaze across the horizon, but actually allowed his eyes to focus one thirty-degree sector at a time, pausing two or three seconds before moving on to the next sector. If he just swept his gaze across the horizon without stopping, the physiology of the human eye was such that he was bound to miss a target ahead.

Something was out there.

Capitán Molinar squinted his eyes, trying to focus on a black dot that had appeared in the distance ahead and to starboard. He ran his hand over his eyes, wiping the sweat he'd already built up.

"Pass me the binoculars," he pointed to a set of grease-smeared yellow Barska marine binoculars resting on the panel next to the helm.

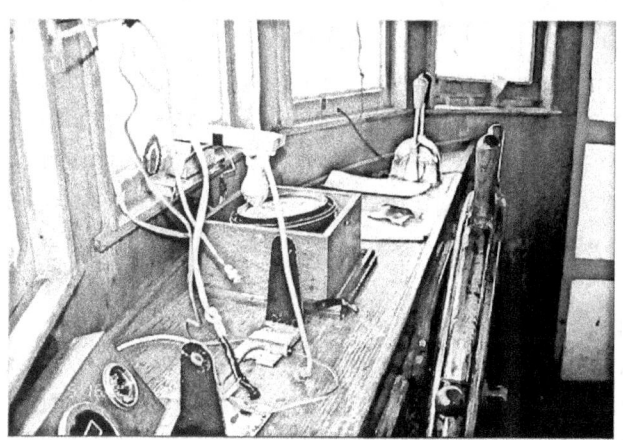

The first mate stood, stretching his neck in an effort to detect whatever it was that had caught *Capitán* Molinar's attention. Nothing was readily visible to the naked eye. He handed the heavy yellow binoculars to his Skipper.

Capitán Molinar accepted the binoculars, lifting them to his face, directing them toward the black dot he'd detected in the distance. "Looks like a *panga*," he voiced after a moment.

His first mate still couldn't see anything, although searching in the same general direction where the binoculars were pointing. "A *panga*?"

The *panga* was a small open boat, powered by outboards and commonly used in Mexico and other countries for fishing, transportation and in some cases, piracy. *Pangas* were normally operated directly from beaches, were between twenty and thirty feet in length, and were capable of traveling at speeds in excess of forty miles per hour. Faster, if the owners were involved in questionable activities such as smuggling and they saw fit to add additional outboards.

"Yes, a *panga*. Probably out fishing." Shrimp boat captains did not like *pangas*. These small skiffs represented a threat to their livelihood. Thousands of these *pangas* fished illegally in the swallow waters near the coastlines all year round, catching shrimp during those months when fishing was prohibited by the Mexican government. The months without the letter "r" were those months when shrimp reproduced, May, June, July and August. During those months, commercial fishing was prohibited and, at least theoretically be shut down in order to allow the shrimp to reproduce.

Considering that one single female shrimp could produce more than 600,000 eggs, it was easily appreciated that capturing female shrimp during the reproduction months could create a real problem for the fishing industry. Yet, that made absolutely no difference to the uneducated fishermen who made their living operating modest *pangas*. They fished all year round in the shallow waters near the coast, using hand-flung nets, and couldn't care less about the reproductory cycle of the shrimp, the Mexican government, or the law. The product was there, they needed to feed their families and hence, they caught it. And damned anyone who tried stopping them.

Two or three of these illegal operations were not a threat to anyone, merely some poor fishermen trying to feed their families. But rumor had it that the number of *pangas* in the Sea of Cortés had increased to over 100,000 in recent years. That number of illegal fishermen depleting the pregnant shrimp population was a definite threat to the owners and operators of the commercial shrimp fleet.

Shrimp boat captains did not like *pangas*.

"Looks like it's two of them," *Capitán* Molinar said more to himself than for the benefit of his first mate.

"I see it now!" Lalo, his first mate, exclaimed.

"Can't tell which way they're going," the old salt added. He kept the yellow Barska binoculars trained on the target. It was unusual for *pangas* to venture too far from shore. Generally, they fished near the beach, using nets to capture shrimp which, during the beginning of the season, reproduced in the shallow waters near land. As the season progressed into the months of November and December, the shrimp would move offshore into deeper waters, placing themselves out of the reach of most *pangas*. It was then that shrimp boats such as the *Concepción* could make a profit, dragging their enormous nets along the bottom of the sea, at depths which were out of reach for the *pangas*.

Since anyone wanting to travel by *panga* would generally stay close to shore, it was rather odd, seeing those skiffs out at sea.

Five more minutes passed.

"It seems that those *cabrones* are headed in this direction," *Capitán* Molinar remarked. The fact that the target kept increasing in size clearly indicated that his shrimp boat and the *pangas* were closing in on each other.

"Maybe it's the whores," Lalo, the first mate offered. *Pangas* were used by many enterprising young men to make a profit selling prostitutes, tequila and marijuana to the anchored crews during the day. The 'goods' were transported out to the shrimp boats and the products and services were bartered in exchange for shrimp.

A great disservice to the owners of the shrimp boats, that much was obvious, but the crews couldn't care less.

Fringe benefits.

Running into some very motivated entrepreneur was not unheard of. Some of these rather primitive businessmen had initiative, deciding to get a jump on the competition by steaming out to meet the shrimp boats as they converged towards Kino Bay,

Providing the fishermen with prostitutes, booze and drugs was very lucrative, and if some ships could be approached before they dropped anchor, so much the better.

"Yeah, maybe it's the whores," *Capitán* Molinar agreed. His powerful binoculars were now showing him the target was not one *panga,* but three. And they definitely were headed toward him. What the hell.

Capitán Molinar was definitely fatigued but, even then, his tired mind was searching for possible explanations for three pangas to be this far out at sea, racing towards the *Concepción.*

He placed his cup of coffee down on the panel. "Lalo, go back downstairs and get me the carbine."

His first mate couldn't have been more surprised. "The carbine? Why? What'd ya think is happening?"

"Just bring me the goddamned thing!"

"Of course," the first mate rapidly disappeared down into the cabin again.

They could be drug runners, *Capitán* Molinar pondered, but that seemed unlikely, seeing how they were southbound. If they were running drugs, they'd be steaming north, towards Rio Colorado and the United States.

Contrary to what his first mate thought, if a whore *panga* was involved, it would involve only one *panga*, not three.   So, who else could be headed toward his ship?

The first mate reappeared alongside *Capitán* Molinar, carrying a Korean War vintage M1 carbine. Weapons of any sort were strictly forbidden onboard shrimp boats by regulations of the Mexican Navy, under penalty of confiscation of the boat, but *Capitán* Molinar didn't give a damn. The *Concepción* was not his; it belonged to Don Carlos Esquivel, so if the ship were to be impounded by the Mexican Navy, it would be no loss to him other than that of his job.

If anyone was going to hurt him or his crew, however, he had to have *some* means of defending the ship. Consequently, Capitán Molinar disobeyed the laws of the sea and always had available the Korean relic. In his opinion, he could always get out of jail but he could not get out of a hole in the ground.

"Thank you," he offered, receiving the carbine. His first mate also handed him a metal magazine holding 15-rounds. Not that there was any real reason to expect trouble though, but one never knew, and it was always better to solve situations from behind the business end of a gun.

The captain inserted the magazine, chambered one round, and leaned the carbine against the panel in front of him. He raised the binoculars to his face once more. "Go wake the men," he ordered.

Ten minutes later, three white *pangas* approached the *Concepción*, reducing speed as their distance closed to within fifty yards. The sound of their outboards could now be heard very clearly.

"*Mierda!*" Capitán Molinar shouted. "Those assholes are armed!" He could clearly see five or so men in each *panga* and they appeared to be carrying guns. Long guns. Rapidly counting, he realized they were facing at least a dozen weapons of God-knew what type. The *pangas* were too close and rolling in the seas, making visual contact difficult through the binocs.

One of the *pangas* approached within ten yards, its engine barely over idle. The men in it wore black ski masks,

Capitán Molinar felt his stomach clench.

"*You, on the ship, stop your engine!*" the voice boomed over the morning air. One of the men on the panga was holding a megaphone.

"*Stop the engine immediately and we won't hurt you!*"

With over three tons of beautiful Blue shrimp onboard the *Concepción*, *Capitán* Molinar knew in an instant what those bastards wanted.

They wanted *his* shrimp.

He briefly considered shooting the man with his carbine, then immediately discarded the idea. One against twelve? No way. And he wasn't such a good shot, anyway. The price of ammunition for the carbine was high and, although he'd intended to go target shooting in the desert to get good with the gun, he'd never done it because of the cost involved. Ammunition wasn't cheap.

"I'm ordering you to kill your engine now! Obey or we will shoot! We don't want to hurt you; we just want your shrimp!"

All six members of his crew were now awake and packed together in the small bridge, watching in horror as the pangas approached.

Capitán Molinar made a decision. He was not going to place his crew at risk. Reaching for the throttle he pulled it back to idle, allowing the *Concepción* to slow. "Hide this down below," he ordered his first mate, handing him the carbine, keeping it low and out of sight from the pangas.

The man with the megaphone signaled for his buddy controlling the outboard to get moving and the panga nudged closer to the *Concepción*.

The seas were very calm and the air temperature was already at 105. The leading *panga* paralleled the *Concepción* on its starboard side and four rough men rapidly boarded the shrimp boat. All wore black ski masks and carried what appeared to be AK-47 assault weapons, known in Mexican slang as *cuerno de chivo*, meaning "ram's horn," in reference to the shape of its curved ammunition magazine.

Capitán Molinar immediately recognized the AK-47s, mentally congratulating himself for not having used his carbine. Twelve of those guns returning fire would have made shreds of everyone aboard.

A second *panga* approached the *Concepción* from the port side, allowing more men to board. One of the *panga* men, a big guy with an enormous belly and a pistol strapped to his belt, approached the bridge from behind. "Come outside! All of you, now!"

Capitán Molinar and his crew began walking out from the bridge, through the doors on either side, slowly heading towards the stern.

"Down into the engine room!" the *panga* man shouted. He'd removed his pistol from the holster and was weaving it menacingly at the fishermen.

The design of the *Concepción* had the engine room located in the front of the ship, with a very long shaft running the length of the boat connecting the engine to the propeller. The cargo hold was in the back of the ship, the design intended to prevent the precious shrimp from suffering contamination from oil or diesel emanating from the engine room.

The engine room and the cargo hold could only be accessed through two separate deck hatches big enough to fit one man at a time. The 75-foot *Concepción* was built entirely of steel, and its hatch covers were also constructed of half-inch thick metal plate.

The crew headed towards the bow, visibly frightened by the armed men, descending one by one into the engine room of the 125-ton ship.

"What're you gonna do?" *Capitán* Molinar asked the armed man in front of him.

"What the hell do you think we're gonna do, old man? We're gonna take your shrimp, that's what we're gonna do! Now get your ass down there with the rest of your crew before I shoot you!" The panga man swung his AK-47 menacingly at the captain in one rapid motion, pushing the nuzzle of the weapon against the man's chest.

Capitán Molinar caught a glimpse of the back of his ship, where some of the pirates had already opened the cargo hold hatch and were passing up red and green plastic crates full of frozen shrimp.

His shrimp.

He greeted his teeth, walking away toward the engine room hatch, descending into the belly of his ship. No sooner had he reached the bottom of the ladder when the hatch was closed above him and his men with a loud metallic clang. Then they all heard the latches being thrown, indicating that the hatch had been locked from above.

Not really a problem, he knew, since the hatch had handles which would permit the crew to open it from inside once the pirates left.

"Who are those sonsofbitches?" a sailor asked.

"Yeah, who are those *cabrones*," another voiced. The temperature inside the engine room was approaching 120 degrees.

"Shut down the engine!" *Capitán* Molinar ordered. His engine man, Esteban, rapidly hit the cutoff switch, effectively shutting off the flow of diesel to the powerful Marine Caterpillar engine. The men were perspiring copiously, having to wipe the sweat away from their faces every few seconds. The engine room was constructed entirely of metal, with no windows and no other exits except for the overhead hatch the men had used to enter. Two bare 100-Watt light bulbs hanging from the ceiling provided illumination. The light bulbs were powered directly from the batteries, so the engine generator shutting down did not affect them.

"These bastards are pirates," *Capitán* Molinar roared. "They are nothing more than fucking pirates. They're stealing our shrimp at this very moment."

The crew echoed his announcement with a barrage of profanity and resentment directed at the men outside.

"Why don't we go outside and kick the shit outta them?"

"Yeah, we can't let them rob us like this!"

"Why did we stop, couldn't we just have ignored them?"

Capitán Molinar shouted louder than the rest. "Quiet, goddammit! We're gonna get out of this but we need to keep our cool. And no, we're not going to fight these assholes, in case you didn't notice, they're carrying assault rifles. We don't have a chance against them. They're just gonna take the shrimp and that's that. Nothing we can do about it. We'll just have to fish harder the next few nights to recover the shrimp they're stealing."

"How can they take our three tons of shrimp on a couple of pangas? There's no way they will be able to fit our shrimp in their *pangas*."

"Eduardo," *Capitán* Molinar explained, "they have three *pangas*, and each can easily carry one ton."

The engine had quit, but the residual heat from the metal was dissipating into the engine room with loud hissing sounds, further aggravating the situation for the fishermen.

"Everybody here?" *Capitán* Molinar was perspiring copiously, just like the rest of his men. He could feel the back of his shirt glued to his body.

"Everyone's here," Lalo, the first mate reported.

"Anybody have any water?" *Capitán* Molinar asked.

Heads shook around the engine room.

"Anybody have any weapons? Knives? Anything?"

The men quieted down. Nobody had weapons, nor water.

The metal construction of the ship prevented sounds from carrying too far. Consequently, the noise generated by the pirates offloading the shrimp into their pangas was totally muffled and none of it could be heard below decks.

Capitán Molinar analyzed their situation with concern. The temperature in the engine room was climbing, and as the morning progressed it was bound to get worse. Daily temperatures these days could climb as high as 119 degrees in the shade in this area of the world, which meant that, inside the metal hull of the *Concepción,* the engine room would easily reach 140 degrees or thereabouts.

Not a good prospect. Especially without water.

It was a race against time. The longer the pirates took to depart, the hotter it would become in the engine room. The engine heat was rapidly dissipating into the tight quarters, superheating the air even more. Not that there was much they could do, anyway. They just had to bid their time and go outside after enough time had passed so the pirates would be gone.

Capitán Molinar thought about the $57,000 pesos, nearly three thousand dollars that he would have earned had he delivered the three tons of shrimp the pirates were removing from his ship. In his hometown that sum made him a very wealthy man. His wife, Lupe, would've been very happy hearing that the first few days of the season had turned out so well.

What the devil! No use being upset: at least they hadn't gotten shot.

Time passed with painful slowness. First one hour. The temperature inside the engine room kept climbing, making respiration difficult. Then a second hour. The men were scattered along the floor of the engine room, trying to move as little as possible in order to minimize the generation of body heat. The exhaustion from lack of sleep combined with the heat was making the men all very lethargic.

After what seemed like the third hour, *Capitán* Molinar decided it was time to take a peek. If those bastards were still on deck, what would they do if they saw the engine room hatch opening? Would they open fire and shoot all of them?

Maybe.

He considered waiting another hour, but the heat in the engine room had become too extreme to ignore. They had to go outside.

"Let's go see if these sonsabitches are gone." He stood, heading for the ladder. The rest of the men stirred and slowly began getting to their feet. The air was horribly hot and putrid.

Capitán Molinar made his way to the ladder, slowly pulling himself upward until his hand reached the handles on the inside of the latch. Holding on to the ladder with one hand, he pulled hard to release the door mechanism.

The handle didn't budge.

"*What the fuck...*" He applied more force to the handle.

Nothing.

Capitán Molinar began to panic, feeling a knot rising in his throat. He pulled again.

The metal handle did not move even a fraction of an inch.

"*Sonofabitch!*"

The men had increasingly worried expressions.

"It's not opening?"

"*Capitán*, do you need some help?"

Capitán Molinar put his entire weight behind a powerful pull.

Again, nothing.

"These sonsabitches locked the door with something from the outside!"

The men grew increasingly vocal.

"Locked the door? How!?"

Capitán Molinar descended into the engine room. "Go ahead, try it. All of you, give that hatch a shot. I don't know what the hell the problem is, but I'm gonna find out."

The men took turns ascending the ladder, attempting to open the latch. Not one could budge it. Panic began manifesting its ugly presence among the sailors.

"They locked us in!"

"Oh God, *we're gonna die!*"

Capitán Molinar leaned against the metal wall of the engine room. He focused on the light bulbs. How long would those continue to function before the batteries died? The engine room would be in total darkness without the bulbs, since there was no other way for light to enter.

The walls of the engine room were an integral part of the hull, made of one-inch thick steel plate. There was absolutely no way in hell they'd be able to cut their way out. The men would have to concentrate their efforts on the hatch that was their only hope.

"Machinist!" *Capitán* Molinar shouted, "show me what tools you have down here!"

The air temperature inside the engine room had reached 122 degrees and was still climbing. The small room had become saturated with water vapor from the perspiration of the men, rendering the air unable to hold additional moisture.

A human steam bath.

Breathing was becoming very uncomfortable. With each lungful of hot air, the men became more frantic. The meaning of it was simple: from that point on, any sweat produced by the men would simply not evaporate, negating the cooling effect that perspiration provides when it evaporates. The sweat would simply condense into drops and remain on the skin of the unfortunate sailors.

Physiologic responses to heat include an increase in cardiac output and blood flow to the skin, which is the major heat-dissipating organ; dilatation of the peripheral venous system; and stimulation of the endocrine sweat glands to produce more sweat.

The skin can transfer heat to the environment through evaporation. At high temperatures the most effective mechanism for heat loss is evaporation, which refers to the conversion of a liquid to a gaseous phase.

The process of evaporation consumes energy. This energy is taken from the human body, inducing a temperature drop, which refreshes the body.

Unfortunately for the men trapped in the engine room, once the humidity content of the air reached around 75%, the air became saturated and, therefore, unable to hold additional moisture. For all practical purposes, this prevented any further cooling effect on the skin of the men.

The temperature of the bodies of the sailors trapped in the engine room of the shrimp boat approached one hundred and four degrees. Once their bodies reached such extreme temperatures, the men began suffering from hyperthermia. First, they experienced a rapid, strong pulse with a throbbing headache. Some of the men succumbed to nausea and began to vomit. One by one, the sailors became confused; they collapsed and began to lose consciousness.

Heat stroke was setting in on the crew of the *Concepción*.

On a cellular level, heat directly influences the body by interfering with cellular activity. If the heat continues unchecked, the cell will succumb and die. A victim of heat stroke will die within minutes if proper medical treatment is not procured immediately.

The crew members trapped in the engine room had no hope of receiving proper medical treatment anytime soon.

Capitán Molinar was older than the rest of his crew, but he was strong as a bull. Sweat poured down over his eyebrows, eyelids and past his eyes. He observed his men attempting to yank the hatch free from whatever was holding it locked, to no avail. His thinking had slowed to a crawl. His ears were ringing. That amazed him. And in such a short time! It really felt like a six-Corona buzz. He crouched down on one knee. His breathing had become laborious and he was breathing in short gasps, not unlike a future mother practicing Lamaze. He wiped the perspiration from his eyes, glancing around at his men. Four had already tumbled to the floor, but he wasn't sure whether they were resting or had passed out. Heat exhaustion, he thought. Just short of heat stroke. He wondered if he should just lie down and take a brief nap. Perhaps eventually, someone would come and rescue them. If he took a quick power nap, nothing bad could really happen, could it? If they didn't exert themselves, they could probably last for days or at least until another shrimp boat spotted them and came over to investigate. Hell, the light bulbs hanging from the ceiling could last for days powered by the huge batteries.

Once a person's core temperature climbs above 104 degrees, that individual is in serious danger. High internal temperatures lead to increased pressure in the skull, and decreased blood flow to the brain. Doctors generally diagnose "heatstroke" when the heat starts to affect the central nervous system. Additionally, extreme heat damages tissue in different areas of the body, and this tissue may also enter the bloodstream and lead to rapid kidney failure. Very high internal temperatures above 120 degrees literally destroy cells in the body through direct heat damage in a matter of minutes.

Capitán Molinar finally decided to lean against the side of the hull and perhaps allow himself to catch a very short nap. He was no longer hot nor anxious. What could it hurt for him to take a quick nap? They weren't going to be able to open the hatch, anyway. Not until some other crew came by to help. He might as well take a quick snooze. A short nap wouldn't hurt anything; they all might as well enjoy a siesta until their rescuers appeared.

Lalo Guero, at nineteen the youngest member of the crew, finally accepted the reality they were not going to be able to force the hatch open. He watched the captain and the other seven sailors wrestle the latch with no success. There was no other way out of the engine room and, although the young fisherman had no formal education, he was smart enough to realize the heat in the engine room would eventually kill all of them if they didn't take some kind of action. He pulled his Samsung Galaxy smartphone from his pocket. It still contained a good charge, although the signal icon was not showing any bars at all.

No signal.

Of course, there'd be no signal down in the engine room. The entire ship was metal. *Gawd*, if he could only get a signal and call his brother who lived in Kino Bay. Lalo would ask his brother to jump on a panga with a good outboard motor and head out to help. Lalo was from a poor family, yet he'd worked construction for months before the start of the fishing season to purchase his cellphone.

Which now was totally useless.

The young seaman rested his back against the metal hull of the shrimp boat, staring at the big diesel engine. He studied the engine. At least, thank God, the exhaust fumes from the engine were not being vented into the engine room. That surely would've have killed them all by now. He observed the exhaust manifold, following it with his eyes. The manifold converged into a funnel, a chimney venting to the outside world.

An idea suddenly came to him. Guero stood, looking for the engine room mechanic. "Chavo!" He cried out. "Chavo, do you have any copper wire down here?"

One of the older sailors leaning against the hull slowly opened his eyes. "What?"

"Your copper wire man, do you have any of it down here?"

The mechanic pointed to his tool box. "Ya, in the box."

Guero clambered over the sprawled limbs of his shipmates to reach the mechanic's toolbox. Opening it, he became deliriously happy to find a big coil of copper wire. Hundreds of feet of beautiful, shiny copper wire.

Thank you, God.

He retrieved the copper wire and a small saw. "I'm gonna save us all," the young sailor announced. He stood next to the engine, touching the funnel connecting the engine exhaust to the outside world. It was too hot to touch.

No matter, he had to do it.

Guero used the saw to cut into the exhaust funnel. Ten minutes later he was exhausted, sweating profusely and barely able to talk, but he'd cut an opening in the funnel wide enough to thread the copper wire through it.

The youngest man in the crew pushed several yards of copper wire up into the stack, then snipped the wire with a pair of cutters. Guero then stuck the end of the copper wire into the headset jack in his cellphone.

The signal icon glared back at him with two out of four bars announcing the presence of a signal.

There was a God.

2

Overlooking the Sea of Cortés

Christian Gibson sipped from the large glass of freshly-squeezed orange juice, admiring the view ahead. The waters of the Sea of Cortés offered a beautiful combination of Baby Blue and Cerulean Blue.

"This is life!" he exclaimed, enjoying the moment.

"Yes, it is," Elaine agreed. His very beautiful wife of fifteen years was his traveling companion and everlasting friend.

They'd been on a short three-day vacation in the small fishing village of Rock Port, in the northernmost part of the Sea of Cortés, or Gulf of California, as some preferred.

Having lived in Arizona over ten years, this had been the family's first chance to visit the enchanting fishermen's village, four-hour drive south of Phoenix. The two of them and their two young daughters had thoroughly enjoyed the visit, and now, preparing for the drive back home, Elaine had investigated where to go for a good Mexican breakfast, her natural curiosity paying off. One of the locals had suggested the Playa Encanto Hotel, located ten minutes from the little house where they'd spent the previous three days.

The family drove to the hotel on their way out of town and discovered a welcoming outdoor restaurant overlooking the sea, where they enjoyed a delicious breakfast of *huevos rancheros* with all the trimmings. All of them, of course, except the youngest, who hated eggs and enjoyed hot pancakes, instead.

"Well, the girls and I are definitely sold on this place. How about you?" Elaine was in her late forties, a slim, attractive brunette with captivating blue eyes. In her professional life she had been a very successful computer Systems Engineer and a respected manager for a computer company in Los Angeles. She also had a Bachelor of Arts degree, so she was that rare combination of intellect, looks, precision and art knowledge.

"Definitely," Christian agreed. "We're coming back here first chance we get."

A waiter in his late twenties dressed in white pants and a starched white short-sleeved shirt approached their table. The service had been absolutely splendid. "May I get you anything else, *señor*? Some coffee? Another orange juice?"

The waiter addressed them in Spanish, which was not really an obstacle, since Christian was fully fluent. Having grown up in the Canal Zone, in

Panama, Spanish had easily become his second language.

Christian quickly eyed the juice glasses and the empty plates on the table. "Girls, do you want anything else? Some dessert?"

His three women turned down any request for additional food.

"I'll have a coffee, please. Decaf." Elaine interjected.

"*Un café decaf, por favor,*" Christian relayed to the waiter. In Mexico, it was customary for the man of the table to speak to the waiter. Any women at the table would pass their wishes to their man, who would in turn order. This custom was to prevent women from speaking directly to the waiters. Old cultural traditions likely dating back to Spanish colonial days, intended for the protection of the ladies.

"*Si, señor,*" the waiter departed at a double pace.

Christian couldn't help but notice the extraordinary service they'd received everywhere in the fishing village. These people were really friendly and sure knew how to wait on tables. He relaxed back in his chair, admiring the view ahead of them, the calm sea and the boats at anchor. There were a dozen fishing boats anchored a few hundred yards offshore.

It turned out the waiter's name was Ramón. After Ramón deposited a black decaf coffee in front of Elaine, along with a small metal pitcher of cream, Christian questioned him.

"What kind of boats are those?"

Ramón flashed a bright smile, leaning on the back of one of the chairs with both hands. "Those are shrimp boats, *señor.*"

"Shrimp boats? Who owns them?"

"They're owned by the *coperativas, señor.*"

"The what?"

"The *coperativas, señor.*"

"And what are those?"

Ramón looked at Elaine, then smiled. "They are the owners of the boats."

"Well, that was clear as mud," Christian shrugged. The concept of *coperativa* was foreign to Christian. He had absolutely no idea what a *coperativa* was, but realized the waiter was not overly educated, so it would be rude to keep asking him something which, to him at least, appeared self-evident.

"How come they're not out fishing?"

The waiter smiled again, a perfect smile with a perfect set of teeth. Dang, Christian thought, I should look up his dentist.

"They don't fish in the daytime. In the daytime they sleep. The shrimp only come out at night." Ramón looked as if he'd just explained the obvious to a child.

That was new. Christian loved shrimp, had loved the flavor all his life, and was also enamored with the movie 'Forrest Gump,' with its amazing story of shrimping in the Gulf of Mexico. But he had absolutely not a clue about fishing for shrimp. Only come out at night? No shit.

"And how do you happen to know this?"

Ramón was built very strong, rather unusual for a simple waiter, Christian observed.

"I'm a shrimp fisherman," Ramón blurted.

That explained the physique.

"No kidding! And what're you doing here being a waiter instead of being a crewmember out there on one of those boats?"

Ramón paused, as if evaluating how much he should share with the gringo at the table.

"I'm getting married, *señor,* so I have to work hard to make money for my bride. *"*

"Fishing for shrimp doesn't make you enough money to take care of her?"

"No, I make more money working here in the hotel. And I can work here all year long. On the shrimp boats I only get work during the season, so the other half of the year I'm unemployed and the hotel won't hire me part-time."

Christian pondered the information. Poor bastard, having to wait tables in order to marry. No way waiting tables could be nearly as exciting as being on one of those boats out there.

"My future father-in-law is a shrimp boat captain," Ramón added.

"Really? And he doesn't mind you working here instead of on the boat with him?"

"No, *señor,* he prefers that I make more money all year long so I can support his daughter."

"I understand," Christian expressed, nodding. "So, your father-in–law is on one of those boats out there?"

"No, he's south from here, five or six hours away."

"Can anyone buy one of those boats?"

The waiter paused. "Yes, of course. The *coperativas* used to be the owners of all the boats, but now the banks are taking them back—repossessing them. You could buy one from a bank, I guess."

Christian's interest ignited. "From a bank? Why are they taking them back? And how much does one of those boats cost?"

Ramón hesitated momentarily before answering, "Aah...I think they cost around fifty thousand American dollars, and the banks are taking them back 'cause the *coperativas* are not making the payments on their loans. But I've heard if a shrimp boat is run properly it can make its owner lots of money, sumthin' like forty thousand dollars."

Fifty Grand to buy one? Defaulting on their loans? Interesting. Profit of forty thousand? That amounted to a really good return on investment.

"Ramón, when's your father-in-law going to be home again?

"I don't know. He doesn't have a set schedule. He comes back whenever he needs to land some of the shrimp or if he has mechanical difficulties."

Christian took a few minutes translating his conversation with Ramón, since his wife was not fully fluent in Spanish. He knew people unfamiliar with languages were not aware that there are two types of interpreting modes which can be used in normal conversation. The first is known as 'simultaneous translation,' which is conducted at the same time as the principal is talking. This type of translation is best suited for places where there are headsets and microphones available, of the type they use at the United Nations. Without the hardware it is almost impossible to conduct simultaneous translation, since everyone is talking at the same time.

The second type of interpreting is known as 'consecutive interpretation,' and, in this mode, the principal speaks for a minute or so before pausing, allowing the translator opportunity to summarize what has just been said. This type of translation does not require hardware.

Christian practiced consecutive interpretation with his wife anytime they were in Mexico.

He was most definitely becoming interested in the shrimp boats.

"Ramón, I would very much like to have a conversation with your father-in-law. Is there any way you can reach him so he can let you know when's the next time he'll be here in town?"

"I can't call him, but he will call home over the next few days and talk to his wife with his cellphone. I can pass the message to him that you wish to talk."

"I really appreciate this. When do you think this will take place? In your opinion?"

"Like I said, I don't know, *señor.* It could be any day."

"All right, let's do this. Do you have a phone number where I can reach you from Arizona?"

Ramón thought about this for a moment. "No, *señor,* I don't have a telephone. But what I can do is leave word at the reception here in the hotel and, if you call them from Arizona, they will inform you of the next date for my father-in-law to arrive in port."

That would work. "Okay, let's leave it at that, then. I'll call here daily and when you hear from your father-in-law, you will leave me a message at the front desk informing me of the date he will be here. What is your future father-in-law's name?"

"His name is Santiago Longoria."

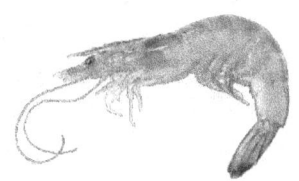

"Were you really interested in the shrimp boats or were you just making conversation with the waiter?" The road ahead of them leading towards the U.S. border was straight and empty of traffic. The Great Sonoran Desert resembled what it might be like driving on the moon.

Christian kept the Jeep Cherokee at sixty-five, with the cruise control engaged.

"Tell you the truth, I'm really kind of interested." He glanced at his wife. "I didn't know private individuals could buy into shrimp boats. From what I've always heard, the Mexican government owns the shrimping business. I need to find out more."

"Really, how feasible would that be for us to consider entering that business?"

"At this point, I don't know. But if it's true that one can buy a shrimp boat for about fifty thousand, I'm definitely interested."

"Why?"

"It could be a productive business. Besides, I love the sea and it would be really bitchin' owning a shrimp boat."

"But the waiter said the fishermen are losing their boats to the banks. If it's such a profitable business, how come they're sinking?"

"Sweetheart, I have no idea. This requires some further analysis."

"And you really are thinking of driving back here to meet with that boat captain?"

"Yes, I believe that man might be able to provide me with additional information about this idea of mine."

"Okay, I'm willing to learn more about this, if you're so interested."

He smiled at his wife of fifteen years. Her support was invaluable to him; she was always there regardless of the crazy-ass ideas he kept pursuing.

Christian was an aerospace engineer and had been an airline pilot for a major airline, but unfortunately lost his medical certificate due to an unexpected diagnosis of diabetes. Since losing his medical the previous year had rendered him instantly unemployed, he'd been courting the Boeing company, in Seattle, hoping for an offer of employment, but so far, he had not heard back from them.

Without question, however, running a commercial fishing boat was far more exciting than sitting in some office in Seattle, supervising a bunch of techies.

3

Office of the Harbormaster
Port of Guaymas, the Sea of Cortés

"*Comandante*, we got a call just a little while ago from a ship owner, an *armador* here in town, claiming that he hasn't heard anything from one of his shrimp boats which should've called in earlier today."

The Harbormaster, known as the *Comandante*, gave his aide a perfunctory glance. "Oh? And, so what?" The high temperature in the port office of the *Comandancia* rendered the air hot and miserable. The *Comandante* was in his late fifties, about fifty pounds overweight and sweating profusely in his tan uniform shirt two sizes too small. He was an hour late showing up at the office, but what the heck, he'd stopped to have some breakfast on the way in and time had flown. And besides, he was the boss there. Nobody was going to harass him for being late.

Placing his hat on the hanger by the door, he walked to his desk and sat down, reaching to turn on the switch on a small fan resting on his desk. The fan didn't move much air, so the *Comandante* once again cursed his job. The government had not issued them the funds necessary to repair their air conditioning unit and that made everyday life in the office as bad as working in the salt mines.

"The ship owner who called wanted to know if we could send out our fast boat looking for his ship. He said the captain on that shrimp boat is religious about calling in each morning from his cellphone, but apparently he missed his call this morning."

The *Comandante* grunted. Yeah, right, send out our fast boat. What the hell were these ship owners thinking? Aside from the fact that there was no money available to buy diesel for the fast boat assigned to his office, what'd these rich bastards think? That the Navy boat was at their disposal for whatever they dreamed up?

"Who was the *armador*?"

"Don Carlos Esquivel," the aide responded.

The *Comandante* sat up. Don Esquivel was a very wealthy and influential man in the relatively small community of Guaymas, a man to be respected. He owned nine or ten shrimp boats, if his memory served him right. "What time did he call?"

"About an hour ago, boss."

"Did you tell him you'd be passing this on to me?"

"Yes sir. I explained to Don Esquivel that I would let you know about his call as soon as you came in."

"Did he leave you his number?

The aide promptly strode over to his boss' desk, handing him a yellow Post-It note with a number scrawled on it.

The *Comandante* reached for the black phone on his desk and dialed the number.

"Hello?" the voice at the other end came across loud and clear and definitely unfriendly.

"Don Esquivel?" the *Comandante* asked.

"Yeah. And who's this?"

"Don Esquivel, this is *Comandante* Urrutia, the Harbormaster. My aide told me you called."

"Ah, *Comandante*, yes, thank you for calling me back. As I explained to your assistant a little while ago, one of my shrimp boats has been out of touch since they reported in yesterday. Its skipper, *Capitán* Molinar is a very responsible man. He never fails to call me in the mornings to give me a tally on the catch of the previous night. He didn't call me so, as you can probably imagine, I'm somewhat concerned."

"I see, did you try calling him on the two-meter radio?"

"Yes, of course I did. Wasn't able to reach him. Normally, he uses his cellphone to contact me, and also his family, but our manager spoke with his wife this morning and she hadn't heard from him either."

"I see," the *Comandante* repeated.

He really didn't.

Why all the commotion? These fishermen were anything but dependable. Don Esquivel's crew was probably at anchor somewhere whoring and smoking marihuana out of sight of the owner. One missed call didn't qualify as an emergency around these parts.

"Is there any chance you could send out your fast boat to look for the *Concepción?*"

"I'm afraid that's not gonna be possible, sir. The fast boat is out of service due to mechanical difficulties at this time." The *Comandante* wasn't in the mood to explain to this rich puke that there was no diesel to run the boat. There was no diesel because the modest budget allocated to his office for the purchase of diesel fuel had found its way into the pockets of the Harbormaster months ago. The diesel allowance provided by the government every three months was seldom spent on diesel. The generally accepted, if unspoken, practice was that the *Comandante* of the port considered the diesel cash as part of his compensation package. Why waste diesel motoring around without a purpose? It just didn't make sense, wasting good money that way.

Don Esquivel was obviously taken by surprise at the news. "Mechanical difficulties? So, you don't have a boat to put out to sea? How about a *panga*?"

"No, we don't got a panga either, sir." As he spoke, the *Comandante* rapidly reconsidered the situation. Pissing off a rich guy like Don Esquivel maybe wasn't such a good idea after all. One never knew what these *armadores*—shipbuilders—were capable of doing once they got a wild hair up their asses. "What I can offer, if you like, is I'll send one of my men up on the hill with a multiband radio and we'll try contacting other ships from there, asking if any of them has seen your ship."

Shrimp boats in the Sea of Cortés were normally equipped with two types or radio, one known as a two-meter radio, a short-range device, and a second type known as multiband, using marine frequencies, used for long-range communications.

"Thank you, *Comandante*. There is no way you can get your fast boat repaired anytime soon? What kinda mechanical problems are you having? Perhaps I could have one of my mechanics come over and take a look? If it's not too serious, I might be able to repair it for you. I'm perfectly willing to provide you credit. I can bill the government later for the repairs."

"Aah, thank you, Don Esquivel, ah, I don't exactly know what the issue is with the fast boat, but I couldn't accept your generous and gracious offer to help. The maintenance on the fast boat is up to us." The *Comandante* was getting annoyed.

"*Comandante,* if it's something simple, I could have my mechanics fix it and then I'd be really grateful if you could send your boat out to the area where the *Concepción* had been fishing."

"I've not been told what the exact mechanical problems are with our boat," he lied. "So, I couldn't tell you what repairs are needed."

"Well, can you find out?"

Crap. Obnoxious dickhead. Didn't this dumbass know when to take 'no' for an answer? Things were starting to get difficult. "Sure, I can do that. Let me find out what the problem is and I'll call you back."

"Thank you *Comandante*. I await your call."

"Pushy sonofabitch!" The *Comandante* cursed, slamming the phone down. He made certain the line was dead before cursing. He quickly weighed his alternatives.

He could simply ignore Don Esquivel, but that had the potential of having ugly consequences. In reality, there was nothing wrong with the fast boat. He could have his aide run over to the marina and sabotage the boat, break something, then call back Don Esquivel and accept his offer to help. But the fact remained that the boat had no fuel. How could he deal with that?

"Raul!" he barked. His aide looked up from his desk by the door, startled.

"Yessir?"

"Go down to the marina, find our mechanic and have him remove the generator and the battery from the fast boat. Have him bring those two parts back here. And ask him not to mention this to anyone. Got it?"

The aide repeated the instructions.

"Take the Suburban. Here's the keys."

The *Comandante* walked over to the small refrigerator humming in the back of his office, grabbing a cold Coca-Cola bottle from it. The temperature in the damned office was getting very hot, even that early in the morning. He waited half hour before reaching for the phone again.

"Yes?"

"Don Esquivel?"

"Yes, *Comandante*, what have you found out?"

"Sir, the problem with the fast boat seems to be electric and we have someone looking at it at this very moment. If your mechanic could give it a quick check then, perhaps, we could get it fired up and send it out to look for your ship."

"Happy to do that. Mario, one of my mechanics, will drive down to the marina to check it out right away."

"Don Esquivel, don't you have other ships in the area where the *Concepción* has been fishing?"

"No, we don't. What do you think, we are—stupid? Of course, we already thought of that. Our closest ship to the *Concepción* is over ten hours away from that area. That is why we need your fast boat. Last we heard from our ship, they were steaming towards Bahia de Kino, which is a reasonable distance from here."

"No, no, I wasn't implying anything, I was merely asking."

"Fine. I'll call you back once my mechanic lets me know what's wrong with your fast boat."

"Don Esquivel?"

"Yes, what is it?" The man's tone was unfriendly.

"There's another small issue."

"What small issue?"

"The issue of fuel. We're at the end of the trimester, and we've already used all the diesel allotment given to us."

"Are you telling me you don't have diesel for the fast boat?"

"Yeah, that's precisely what I'm sayin', sir."

"Not a problem. I'll have my mechanic look over your boat and if he's able to get it going, we'll put diesel in it."

"That should work. Do you still want me to send someone up on the hill to use the radios and contact other fishing boats?"

"Yes, please, you do that."

The *Comandante* hung up. That'd been a close call. He briefly wondered the odds of Don Esquivel contacting his superiors in Mexico City and mentioning anything about the diesel. Not likely. He wiped the sweat off his eyelids, exhaling with a feeling of relief. He needed another Coca-Cola.

Two hours later, the fast boat with a new battery and generator left the port of Guaymas, heading north at better than thirty knots.

4

Phoenix, Arizona.

"So, you're telling me that anybody can go to the Sea of Cortés and buy a shrimp boat now."

"No, not anybody, you'd have to be born in Mexico in order to do that." Christian poured a couple of one-inch shots of Tullamore Dew Irish whisky into two glasses, passing one to his friend.

Brad Murray accepted the drink, admiring the honey-colored whisky. He downed it in one quick gulp, appreciating the color of the pink bougainvillea flowers in Christian's garden, feeling the warming effect of the 'Irish Milk' going down. "And this waiter down there told you that one could make forty thousand dollars a year with a fifty-thousand-dollar fishing boat?"

"Yeah, he said around fifty-thousand, but I'm not sure that waiter knew what the Dickens he was talking about so don't take those figures to heart just yet. I've been researching all I can about the Mexican shrimp industry, and it does appear there's something very interesting going on down there just now."

"'Interesting' as in what?" Murray reached for the whisky bottle. He was an Irishman and whisky was the elixir of life.

"Interesting as in 'opportunity to make money.' I've been calling Mexico City for two days and I'm starting to get a picture of what's going on down there. Mexico has a tremendous fishing industry, and shrimp is king down there. It appears that the entire shrimping industry has been in the hands of these groups called *coperativas*, some sort of fishing unions that owned everything: the shrimp boats, the processing plants, the fishing gear."

"And they don't now?" Murray poured himself another whisky.

"I'm not too sure about that yet. From what information I've been able to gather talking to the department of fisheries in Mexico City, it appears that the *coperativas* are disintegrating and the banks are repossessing everything; the ships, the processing plants, the fishing permits."

"And what's that got to do with us?"

"I was told private individuals have not been allowed to own shrimp boats in the Sea of Cortés for a couple of decades. Apparently, only the *coperativas* could own the fishing permits and the boats, but now they've defaulted on their loans and the banks are eager to sell everything to anyone interested who can show up with a suitcase full of cash."

"No shit?"

"Yep. I learned there are nearly three-hundred and fifty shrimp boats fishing in the Sea of Cortés, or somethin' like that, and each one of those trawlers has a fishing permit. Apparently, the government of Mexico is not giving out any additional fishing permits to anyone. What's out there is all there is. The permits are transferable from one shrimp boat to another, so if a boat sinks and you build a replacement, in theory you could transfer the permit to the new boat."

Brad Murray poured himself another shot of Tullamore Dew.

Christian was amazed at the drinking ability of his good friend. Brad was forty-three, just as he was, but he could drink all day and night and not show any signs of being drunk. Christian had already made the mistake of trying to drink Brad under the table a couple of times, which turned out to be a very bad idea. God gave the Irish whisky so they wouldn't rule the world, or so they say. And Brad Murray was all Irish.

The man must have two livers.

"So, they're controlling the supply of shrimp very tightly." Brad Murray was an analyst for one of the largest credit card companies in the world and he had a very logical, calculating mind.

"Yeah. Nobody else is allowed to fish in Mexican waters. Only Mexicans."

"And according to this one waiter...what's his name?"

"Ramón. His name is Ramón."

"Okay, so, according to this Ramón guy, a fifty-thousand-dollar shrimp boat can produce nearly that much in profits in one year. That sounds hard to believe."

"It would be if it wasn't Mexico. Everything's possible down there." Christian reached for some documents from among the pile of papers flooding his kitchen table. "Check this out. The annual production of Mexican shrimp has been declining rapidly over the past six years. I haven't been able to find anything wrong with the shrimp, so it appears that the fishing fleet is just not doing things right for some reason."

"And so, what you're sayin' is that any private Mexican private bloke with enough cash can now show up at the bank down there and buy a boat? Just like that?"

"I'm not really sure that's exactly how it works, but yeah, that's about what I think is going down."

"What's the next step?" Brad Murray had a positive, likeable personality. His Cockney accent contradicted his Irishness. Though born in Ireland, he was raised in London, which confused just about everybody.

"The next step? We drive down to Rock Port and meet with a shrimp boat captain and pick his brain for information."

"The father-in-law of this guy, Ramón?"

"Precisely."

"All right. I'm game. When do we go?"

5

On a highway headed for Old Mexico in the Sonoran Desert.

The desert road leading south from Gila Bend toward the Mexican border at Sonoita was as straight as one of the runways at Sky Harbor International airport. Christian had the 1984 red Mustang convertible on cruise control at seventy. The convertible top was up because the air temperature, approaching 118 degrees, was hot enough to catch their hair on fire. Or so it felt.

"This guy, Longoria, is going to be there before we arrive?" Brad Murray barely fit in the small Mustang. His six-foot three frame was not designed for small cars.

"Yeah. Ramón said his future father-in-law had been fishing five hours south of Rock Port, and they finally made contact by radio. *Capitán* Longoria agreed to meet with us and he's been steamin' north since early this morning."

"This captain agreed to meet with us even though he was five hours away? That's a nice guy."

"I don't know about that, but Ramón must've told him that some gringos showed interest in buying a boat, and maybe he's thinking he could work for us. The sweet smell of money, remember? This captain's been fishing for many years, so he's probably experienced enough to give us some good info."

"That's possible." Brad Murray didn't speak any Spanish but he had a contagiously enthusiastic personality, the ideal companion for any adventure.

"I found out the shrimping season spans from September through April, although that can vary, as well. The Mexican government prohibits fishing from May through the end of August in order to allow the shrimp to reproduce. They call this the 'Veda'. I think that means something like 'closure.'"

"That's smart."

"No kiddin'. That way they protect their shrimp. I read that the Japanese are always trespassing into territorial waters of many countries, fishing where they're not allowed, but here in the Sea of Cortés they have a hard time poaching because this sea is nearly a thousand miles long and surrounded on both sides by Mexico. Any Japanese ship entering the gulf would be a sitting duck for the Mexican navy."

Murray grunted. "First, they overfish their own waters and then come over here and empty our oceans of fish," Brad Murray was annoyed. He had no love for the Japanese. Having lived in the U.K. a long time, he was all too familiar with the horror stories of the Bataan Death March and the other cruelties imposed by the Japanese on British soldiers during WWII, behavior which many Brits simply refused to forget. "What'd the Mexicans do if they catch some of those Japs fishing in their waters?"

"I read about one such incident last year," Christian shared. "Apparently, the Mexican Navy intercepted a Japanese shrimp boat fishing illegally and arrested the crew. The ship was impounded and the crew were sent to Mexico City and delivered to the Japanese embassy to be repatriated at their own expense. The Japanese government 'violently protested' this flagrant violation of human rights and demanded the return of their shrimp boat."

"You're shittin' me."

"No. I'm not shitting you. The nerve of the Japs. So, anyway, the Mexicans simply laughed and refused to return the fishing boat. I guess some rich politician in Mexico is now the proud owner of a Japanese trawler renamed something like *Conchita*."

"Good for them. So, the Japs found someone with more nerve than they have."

"Elaine and I hit the ASU library for some books on commercial shrimping and found lots of good stuff. The Food and Agriculture Organization had an excellent technical manual with a very good description on what to do in case one gets involved in fishing as a business, what kind of vessel to use, what type of nets."

"Did you read about the *coperativas* in those books?" Brad Murray glanced in the distance. A military fighter plane of some kind had suddenly made an appearance about a mile down the road, flying very low and crossing the highway from left to right at breakneck speed. "Look at that!"

Christian saw it too. "It's an A-10 Warthog. It's a ground support fighter. The military use this area for shooting practice. This entire area between Gila Bend and Ajo is a hot military operations area."

"Incredible. Are we gonna get shot?"

"Naw," Christian laughed. "They do bomb runs and strafing at selected areas away from this highway."

"Isn't this where the 'Organ Pipe' national reserve is?" Murray referred to an area in Southwestern Arizona known as the Organ Pipe National Monument, a biosphere reserve where enormous Saguaro cactus and all kinds of flowers grew wild. The park shared a border with the Mexican state of Sonora.

"I'm not sure where the reserve begins, but I think it's somewhere around these parts. I read somewhere that the land for the Organ Pipe reserve had been donated by the Arizona government during Prohibition with the intent of improving the road we're on. This road made contraband alcohol easier to import from Mexico."

"Aah, the elixir of life," Brad offered, "those Arizona boys back in those days had their priorities straight."

Christian smiled at his friend's view. The Irish may not know what they want, but they're willing to die for it. Provided there's beer or whisky available, anyway.

"In answer to your question about the *coperativas*, no, we weren't able to find squat about those in any of the books from ASU. But I called the Department of Fisheries in Mexico City and was given the official version of what they claim is going on.

According to those guys in the capital, the government of Mexico 'gave' the fishing industry to the fishermen decades ago. In my opinion, that must've been a move towards socialism that the government of Mexico made, perhaps as an act of thumbing their noses at their big neighbor to the north. Those were the days when Mexican presidents leaned left, just because Uncle Sam leaned right."

Brad Murray reached behind Christian's seat, retrieving two ice-cold cans of Coke. Popping both open, he handed one to Christian.

"Thanks. Anyway, it seems that the fishing industry in the Sea of Cortés became corrupt to the core and began falling apart at the seams. Apparently, that's the reason why the government and the banks are now trying to take it away from the fishermen and give it back to the private sector."

"And that would be us," Brad Murray stated.

"Yeah, that's us, hopefully. Lessee if we can go make us some money. Tons of it."

6

At the Playa Encanto Hotel overlooking the Sea of Cortés

"*Capitán* Longoria?" Christian and Brad Murray shook hands with the man. Longoria was a big man, overweight and dark-skinned. He probably had mostly Aztec blood in him, Christian thought. The man sported a dark mustache matching his dark head of hair. He appeared to be in his mid-fifties and wore a simple white button-down short-sleeved shirt and black pants. He had a strong handshake.

"*Mucho gusto*," Longoria greeted, shaking the hands of the two men. The waiter, Ramón, had met them in the lobby, and led the way to the back of the hotel, where there was a large open-air patio dining area furnished with white plastic tables elegantly covered with linen table cloths. The patio faced the calm turquoise waters of the Sea of Cortés.

"*Capitán* Longoria, first of all, we'd like to thank you for meeting here with us today. I understand from your son-in-law that you had to come quite a ways."

"Naw, I was jus' fishin' south of here. Near the Island of San Jorge."

Christian had absolutely no idea where that island was but apparently Longoria thought it was common knowledge. And maybe it *was* among fishermen.

Ramón stood next to the table and handed paper menus to the three men. "What can I get ya all to eat?"

Because Longoria obviously didn't speak a word of English, Christian communicated with the man in Spanish, pausing frequently to interpret for Brad Murray.

The ambient temperature was well over one hundred degrees. Although the fishing village was on the white beaches of the Sea of Cortés, the scorching temperatures of the Sonoran Desert still prevailed during the summer months. The only saving grace was what appeared to be a ten-knot breeze blowing from the south.

"I'll have three scrambled eggs with the *carne asada*," Brad Murray ordered.

"And how'd you like that cooked, *señor*?"

"Medium rare, please. And can you bring me a beer. What kind you have?"

"We have Corona, Pacifico, Dos Equis, Modelo."

"Bring me a Pacifico."

Christian gestured for Ramón to get Longoria's order next.

"And you, *jefe*?" Ramón asked his future father-in-law.

Longoria tossed the menu onto the table without glancing at it. "I'll have some pork chops with potatoes and some tomatoes. And bring me a Corona, but not one of those little miniature ones, Bring me a big one."

Christian was thirsty, and although the table had been set with three glasses of water with ice in them, he knew better than to drink water or use ice in Mexico. "Your cheese-stuffed shrimp wrapped in bacon sounds terrific. Bring me that. And I'll have a Coke. In the bottle, please, without any ice."

Ramón finished jotting notes on his little pad, nodded, and disappeared.

"So, you're a shrimp boat captain?" Christian felt the back of his shirt sticking to his skin. Infernal heat, he thought, just like in Phoenix. But with humidity.

"Yessir," Longoria was sweating profusely, as well.

"And you've been doing this for a long time?"

"Thirty-five years."

"Is it your own boat?"

Longoria used the linen napkin to wipe the perspiration from his forehead. "No, I wish," he laughed. "No, I don't have a boat, it belongs to an *armador*."

Christian translated.

"What's an *armador*?" Brad Murray asked.

"That's what they call the ship owners and the ship builders," Christian explained. I think it actually means 'the one who builds it,' because I assume in the old days the builder of a ship was also the owner-operator."

Ramón reappeared holding a round metal tray with drinks balanced on it. He distributed the cold beverages. "The food will be out soon."

Brad Murray removed the lime wedge from the neck of the bottle of his Pacifico, sucking on it before taking a long swig of beer. "Aaaah, the nectar of the gods!"

"I understand from Ramón that there's a bunch of shrimp boats up for sale?"

"Yeah, that's correct."

"And who's selling them, the banks?"

"The banks and the *coperativas*," Longoria replied. He drank half his beer in one continuous gulp.

"And private individuals are allowed to buy these boats?"

"Yes."

"But, before, only the *coperativas* could own and operate shrimp boats?"

Longoria signaled his future son-in-law to bring another round of drinks. "That is correct."

"And each boat has its own fishing permit?" Christian drank half his Coke without pausing to breathe. The heat was intense.

"Yeah, each boat's got its own fishing permits."

"Can you tell us a little bit about the history of shrimping here in town?"

"The history?"

"Yes, like how long has shrimp fishing been going on here? Who owns all those boats out there, where'd they come from?"

"Yeah, sure."

The man looked anything but sure.

"There's been shrimp boats here since forever."

Christian waited for more. Nothing else came. Better try another angle. "Okay, what are the *coperativas*?"

"The *coperativas*? They're fishing companies. They're the ones who own the boats."

"And how long have they existed?"

"I'm not sure exactly. If I remember correctly, they started back in 1982 or sumthin' like that."

"And before that, who owned the shrimp boats?"

Longoria paused, obviously relieved at the arrival of his future son-in-law with another round of drinks. "Before the *coperativas*, the shrimp boats belonged to the *armadores*."

That was confusing. "You mean before the *coperativas* the shrimp boats belonged to private owners?"

"Yeah, that's what I meant."

"And then who created the *coperativas*?"

Longoria drank another long gulp of his second beer. "Those were created by the government. I think."

"And why would the government create the *coperativas*?"

"Because the President thought that the fishin' belonged to the fishermen."

"Can you explain that a little bit more?"

Longoria looked at his hands, placing the second beer bottle atop the table. "I'm no expert on this, mind you. But if I remember right, before 1982 the shrimping industry belonged to the folks who owned the boats and the shipyards, and they paid the crews very low wages. They just took advantage of the fishermen."

Ramón materialized, accompanied by two other young men carrying several trays of food. The men paused while the waiters arranged plates with steaming hot delicious-smelling, food in front of each.

"This looks fantastic," Brad Murray expressed. "And that was fast."

"That's 'cause we're here ahead of their lunch hour," Christian explained. "Lunch time in Mexico is from three in the afternoon on. We're here two hours ahead of their lunch hour, so they're not real busy in the kitchen just yet."

The waiters placed plastic baskets containing French bread and corn and flower tortillas on the table. Christian admired his plate containing six enormous shrimp each individually wrapped in crispy bacon and stuffed with yellow cheese, each piece of culinary artwork held together with wooden toothpicks.

Longoria reached for the tortillas, helping himself to pork chops which he quickly made into tacos by cutting the meat into small pieces with his knife.

"So, you were saying the government found that private owners were exploiting the fishermen and that's why the president of Mexico handed over the industry to the fishermen?"

Longoria looked up with a mouthful of tortilla and pork, nodding. "Yeah. That's when the president gave the fishing industry to the fishermen."

"What'd you mean 'gave it to the fishermen'?" Christian was in flavor heaven. The combination of the huge shrimp with the taste of bacon was extraordinary.

"The government said only *coperativas* could own shrimp boats, so groups of fishermen got together and formed many *coperativas*."

"Where'd they get the money to buy the boats?" Christian felt refreshed after finishing his second Coke.

"The government gave the *coperativas* bank credits to buy the boats," Longoria continued. "Each *coperativa* was allowed to buy a limited number of boats, depending on how many members it had."

"And who were these members?"

"The fishermen. We were the members."

Christian tried to digest this information. The government of Mexico had obviously taken the fishing industry away from the private sector, transferring it into the hands of the fishermen. "And then, what happened? The fishermen became the owners?"

Longoria finished his second beer, lifting the empty bottle, signaling to a waiter standing by the back wall to bring another round. "Yeah, the fishermen became the owners."

"And that was fifteen years ago, so what happened? Why are all the *coperativas* going out of business now? Did somethin' happen to the shrimp? Is there some kind of disease? Is the catch diminishing every year for some reason? I mean, if one is making money catching shrimp why, in God's name, would they want to abandon the business?"

Longoria licked his fingers while polishing off another pork taco. He shook his head. "No, nuthin' wrong with the shrimp. It was just the *coperativas* didn't work."

Christian waited expectantly for additional information but instead, Longoria took another bite of his food. He translated for Brad Murray.

"When the government gave us the shrimp boats," Longoria finally continued, "everyone was deliriously happy. We were all going to be owners." He followed the taco with a swig of beer. "Since not everyone could be a crewmember on the shrimp boats, most of the members had to stay behind and become managers and do all the stuff one does on land while the shrimp boats are out fishin'."

"What do you mean? Every member of a *coperativa* was part-owner of a ship?"

"Yes, if you were a member, you were also a part-owner and you were entitled to an equal share of the profits."

"So basically, the government handed the fishermen a bunch of shrimp boats and told them to run the show."

"Run the show?"

"It's an expression. It means you guys were in charge of everything."

"Yeah, the fishermen were in charge."

"And where'd these boats come from? The shrimp boats?"

Christian was beginning to realize that Longoria was clearly not extremely eloquent or educated. Getting information from this dude was painful.

"The boats came from the *armadores*," he responded.

"I don't understand."

Longoria stopped eating. "The government took the shrimp boats from the *armadores* and gave them to the fishermen."

"Just like that? Did the government pay the armadores for their boats, or they just took 'em?"

Longoria put his tortilla down, looking to wipe his oily fingers with a napkin. He appeared to finally realize that he'd better answer some of the questions these gringos were asking or he was not going to be allowed to eat in peace. "Yeah, the government paid the *armadores* for their ships. But hey, they didn't steal 'em or anythin' like that."

"And then they made these ships available to the *coperativas*."

"That's right."

"How were the poor fishermen able to pay for these shrimp boats?"

"I told you, the government banks gave out loans to any *coperativa* interested in buyin' 'em."

"What did the *coperativas* do then? Hire managers and accountants and mechanics to run the boats?"

"Ah, no. The fishermen did all that."

Christian was starting to get the picture and it wasn't pretty. "You're telling me the fishermen ran everything?"

"That's how it happened. All the members of each *coperativa* wanted to go out fishing on the boats, of course, but that wasn't possible 'cause there were too many members. So, the ones who stayed behind, like I said, learned how to take care of everythin' else."

"The co-ops didn't hire managers and lawyers and accountants and all the rest of what's needed to run a company?"

"No, no, that wasn't necessary. Like I said, there were so many members who joined the *coperativas*. Some of the members became managers, some accountants... there was a job for everyone."

Christian was starting to get the picture indeed. The government of Mexico had basically nationalized the shrimping industry, taking it from the educated elite and handed it over to a bunch of fishermen, most of whom probably didn't even know how to read or write.

A real smart move.

"He translated for Brad Murray.

"You gotta be kiddin' me!" Murray couldn't understand anything of the conversation but, once Christian explained, he was equally baffled.

"What happened next?" Christian noticed Longoria was putting away beer twice as fast as Brad Murray. The sailor drinking the Irishman under the table?

"Everyone was very happy to become owners, that's what happened," Longoria explained. "The fishermen were delighted to be rid of their former bosses. Each ship got a crew and they all went out fishin'. 'Cause they were all owners now, they fished hard and better than ever before. I was a young man back then. I remember that first trip out we caught nearly seven tons of shrimp."

"Is seven tons a good amount for a first trip?"

"Oh, yeah. A very good amount."

Longoria eyed his food and began preparing himself another taco, adding meat and beans to a couple of corn tortillas. "All the ships returned to port after a few weeks out fishin' on those first trips as owners, and the members of the *coperativas* who'd stayed behind on land helped unload them shrimp boats and transport all the captured shrimp to the processing plants. There were three processing plants here in town back then."

All three men were perspiring heavily. An umbrella afforded protection from the direct sun, but notwithstanding, even in the shade the desert air temperature was brutal.

"The captains and their crews were proud of how much shrimp they brought back on that first trip. Everyone worked hard to unload the boats, refuel them and put provisions back on. The government had provided cash credits to buy all these things. They were all back out to sea in record time. The general enthusiasm was at a very high level."

The captain resumed eating his taco, talking through mouthfuls of food, chewing and talking at the same time. Small pieces of tortilla flew out of his mouth as he continued. "The ships all left port again and steamed out to sea. The fishermen who'd stayed behind managing the *coperativas* sold the shrimp from those first trips to the government and were stupefied at how much money they received. They had never seen so much cash. So, they took the money and kept it. They bought houses, pickup trucks and women."

Christian translated.

"Bloody thieves!" Brad Murray blurted.

"None of the crews were paid anything from those first trips. When the boats returned to port after several trips, the managers once again sold the shrimp, keeping half the money. They distributed the other half to the crews, but this made the fishermen who were crewing the ships very angry. The leaders in charge of the *coperativas* rapidly fabricated stories about how the government was slow to pay, how the shrimp had not been of export quality, how the payments to the banks had eaten up all the profits."

Christian admired the sea in front of the hotel. It was calm, with a dozen shrimp boats at anchor in the distance.

"The crews eventually caught on to what was happening. It wasn't hard to see the picture. The managers of the *coperativas* had suddenly become quite wealthy, which in small villages does not go unnoticed. Everyone could see the self-appointed leaders of the *coperativas* had become rich overnight. New houses, new trucks, new clothes. One can't hide money in these parts. Especially money made off the backs of the fishermen."

"What happened then? Did the crews lynch the managers for stealing the money?"

Longoria glanced at the gringo in front of him with mild curiosity. "Lynch them? No. they didn't lynch them. What happened then, the crews began selling the shrimp themselves out at sea for half the market price or less. They realized the managers were going to help themselves to half of the cash from the sales no matter what, so they got creative. There's always folks out there willin' to buy the shrimp on the black market."

"What'ya mean 'the black market'? Didn't you say the government was buying the shrimp from the *coperativas*?"

"Yes, the government normally bought the catch."

"And the black market was not the government?"

"No, no. The black market was a bunch of people who bought the shrimp at half price and sold it themselves all over the country."

"The crews were selling the shrimp at half price?"

"They sure were. As time passed, the amount of shrimp being unloaded from the fleet became progressively smaller. The leaders of the *coperativas* were still boldly helping themselves to half the money from the sales, so what was left wasn't sufficient to pay the crews and buy diesel, much less make payments to the banks. Not to speak of providing maintenance for the boats."

What'd the government expect? Christian mused. Give an entire industry to a bunch of uneducated people and the outcome was not just predictable, it was inevitable.

"The situation became worse as time passed. Everyone was out to make a peso. Say you needed a new generator checked out. The *coperativa* managers would have the generator removed from a ship and taken to a local electric shop. The owner of the shop would swap the new generator for an old one and that old one would be returned to the ship. The charge for 'repairing' the generator would be ridiculously high, and the shop owner, in cahoots with the managers, would then sell the original new generator on the side, making more money."

"Incredible."

"After a while thing settled down and everyone accepted the corrupt system as the new normal way to operate. The crews caught shrimp, then sold half of it at sea. The remaining catch was brought back to port where it was sold by the managers, who kept half of the profit. The rest was distributed to the crews and used to buy some diesel and supplies."

"And this happened everywhere?"

"Yeah, everywhere. Here in the Sea of Cortés and in the Gulf of Mexico. The were able to maintain a certain level of operations like that, but since half the profits were taken by the managers, there was never any money to repair ships or provide maintenance. Predictably, the shrimp boats began deteriorating. At first the banks gave loans to take care of the maintenance, but the co-op managers kept half of that money for themselves, as well. Eventually, the bank loans dried up. As the years passed, the shrimp boats began having all sorts of mechanical problems and many stopped fishing, because there was no money to fix them."

Longoria finished the last bit of food on his plate, pushed back from the table to give his voluminous belly more room, and sighed contently.

"Do these boats run on diesel?" Christian had heard of the corruption in the shrimping industry, but he'd really no idea the extent to which it had permeated a potentially profitable industry. What the hell had made the government of Mexico give the business to the fishermen? And what could it possibly stand to gain from it? A very noble gesture, indeed, letting the fishermen own their livelihood, but the reality of life dictates that, in order to run any industry, one needs educated professionals trained in different disciplines: managers, bankers, accountants, engineers. Infrastructure, in other words. From what he'd seen so far, Christian wondered if some of these fishermen even knew how to use toilet paper, let alone run an industry. Putting these people in charge of everything was a guarantee that everything would eventually go to shit.

"Yessir, these are big diesels, Caterpillar, Cummings."

"How much fuel do you burn a day?"

"If we're running somewhere, we burn about 1200 litters a day. Trawling, pulling the nets, we burn around 1400 liters a day."

Christian rapidly punched some numbers into his Casio calculator watch. These guys burned somewhere in the neighborhood of four hundred gallons per day.

"Then the *coperativas* were able to keep going even with the managers helping themselves to everything they could?"

"They survived for many years. The government helped with a plan they had of providing loans to the *coperativas* to buy diesel and pay for some maintenance at the start of each season. The managers could not steal this money because everyone was watching. The government agency buying the shrimp from the *coperativas* would provide a loan to each ship, then these loans would be paid back to the government from all the shrimp sold during the season. The *coperativas* had no other choice but to sell all their production to the government, so what the feds did was deduct one dollar per pound of shrimp landed. These loans were paid off without fail because they were taken right off the top from the sales. The thieves never got their hands on this money."

"How much were the loans?"

"I think about a quarter of a million pesos per boat."

Christian worked his calculator. About thirteen thousand dollars per ship.

At a dollar per pound, that meant the *coperativas* were paying off their loans at the rate of $2,000 per ton of shrimp landed. From the statistics he'd read published by the Department of Fisheries, the average production of a shrimp boat these days was around twelve tons per season. That meant that even at break-even production there was enough money to pay off the pre-season loans.

"So, how come the government is bringing in private investors now?"

"Private investors?" Longoria repeated.

"Yeah, private owners. Not *coperativas*."

"Ah! Yeah. The *coperativas* just can't pay off their loans any longer."

"What loans?"

"The loans they took out to buy the shrimp boats. As the years passed and the boats deteriorated more, managers began taking out equity lines of credit on their homes and trucks and using the money to pay for maintenance and purchase diesel, but ultimately nothing worked and many ships could no longer fish. People lost their houses to the banks because they could not repay their loans."

From an engineering point of view, the story Longoria was telling made perfect sense. A complete fuckup. The only thing that didn't make sense was why the Mexican government would give away the store to the fishermen.

"And now what's happening?

Longoria wiped his mouth with his napkin before dabbing his forehead with it. "Now, the *coperativas* are dying. This past year, the banks have taken many of the shrimp boats back and more are defaulting on the loans. The processing plants are closing. Last year, the government finally had enough of the corruption and sent in the military to take over two of the three processing plants here in town, and repossessed dozens of shrimp boats because they were so far behind in their payments to the government banks."

Longoria belched before proceeding. "That was not a good thing. The army shut down the plants, threw out all the employees, and placed chains and padlocks on the doors. It was hot and the plants had several tons of shrimp being processed when this happened, so the shrimp spoiled when the electricity was cut off. The whole town smelled of rotting shrimp.

Everyone who worked at the plants and on those shrimp boats were out of a job as far as the fishing industry was concerned. This affected more than just the ship crews because the entire town lived off the businesses that supplied the boats, such as fishing gear suppliers, small repair shops and supermarkets. Since many of the shrimp boat captains had also taken out cash from the equity on their homes to buy diesel and keep the operation going, at the request of their leaders, suddenly finding themselves unemployed made them lose their homes."

Christian began wondering if it would be possible to make money with a shrimp boat in view of what was happening.

"The town of Rock Port slowly began to die, with people leaving by the hundreds. People began referring to their town as 'Dead Port'."

Christian nodded. A very sad outcome, yet totally predictable. A disaster for everyone involved in fishing. Maybe now the government of Mexico finally saw the light and realized that uneducated fishermen could not possibly run an entire industry. Perhaps it finally decided to sell the shrimp boats with their permits back to private individuals who at least were educated and could actually read, write and understand costs and revenues and yields. Regardless of the past, it should be possible to turn a profit from shrimp. For heaven's sakes, the shrimp was out there swimming, just waiting to be caught.

And it was free.

"*Capitán* Longoria," Christian asked. "Would you like some dessert?"

The sea captain looked uncertainly for a waiter. "Sure, that and some coffee would be good."

Christian raised his arm, attracting the attention of a waiter who'd been standing by the bar.

"Si, *señor?*"

"Bring us a dessert menu, please."

"We don't have one, *señor*. I can bring you flan or ice cream."

Longoria addressed the waiter. "Just bring me a flan and some black coffee."

"And for you?" the waiter paused holding his pad and pencil at the ready.

Christian asked Brad Murray about dessert and the Irishman just shook his head, smiling, taking a long draw from another beer.

"No dessert for us."

The waiter left in a hurry.

"Thank you for the very interesting information, *Capitán.*" In Mexico it was customary to address a professional by his title. Not doing so would certainly be considered an insult.

Longoria nodded his head in appreciation.

"How much are these ships? How much would I have to put together to buy one?"

Longoria looked as his hands, as if trying to come up with the best answer. "It depends. Some are expensive, some aren't."

"Your future son-in-law told us they cost around fifty-thousand American dollars. Was he wrong?"

Longoria seemed uncomfortable. He must've been calculating how much fifty thousand dollars was in pesos.

"No, no. he wasn't wrong. There are some for that price."

"He also told us that one of these ships can produce nearly fifty thousand dollars profit in one season. Does that sound realistic?"

"Yes, these shrimp boats can make a lot of money for their owners."

Christian realized that maybe he was asking the wrong man. The shrimp boat captain didn't seem to know a damned thing about profits and costs. He just ran the boat. Maybe it was time to find a ship owner and have a chat.

"Who buys your shrimp?"

Longoria blew his nose on his linen napkin. "Ocean Fruit does."

"And who's that?" Christian realized that getting information out of this guy was like pulling teeth.

"It's the company that buys all the fish and all the shrimp. All over the Sea of Cortés."

"Who owns Ocean Fruit?"

"Nobody owns it. I mean, the government owns it."

"The ship owners sell all the production to that company?"

"No, not all of it. Only the export-quality shrimp. The small stuff, the *chatarra*, or junk, Ocean Fruit don't buy that."

Christian translated for Brad Murray. "*Chatarra* is a Spanish word meaning 'junk.'"

This was getting interesting. The government bought the shrimp? At what price?

"How much of your catch is *chatarra*?"

Longoria looked up. "Ah, just a small part of it."

"What'd you do with it? Keep it?"

"No, we don't keep it, we sell it separately."

"Okay, so Ocean Fruit buys all your export-quality shrimp. Do they pay you a fair price?

"Longoria once again appeared lost. "Yeah, I suppose they do."

7

On a highway in the Sonoran Desert driving north.

"So, what'd you think?"

"I'm interested," Brad Murray voiced. They were headed north on the road to the U.S. border, a one-hour drive inside Mexico.

"It seems there's opportunity here, wouldn't you say?"

"Yeah.   Provided all that Longoria told us checks out."

"The guy didn't seem too bright, did he?" Christian had the red Mustang on cruise control

"No, but I guess we can get some more information from those guys he mentioned. What were their names?"

"You mean the guys selling their ships?"

"Yeah, those."

"The Vega brothers."

Longoria had divulged there were many shrimp boats for sale in town but not all were in 'good' condition. Of course, the man's definition of what 'good condition' was remained to be seen. Those boats which had been repoed by the banks were in lousy shape, not having received any maintenance forever. Some *coperativas* in town were selling their ships and those were in better condition. The co-ops were still operating their shrimp boats, so they had to at least be in running shape. Longoria gave them the contact information for two of those co-ops, one in Rock Port and the other one in Rio Colorado, another fishing village across the gulf.

"What did you think about the history behind the co-ops?" Christian asked.

"Corruption and ignorance at its finest," Brad Murray stated. "Not exclusive to the Sea of Cortés, either. This situation could've taken place in any country in the world."

"I agree. The issues that brought down the shrimp production were with the people, not the shrimp. I figure if we got our hands on a couple of those boats and ran 'em like a business, we could probably see some good profits from them."

"I tend to agree with you but with some reservation. We need to dig further and obtain some real numbers here. So, what's the next step?"

"I guess we should also find out if we can have a new shrimp boat built. Those rust buckets they're operating down there scare me."

"They don't believe in maintenance, do they?" As an analyst for the credit card company, Brad Murray's world was one of order and precision.

"It doesn't seem that way. Longoria said some of those ships are twenty-five years old."

"It seems to me having a new ship built would be the way to go," Brad Murray released his seatbelt, reaching into his pants' pocket for his passport. The town of Sonoita was in view. With its population of 13,000, the Mexican border town stood on the US-Mexico border, facing Lukeville, Arizona.

Unincorporated Lukeville, population thirty-five, consisted of a border entry point, a gas station, a duty-free shop and some outlets selling Mexican auto insurance.

A real metropolis.

The men approached the border crossing point. Two cars were ahead of them.

"We didn't really find out much from this Longoria character, did we?" Brad Murray pointed out.

"No, he didn't seem to know much about anything, but he did give us a good picture of why we are now able to buy shrimp boats down here."

"True. Did it occur to you, however, that this guy was out fishing five or six hours south of Rock Port and that he navigated all the way there to meet us? And then after lunch he steamed back another five or six hours to return to the fishing grounds?"

"So what?"

"Think of the diesel he burned doing that. Do you think the ship owner is aware Longoria burned his fuel doing this? "

"Yeah, that's somethin' to think about." Not a very considerate attitude towards his employer, that's for sure."

They pulled up to the border crossing point.

"Mornin'. Your citizenship?" The Customs and Immigration officer asked.

"U.S.," Christian responded, accepting Brad's passport and passing both of them to the man in the booth. The temperature was approaching 120 degrees, so the man must've been cooking like a turkey at Thanksgiving inside his glass cage, although Christian noticed some air conditioning vents on the ceiling of the booth. Probably not enough to cool the guy's head, even.

"What was the purpose of your visit to Mexico?" the officer asked, looking at his computer screen while holding the two passports open in front of him.

"Came down to look at some shrimp boats," Christian replied.

The officer gave the two men a cursory look, giving no sign that he'd heard. "Where do you live?"

"Phoenix."

The officer glanced at Brad Murray. "What is your citizenship?"

"American."

"Where do you live?"

"Phoenix."

"Is this your car?" The officer asked Christian.

"Yes, it is."

The Customs and Immigration officer handed back the passports. "Have a nice day."

Christian accepted the passports, pulling away from the checkpoint and driving into the local gas station across the road.

"Let's gas up. I don't like putting Mexican gas in my car, it has too much sulfur and we don't have enough juice to make it home without getting some fuel."

"Man," Brad Murray expressed. "I can't even imagine being stationed in this dump. I feel sorry for that poor bastard."

"Feel sorry for the poor bastards crossing the border illegally around this area. Imagine having to walk all day in this friggin' heat."

Both men were sweating profusely, although standing in the shade by the pumps.

"I don't even wanna think about that," Brad Murray replied. I'm goin' inside to get us some drinks. Anything in particular?"

"Pepsi. Thanks. And don't pour any goddamn whisky in it."

"What'd ya mean, you implying I'm a drunk?"

"Naw, just an Irishman. I know you don't get drunk; you just enjoy your whisky."

"Precisely."

8

Phoenix, Arizona

"Hullo?" Christian sat in his kitchen overlooking a turquoise swimming pool under a perfectly blue desert sky. The temperature in his kitchen was a delicious 75 degrees. The exterior thermometer hanging in the shade under the patio cover read 119 degrees.

"*Bueno?*" the woman's voice replied.

"Where am I calling?"

"You're calling Bisset Shipyards. How may I help you?"

"Is Mr. Bisset in?" Bisset was shown as the owner of the shipyard on his poorly-constructed website. Christian had been researching shipyards in

Rock Port all weekend. By Monday he had a list of shipyards in Rock Port and Guaymas that he intended to call.

There was a long pause while the secretary found her boss.

"Francisco Bisset speaking!"

"Mr. Bisset, my name is Christian Gibson and I'm calling you from Phoenix. I understand that you're a ship builder?"

The shipyard owner paused. "Yes, and how may I be of service?"

"I understand that it's now possible to purchase a shrimp boat as a member of the private sector and I'm interested in the possibility of acquiring one."

The shipyard owner's voice was neutral. Not friendly, not hostile, just neutral.

"I see. I don't have any shrimp boats for sale. But I can build you one."

"You can build me one?"

"Yes, that's what I do."

"You can build me a new shrimp boat."

"Yes."

"And how much would that cost?"

"It's hard to tell. Depends on many things. Are you here in Rock Port?"

"No, I'm in Arizona."

"Well, can you come down and see me? Then we can talk."

Christian suspected he wasn't going to get much out of this guy by phone. "I can be there tomorrow."

"Very well!" The shipbuilder's voice became a click friendlier. "Just come to my office when you arrive here. Do you know where we're at?"

"No."

"Just ask anyone once you're in town. Everyone knows us. We're right by the water."

Christian ended the conversation with the usual long formalities predominant in the Mexican culture. Then he dialed Brad Murray.

9

Rock Port, Sea of Cortés

Christian parked the Mustang in a small dirt parking lot adjacent to an old concrete building. An enormous rusty metal fishing boat of some sort sat propped up on wooden beams behind the building. He couldn't see the water from the parking lot, but knew they were really close to the sea. The smell of salt was strong in the air. He'd read that the Sea of Cortés was one of the saltiest bodies of water in the world. The tides were also pretty extreme, with more than ten-foot differences between high and low tide. At low tide, a multitude of marine life ended up marooned in tidepools and the intense heat of the Sonoran Desert sun cooked the stranded oysters, clams, crabs and other creatures, giving the air an intense fishy smell.

When the Hoover dam was built in the United States in 1936, the flow of fresh water into the Sea of Cortés diminished dramatically. After millions of years of fresh water mixing with the sea water, the environment changed. This made the Sea of Cortés a very salty body of water, with a salinity far above that of other seas. High desert temperatures also contributed to the salinity due to constant evaporation.

Brad Murray climbed out of the Mustang, studying the surrounding structures. A weathered, hand-painted metal sign hanging on the side of one of the buildings read "*Astilleros Bisset*" in brown letters.

"Bisset Shipyards!" Brad Murray announced.

The air was suffocating. There was no breeze and the desert floor seemed to radiate heat.

"Impressive," Christian exclaimed, surveying the place. He checked out the single fishing boat visible next to the building. It was obviously of metal construction but it appeared rusted and unfinished. No paint and no glass in the windows. He wasn't sure if the boat was a new boat still under construction or an old one undergoing maintenance.

They entered a door beneath the sign. A young woman sat at a desk in a small office.

"Good morning. May I help you?" A rotary fan on the desk blew stale air at her.

"We're here to see Mr. Bisset. My name's Gibson."

"Allow me, please." She disappeared up a set of stairs.

Christian checked out the office: a mess of papers strewn over several tables; no computer monitors in sight anywhere.

"Mr. Bisset would like you to come upstairs, please."

Francisco Bisset was in his mid-forties, short and strong, a mixture of Spanish and Aztec blood. His white open-collar shirt was soaked, sticking to his chest. The window air conditioner struggled but was evidently unable to cool the little office much. "Good morning, *señores!*" He stepped forward from behind his desk to greet the gringo visitors.

They shook hands.

"Have a seat," Bisset invited, pointing to two hard wooden chairs. "Did ya have trouble finding us?"

"No, no trouble."

"Can I get you a soda or some water?"

"No, we're fine, thanks."

"So, how can I help you? You want me to build you a ship?"

Christian didn't like the guy right from the start. Too much in your face, just another used car salesman. "We'd like to get some information first, before we can talk about building a ship."

"What kinda information?"

"We're considering the purchase of a shrimp boat, but the ones we've seen around these parts seem a little beat up. We've learned that some of these boats are over twenty-five years old."

"That's right. Most of the fleet is getting up there in years."

"We sorta figured getting a new boat maybe the way to go."

"Absolutely. I can build you one for five hundred thousand American dollars."

Christian and Brad Murray exchanged glances.

"Just like that?"

"Yes, of course, no problem. I can build you a beautiful ship, with everything you need to go fishing. Big Cat engine, you'll be able to pull big nets. Electronics, everything."

"Do you have used boats for sale?"

"Used boats? No, no. I only build new ones."

"Five hundred thousand dollars is a lot of money," Brad Murray put in.

Bisset looked at the big Irishman, surprised that he'd spoken. From the look on Bisset's face, it appeared the shipbuilder understood some English.

"Half a million dollars is a little more than we'd thought," Christian added. "How much are they asking for one of those old boats out there?"

"You mean a used one?"

"Yeah, one of those anchored right out front."

"Depends on the size of the ship and the condition. Two-hundred and fifty, three-hundred thousand, maybe."

Now it was Christian's turn to be surprised. Three-hundred thousand!? What the hell happened to the fifty-thousand-dollar ships? He had a horrible suspicion that the waiter, Ramón had his head up his ass after all.

"That seems like an awful lot of money for a rusty old bucket," Christian replied.

Bisset never smiled; he seemed to take himself rather seriously. "That's because you're not really paying for the boat. You're paying for the fishing permit."

"What do you mean?"

"The price you pay for a shrimp boat is mostly for the permit. Most of those boats out there are not worth twenty-thousand American dollars."

"You said it would cost us half a million dollars for you to build us a new ship. Does that include the fishing permit?

Bisset became slightly uncomfortable. "Uh, no. That's just the price for the boat."

"And what about the fishing permit, then? How do we get that and how much would it cost?"

Bisset hesitated. "Ah, that would have to be seen, I'd have to check with my contacts in Mexico City…"

It was painfully obvious the man was lying.

"Wait. Are you saying that, in addition to paying half a million bucks to have you build a new shrimp boat, that we'd have to on top of that, add the price of a fishing permit that could cost over two-hundred thousand dollars?"

"Where did you hear that amount? Yes, no. it depends," Bisset was obviously flustered.

"You just said that most of the price for an old shrimp boat is in the permit."

"Yeah, that's true. I'd have to find out how to obtain a fishing permit for you in Mexico City."

"At what price?"

"I don't know, it'll depend on many factors."

"Are fishing permits transferable between shrimp boats?"

"How'd you mean?"

"What happens when a shrimp boat is no longer seaworthy? What happens to the fishing permit for that vessel?" Christian was starting to smell a rat in the room. This character, Bisset, was not being totally straight.

"When that happens, then yes, the permit can be transferred."

"You're saying, then, we could buy one of those old rust buckets out there and transfer the fishing permit to a new ship that you can build for us?"

Bisset appeared visibly relieved. "Yeah, yeah. One could do that, too."

Christian translated for Brad Murray.

"Blast him. Now he's talking almost eight-hundred thousand dollars for a new shrimp boat!"

Christian addressed Bisset again. "In your opinion, then, what's more convenient: try obtaining new fishing permits in Mexico City or just buy an old ship and transfer the fishing permit to the new one?"

"Transferring the permit would be a lot simpler."

"And how long would it take for you to build a new ship for us?"

Bisset smiled, once again allowing himself to savor the possibility of seeing some good money from these two gringos after all. "Ah, I'd say it'd take me about seven months to build one."

"Seven months," Christian glanced at Brad Murray. "That would mean we'd be unable to fish this coming season. Basically, we'd lose one season."

Bisset seemed taken back by the logic. He quickly dismissed the concern. "Sure, but it takes time to build a new ship. And new ships don't have mechanical problems. Breakdowns early in the season can be very costly."

"And if we applied for a new fishing permit for the ship you can build for us, wouldn't that be cheaper than buying an old ship? After all, if we buy a ship just for the permit and then discard the ship, wouldn't we be losing the twenty thousand dollars you said the ship is worth?"

The shipyard owner hesitated, letting the statement sink in. "Yes, but you'd get some money back from selling the metal of the old ship."

"But you think it's possible to get a new fishing permit from Mexico City—with your contacts, of course."

"Yes, I'd have to get in touch with the people I know over there..."

"We thought the older ships went for around fifty-thousand."

"Fifty-thousand? Who told you that? The fishing gear alone is worth nearly that much."

"Let me see if I understand you correctly. If we buy an old ship, the fishing permit comes with it and it can only be used on that ship."

"Yes." Bisset lit up a cigarette.

"And if we hire you to build us a new ship, you can apply for fishing permits for us, or we could also buy an older ship, junk it, and use its permit for the new ship."

"Yes. That's how it works."

"And that is legal?"

Bisset assumed a look of indignant honesty. "Of course, it's legal."

"And does the five-hundred thousand dollars you quoted us include the fishing gear and the electronics and everything else needed to go fishin'?"

Bisset didn't hesitate. "Yes, it does. Everythin' included."

Christian signaled to Brad Murray. Time to leave.

"We thank you very much for your time," he stood, offering his hand to Bisset. "We'll analyze what you've told us and let you know what we decide."

"Don't take too long to decide. I've got two other ship contracts pending and if I start on those two, yours will take a lot longer to complete."

Sure, Christian thought, glancing at the deserted shipyard without a soul in sight. *You're so goddamned busy we better drive to our bank in Phoenix right now to get you half a mil in cash so you can start. Sure as shit wouldn't want to lose our place in line.*

The shipbuilder accompanied them to the parking lot. "Where you staying?"

"We're staying at the *Plaza Oceano Azul* hotel."

"Excellent choice. Call me if you need any more details. I'll be here all day."

Bisset was beaming. Christian was not a cynic, but the guy's behavior was just too obvious. He was probably jubilant at the thought of having bagged two rich Americans who were going to provide him with some urgently needed cash.

The pair drove the Mustang to a small seafood restaurant overlooking the Sea of Cortés, in the area of the fish market. The place was wide open, with no windows of any kind, in possible expectation of a breeze that wasn't there.

They sat at a table covered with a white and red linen tablecloth. A waiter appeared almost instantly. "Good morning!" the young waiter greeted, in English, placing two red plastic glasses of water with ice in front of the men. He handed them menus.

"We're going to have lunch," Christian informed him. "But first we'd like two Pacificos, please."

"Right away, sir," the waiter departed.

Brad Murray glanced around. The restaurant was decorated with very bright colors, paper-mâché parrots, beautifully painted chairs and flowers. Lots of flowers.

"Don't drink the water," Christian cautioned.

"I know. I love that Pacifico beer. What kinda beer is it anyway?"

Christian reached for some chips to dip in the red salsa bowl parked in the middle of the table.

"It's a pilsner beer. It's from Mazatlán, another port south of here. I think I heard that it was first brewed by some Germans years ago. But I think I heard on CNN that Anheuser-Bush now owns it."

"Figures. Pretty soon there'll be only one giant corporation owning everything in the world. They'll call it Big Daddy."

"No kiddin'. What'd you think of Bisset?"

"He doesn't smell like Honest Abe to me."

"Five-hundred thousand for a new boat? The guy's out of his mind."

"Yeah, and how about those prices he quoted for some of the old boats?"

"Very high. But then again, it could be possible. We haven't really obtained any reliable pricing information from anyone else here yet. That waiter, Ramón, probably didn't have the slightest idea what the hell he was talking about. I searched the Internet for shrimp boats selling in the Gulf of Mexico, Louisiana and Florida, and found some old ships goin' anywhere from thirty thousand and up."

"Old ones like these?"

"In a way. But of course, American maintenance is something entirely different from what I'm seeing here. Those American ships selling around the Gulf of Mexico seemed in good shape, nice paint and all."

"Not like these old rust buckets around here, eh?"

"No, not like these."

The waiter reappeared, placing two Pacifico beers in front of them, each with a wedge of lime inserted in it. "Would you like to order some food?"

"Yes, give us a coupla minutes," Christian instructed.

The waiter left and Murray pushed the lime wedge into his bottle with his thumb, gulping down the golden liquid with great gusto.

"If the older ships are selling for a quarter of a million apiece, it may be a better idea just getting our hands on two of those instead of having Bisset build an entirely new ship. I don't know enough yet, but logic seems to dictate that two ships could catch more shrimp than just one," Christian drank half his beer, feeling instantly refreshed.

"Makes sense. I wouldn't wanna trust that Bisset fellow with ten bucks, let alone half a million.

He just doesn't give out good vibes. I don't think I'd even trust him enough to wash my car."

"Yeah, I felt the same. He was just a little too eager. And, of course, it remains to be seen whether he'd be able to secure a fishing permit for a new ship on his own. From what I was told by the Department of Fisheries in Mexico City, the government is not issuing any more fishing permits."

"You think he was bullshitting us just to get the contract for a new ship?"

"Naw, you think? The thought crossed my mind, yes. His didn't seem to me like a thriving shipyard with feverish activity."

The waiter returned again. "What can I bring you?"

Christian picked up the menu, rapidly scanning it. It was in English and Spanish. "Brad, the menu is in English."

"Bring me the seafood soup," Christian ordered. The menu described it as a 'succulent mixture of seafood in a tomato broth.'

"And for you, *señor?*" the waiter addressed Murray.

"Bring me the fish filet with garlic, this one right here. And two more Pacificos."

The waiter wrote it all down and left.

"Yeah, he didn't seem to have much business, did he?" Brad Murray finished his beer in one long draw.

"No, other than a coupla stray dogs, I didn't see any action in his shipyard. There's a couple of other shipyards in town, though. We should hit those, too."

"Good idea. And what about going to that co-op Longoria told us about? The one with the brothers with the sixteen ships?"

"Yes, we definitely should get in touch with those guys. They're selling used boats and we need more information. I'll call them from the hotel after we've had our lunch. Maybe we can talk to them this evening or tomorrow morning.

Lunch arrived and it was entirely up to expectations. Two waiters placed hot plates containing exquisite food in front of the men.

10

Planning the fleet

"What do we know so far?" Christian asked.

"Seems to me building a new ship is not a realistic proposition," Brad Murray pointed out.

Elaine agreed. "From the way you guys describe him, that guy, Bisset, cannot be trusted."

They were enjoying beers sitting at a table by the pool at Christian's home in the beautiful April Arizona weather.

"Yeah," Christian added, "I'm really not interested in giving that guy any business. He gives out brutally dishonest vibes."

"And five hundred thousand for a boat is very high. Particularly since it wouldn't have a fishing license," Brad Murray noted.

"Right. From what we've gathered so far, it appears we can buy some of those used ships for two-hundred to two-hundred and fifty thousand apiece. And that includes shrimping permits *and* fishing permits."

"What do you mean 'permits', as in more than one?" Elaine questioned.

"It seems that most of the ships in the Sea of Cortés have two fishing permits, one for shrimp and a second one for fish. I don't know yet if the second permit is a factor or if those boats catch any fish in addition to the shrimp."

"Okay, so we all agree that waiter, Ramon, didn't have the slightest friggin idea what he was talking about when he told us the price of a shrimp boat was fifty-thousand." Christian sipped a Heineken from a can.

"That's obvious." Brad Murray popped a second beer can. "That idiot can eat my shorts. He didn't have a fucking clue what he was talking about. Based on the numbers we got so far from the Mexican Ministry of Fisheries, it seems that those older boats can produce anywhere from sixteen to eighteen tons of shrimp per season."

"Yeah, that seems to be the norm. And don't forget those are only the official figures. I don't think the ship owners are really sharing with their government the entire truth about their production."

"In other words, you think the annual production per ship is more than the sixteen to eighteen tons?"

"Yes. Since they have to sell all their export-quality shrimp to the government, I suspect the smaller shrimp gets sold behind the scenes and their government never really hears about it."

"All right," Elaine asked, "how much more production do you think they're hiding, then?"

"From what we've learned, it seems that twenty percent of the catch is not export-quality shrimp. I believe that's the amount they're not reporting. They call this '*chatarra*,' junk," Christian explained. "I think they sell it for around seven thousand dollars a ton, as compared to fifteen thousand per ton for the big Blues."

"All right. So, from what we've been able to determine, twelve tons of shrimp seems to be the break-even point for the season for one boat. If we manage to produce eighteen tons per ship, plus say three tons of *chatarra*, what would we be looking at for numbers?" Elaine asked.

Brad Murray looked at a spiral notebook on the table in front of him. "With five tons over break-even per season for each boat of export-quality product, selling the shrimp at an average of $16,000 per ton, that would generate $80,000 above and beyond operating costs. Add another $21,000 from the chatarra, and ballpark I would say each boat could generate about one hundred thousand dollars clear of dust each season. Give or take."

"Where did you get the figure of $16,000 per ton for the price of the shrimp?" Christian asked.

"The shrimp sells for about $15,000 per ton early in the season, but since they continue to grow, so the price goes up all the way to $20,000 per ton around December. Average it out and it comes out somewhere around $16,000 just to be conservative. I got that through Google."

"Fine. So, we're looking at around $100,000 in earnings per shrimp boat each season."

Murray consulted his spiral notebook again. "That is correct. Of course, we'll be able to fine-tune those numbers once we acquire some experience in the business."

"Let's say we buy three used boats," Elaine offered, "and assume we pay a quarter of a million dollars for each. That's $750,000 for the fleet. Then we have to add the cost of diesel, crews, fishing gear, and all the other good things needed to go fishing. I'd say we need a million dollars to get this thing moving."

The men nodded.

"So, you're thinking with a million-dollar investment we can generate about $300,000 in annual return on investment."

"That's what it looks like," Brad Murray agreed.

"In theory—at least—the investment could be recovered in three-and one-half years," Elaine pointed out. "With a profit of 300 thousand per year thereafter."

Elaine was an incredibly valuable element of the team. Her computer systems engineering background gave her a tremendous advantage in business. And she had a sharp mind for logic and numbers.

"In a nutshell, yes." Brad Murray sighed.

"Don't forget that the Mexican taxes are substantially less than our taxes here in the States," Christian added.

"Yes, that is without doubt a strong added incentive," Elaine agreed. "So, basically we need to figure out how to come up with a million dollars."

"When you put it like that, it scares the shit out of me," Brad Murray commented.

"We can't come up with that ourselves, of course," Christian pointed out. "But, we have friends."

"Are you saying we should get ourselves some investors?" Elaine was blunt.

"Yeah, some investors and maybe some partners. We're gonna have to think about this."

"And why would anybody want to invest anything in the Sea of Cortés with the three of us, who know nothing about shrimping?"

"That's not exactly true. We didn't know much about shrimping in the beginning. But we're starting to learn the business. And besides, there seem to be some pretty good angles to this operation."

Elaine poured herself some Chardonnay, lighting up a Misty ultralight. "Good angles you say? Such as?"

"Well, this opportunity is not available to your average American. As we found out, only Mexican citizens can own fishing boats and permits. And only Mexicans can establish corporations down there. So, as an American investor, being invited to participate in a business enterprise such as this one is not an everyday occurrence. It could be considered a privilege."

Brad had been born in Mexico City when his father had lived there during medical school. The accident of birth unexpectedly provided them access to the shrimping industry in Mexico.

"Okay, I'll give you that. But what about the risks?" Elaine was the eternal devil's advocate.

"We don't know what those are yet. What we do know is this. If someone decides to invest capital in our shrimping business, we can pay them their dividends in Mexico, in hard cash. That should attract some bees to the honey."

"Are you saying what I think you're saying?" Brad Murray popped another Heineken.

"And what is it you think I'm saying, Brad?"

"If I'm hearing you correctly, you're implying we can pay out dividends to the partners without them having to pay taxes here at home. Which, I might add, is not a very good idea."

"No, I'm not saying that at all. Whether our investors pay their taxes to Uncle Sam or not is not our responsibility, nor that of our business. Investors can decide what to do with their own financial affairs. All I'm saying is we pay them dividends in Mexico in U.S. dollars. We invite them down there twice a year, treat them to a nice dinner with Mariachis, hand them a white envelope full of cash, they sign a receipt and that's the last we hear about it. They can then take their money and leave it in a bank account in Mexico or they can bring it back here and declare it."

"But you realize the implications." Brad Murray was a straight arrow. Dodging taxes was not something he would even consider doing. Not ever.

"What implications? Are you suggesting that just because we pay investors in cash in Mexico, we are advising them to hide the cash and not give Uncle Sam his fair share?"

"That's exactly what I'm suggesting, Christian. Any advice to avoid taxation can be construed as illegal. Look what happened to that old chap, Al Capone."

"But we would never suggest such a thing. As honest citizens, we will declare any earnings paid to ourselves from the production from our shrimp boats, and we will pay taxes on those earnings. After first deducting any taxes paid to the Mexicans, of course. And our partners and investors will be free to do the very same thing. We're not lawyers and will not be advising anyone what to do with their earnings. It would be entirely up to the individual how they want to handle their own personal financial affairs. It would be totally unbecoming for us to presume we can give tax advice to anyone."

"You know what I mean. Offering people hard cash paid in Mexico is an invitation to cheat. Marginally legal, if you ask me."

"Perhaps, but we're not gonna spell it out like that. And you're right, Brad. The idea of receiving dividends in Mexico in the form of greenbacks could be a very strong lure for many people to invest with us."

"What are we gonna do? Put out a general request for venture capital? Why can't we just setup a corporation here in the States and capitalize it with an initial public offering?" Brad Murray was rapidly considering alternatives.

"First of all," Christian explained, "I read somewhere that it's illegal to solicit venture capital from strangers unless one follows some very strict guidelines. When approaching strangers asking them for money, our government has some very Spartan guidelines that need to be followed to keep it legal. A business prospectus needs to be put together if one is dealing with strangers, and it has to follow a very unimaginative template. Then, a financial institution such as a bank needs to be hired to manage the entire enchilada. If the business appears to have potential, a bank could possibly be talked into putting together the initial public offering, as you mentioned."

"And what is wrong with that?"

"Nothing's wrong with that, other that it would be practically impossible for us to attain such an IPO."

"Why?"

"Because, first of all, doing all of that is horrendously expensive. And it's just another gamble. We could spend hundreds of thousands putting the business prospectus and financial package together, and even then, we still might not get to become a public company. Plus, the amount of money we're trying to put together here is miniscule. Public offerings are usually made for much larger sums. The financial institutions would laugh at us, trying to go public with a corporation needing only one million."

"One million is ridiculous? Holly shit. What other options do we have then?"

"We need to approach only people we know. As long as they're not total strangers, we can propose our own business plan to them and remain within the confines of the law."

"And that is legal?"

"That is legal. Doing it this way, we can put together our own business prospectus any way we damned please."

"And you think we can attract enough interest?"

"I believe so, yes."

"Then what are we waiting for? Let's put together a list of names of everyone we know who may be interested!"

"Jesus Christ," Christian laughed. "We're becoming the characters in the Forrest Gump movie.

"Another issue we need to review," Elaine put in. "The majority of the fishing trawlers operating in the Sea of Cortés have cargo holds cooled by freon. This type of refrigeration freezes the shrimp over a period of a few hours. Consequently, the heads on the shrimp cannot be left attached to the bodies, because most of the organs of the shrimp are in its head, the lungs, stomach, intestines. If left with the heads attached, the organs of the shrimp would spoil faster than the bodies would freeze, thereby ruining the catch. There are shrimp boats out there in other parts of the world equipped with what they call flash-freeze equipment. Those trawlers freeze the shrimp instantly. Being able to flash-freeze the product is an advantage because then the heads become part of the catch, increasing production by one third, since production is sold based on weight. Also, shrimp with their heads on bring in more money because chefs in Europe use them to decorate their seafood platters."

"Blimey," Brad Murray observed. "Why don't we get ourselves some of those ships equipped with flash freezing capacity then?"

"Because, Brad, there are none of those ships fishing in the Sea of Cortés. The cooling system for flash-freezing shrimp is incredibly expensive. Using that system freezes the product instantaneously, allowing for one third more revenue. But from what I've read, the cost of installing a system like that on a boat runs about half a million bucks."

"And the ships have to be bigger and newer than what they have for sale in this part of the world."

"Okay, so that's out." Murray sipped some Crown Royal. "What about the subsidy on the fuel for our boats?

"That's a different story," Elaine explained. "Based on my conversations with the folks at the Ministry of Fisheries in Mexico City, it appears the Mexican government subsidizes the fishing industry by selling marine diesel at one-third its market price to anyone engaged in commercial fishing."

"Why would they do that?"

"It's their way of supporting the fishing industry. Marine diesel sells for about three bucks per gallon around the Sea of Cortés, yet commercial fishermen get it for less than a dollar per gallon. This is a very important element for us. Diesel is our highest cost, considering three ships running those huge diesel engines twenty-four-seven burn thousands of gallons of fuel during one season. Bottom line, without that subsidy, fishing for shrimp would not be a profitable business. Once we include the subsidy into our business model, we see that we can produce about $100,000 earnings per ship each season. If the subsidy was unavailable, we would just break even. In other words, we'd be a non-profit organization."

"No shit," Christian interjected. "If we decide to go ahead with this project, we'll be putting a lot of money at stake basing it on the willingness of the Mexican government to continue the subsidies."

"I thought of that as well," Elaine pointed out, "but historically, the Mexican government has been subsidizing their fishing industry since WWII. Remember, Mexico is very rich with oil and they produce their own marine diesel, so I guess they can charge whatever they want for it. I don't see any likely reason why, all of a sudden, the diesel subsidy would just stop out of the blue."

"So, how does this work? We get a special price at the pump?"

"No, we pay three bucks a gallon all season, same as everyone else, then every three months the government issues us a check reimbursing us for the overpayment."

"Hence, we have to come up with the cash up front to refuel each time?"

"That is correct," Elaine indicated. "But we won't be using as much diesel as all the other shrimp trawlers fishing in the Sea of Cortés, either."

"Why not?" Christian asked.

"Because we won't be fishing during the entire seven months of the shrimping season. Shrimping is kinda like harvesting corn. When it's time to harvest the corn, all the huge combines go out and pick the fields clean in just a few days. All that's left after the combines sweep the fields are the small patches of corn by the roads or rivers, and these need to be harvested by hand. Same thing with the shrimp. Once the season starts and the big fishing trawlers go out, they sweep everything clean the first three months of the season. After that, there is very little shrimp to be had. Although the season runs September to April, fishing after November is not a good strategy. Sending the ships out after November would not make financial sense. They would burn diesel and be at risk of suffering a mechanical breakdown, all of which detracts from the profits for the season."

"Why just three months?" Murray questioned.

"December is a bad month for fishing in the Sea of Cortés. The first week in December those good folks celebrate the holiday of the Virgin Mary; I believe that's on the eleventh of December. The crews want to be home for that. Then, Christmas is just around the corner, so they also want to be home for the Holidays, understandably so. All of it followed by the celebration of New Year's Eve. And adding to it is the celebration of the three Wise Men visiting baby Jesus on the 6th of January."

"Boy, those people take their holidays serious!" Christian exclaimed.

"They sure as hell do, so as you can see, fishing in December would be non-productive, since the crews would have very few days at sea, and that's only if the owner of the ships forced the issue. And, anyhow, once January comes around, there is very little product left to catch. About 90% of production takes place before December, during the initial three months of the season. The other five months produce ten percent of the catch—at best. That is why, our ships would only go out fishing the first three months and let the rest of the fleet go out to sea the rest of the season."

"You think the crews would be good with that?" Brad Murray thought out loud.

"I don't see why not. Remember, we found out the crews get paid a percentage of the catch. The months when they catch the most shrimp, they make the most money. By fishing only three months out of a seven-month season, they will be taking home 90% of what they would take home if they worked an additional five months."

11

Casa del Pescador Restaurant
Rock Port, Sea of Cortés

"*Blimey*, it seems to me all I've done in this town since we arrived is eat!" Brad Murray dropped himself onto a bright pink wooden chair in the outdoor patio of the restaurant at the top of the hill. The restaurant sat atop the highest point in town, and the view was truly breathtaking. The Sea of Cortés extended to the horizon outside the balcony.

They ordered margaritas and admired the beautiful décor of the Casa del Pescador restaurant. They'd been told this was the best place in town at sunset.

"What time are those guys meeting us?" Murray liked the restaurant. Colorful and clean.

"They should be here in about ten minutes," Christian replied, glancing at his watch. "Three brothers coming over. Arturo, Rodolfo and I can't remember the other guy's name. I think it was Ramiro."

"Five of us. The table should be big enough to accommodate all of us."

"We'll be all right," Christian confidently asserted.

"They seemed nice on the phone?"

"Yeah, very nice. Courteous."

The margaritas came and the men accepted one each.

"Slainte!" Brad Murray toasted.

"*Salud!*" Christian replied. "To our dreams!"

The margaritas were served on the rocks with lots of salt on the edges. Christian wondered if these good people also served the Scottsdale, Arizona, version of a margarita, the one that resembled a Dairy Queen slush for kids.

"That must be them," Brad Murray pointed towards the main entrance. Three men approached the hostess' podium, all three wearing Mexican cowboy hats made of some white straw or wicker.

Christian stood, waving at the strangers.

The strangers waved back, smiling big from behind three black handlebar moustaches, starting in their direction.

The men introduced themselves as the 'Vega' brothers. Two of them were tall, the third one was of medium built and about the same height as Christian.

"Delighted to make your acquaintance," they echoed, everyone shaking hands. None of them spoke two words of English, Christian noticed, resigning himself to some more consecutive interpreting during dinner.

"Thank you for joining us for dinner," Christian began. "Sorry about the short notice."

The three brothers ordered tequila and beers and never removed their cowboy hats.

They wore blue jeans with cowboy boots and white long-sleeved cotton shirts. The men appeared to be in their mid-fifties.

"You interested in our shrimp boats?" The one named Rodolfo asked. He had a full head of disheveled black hair and bloodshot eyes.

Christian liked a man who cut right to the chase.

"Yes, we understand that private owners can now buy ships and permits." It was more a statement than a question.

"Yes, yes, that's correct. Anyone can own a shrimp boat now."

"And you gentlemen have some for sale?"

Rodolfo downed two shots of tequila *Patrón* in rapid succession, followed by half a glass of beer, then nodded vigorously. "Yeah, we have sixteen boats. How many you lookin' to buy?"

"Not sure. We went over to see Francisco Bisset at his shipyard. He was trying to convince us to build a new boat with him instead of buying older boats."

The brothers made no comment, but glanced at each other, the unspoken words saying much about Bisset.

"Bisset told us he could build us a ship and get a fishing permit for it."

"Bisset is full of shit," Rodolfo spat. "He can't get you a fishing permit."

"He said he'd check with his contacts in Mexico City," Christian added.

"His contacts? What contacts? That idiot has no contacts. And he knows damned well that the Ministry of Fisheries ain't giving out fishing permits to anyone."

Murray and Christian exchanged glances.

"He's just trying to take your money to build you a ship. He doesn't give a crap about your fishing permit," Rodolfo explained. The man appeared younger up close, perhaps in his mid-forties, tall and strong, but with a beer belly sticking out of his belt. He smiled a lot.

"You mean he lied?" Christian stated the obvious.

"Of course, he lied! What planet do you come from? He sees two rich gringos dropping on his lap with wallets full of money, What'ya think he was gonna say?"

Christian thought better than speaking badly against Bisset. For all he knew, that shipbuilder could be a blood relative of these guys. "As an alternative, we were told that you gentlemen have some shrimp boats for sale. Happy to hear that's the case."

Arturo spoke up. "We do. How many you looking to buy?" He repeated.

"Three for now," Christian responded. He didn't know whether he should say three or ten. But three was the number they had been contemplating to start their fleet, so three it was.

"Yeah, we can sell you three boats."

Christian was surprised. It wasn't like Mexicans going right to the point. "How much are they going for?"

"Depends which ones you want," Rodolfo replied.

"I understand. But what is the range? I need to have some idea of the prices for my associates back in Arizona."

The brothers looked at each other.

Rodolfo spoke again. Apparently, he was the mouthpiece for the group. "Around two-hundred fifty thousand, I'd say."

No kidding. Christian was slightly annoyed and disappointed by the high prices. Somehow, he'd harbored secret hopes that the waiter, Ramón—against all logic—had been closer to the true figures. However, he was already sold on the idea of operating shrimp boats, so they'd just have to analyze the numbers a little more closely. "And for those prices, is everything' included?"

"Sure, everything's included," Rodolfo confirmed, a little too quickly.

Christian wondered exactly what 'everything" meant. He wanted to ask, but it occurred to him that maybe it was too early in the game to do that. No need to get too picky with these dudes just yet. "How many ships do you gentlemen have?"

Rodolfo tossed back another shot of tequila. "Sixteen. We have sixteen trawlers, but we need to get rid of some. The bank's on our asses about the payments, and we're not making it."

Christian already knew enough about the fishing industry in the Sea of Cortés to realize that the lack of formal education had been the primary reason for the demise of the *coperativas*. He decided not to ask the Vegas why they had been unable to continue making their payments on their ships. No need to embarrass them.

"Where are you guys from?" Changing the topic might be the best policy.

"We're from Sinaloa," Arturo replied. He was the tallest of the three brothers. Sinaloa was a state in Mexico south of the state of Sonora, which in turn was the state bordering with Arizona.

"Your family in Sinaloa, are they fishermen?"

That got a laugh from two of the brothers and a smile from the third. "No, we're the only fishermen in the family. Our folks back home are not in the fishing business."

"They're in agriculture," Rodolfo added.

"Which of your boats are you interested in selling?" Christian inquired.

"You want three of 'em?" Rodolfo replied. "You can take your pick. Go look at our sixteen boats and just choose the three that you like best."

Christian was surprised at how easy this was turning out. "You don't care which three we select?"

"Nope," Rodolfo stated.

"Where are they now?"

"All of our boats are at the marina. Season's over and they ain't goin' nowhere."

"When could we take a look at them?" Christian translated for Brad Murray.

"Whenever you want," Rodolfo responded, quite accommodating.

"Tomorrow be okay?"

"Sure. We'll let our watchman know. We can meet you at the docks. What time did you have in mind?"

"Would early in the morning work?"

"Yep. What time?"

"Nine?"

"Nine sounds just fine."

"If we select three ships we like, can we take them out of the water to have them inspected?"

Rodolfo seemed to be the spokesman for his two brothers. "Of course, that won't be a problem."

"How do we set that up?"

"We'll talk to Federico García. He's the owner of the shipyard we use for maintenance and repairs. He will accommodate us."

Christian had a good feeling. These three brothers seemed to be gentle souls and they acted so cordial and cooperative.

"We are acquainted with a naval architect working for the local Cummings dealership. Do you want us to try getting hold of him, see if he can be there tomorrow to give you his opinion about the condition of the boats?" Rodolfo offered.

"He can give you a report on each of the boats," the brother who introduced himself as Ramiro put in. "That way you can have a written description on the condition of each trawler."

"That is an excellent idea, thank you. Yes, if you could get hold of your naval architect and ask him to inspect the ships for us, we'd really be grateful."

Later that night, Christian updated Elaine by phone. "Looks like we are moving ahead with this project."

"What did you two find out about these brothers Vega? Are they for real?"

"They seem to be, yeah." Christian relayed the conversation they had at dinner with the fleet owners.

"And they're going to let you choose three boats from among the sixteen they own?"

"That's what they said."

"That sounds almost too good to be true."

"My skeptic wife."

"Think about it...don't you find it odd these guys are willing to sell any of their boats? Logic dictates some would be in better shape than others."

"We're not buying anything yet. We're merely going to select three and take them out of the water to check them out." He told her about the marine architect.

"And who's going to pay for all this? Or did you even ask?"

"Tell you the truth, we didn't ask but I figured if the Vega brothers are anxious to sell, they'll foot the bill for the cost of lifting the ships out of the water and to pay the architect for the inspections."

"Make sure you ask all that up front before we get stuck with a monstrous bill."

"Very good suggestion."

"So, building new ships is out of the question?"

"I believe so. The guy Bisset at the shipyard seems to be a two-bit crook, and according to the Vega brothers, Bisset would never be able to procure a fishing permit for any boat he built for us."

"What a dishonest shithead."

"Aah, so poetically put. Yes, we're going to check out those trawlers in the morning. We still don't know how much they want for them. The brother Rodolfo said it would depend on which ones we pick."

Two days later the gang sat around Elaine's kitchen in Phoenix, drinking Guatemalan coffee.

"According to this written report, the naval architect indicates his inspection didn't find any major problems with any of the three trawlers we selected."

"And the Vega brothers gave you these prices."

"They did, $250,000 each for two of the boats and $230,000 for the third."

"Why the price difference?"

"It appears the smaller of the three ships has a smaller engine. Hence the difference in price."

"And you guys are satisfied with these boats?"

"From what we could tell, they looked better than the rest. Less rust. And two out of three have huge engines, which means they can drag bigger nets, which translates into more production."

"Are the Vega brothers willing to wait a month or so while we put the capital together?"

"Not that they have too much of a choice. No one else is scrambling to buy their ships and the banks are breathing down their necks."

"We need to confirm that."

Christian agreed to call Rodolfo in the morning with an offer. "Where are we with our business prospectus?"

"It's nearly done. A little fine-tuning now that we have identified the ships and the cost of acquisition and we'll be able to contact every friend we have with the proposal."

"We're still talking a million dollars for startup?"

"Seems that way," Elaine confirmed.

The following day, Christian called Rodolfo Vega with their offer to purchase the ships and all the gear needed to go trawling for shrimp. Rodolfo Vega seemed happy to hear the news until he learned how long it would take to put the venture capital together. He requested a fifty thousand dollar down payment to be paid immediately. Rodolfo explained the banks would probably wait a month to receive the proceeds of the sale from the three trawlers, provided they could see some immediate cash.

Christian presented the request to Brad and Elaine.

"I'm sure we can come up with fifty thou between us," Murray agreed. "It makes sense that the Mexican banks would want to see some earnest money before they agree to wait an entire month for payment."

"What's the worst-case scenario?" Elaine asked. "If we fail miserably with our prospectus and are ultimately unable to put together the financing needed for this adventure, we would be out fifty thousand."

"We can live with that," Christian confirmed.

He called Rodolfo back, informing him they accepted his terms. Christian and Brad Murray would personally deliver the fifty thousand in a couple of days via an international cashier's check.

"I'm driving out to Costco to buy us a bottle of Dom Perignon," Brad Murray announced. "This calls for a celebration. Let the games begin!"

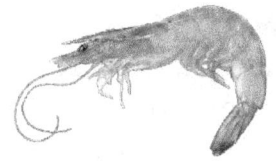

Two weeks later, Elaine called a meeting at home.

"It's only taken two weeks, but we've managed to spark tremendous interest in our commercial fishing project."

Christian and Murray took seats around the kitchen table, armed with Coronas.

"I'm all ears," the latter said.

"Since you two put me in charge of the financial aspect of this endeavor, I'm happy to report we've met our goals and surpassed our expectations."

Elaine had taken on the task of sending out the prospectus to thirty of their good friends and acquaintances. She was in charge of contacting the potential venture capitalists, explaining the prospectus and clearing any questions they might have.

The lure of cash payoffs as a return on investment attracted many more interested parties than they had expected.

"As you know, we contacted thirty potential investors." She glanced at the two men. "I'm delighted to inform you twenty-six of our friends and acquaintances have expressed interest and have verbally committed to investing with us. "

"Twenty-six, wow! Are you saying we have the million dollars necessary to buy the three boats and launch our first season?" Brad Murray asked.

"Yes! And we don't need all twenty-six investors. We put the capital together with just nine."

"Nine investors?"

"Yes! The others were told thank you for your support, but we can't use your money at this time."

"So how did you select the nine?"

I picked those folks we should all be able to get along with and who were prepared to invest a sizeable amount. Having too many investors complicates things."

"That is fantastic!" Christian exclaimed. "And they agreed to come in as venture capitalists, not owners?"

"They did," Elaine smiled. "You were right, I don't know if it was the lure of the sea or the sweet smell of cash being paid overseas, but regardless, we have nine in the bag and we can launch."

"That is terrific! I will immediately contact the Vegas and setup a meeting to pay them."

"How are we going to transfer the funds to them?" Brad Murray put in.

"We're gonna do it the same way we did with the first fifty-thousand. We'll buy international cashier's checks here and take them to the Vegas. They can deposit them in their Mexican bank accounts and from there they can pay off the loans on the boats. I'll call the attorney we hired in Rock Port so he can write up the final purchase contract."

"Don't we need a notary as well?" Elaine asked.

"No, in Mexico notaries are also attorneys. We located one down there, the notary who drafted the contract for the fifty-thousand dollar advance we gave the Vegas."

"So, we're in business?" Brad Murray's face was illuminated with enthusiasm.

"It appears we are. Great job, honey!!"

"Now, all we need to do is put this thing together and pray our rookie year doesn't turn out to be too costly for us," Elaine stated.

12

At the docks in Rock Port
Sea of Cortés

Capitán Cruz examined the aft deck of his shrimp trawler, the *Orca*. The men were still loading supplies onto the trawler. The company's dark blue Ford F-150 pickup was parked alongside the ship on the concrete dock, loaded with most of the food and beverage supplies needed for a thirty-day cruise. This was the best time of day to load supplies, since it was daytime and the tide was at its highest point. Twice a day, the tides changed the environment at the docks. During low tides it was practically impossible to load a ship fast. The tide extremes varied, but in general they fluctuated around ten feet.

The only way to load the trawler during low tide was by means of the winch and a metal cage which was used to lower men and supplies down to the ship. Cruz had been hired by the gringos the previous season, so he held something of an employment record in that area of the world, where most captains didn't even last one season with the same ship.

Capitán Cruz liked the *Orca*, with its 435-horsepower Caterpillar engine and its sleek hull. So far this season he'd done extremely well. He was happy. Four tons of blue shrimp had definitely rewarded his first trip with a gold seal. The owners had been pleased. And he'd made $5,200 American dollars from that trip. He liked being paid in dollars, since the Mexican peso continuously fluctuated in international markets. Being paid in pesos was not good. Most of the ship owners in the region insisted on paying their crews in pesos, because that left an additional margin of profit in their greedy pockets. This was due to the exchange rate, since buying and selling dollars was a lucrative business. The crews hated being paid in pesos because they knew they were being scalped by the ship owners, but didn't have much of a choice. There were many more sailors than there were jobs.

Capitán Cruz was in his mid-thirties, of slender body, skinny but strong. His blood was equal parts Spaniard and Aztec, and he loved his job. The eight members of his crew had been hand-picked by him, and he trusted most of them as much as pirates anywhere could be trusted. His freshly-shaven face with discerning eyes scanned the situation in the back of the boat.

Once they had all their supplies onboard, the captain would run a quick check to ensure the *Orca* was ready to set sail. The second trip of the season was never as rewarding as the first, but he held hopes of catching at least another two or three tons of the delicious Blue shrimp. The fourteen tons of shrimp he'd produced the previous season had left him with over eighteen-thousand American dollars in gross pay. Even after all the deductions, he'd still been able to take home nearly fifteen thousand.

That made him a very wealthy man in his modest village. And to think that he'd produced that much in just three months. This company of the gringos only fished the first three months of the shrimping season, so he was unemployed after November. This strategy was new to *Capitán* Cruz, and at first, he'd been surprised, but eventually he'd come to understand that not fishing after the end of November made sense. The shrimp was not there after November in quantities large enough to warrant taking out the shrimp boat.

"Goddammit, get those supplies loaded up! Clear the aft deck! We don't have all day, the tide's going to start down!" Cruz was known for being a lucky captain. Lucky meaning simply that he found the shrimp. He was also known for running a tight ship. The ship owners trusted him with their trawler and he went out of his way to avoid causing any sort of trouble. Other captains pulled stunts once they were out of sight, like continuously selling crates of shrimp to the *pangas* or trading shrimp for prostitutes and tequila any chance they got, but Cruz didn't allow any such nonsense during the season.

Cruz was married with four children and wanted to keep his job. He made more money than anyone else on his crew and that made him treasure his position. Most fishermen in the Sea of Cortés made little money, but expected some perks from their jobs: free fish for their families, and hookers and marihuana for themselves.

Those men working with *Capitán* Cruz knew how he operated. They knew their skipper would reward them with the perks they coveted, but only as the end of shrimping approached in late November. At that point, if the ship's production had been satisfactory, Cruz would drop anchor near Bahia de Kino and allow a dozen cases of shrimp to be bartered for women and whisky or tequila, as the case was in that part of the world.

Cruz entered the tiny bridge of his shrimp boat. Bolaños, his first mate, was already there. The scalding 115-degree temperature on the bridge had both men perspiring heavily. Their shirts glued to their backs, the armpits of their shirts totally soaked.

"So, we got the diesel onboard, the nets are all ready, and you made sure the motor oil was stored in the engine room?"

"*Si, Capitán,*" his first mate replied. Bolaños was dark, tall and overweight. His looks would've allowed him to pass as an Apache or a Navajo native American at any of the casinos on the reservations in Arizona. "The oil's in the engine room. We got everythin' we need."

"Did you check the *salmuera*?"

"Yes. Salt's in there and it's cooling."

The *salmuera*—brine—was a combination of fresh water and coarse salt mixed inside a 200-gallon open tank sitting on the aft deck. The tank was equipped with Freon coils inside, which cooled the water. The brine tank was used to pre-cool the shrimp in crates before it was lowered into the cargo hold. Although shrimp were cold-blooded, they still retained enough residual heat to warm up the refrigerated cargo hold. A quick dip in the *salmuera* prior to lowering the shrimp into the cargo hold helped keep down the temperature in the refrigerated room.

"Did the men get their cash advances to their wives?" Cruz demanded.

"They did, Boss, yes."

Giving the crews some cash up front was customary before sailing off on a fishing trip.

"Let's get ready to set sail as soon as those guys are done unloading the truck. Go ahead and start the engine. Let's start freezing the cargo hold."

Bolaños pressed a large red button on the dash and the roar of the Big Cat reached their ears. The engine vibration underfoot confirmed that the powerful diesel had come alive. Black smoke erupted from the eight-inch exhaust pipe behind the bridge. The refrigeration unit driven by the ship's engine would start pumping cold refrigerated air into the cargo hold immediately. It might take the Freon-based system thirty hours to completely cool the storage area for the shrimp, so the sooner one started, the better.

The five sailors loading supplies from the company's pickup truck looked up at the smoke-belching and increased their efforts to get everything loaded faster.

Capitán Cruz reviewed his paperwork. He'd enough diesel to last him up to thirty days. Naturally, the odds of being out thirty days were not really good. Something or other was going to fail long before they'd be out a month. These were old ships and something was inevitably going to break.

The release issued by the harbormaster was on the clipboard. Everything was as it should be. Now, if only these lazy fishermen would get a move on and finish loading the supplies, they'd steam away towards the southern fishing grounds. He knew exactly the spot where they'd drop the nets. He'd created a waypoint on the GPS which would allow him to find the exact same spot where his crew had caught plenty of shrimp the previous trip.

They would reach that spot by tomorrow afternoon. *Capitán* Cruz was young, ambitious, and actually very grateful to have landed this job with the gringos. They paid better than anyone else in the entire Sea of Cortés and, as long as they didn't feel they were being screwed too much by the crews, they'd probably stick around, hopefully for a long time. And *Capitán* Cruz wanted to be there with them the entire way.

"Did you make sure the turtle excluder device was sewn back on that net Juan repaired?"

"Yessir," Bolaños replied. One of their nets had been damaged by something sharp on the seafloor, and it had to be repaired.

Capitán Cruz was not about to get nailed by the Mexican navy for fishing without the TED. He was very much aware that the penalty for fishing without the turtle excluder device was the loss of the ship. Which translated into the loss of his job. Some of the other captains foolishly believed that using the excluders was detrimental to the amount of shrimp they could catch.

It was a common misconception that a lot of shrimp would escape from the trapdoor where the turtles also escaped when trapped by the nets. The loss was really nothing significant, along the lines of one percent of the catch, but try explaining that to some of the stubborn old-timers.

Since the TEDs were hand-sewn onto the nets it was practically impossible to remove and reinstall a TED on a net that was being used without spending several hours doing it. Those several hours were normally not available when a ship of the Mexican navy appeared on the horizon. *Capitán* Cruz didn't like playing games. The rules were quite clear: no women, booze, drugs or guns on his ship while they were at work.

No exceptions.

Once the trip was finished, however, it was another story. He could then indulge the men. *Capitán* Cruz didn't follow the letter of the law out of any respect for the law; he followed it because he didn't want to get caught and lose his job. Once he felt confident that their mission had been accomplished, he'd have no second thoughts about stealing some of the shrimp to take care of his men. But, naturally, he did not look at it as 'stealing.'

A deckhand stood in front of the side door to the bridge. "*Capitán*," we're done. Just need to drive the truck back to the office and we can leave." The man was short but powerfully built. And he was totally drenched in sweat.

Capitán Cruz looked up from the clipboard. "Good. Return the truck and hurry up and get back here. Tide's goin' out and we need to leave." *Capitán* Cruz glanced at the company's other two ships tied up to the docks ahead of him. He'd be the first one to leave.

The rumbling of the powerful Caterpillar engine sounded like a tiger purring in *Capitán* Cruz's ears. He shouted orders from the side door to the crew. "Let's get those lines off! We're pushing out!"

The ship began moving under its own power. At the last minute before they became totally separated from the docks, the man who drove the company pick up back to the office appeared running as fast as he could, jumping on the aft deck. Twenty seconds later, and he would've been unable to jump the gap. Had that occurred, the man would've had to rent a *panga* out of his own money to catch up with his ship.

Capitán Cruz kept the ship at a slow pace, maneuvering out of the narrow inlet. The ship felt heavy, but steady. Not a cloud in the sky ahead. The seas were calm and the breeze generated by the ship motoring at five knots brought a feeling of relief from the scorching temperatures of the Sonoran Desert in September.

Life was good.

Thirty minutes later and roughly six miles from the white sandy beaches paralleling their course,

Capitán Cruz ordered Bolaños, his first mate, to take the helm. The trawler steamed at ten knots in calm seas.

The skipper descended to the crew area located directly behind and below the bridge. It was his own personal policy to go through his crew's belongings at the start of each trip. Although the fishermen working with him were certainly aware of the rules, it wasn't unheard of for some to simply ignore them. *Capitán* Cruz had found many violations over his years as a shrimp boat captain. One sailor had brought his sister aboard once. She'd just wanted to come along to see how a shrimp boat worked. And perhaps make a little extra money on the side selling her favors to the rest of the crew.

The crew cabin was tiny and it was hotter than a sauna. *Capitán* Cruz was perspiring so much his sweat poured down on the sailors' humble belongings as he rummaged through them. He moved from one locker to the next. Nothing illegal. Couple of porno magazines, cigarettes and some chewing tobacco. Nothing really to worry about.

He opened the last locker.

Goddammit!

A six-pack of Tecate beer cans stared back at him. The gold and black cans sat half-wrapped in a white cotton T-shirt. The cans were still cold to touch, sign that they'd been recently purchased.

Capitán Cruz grabbed the six-pack, walking out on the aft deck. Some of his men were busy stashing the supplies into every available space they could find.

"Linares!" *Capitán* Cruz shouted. Linares was the youngest member of the crew, barely nineteen. His job was helping the others in every way possible when they trawled for shrimp. He also made the least amount of money of anyone in the crew.

"Yes, *Capitán?*" The young sailor responded, stepping forward from the area of the deck where he'd been busy clearing supplies.

"Are these yours?" *Capitán* Cruz demanded, holding the six-pack of beer at arm's length in front of the young sailor's nose.

The look on the kid's face confirmed ownership of the beer. His mouth opened as if to say something.

Capitán Cruz's face showed his anger. "Go get your shit and bring it up here."

"*Capitán*, I'm very sorry, it's only six beers. I thought if we're gonna be gone a whole month..."

"Get your gear and bring it here, NOW!"

The sailor cowered, walking a wide arc around his skipper. He disappeared through the cabin door.

Capitán Cruz stood his ground, staring at his men, one by one. The men lowered their eyes, not wanting to become part of the confrontation. *Capitán* Cruz's reputation with rule-breakers was well-known among some of the crew. Nobody wanted to engage in a fist fight.

The young sailor returned, holding a half-zipped green canvas backpack with white T-shirts and underwear partially stuffed in it.

Capitán Cruz reached for the man's backpack. "Gimme that!" with one quick motion the skipper yanked the backpack from the hands of the sailor, launching it overboard twenty feet away from the boat. The six-pack of Tecate followed, plunging in the ocean.

The young sailor was too surprised to say anything.

Capitán Cruz then stepped closer to the sailor, grabbing him with both hands by the belt from each side of his waist, then using his own body weight, propelled the young man overboard.

The surprised sailor screamed once, performing a nearly perfect summersault, hitting the water head first.

"Nobody!" *Capitán* Cruz yelled, "*nobody* breaks my rules on *my* boat! Is that clear?" The expression on his face left no room for doubt.

It was clear all right.

None of the fishermen replied. A couple of them barely cast a glance towards the stern of the boat, where the head of the unfortunate sailor was bobbing in the wake. No one made an effort to throw a life preserver to the unfortunate sailor already struggling against the prop-wash and the current. No one called 'man overboard.'

Those were the unspoken, implacable rules of the pirates of the Sea of Cortés.

Many hours later, totally exhausted, the young sailor reached the beach near *Las Flores*, a residential luxury neighborhood south of Rock Port. He was exhausted from the exertion, yet he walked nearly two additional miles to the office of his *coperativa*, the one that had provided him with the job.

"I want my pay!" the young sailor demanded, no longer wet. The two-mile walk in the desert heat had dried his clothes.

"And who are you?" The clerk behind the desk asked, only partially interested.

"My name's Linares. I was working on the *Orca* these past three days. I want my pay."

"The *Orca* you say? She just sailed this morning. What are you doin' here if you're supposed to be onboard?" The *coperativa* clerk was a big man, over two hundred pounds.

"*Capitán* Cruz threw me off the ship."

"He threw you off the fucking ship? And why in the devil's name would he do that?" the man looked at the sailor suspiciously.

"I had some beer with me and he threw me overboard."

"You had beer with you? What are you, stupid? You know you're not allowed to take beer on the ship!"

"I don't care. I just want my pay."

"I can't pay you."

The young man leaned forward on the desk. "What? Why not? I worked three days provisioning that ship. I want my pay. Now."

"It doesn't work that way, buddy. We can't pay you shit until the *Orca* returns to port. Once we know how much shrimp they brought, then we can plug that number into the computer and it'll tell me how much your pay is. Until that happens, I can't pay you. You're shit outta luck."

"This sucks!" the young sailor leaned closer to the big clerk.

The clerk stood. He towered more than a foot over the sailor. "I don't give a shit what you think! Get your ass outta here before I throw you out!"

"I want my pay!"

"And I already told you that you're gonna have to wait until the *Orca* returns from its trip. Now beat it or like I said, I will throw your sorry ass outta here myself."

The young sailor backed off, realizing a fight with the big clerk was going to be a losing proposition. Leaving the *coperativa* he walked to a nearby gas station. The young man filled two glass bottles with gasoline, paying the attendant some pesos. He then walked to the docks, stuffing a rag into each bottle. The company's two other ships, the *San Felipe* and the *Conquistador* were there, tied to the docks. Their crews had them almost ready to sail the following morning and were resting below decks after a long day in the heat. Nobody was in sight. The ships were five feet lower than the docks due to the receding tides.

The night watchman was a humble man in his fifties. He was paid very little, but at least he was glad to have the job. He sat on a wooden stool against a wall, watching the sun slowly descend towards the sea. Suddenly, a young man appeared, walking rapidly toward the two ships tied to the docks. The young man carried a glass bottle in each hand, their tops on fire, with flames trailing behind.

As fast as he could, the night watchman jumped up, sprinting and tackling the young man from behind. The impact forced the young man to release the bottles, both of which crashed on the concrete docks, showering the area with burning gasoline. Both men screaming at each other.

The crews on the two docked ships raced out, attracted by the commotion.

"What in the name of the Virgin Mary is going on here?" *Capitán* Tuero took in the scene: the flames burning on the dock, the black smoke, the watchman holding some guy by the shirt. *Capitán* Tuero realized in a split second that the burning stuff, whatever it was, had been intended for his ship. The *San Felipe* was all metal, so a Molotov cocktail wouldn't burn it, but the twenty-thousand dollars' worth of nets and fishing gear piled up on the stern sure as hell would. "I recognize you! You're Linares! You were on the *Orca*. What the devil are you doin' here?"

The young man didn't respond.

"You wanted to burn my ship didn't ya?" *Capitán* Tuero barked, reaching for the young sailor. "Leave him to me," he ordered the night watchman, pushing the man off.

Capitán Tuero had hung around gyms most of his life and had boxed with and without gloves when he was a young man. His boxing skills were better than amateur. And he had every intention of using them to teach this young shit a lesson.

The men made a circle around their captain. The crews from both shrimp boats joined the scene.

Capitán Tuero punched the kid in the face, then did it again. Linares fell back against the circle of sailors. The sailors pushed him back up. The ship's captain continued punishing the young man with multiple blows to the face and chest and stomach. Blood flowed from the sailor's mouth and nose.

A police car appeared, screeching to a halt on the concrete docks, two armed policemen jumping out. "Stop it! Right now! Stop this fight or we take you all in!"

The beating stopped.

"What is happening here!?" one of the two cops demanded.

Capitán Tuero faced the police officer, breathing hard. "This little sonofabitch tried to torch my ship!" pointing at the still burning gasoline on the docks, black smoke billowing from the spot.

The two cops took in the situation, as well as the crowd of men standing around. "What do you want to do, *Capitán?*"

"I wanna beat the crap out of this little shit."

"Make a circle!" The cop ordered.

The men closed the circle around their captain and around the young sailor. *Capitán* Tuero resumed punching the kid with deliberate, professional hits, swinging at the face and the chest. He delivered a good dozen blows until Linares, bleeding and in desperation jumped the circle of men and ran away from the docks fast enough to prevent anybody from catching him.

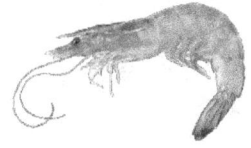

Two weeks later to the day, Christian was sitting at his desk in the company's small office in Rock Port writing checks. He was planning on staying in town overnight and having a nice dinner up on the cliff at the *Casa del Pescador* restaurant. Javier Arenas, his manager sat across from him. The front door opened; a middle-aged local man wearing a shoddy green suit with an orange tie walked in. The guy was disturbingly out of place.

"Good afternoon," he greeted. He was sweating profusely and his cheap suit was wrinkled and stained.

"How can we help you?" Arenas stood rapidly, protective of Christian. In that town one never knew when a pissed off sailor would try his hand with the knife.

The man extended a business card to Arenas. "I'm *Licenciado* Jose Iturbide. I'm an attorney and I wish to talk to the man in charge."

Christian stood and introduced himself. "Have a seat," he directed. "What can we do for you, Mr. Iturbide?"

Christian intentionally did not address the man with his title of *Licenciado*—lawyer—which, in Mexico, was a significant breach of etiquette...a subtle statement stablishing the status of who was in charge and who was subordinate.

The attorney was still sweating heavily despite the cold air in the office. "I'm here regarding a client of mine, one Esteban Linares, who was thrown overboard from one of your ships and then viciously assaulted by one of your captains."

Christian and Javier Arenas exchanged looks.

"Javier, was that the kid who brought beer onboard one of our ships?"

"Yessir. Cruz threw him off the ship for doing that."

"As you're well aware, sir," the attorney chimed in, "these waters are extremely hazardous. We have great hammerhead, bull sharks, tiger sharks, great barracuda..."

"I know, I know, you don't have to recite to me the list of dangers in the Sea of Cortés. Your client, you say?"

"Yes. Mr. Linares is my client."

Christian was a little surprised and insulted. He hadn't expected the ungrateful little creep to sic a lawyer on him. "Javier, did Samuel cut the check I ordered for Linares?"

"Yea. Twelve hundred dollars. Linares lives with his mother. I took the check to him myself last week and he already cashed it."

Christian turned to the attorney. "Mr. Iturbide, your client took beer aboard one of our ships. As you know, it is against Navy regulations to have any sort of liquor on a shrimp boat. You know what the penalties are if the Navy discovers any sort of booze on a ship. I don't have to tell you that. Mr. Linares was the youngest member of the crew, also the least experienced and, consequently, his pay was the lowest among the nine crewmembers. If the ship he was on performs really well this season, Mr. Linares could've maybe earned around one thousand dollars for the three months that we fish.

The attorney merely sat there, listening. He was hugging a brown briefcase, holding it against his chest like a high school girl holding her books. He was deeply intimidated by these rich men from the Other Side.

"Out of the goodness of our hearts, we decided to give the young man a check for the whole amount he would've made if he'd stayed with the ship the entire three months, and more. We didn't have to do this, but we did it because I was told that the young man supports his mother, and I admire that. It was an act of kindness. Otherwise, the pay that he'd earned working for us three days prior to sailing would've been around fifty dollars. Now I see that we might've made a mistake being generous to the little punk."

"I understand, but you gave orders to have him tossed overboard in shark-infested waters, putting his life in danger," the attorney interrupted.

Christian laughed. "I gave no such orders. Every crewmember on that ship can testify to that. So, don't go there."

"My client is suing you for fifty thousand dollars," the attorney blurted out. He appeared very uncomfortable, looking at the two men in front of him with nervous, darting eyes. He was a fishing village attorney and he'd heard many stories about these men from the Other Side, from the north, powerful men with lots of money, who could make life very difficult for anyone stupid enough to go against them. Being in their presence made him understandably skittish.

Christian laughed again. Aah, these people were so transparent. And so corrupt. He reached for his checkbook, filling in a check. "Here," he stated, passing the check to the attorney across the desk. "That's all you're getting. If that's not enough, then give it back and we'll fight this out in court and you'll work for free, because I assure you there's no way that you're going to win this."

The attorney read the check, his face breaking into a big smile. "Thank you, *Capitán*, thank you very much. I will speak to my client and I guarantee you he'll understand that you were very generous with him and that he shouldn't be bothering nice people like you." The man stood, extending his hand. "Thank you again. Have a good evening." He shook hands with Javier Arenas then left the office.

"That filthy sonofawhore," Javier exclaimed.

"Hey, no harm done. We're rid of him."

"How much did you give him, Boss?"

"Five hundred dollars. Which he's going to go deposit in his own checking account first thing tomorrow morning and probably buy his wife and girlfriend each a present before going out to get drunk."

"That was too much money."

"Yeah, maybe. But I really don't want any more legal problems here. If we let this thing go, I suspect it would cost us more than the five hundred I gave the man. Money well spent. You've fished these waters before, Javier, how bad is it with the sharks?"

"You mean Linares' long swim?

"Yeah. How bad was that? What were his chances?"

Javier Arenas smiled from behind his moustache, his cowboy hat and his clear blue eyes. "He's pretty goddamned lucky to be alive. There's some big sharks out there, Boss. I wouldn't have bet a fish taco that he'd make it back in one piece."

"And Cruz knows this too?"

"Of course, Cruz knows this."

"You better have a talk with Cruz. Tell him not to be doin' this anymore. If he finds anything illegal on his ship, wait until the next time he makes port and we'll put the sailor in jail. But tell him not to throw anybody else off his ship."

"Yes Boss."

"Remind our captain of something I read once, that good judgement comes from experience, and experience? Well, that comes from bad judgement. Pitching that kid overboard was definitely bad judgement."

Christian realized the sky was turning amber, time to head to his favorite restaurant on the hill for some spaghetti with shrimp and a beer or two.

13

Angel the Shrimp

The temperature and salinity of the water were just perfect in the Sea of Cortés. The female Blue shrimp each began their task of depositing over 600,000 eggs along the silty bottom of the Sea of Cortés just south of the delta of the Colorado river.

The high salinity of the seawater diminished considerably where it blended with the millions of gallons of fresh water pouring down from the Colorado river. Female shrimp much preferred areas of low salinity to deposit their offspring.

Millions of other female Blue shrimp released their eggs in the same area, around the same time, collectively depositing a number of eggs far more numerous than the entire population of Planet Earth.

The eggs floated towards the marshes along the beaches of the Sea of Cortés, pushed by the local currents.

Within twenty-four hours, the eggs hatched and the larvae continued their journey toward the shallow waters nearer the marshes.

Thousands of marine predators sitting higher on the food chain heard the dinner bell, and converged from all directions on the billions of larvae headed for the marshes.

Due to their small size and abundance, shrimp were prey to numerous predators in the Sea of Cortés, both in the water and out. Shrimp were eaten by fish, crustaceans such as crabs, sea urchins, starfish, sea-birds, whales, dolphins, sharks, humans, plus many other animal species as well. All of these predators followed the dinner invitation, converging on the cloud of shrimp egg and larvae floating toward shore, devouring the future shrimp population by the uncounted millions.

Among those millions of new arrivals was Angel, a Blue shrimp larva being transported by the current toward shallow waters.

Angel was lucky. By random chance he had remained in the middle of the cloud, sheltered from outside predators by millions of other larvae which were being devoured first, before Angel's existence could be cut short in the mouth of a ravenous fish.

The marshes provided shelter and food for survival of the young juveniles. The lucky ones able to reach the shallow waters near the shore would thrive. Only a third of all the larvae would survive the journey, their ranks decimated by hungry sea inhabitants searching for food.

Angel had no idea who he was or what he was. He operated following a very basic program nature had given him to ensure his survival during the two short years of his lifespan here on earth. Being one of the lucky ones, Angel arrived in the area near the shore as a young juvenile, not yet fully grown, but already shaped like a shrimp, with ten slender long walking legs, and five pairs of swimming legs located on the front surface of his abdomen.

14

Just another fraud

The *Maria Cristina,* a shrimp trawler painted white but with generous amounts of rust streaking along her hull, steamed under cloudy gray skies just north of La Paz, Baja California, at ten knots.

Her skipper, *Capitán* Escobar, glanced at his GPS and his marine navigation chart. The gulf was deep enough there. The Sea of Cortés was never deeper than 600 feet in the northern part, but down here approaching the southern tip of Baja, there were areas where the depth of the water approached an abysmal 10,000 feet.

Capitán Escobar estimated their current position to be over one of those deep areas.

It was time.

He left his Second Mate at the wheel, stepping out in the drizzle to scan the area visually. He didn't want any other ships to be in the vicinity when he played out his plan. Visibility was under one mile in drizzle and fog, and he didn't spot any other boats near his.

Good.

"Let's get the men off their bunks and run through a pirate boarding drill," he ordered his first mate.

"*What?* Now?"

"Yes! Now! We need to be prepared in case we're boarded by pirates at any time. This weather is conducive to piracy," he added. He had absolutely no idea whether the weather was conductive to piracy, but it sounded good.

His first mate reluctantly left the small wheelhouse, stepping down into the main cabin area of the shrimp boat. The men slowly removed themselves from their bunks where they had been resting after a long night traveling south. The drizzle became light rain.

"Men! Everyone in the cargo hold, now!" The plan was to hide in the cargo hold and lock the hatch from the inside. That way, any potential pirates would not have access to the three tons of shrimp and the crew would be safe inside the all-metal cargo hold. If the pirates blocked the hatch from outside in an attempt to trap the crew, an acetylene torch had been placed in the cargo hold. With it, the crew could literally cut their way out through the hull or the deck.

The eight sailors descended into the freezing air of the cargo hold one at a time, not yet totally awake. They wore T-shirts and light sweaters, none of them dressed for a prolonged stay at twenty below zero. All had been through these drills before, and knew that they wouldn't be spending more than five minutes in the hold. The first mate was the last man in. The Skipper didn't follow them. They were used to this, as well.

Someone had to test the hatch to make sure it couldn't be opened from the outside. The idea was to have the sailors lock themselves in the cargo hold, keeping the pirates out.

Once the last man descended into the hold, *Capitán* Escobar quickly removed a large Yale lock from his pants' pocket, snapping it on the hatch. Now the men were locked below.

There. Now to action.

The fifty-four-year-old sailor rapidly went to a tarp located on the roof of the main cabin. Removing the tarp, he retrieved a large yellow bag. The bag was labeled: RAFT.

Capitán Escobar tied a rope extending from the yellow bag to one of the *tangones*, a boom used to drag their nets. He then pitched the yellow bag overboard. The raft immediately inflated. He visited the wheelhouse one last time, glancing at the place that'd been his office for the past three years. Nothing there he wanted to take with him. He closed the throttle, effectively slowing the advance of the trawler. Reaching behind one of the seats, he removed a very large crescent wrench.

Exiting the wheelhouse, *Capitán* Escobar got hold of the rope, pulling the raft closer to his ship. The yellow raft could hold ten people in great comfort and safety. It had an inflatable top, which guaranteed that even if it was rolled over by the waves, its occupants would not fall out. He stepped into the raft, removing his shirt, hat and shoes. The *Maria Cristina* had slowed to a crawl. *Capitán* Escobar donned a diving mask and jumped in the water, the crescent wrench clutched in one hand.

The water-cooled Cummins engine of the *Maria Cristina* was equipped with an external radiator attached to the hull, nearly twenty feet in length. This external radiator was designed with two pipes penetrating the hull, allowing for the circulation of cooled water. It was to these two pipes that *Capitán* Escobar directed his attention in the warm waters of the Sea of Cortés.

He had to surface several times to get air but, in less than five minutes, he had loosened both pipes. This allowed seawater to enter the hull of the ship at a rate of nearly one hundred gallons per minute.

Capitán Escobar climbed back on the yellow raft, drying himself with a towel he had stored in the raft the day before. He slipped on a sweat shirt and dropped a sea anchor into the water, allowing the yellow round raft to be pulled away from the shrimp trawler. He was still attached to the *Maria* Cristina by a lanyard, which was fine by him. He wanted to stick around to make sure the goddamned boat actually sank.

The men trapped in the cargo hold would not have enough time to cut their way out of there before the ship went down.

The ship's owner, Carlos Iturbide, had approached *Capitán* Escobar weeks before.

"*Capitán*," Carlos Iturbide had confided. "We need to talk."

They had gone into the ship owner's little office in the city of Ciudad Obregon.

"*Capitán* Escobar, as you know, the *Maria Cristina* is in very sad shape. I don't have the money to prepare her for the upcoming season and this is a very real problem. Ocean Fruit won't lend me any more money for maintenance because I still owe them a bunch from last season."

Escobar said nothing.

"Extreme problems call for extreme solutions," Carlos Iturbide stated.

Escobar just sat there, looking at him. "What I'm saying is we need to do something about it."

"Sure."

"If you take her out fishing, she will not make it through the season. You know that."

Escobar knew the trawler was in bad shape but didn't really think it was going to sink anytime soon. It could probably continue to fish two or three more seasons, even without any serious maintenance. "What'd ya have in mind, Boss?"

Carlos Iturbide studied the face of his captain. He'd always considered all his captains to be prostitutes, pirates, men who would do anything for money. "What I have in mind is, if she happened to sink, then the insurance company would pay me a shitload of money for her."

Escobar analyzed the information his boss was giving him. "I don't think she's gonna sink anytime soon, Boss."

"Maybe not by herself, she's not. But if we give her a little push then, perhaps, she could sink."

Capitán Escobar understood. "I see."

"Well, what do you say? Don't you agree with me?" Carlos Iturbide was the descendant of Spaniards who had settled in Ciudad Obregon centuries earlier. He was in his late fifties, totally out of shape, dressed meticulously and displaying the fastidious behavior of Mexican Spaniards.

"Yes, I agree with you that she could sink."

"Good! How about fifteen thousand dollars for you?"

Capitán Escobar swallowed. That was more money that he could make fishing an entire season. "Tax free?"

Carlos Iturbide smiled. The cat was in the bag. "Yes, tax free."

"Consider it done."

"Very good, then. You need to do it the first trip of the season."

"Why the first trip?"

"I'm sure you know most pirate attacks occur during the first trip of the season. That's when you have the most product on your ship."

"Pirate attacks? Nobody said nuthin about no pirates."

"Relax, there will be no pirate attacks. Not real, anyhow. After the *Maria Cristina* sinks, I have to file a claim with the insurance company, and these guys are not stupid. I'll allege that your ship was attacked by pirates and file a claim for the ship, the shrimp and the crew."

"The crew?"

"Yes, of course, the crew. The ship has to sink with the crew, otherwise it's not believable. You really weren't thinking of having your crew support our story that pirates sank the ship, were you?"

"You didn't say nuthin about the crew."

"Think about it. There's no way we're going to convince the crew to back up our story. Even if we paid them all off, someone would eventually spill the beans. Then you and I would spend the rest of our very unhappy lives in prison."

"I see. That's different. I want thirty thousand dollars then."

Carlos Iturbide wanted to reach out and choke the captain. Insolent uneducated extortionist!

"Thirty thousand!?"

"Yes. For that, I'll sink your ship along with the other crewmembers."

Carlos Iturbide did some quick calculations in his head. He could file a claim for $250,000 for the ship, plus say three tons of shrimp, another $45,000. Another $25,000 in diesel. And maybe he could get $20,000 for each crew. He would give $5,000 to the families of each sailor, pocketing the rest. That would leave him with about $440,000 from where he could take out thirty Grand to pay this bastard, Escobar.

Or not.

"Deal."

Capitán Escobar sat in the rolling raft, watching coldly as the last part of the *Maria Cristina* disappeared below the warm waters of the Sea of Cortés, taking with her the entire crew. She had been built thirty-seven years earlier and had served a long list of captains over those years, capturing hundreds of tons of shrimp for its multiple owners, the last of which had been Carlos Iturbide, distinguished gentleman from the city of Ciudad Obregon.

Capitán Escobar opened the water-proof bag, removing a powerful Uniden submersible two-way radio with a fifty-mile range and a portable Garmin GPS. His son-in-law, Paco, had the same equipment and would be expecting the call. Paco was very dependable and they had arranged for him to rent a *panga* and pick up his father-in-law once the operation was complete. With the *Maria Cristina* now on its way to the bottom of the Sea of Cortés ten thousand feet below, it was time to go home.

Capitán Escobar would become an instant celebrity in his village as the only survivor of a terrible pirate attack that left eight crew members dead. He started thinking about things to do during his upcoming retirement.

Fifteen miles away was an entirely different man, Camilo Salcedo, twenty-one, young and strong and full of dreams, originally from the state of Sinaloa. He sat in his *panga* while writing down the coordinates he just heard over the hand-held receiver. The latitude and longitude of the GPS position of *Capitán* Escobar. He reached for the AK-47 assault rifle at his feet, sliding the first round into the chamber. The weapon had a 30-round magazine and two additional mags were in the duffle bag at his feet.

He started the engine of his panga in the dark, attaching his GPS receiver against a strip of Velcro duct-taped to his pants. He sure didn't want that GPS sliding off anywhere. Hernan Urrutia, a good friend of his, who just happened to be the personal driver for Don Carlos Iturbide, had commissioned him for this task. He didn't know why, but all he had to do was take out a man in a yellow raft and another dude in a panga and send them both to the bottom, along with their boats and their gear. Easy as eating *enchiladas*. The sharks would take care of any final cleanup necessary after he was done.

And for all this, he would get paid a fortune. One thousand dollars.   And perhaps more jobs like this could materialize in the future if his employers found that he was reliable. He eagerly gunned the engine, accelerating into the haze.

Carlos Iturbide, businessman extraordinaire, shrimp boat owner, pig farmer. A man of many talents. He was happy and in the mood for celebration. The *Maria Cristina*, that old bucket of rust had finally found her final resting place at the bottom of the Sea of Cortés. Iturbide had been able to successfully orchestrate the untimely demise of the ship and her crew, followed by the cleaning up of loose ends with the elimination of Captain Escobar. That greedy bastard.

Carlos Iturbide smiled. It'd been three months since the *Maria Cristina* sank and the insurance company had finally completed its investigation of the accident and made the payment for the loss of life and the sinking of the vessel. Pirates, of course, had been blamed for the tragedy. There were no witnesses really, and the insurance company—as expected—had taken its own sweet time doing its due diligence before grudgingly paying for the loses.

The insurance adjuster from Mexico City had investigated Iturbide and his financial situation, searching for possible motivation for insurance fraud, but had been unable to find anything even remotely incriminating. Iturbide was a solid businessman with diverse sources of income, and was quite solvent.

Ultimately, the insurance adjuster had enough of staying in the hotel in Ciudad Obregon, a city he considered too friggin' hot and provincial for his taste. Hence, he authorized payment on the policy and returned to Mexico City.

Now Carlos Iturbide was half a million dollars richer and life was good.

He walked toward a restaurant he liked not too far from his office when a black GMC Hummer came to a sudden stop next to him, skidding on the sand-covered street.

Carlos Iturbide instinctively jerked away from the street, angry at the careless driver. As he turned to yell at the idiot in the Hummer, much to his surprise all the doors opened and four men holding pistols rapidly surrounded him.

"What the fuck??!!"

Before Carlos Iturbide had a chance to react, one of the four men hit him on the back of the head with the butt of his pistol, while the other three grabbed the surprised businessman, forcing him into the Hummer.

Carlos Iturbide had never felt such pain before. He'd always been a gentleman of high social standing in his town, and physical altercations were not something he was familiar with. The blow to the back of his head was horribly painful and had made him see stars. He really had no time to ponder who these thugs were or what they wanted from him. All he knew was they had thrown him into the back seat of the Hummer and were tying his hands with plastic cuffs behind his back. He'd caught a glimpse of his hand and seen it bloodied after reaching to touch the back of his head.

A kidnapping, that's what it was. Carlos Iturbide felt anger at being in that situation, but also relief. They were not going to hurt him, at least not right away. Kidnappers wanted money and he had plenty of that. He would talk to their boss and cut a deal. His anxiety level went down several clicks when he decided he was being abducted.

Carlos Iturbide suddenly felt the calloused hand of one of his kidnapers cupping his chin. The rough hand lifted his head up and backwards, exposing his neck.

At that moment, he felt the tip of a very sharp object pushing against his neck below his right ear.

The pain he felt was out of this world.

The man holding up his chin plunged a narrow, extremely sharp blade into the right side of Iturbide's neck.

The human larynx, or windpipe, is very difficult to actually penetrate, since it's surrounded by skin tissue, cartilage and very fibrous tissue.

But the man calmly attacking Iturbide was strong, and his fisherman knife was sharp as a razor. He had little difficulty inserting the blade to the hilt into the immobile man, then sawing off the Carotid Artery and Jugular Vein.

Although Iturbide was not aware of the gravity of the injury he'd just suffered, he began experiencing sheer terror.

He bled profusely, blood flow to the brain being compromised. Iturbide struggled trying to move his head away from the vice grip the man had on his chin, then began struggling to breathe. Everything around him became white. His hearing faded. Unconsciousness was attained seconds later.

"Did you finish the asshole?" One of the men inquired from the front seat.

"He's done," the man in the back responded, cleaning his nine-inch fishing knife against the shirt of the man whose throat he'd just cut. The ultra-sharp fishing knife had cut through the guy's throat like it did when fileting tuna. The plastic garbage bags on the floor of the Hummer protected the vehicle from most of the blood that emptied through the dude's severed jugular.

"All right, let's go out to the sierras and burn this asshole. We'll bury whatever's left and we can still be back in time for some tequila before all the bars close. You do have the gasoline back there, right?"

"Yeah, I brought plenty of gasoline."

15

Phoenix, Arizona

"The maintenance on these ships is killing us," Brad Murray complained.

"Well, they *are* thirty-five years old." Christian sat around a table in the kitchen of his home with Brad and Elaine.

"You really can't believe these guys," Murray continued. "They just don't know the meaning of the word 'maintenance.' I'm starting to wonder if that word even exists in the Royal Academy Dictionary of the Spanish Language, as published in Madrid. I mean, we took some aluminum fuel lines down for the *San Felipe* and they installed them without priming them or even painting them. The salt in the air down there's enough to corrode the metal in a week. But they don't give a damn. The general attitude seems to be 'the gringos will buy another one and replace it again once it breaks'."

"I know, they're a nightmare to deal with." Christian poured some Crown Royal for him and Brad, Elaine was drinking chilled white Pinot Grigio.

"We've lost too many fishing days steaming back to port to conduct repairs for mechanical failures that should've never occurred at sea in the first place. This happens every trip, but it's particularly damaging on the first trip of the season, which ends up costing us a fortune in lost catch." Brad Murray was distressed. "We're hemorrhaging revenues because of these mechanical problems, look at it this way. We're making an average of one hundred thousand dollars in profits from each ship each season. One day on that first trip of the season, just one day without fishing, can cost us one ton of shrimp. That's fifteen thousand dollars. Plus, the cost of the repairs and the diesel those boys burn going back and forth to port. That's unacceptable. We need to overhaul these ships from head to toe."

"Brad, we can't rebuild the ships inside out, it'd cost way too much," Christian would have preferred taking the ships out of the water in late spring and gutting them, rebuilding them completely, but the cost was in the neighborhood of $150,000 per ship.

Not an option.

"We need to do something. Look at that García dude who owns the shipyard, he's got nine ships, all new, and he never breaks down. Not only he never breaks down, but he's got much bigger engines and nets on those things. He's catching a lot more than we are. By far. What we need is some new ships with more powerful engines so we never break down and with those ships we can pull bigger nets." Brad Murray was a numbers man, and the numbers made much better sense with newer, bigger ships.

"I agree, but at five hundred thousand dollars apiece it's a bitch. And that's not even guaranteeing that we could get fishing permits."

"We could build three new ships, sell the ones we have now for scrap and use their fishing permits on the new ones." Brad was on his third Crown.

"That takes about one and a half million dollars," Christian pointed out. "As you know, that amount is quite difficult to obtain. Venture capitalists aren't interested in such small investments. Neither are commercial banks. It's more than we have, but not enough to interest any serious capitalists."

"Nat, one of our investors, has a contact with an investment firm in San Diego. It's a firm managing retirement funds for airline pilots. They must have a lot of money. Why don't we talk to them?

"They won't give us a million and a half either. it's not enough money to interest anybody."

"So, let's ask for more."

"What'd ya mean?"

"If a million and a half is not enough, let's ask for ten million." Brad poured Elaine more wine.

"Ask for ten million?" Christian repeated. "What for?"

"To build ships. We'll just build more."

Christian gave it some thought. "We're not building twenty ships, that's out of the question. We could never get the fishing permits."

"Then, let's build nine!" Brad was on a roll. "That's only four and a half million. That should get their attention."

"Brad, where in the hell are we going to get six additional fishing permits?"

"I don't know. Ask García. We can have him build nine new ships for us provided he's able to find six additional permits."

"García is well connected," Elaine interjected. "If anyone can find us six additional permits, it would be him."

"We can't borrow four and a half million dollars not knowing if we have fishing permits. That's insane." Christian had learned to be extremely conservative, after being burned every day by just about everyone involved in the shrimping business.

"Okay, I agree," continued Brad. "But what if García could guarantee us the permits as a contingency for building the ships? Put it in the contract?"

"If he was willing to do that, and put it in writing as part of the contract, then perhaps we could talk. However, I very much doubt that he'd do that knowing how difficult, nearly impossible, new permits are to get."

"Think about it," Brad Murray was enthusiastic, ignoring any objections. "Nine new ships. All with bigger engines and bigger nets. No mechanicals at all the first trip. None the second trip. Our profits could easily double."

"Mechanical problems are not our only issue, Brad. I told you about the five hundred bucks I paid to the Mickey Mouse attorney because of that kid Cruz threw overboard."

"Yeah," Elaine agreed. "Whatever happened to that kid?"

"Nothing. He's at home with his mother. According to Javier Arenas, the stupid boy's lucky to be alive. Arenas said the sharks in the area are pretty big and mean. The fact that the kid made it to shore without being attacked is nothing short of a miracle."

"Poor guy!" Elaine stated.

"Poor guy, my ass!" Brad Murray exclaimed. "The idiot knew better than to take beer onto the ship."

"He's just a kid," Elaine insisted.

"Kid or not," Christian explained, "he's lucky to be alive. Just about everything that swims in the Pacific Ocean is born in the Sea of Cortés. Those waters are really dangerous. Not intended for long distance swimming."

"I can't believe he was going to torch our ships," Brad Murray was not happy with these people. "What kinda people are these anyway? One guy throws a kid off the ship in the middle of the goddam sea, and then the kid decides he's going to take revenge against *us!?*"

"Think pirates. Think the island of Tortuga in the Caribbean in the days of buccaneers."

"What island of Tortuga?" Elaine asked.

"Tortuga, the famous island founded by buccaneers in 1630 on an island off Haiti. Pirates and buccaneers lived there and they robbed anyone they came across in the high seas. They pillaged, plundered and pilfered. Just like they do in Rock Port. Our darling fishing village here is the modern equivalent of Tortuga in the Sea of Cortés," Christian stated.

"So, you think pirates still exist?" Murray questioned.

"What the heck kinda question is that, Brad? Of course, they do! They exist along the coast of Indonesia, Somalia and Bangladesh. And they exist here. Did you already forget about the incident with the *Concepción?* Remember? The shrimp boat where the pirates locked the crew in the engine room and they only survived with their lives because of the one sailor who used his cellphone to call for help?"

"No, I didn't forget about those poor bastards."

"And let me tell you, the population of Tortuga were all pirates. All of them. You couldn't turn your back on man, woman or child without getting scalped. Sound familiar?"

Christian had had enough exposure to the villagers in the sleepy town in the Sea of Cortés to form an opinion. They should all be anointed honorary citizens of the island of Tortuga.

"Yeah, I guess those Caribbean pirates of the past sound strangely like the good folks we deal with every day in this here fishing adventure," Brad Murray commented.

"Precisely. The pirates of the Sea of Cortés."

"So, are we insane even talking about building new ships?" Elaine put in.

"That, we certainly are," Christian agreed. "But unfortunately for us, the irresistible lure of the sea has us hooked."

"Don't kid me. Are we really going to search for financing for new ships?"

"Why not? We're already doing this. We're fishing. Yeah, our ships are old and we spend more time fighting the natives and repairing the ships than we do at making money, but what the heck. It's an adventure. Let's make it bigger."

"I'll talk to Nat and call the people with the pilot pensions, see if they're interested." Brad Murray raised his glass, "slancha!"

"In the meantime, I have an idea," Elaine stated.

Both men gave her their attention.

"These ships have big diesel engines, right?"

"That, they do."

"Aside from the maintenance on the actual ships, our mechanics don't seem to be very educated about these big engines. So why don't we do something? I propose we hire someone here in the States who knows diesel engines in depth, someone we can trust, someone who is American and has the highest standards."

The two men eyed her expectantly.

"And who would you have in mind?"

"The perfect fit. My dad!"

"Really?" Brad was truly surprised.

"Yes! Think about it, he's driven big rigs his entire life. He's familiar with Cummins and Caterpillar engines, he has extremely high standards and he just retired after thirty-five years on the road. He's the perfect fit!"

Christian was surprised. Why had he not thought about his own father-in-law? Elaine was right, the old road warrior had spent his entire life around big diesels. He was totally fit to contribute to the fishing adventure.

"But he's living in Nebraska now, isn't that right?"

"So what? Make him an offer! I'm sure he'll jump at the chance to move down here and participate in the shrimping business."

"She's right," Christian addressed Brad. "Her dad could really help us out. He does have very high standards, and long as we're operating these old buckets, we might as well get all the help with can. God knows those boys down in Mexico can't be trusted with the health of our engines."

"And you think your dad would be interested?" Brad asked.

"I don't see why not. He's retired and ever since he divorced that barfly bitch, he doesn't have much to do. Yeah, I think he would be interested."

"That, is a splendid idea," Christian voiced. "Since it looks like we are stuck with our old rust buckets at least for now, I do believe your dad could provide us with some invaluable help. Let's figure out how much we can pay him and then maybe I can give him a call."

16

Blackmailing Pirates

Christian received the call from Javier late in the evening.

"Boss, the *Orca* is on its way back. They're bringing over three tons of good Blue with them."

"Fantastic! Why are they coming back? They couldn't stay out there and catch some more?"

"Her skipper, Alonzo Cruz wants to take on more ice and diesel. He's six hours from Rock Port so he'll arrive here later this evening. He's going to wait at anchor until it's light enough to bring the ship into port in the morning."

Three tons was a very good catch for the first trip of the season. Especially three tons of that most desirable of all shrimp, the Blue.

"Javier, why can't he just go straight to the docks so you can meet them instead of waiting at anchor?"

"It's very windy here, Boss. Cruz's not going to chance bringing the *Orca* into port with low tide and strong surf in the dark."

"So, he's going to just anchor outside the seawall?"

"Yes."

"That worries me."

Javier Arenas knew what this was all about. "Don't worry. They won't steal the shrimp."

Christian was surprised that Arenas had read his mind. "But I do worry. He's gonna have all kinds of *pangas* going out to meet him when he arrives near the port, what's stopping him from selling a few crates?" Each crate full of shrimp represented $700 worth of revenue.

"No, he won't do that. Not with three tons of Blue in his hold. "

Christian wasn't convinced. The numbers didn't add up. Say the skipper sold off one tenth of a ton of shrimp from under them at half price, he would probably get paid $750 for it. However, if he did not steal the shrimp, his legitimate income for that amount of product would be $600. Not too difficult to see which way the apple would fall. There was an edge there for the captain, an edge which Christian was sure the captain might not be able to resist.

"These guys don't like helping themselves to the product once they're in their home port. They'll do it in another port for sure, but not here," Javier reiterated.

"All right, I'll take your word for it. We'll be there tomorrow morning. Go ahead, unload the ship and take the shrimp to the plant, but only if the plant assures you they will process our product when you arrive with it."

"Not to worry, Boss, I know the routine."

Christian and Brad Murray drove down to Rock Port early the following morning, arriving in the fishing village by ten. They drove directly to the docks, finding the *Orca* tied to the concrete docks. The company's blue F-150 was nowhere in sight. The night watchman was standing by the ship.

"Good morning, José," Christian greeted the man in Spanish.

"Good morning Boss," the watchman tilted his baseball cap.

"When did the *Orca* arrive?"

"She docked this morning, *Jefe*, about six."

"Did they unload her yet?"

"Yessir. Javier Arenas was here with three pick-up trucks and took all the product to the plant by seven this morning."

Christian thanked the man, departing the docks in the Bronco II, heading for the processing plant.

"Thank God for Javier Arenas," Brad Murray voiced.

"Yes, we're lucky to have him on our team."

The men parked the little Ford Bronco in front of the plant. The plant was an all-concrete building of around 30,000 square feet with sheet-metal roof and no windows. The slogans and painted posters of the ruling political party in Mexico adorned the outside walls. The two men walked into the front office. A bored secretary greeted them.

"Good morning," Christian said. "We're looking for Javier Arenas. He brought in a load from the *Orca* earlier this morning."

The woman shuffled some papers in front of her, looking up from her chair behind a desk overflowing with paperwork. "Mr. Arenas is inside supervising the processing of your shrimp. Do you know how to get there?"

"Yes, we do. We'll go find him. Thank you."

The secretary did not answer, returning to her paperwork.

They found Arenas inside the plant, wearing a white coverall, face and hair protectors. Multiple metal conveyor belts with steel cylinders were rolling thawed shrimp toward an army of women dressed like nurses about to enter an operating room.

"Good morning, Boss!"

"Good morning, Javier. Did you unload the *Orca*?"

"Yes, Boss, This here is the last of what they brought in."

Christian glanced at the shrimp on the conveyor. Blues, pretty good size.

"Fantastic! How much did they bring?"

"Don't know yet. I'll get the report right after this last batch gets processed. A rough estimate, I'd say over three tons."

Christian did the math. Nearly fifty-thousand dollars in revenues. Very nice. He translated the good news for Brad Murray.

"I love it when I hear good news," the Irishman replied.

"Let's go find the skipper and congratulate him. Javier will stay here watching the processing of the last batch, then he'll bring us the paperwork to the Playa Encanto hotel so we can have some breakfast."

"Sounds good to me."

They drove back to the docks. Parking alongside the *Orca,* they asked one of the sailors if the captain was still aboard.

"No, he went to get us some ice. Should be back shortly, though."

Fifteen minutes later an old Toyota with chalky, sun-damaged, red paint pulled up. The driver dropped off *Capitán* Alonzo Cruz.

The men shook hands.

"So, how did it go?" Christian asked his captain.

Of course, they already knew how it'd gone, but he wanted to give the captain the pleasure of announcing the good news.

Cruz looked at the ship's owner, momentarily wondering if the gringos already knew how much he'd produced. "It went well, I think we brought over three tons of big blues." The man smiled proudly, showing a gold-capped front tooth.

"Well done, Cruz. Javier is already at the plant processing your shrimp."

"Yes, yes. I went to the ice factory to order us some ice. They're gonna bring it out here later today."

"Anything else we can give you for the next trip?"

"No, no. we're good. I sent the cook to buy us some more tortillas and rice. He should be back here anytime now."

"The ship running okay?"

"Yes, she's running fine."

"No mcchanicals?"

"No, sir."

"Cruz, we're going to give you a big-screen TV as a bonus for this load."

The man did not show any enthusiasm at the news. "Aah, I wanted to talk to you about this load."

"What's on your mind?"

"You know how you're paying us $1,200 per ton that we bring in?"

"Yeah?"

"Well, this is really good shrimp I brought in. And lots of it. Over three tons of big Blues."

"Yes, that's right. So?"

"What I would like instead of the TV is to get paid $1,600 per ton instead."

Christian was surprised by the audacity of the man. The captain's percentage of the catch was pre-arranged with the *coperativa* before the season started, and it remained the same throughout the season. It was not customary to modify the pay for the crew after the season started. And shrimp boat captains did not negotiate their own deals. The co-op did it for them.

"Cruz, you know we can't do that. The contract with the *coperativa* is to pay you $1,200 per ton for everything you catch during the season. Which by the way, is more than all the Mexican ship owners pay their captains. You know damned well your colleagues here are only making $1,000 per ton."

"Yes, but I brought big Blue."

"And you'll get paid as we agreed, $1,200 per ton."

"But I should be paid more. I brought bigger shrimp. You get paid more for the big Blues."

"Cruz, yes, we get paid more for the big Blues than we do for other types, but your *coperativa* negotiated the pay rates for you, and that's what we agreed. We can't change it just for you."

"But, that's not right. If I bring you top quality Blues, I should make more."

Christian was getting annoyed. Where in the devil had this guy come up with the idea that he could ask for more? The crew share of the catch was determined by a rather complex formula created by the sailor's own union.

"We can't do that. In order to change the pay rates we'd have to negotiate with your union, and that can't even happen until next summer. And even if we were willing to contemplate paying you more, at the end the answer would still be no. Like I said, you're already getting paid more per ton than any of the other three hundred captains in the Sea of Cortés."

Cruz stared at his boss, realizing his request was not going to fly. "I see."

"Have a good second trip, Cruz. Let Javier Arenas know if you need anything else before you sail. Your money will be at the *coperativa* this afternoon."

"Greedy little shit," Murray commented, as they drove to the Playa Encanto restaurant for some breakfast.

"It's always the same with these guys. You give them a finger and they try grabbing your arm. I would've thought paying them a couple of hundred dollars more per ton would have generated some gratitude and–God forbid—maybe even some loyalty. Boy, was I wrong."

"I don't get it," Brad Murray mulled. "We're providing these dudes some steady employment with a good company that is here to stay so they can plan long term. And it just seems to me that most of these guys don't value that at all and try to screw us every chance they get. Does Cruz know that a civil engineer in this town earns $300 a month?"

"I think what's happening here is that these poor bastards have never had steady long-lasting employment. Something always happens where they lose their jobs and they're back to square one, unemployed and hungry. The concept of anything permanent is so far removed from them that we could operate shrimp boats for twenty years here and every single day they would still be suspicious of us being around next week."

"A real sad situation."

"Yes, it is. This is the Sea of Cortés."

They ordered *carne asada* and eggs at the restaurant overlooking the blue waters of the Sea of Cortés. Javier Arenas joined them, paperwork in hand.

"Here's the report," he announced.

Christian studied the forms. A good report. A little over $50,000 worth of Blue shrimp. Good-sized, too. He gave Javier authorization to drive the report to Ocean Fruit to complete the sale. The manager there would cut Javier Arenas a certified check in dollars for that amount, which Javier would then deposit at the local bank. That afternoon, Javier would take a check to the coperativa, to cover the share due to the crew.

"Make sure all the suppliers are paid," Christian instructed. "We're going to be staying for the night at the Plaza Oceano Azul hotel.

They were not staying the night, but out of an abundance of caution, Christian constantly played that game, since one never knew when some of the locals might be inspired to cut them off at the pass, so to speak. The less the locals knew about their coming and goings, the safer it would be. It was not unusual in that area of the world to be ambushed by men with guns and an agenda.

Christian and Brad Murray left town under the cover of darkness. They drove the red 1984 Mustang convertible in the heat of the desert night, arriving at the US border one hour later. After refueling at the lonely gas station in Gringo Pass, they enjoyed the two-hour northbound drive to the town of Gila Bend, in Arizona. The night was clear and the desert sky held very little humidity, hence a firmament of stars accompanied them during those long miles driving with the top down. The lack of light pollution in the middle of the Sonoran Desert made for a spectacular celestial show.

"Thank God for small favors," Christian stated.

"How's that?"

"We are saving quite a bit of money with the crew meals."

Brad Murray sipped from a cold Coke can. "We are?"

"Yeah, I just saw the receipts for the groceries we boarded on all three ships. It wasn't much. Mostly thin beefsteaks, beans and rice. And tons of tortillas and soft drinks."

"How's that saving us money?"

"Think of it, if the sailors had a regular diet of shrimp it would cost us a fortune. Fortunately— according to Javier—the last thing those men want when they're out working is shrimp. Apparently, after spending all day handling our product, they don't want it for supper. They are perfectly happy with those thin steaks and generous helpings of rice and beans. And gallons of soft drinks."

"No shit."

"Yeah, bottom line, we're saving a small fortune there."

Brad Murray reached into the back seat. "Wanna Coke?"

"Sure. By the way, did I tell you most of the cooks on the shrimp fleets in the Sea of Cortés are gay?"

"What? Fuck no."

"Javier told me that."

"On our boats as well?"

"Yeah. I have no idea what the reasoning is. The interesting part is, the cooks do all the shopping for the provisions for each trip, they cook for the men and they keep their distance. And the crews just seem to accept this without question. Apparently, they're damned good cooks."

"No funny business going on with the cooks trying to hit on the men?"

"No, I asked that. Remember, this is the land of the macho. I could almost guarantee you that if a cook even considered making a move, he would be sliced into a thousand pieces and thrown overboard."

Brad laughed.

"By the way, we've been so damned busy I forgot to tell you. Elaine's dad Curtis is onboard. I spoke with him about coming down here to help us with the maintenance aspect of the business in everything having to do with the engines, and he was instantly interested."

"No shit?"

"Yep. He's flying out tomorrow. He wants to try it on for size, if he likes it, then he'll fly back to Nebraska to get his car and his belongings and move to Phoenix."

"Well, I guess that's good news!"

"Better than good news. Curtis is an expert in these big diesel engines. He's exactly what we needed. He doesn't know crap about ships, but he is the 'diesel whisperer.' Hopefully, his presence will signal the end of these horrendously expensive maintenance reactionary fixes we've been having to deal with."

"Hey, anything that can save us money is welcome. Besides the multitude of expensive repairs we've had to pay due to lack of maintenance, there's also the fact that any day we're not out there fishing, we're losing money."

The following morning the phone rang early at Christian's home.

"Boss? It's Javier."

Oh, shit. That early in the morning it couldn't be anything good. "Yes, Javier, good morning. How is everything going?"

"Boss, we have a small problem."

So, what else was new? "What small problem, Javier? What is it now?"

There was a short pause. Javier was in the habit of doing that when breaking bad news.

"Cruz, Boss. The problem is Cruz."

"Our captain? What's going on with him?"

"Aah, did Cruz talk to you yesterday?"

"About what?"

"About his compensation?"

"You mean, when he wanted to get paid more than what we agreed to pay him?"

"Yes, Boss."

"Yeah, we talked about that. Why?"

"Well, there seems to be a small problem. See, Cruz feels that he should be paid more and because you didn't agree to that, he took all the electronics from the *Orca* home with him last night."

"What?"

"Yeah, he told me this morning that he's not going to be returning those electronics until he gets paid what he demanded."

"You have got to be shitting me."

"No, Boss, I ain't shitting you."

Christian seldom used profanity with his men, and he quickly regretted doing so. "What electronics did he take off the *Orca*?"

"Everything, Boss. The radios, the navigator, the GPS, the sonar, all the antennas."

Christian quickly remembered. Each ship had about $20,000 worth of electronics aboard. And this blackmailing sack of shit had taken all the goodies home with him. He glanced at the time. A little before eight. The border would be open now.

"Javier, please let the Harbormaster know about this. We will be driving down to Rock Port less than an hour from now. Should be arriving there around one. I will go directly to the Harbormaster's when we arrive. I'm going to put Cruz in jail for this."

"Yes *patrón*." Arenas agreed, nervously.

Four and a half hours later, the tan Bronco II slid to a stop in front of the office of the *Capitán de Puerto*—the Harbormaster.

Christian and Brad entered the modest building housing the Mexican naval officer in charge of the port. A uniformed receptionist wearing Navy whites greeted them.

"Afternoon, how may I help you?"

"We're here to see the Harbormaster," Christian explained.

'And who may I say is calling?" The woman took in the two foreigners.

Christian introduced himself and Murray. "We are *armadores*—ship owners—and we have a problem with one of our captains."

"Please, take a seat," the young woman offered, getting up from her desk. She walked to an office in the back. Seconds later, she reappeared followed by a man in his thirties, also sporting Navy whites.

"Gentlemen," Navy man greeted them. "I'm aware of the situation why you're here. Your man, Javier Arenas came by and explained it to me earlier today."

"Good!" Christian nodded. "Then you know why we need your help."

"I'm aware of the situation. Arenas explained your captain is asking for a little more money."

"That is true. However, it's not just 'a little more money,' but regardless, we're unable to change the pay scales for the crews at this time. The man is blackmailing us and holding our electronic equipment hostage. He removed all of our electronics from one of our ships, the *Orca*, last night and is demanding an unreasonable pay increase as a condition to return our property to us."

The Naval officer appeared to be sizing up the two foreigners standing in his front office. "You gentlemen come from the other side with a lot of money. Why not just pay the guy what he asks? It's nothing to you."

Christian couldn't believe his ears. Did the Harbormaster really just suggest they capitulate to the blackmailing captain?

"No, we're not paying him one red cent more than what his contract says. What we're gonna do is go to the *Ministerio Público* right now and file formal charges for robbery."

The Harbormaster did not appear amused. With a serious face the man informed Christian and Murray that filing formal charges wouldn't be necessary, since Cruz, the captain on the *Orca*, had already returned all of the ship's electronics to the bridge within the past hour. Furthermore, Cruz was reported to have stated he'd never held the gear for ransom. He claimed he merely took all the electronic equipment to his home to protect it, just in case thieves targeted the ship while the captain spent the night at home.

Christian was dumbfounded. The rat! Any further conversation with the Harbormaster was not gonna be productive, either. The Navy man was obviously supporting the behavior of the thieving skipper. Probably related to Cruz in some manner. They were all related in this town. He thanked the man for his time then led the way out to the Bronco II.

Brad Murray waited patiently for his friend to update him on the events inside the building.

"Gawdammit," the big Irishman barked. "We drove all the way down here for this? Let's go find the little bastard, I wanna choke him!"

"Naw, you can't choke him. Bad idea. He'll stick a knife in you. We're gonna do somethin' better though. We're gonna fire his ass. Let's go find Javier."

The two men drove the short distance to their local office. Inside, they found Javier and their secretary having coffee.

Javier jumped to his feet when the men entered.

"Is it true Cruz returned our property?" Christian asked, skipping any formalities.

"Yeah, everything's back on the ship. Good morning!"

"And Cruz claims he took the equipment to protect it from being stolen?"

Javier acknowledged this to be the case.

"That sonofabitch is fired," Christian said. Get rid of him and his crew. Don't let him get back on our ship. How soon can you find us another captain?"

Javier breathed a sigh of relief. He'd been very worried all day that the Cruz situation was going to splash him with manure. He liked his job, loved his pay and enjoyed the feeling of power and respect he received from the folks in his hometown as a result of being employed by the gringos. He was envied and that was a new feeling for Javier. He sure as shit didn't want to lose his job because of the stupid behavior of one single captain.

"I'll go find us another crew," Javier replied.

"Good!" Christian smiled at his manager. He liked Javier and trusted him at least as much as he could trust anyone in this place, which really wasn't much.

"Now what?" Brad Murray asked.

"We'll hang around to see who Javier can round up to run our ship. If he can find us a decent captain, we'll interview him and then head back to Phoenix."

17

Rock Port

"Here we are," Javier Arenas announced, opening the front glass door to the small office.

Christian and Brad Murray looked up at Javier and another man entering the office.

"This is the captain the *coperativa* recommended for the *Orca*," Arenas explained.

Christian stood, greeting the stranger in his office. The man was in his mid-thirties and didn't have an ounce of fat on him. He was also a couple of inches shorter and tanned, just like the rest of these guys. And he had pitch black hair.

"My name is Juan Blanco," the stranger announced, offering his hand. "And I'm a Christian."

Christian was slightly surprised at the novel introduction. "Well, my name is Christian, and I'm the boss around here. And while we're at it, let's leave religion out of it, okay?"

They shook hands.

The man appeared somewhat taken back. "Sure."

"So, you're a shrimp boat *Capitán*?"

"Yessir."

"And you have experience?"

"Yessir. Out of San Felipe and Guaymas."

"We need someone we can trust."

"That'd be me."

"Do you have a crew?"

"I do, yes."

Christian evaluated the man. Juan Blanco seemed self-confident enough, looking at Christian straight in the eye. "You're from here?"

"No, *patrón*. Born and raised in Rio Colorado."

"How do you feel about taking command of one of our ships, the *Orca*?"

The man had a smile. "I feel good."

"You want to take the *Orca* tomorrow and go catch us some shrimp?"

"Yessir!" he answered, with real enthusiasm.

"All right, I'm giving you a chance. Get your crew together and have Javier here give you everything you need so you can sail off tomorrow. The Orca is fully equipped, fueled and ready to go."

"Thank you, *Capitán*," Juan Blanco shook hands again. He had a handshake like a vise, strong and dry.

"Ah, one more thing before you go. You can go fishing south of this port anywhere you want, but don't go anywhere north of here. I don't want you fishing up by the delta of the Colorado river. Too much mud on the bottom."

"Yessir. I won't disappoint you."

"Javier, get him setup with the ship, would you? We're going to catch some late lunch and will be at the *Plaza Oceano Azul* for the night."

Javier Arenas acknowledged the instructions, turning to leave. The new skipper, Juan Blanco, followed him out of the office.

Christian gathered his briefcase and walked outside into the blinding heat. If they left right then, he thought, they'd be in Phoenix in time for dinner. The four-hour drive in his little Ford Bronco II would be mostly done in the daylight. As always, caution forced him to lie to his manager about having lunch and going to the local hotel for the night. In order to avoid unpleasant surprises, it was safer not to share their true itinerary with any locals. Mexico was a lovely place, but with 36,000 murders in one year, one had to take some basic precautions if one contemplated having any sort of longevity.

18

Angel the Shrimp
Sea of Cortés

Angel, the shrimp, was now a two-month old adolescent, and although he didn't yet know what he was, nature had programmed in him the instinct to swim out to sea with his billion companions. For some reason, Angel knew it was now time to follow the cloud of shrimp headed toward the middle of the Sea of Cortés.

He was young and strong, and he could swim as fast as any of the others. Something primitive in his brain cautioned against swimming away from the center of the cloud, hence he directed his efforts at remaining inside the cloud, far from its boundary.

Angel had found plenty of food near the shore, and he did not know the sensation of being hungry since plankton was also available in sufficient quantities as the cloud swam away from the shore.

Days later, in the middle of the night Angel, the shrimp, rested half-buried in the sandy bottom of the Sea of Cortés. The entire cloud had landed on the sandy floor and relaxed after a day of swimming.

Angel suddenly sensed collective panic building in the seawater, not something he could identify. Vibration in the water indicated something big was headed their way. Perhaps a whale? Angel had already experienced the dramatic event of a whale feeding on his companions by the bucketful.

A strange disturbance not too far from his location caught his attention. He was not able to identify the source of the vibration, but sensed it was not something good.

Five minutes later, a gigantic trawler net dragged across the sand, its giant maw disturbing the sandy bottom and forcing the shrimp in its path to jump. As soon as the shrimp abandoned their shelter in the sand, they were caught by the net, inescapably condemned to become shrimp cocktail at a restaurant in one of the major capitals in the world.

Angel froze in place, half buried in the sand, not sure what to do. The vibrations created by the dark whale-like animal floating on the surface slowly receded, allowing the bottom of the sea to return to normal. The only phenomenon still disturbing the tranquility of the sea was caused by hundreds of thousands of shrimps trapped in the two nets of the trawler, all screaming desperately for help.

Angel the shrimp had no idea what had just happened, but he could sense the panic emanating from hundreds of thousands of shrimp on the verge of death. Whatever that whale-like creature was on the surface, it was a bad thing. Whales normally ate into the shrimp cloud, Angel having experienced this already, but a whale would swallow shrimp quickly, not giving the victims the opportunity to generate any sound or vibrations. One second, they were swimming free, the next they were inside the digestive system of the whale.

This whale-like thing on the surface was different. That mysterious creature had not swallowed millions of shrimp, it had somehow *captured* them keeping them alive long enough for the schools of shrimp to produce panic and convey it to the rest of the cloud.

Angel the shrimp made the decision to remain buried in the sand if he ever felt that strange creature approaching again. His mission was to keep traveling south, headed for the deeper waters of the Sea of Cortés, where the shrimp cloud could dive down to depths beyond the reach of most predators.

19

The Shrimp Business
Just Another day

Four days later Christian's cellphone rang in Arizona. "Hello?"

"*Capitán?* It's Javier."

"Javier, what's up?" He was getting ready to go out to dinner for a delicious steak in the hot Phoenix evening.

"*Capitán,* the *Orca's* coming back to port."

"Coming back, why?"

"Engine's overheating."

"Oh, crap—that can't be good. There's no reason why that engine should be overheating, is there? We rebuilt the damned thing just two months ago, didn't we?"

"They'll be in port later tonight."

"I can't head out in your direction tonight. I'm getting ready to take my wife out to dinner. I'll be there at eight in the morning tomorrow. Can you please meet the *Orca* and tell them not to land any of the catch until I get there?"

Christian terminated the call then dialed Brad Murray's number. "Brad, we got a problem."

"What is it?"

"The *Orca's* headed back to port. Problems with the engine, it's overheating."

"Dammit."

"That's what I thought too. Wanna head down with me in the morning?"

"Absolutely."

"I'll call Curtis and invite him to join us. This will be his baptism by fire. Curtis, hopefully will diagnose the problem with the *Orca's* engine without wasting too much time."

"Will do. What time we leaving?"

"Four."

"Cripes."

"That way we can be at the border when they open at seven and in Rock Port by eight am."

"Sounds good to me. What could possibly be overheating the engine?"

"I don't know. Only thing I can figure is maybe something broke. Maybe something with the cooling system."

Christian tried to remember the design of the water-cooling system for most of the trawlers fishing in the Sea of Cortés. He seemed to recall the system was relatively simple, with seawater entering the hull, circulating around the engine removing heat and then venting overboard. Not too many things could go wrong with it.

The next morning, the four men left Phoenix while it was still dark. The 212-mile drive to the Mexican fishing village took them four hours, including a quick stop at the Gila Bend McDonalds for some breakfast and a second stop an hour later in the town of Ajo to purchase Mexican auto insurance for the Bronco II. The group pulled up at the docks in Rock Port minutes after eight in the morning.

The *Orca* was there, tied to the dock in front of them.

The company's Ford F-150 pulled up alongside almost simultaneously, a smiling Javier Arenas behind the wheel wearing his cowboy straw hat. Christian wondered what sort of radar the man had, as he seemed to intuit the moment the boss arrived in town. No idea how the hell he did it. He must have some sort of jungle telegraph spread out throughout Rock Port.

"*Buenos dias!*" Javier called.

"Good morning, Javier."

"Did you have a good drive?"

"We did, thank you. Where's the mechanic?"

"Chavo's on his way here."

"And Blanco? Where's the skipper?"

"He went home last night," Javier sounded apologetic.

"He went home? Why? Isn't he from Rio Colorado?" The town of San Luis Rio Colorado was roughly three hours by bus from Rock Port.

"Yeah, he is. He knew it'd take a couple of days to fix the ship, so he went home to his family. He said he'd be back late tomorrow."

"Call him. Have him get his ass back here today. He needs to talk with us."

Javier acknowledged the instruction, reaching for his cellphone.

The *du jour* mechanic appeared, parking his two-door twenty-year old Chrysler next to the company's pickup. The old Chrysler was known as a 'Rock Port convertible,' with its top having been cut off with a torch. Mechanics didn't seem to last long working for the company around these parts. Christian was sure that anytime repairs were needed for any of the three ships, a different mechanic seemed to show up.

Curtis disappeared down into the engine room together with the Mexican mechanic.

Javier Arenas joined them again. "Juan Blanco's on his way back. I reached him at home. He'll be here late this afternoon."

"Good. Thanks. How much shrimp did they bring?"

"They brought just over nine hundred kilograms."

"Have it unloaded and take it to the plant. Stay with it. Don't let it out of your sight until they've processed it."

"Already called Don Sancho at the plant, he's expecting us. He said they can process it right away."

"Well done, Javier."

"Brad, let's go eat breakfast while they check the engine."

They drove off to a small restaurant on the board walk by the sea.

A middle-aged lady with a big smile greeted them, placing menus in front of each. The breeze was pleasurable and the temperature had not yet reached uncomfortable levels. They enjoyed a magnificent view of the blue waters of the Sea of Cortés.

"Bring us some orange juice first, please."

"How'd you like Blanco just taking off last night? The gall of the man! He brings the ship back in need of repairs and doesn't even have the common sense to wait for us this morning. He knew we were coming down. Javier met the ship when they arrived." Christian was annoyed.

"These people never cease to amaze me," Brad Murray stated. "They defy logic. I'd been hoping the *Orca* was going to stay out fishing at least a couple of weeks before we heard of any problems."

The waitress brought them large glasses of freshly squeezed orange juice. "What can I bring you?"

"Bring me some *huevos rancheros*. Flour tortillas on the side, please."

Brad read from the menu, "I'll have a steak and eggs. *Carne asada*."

"How do you like your steak?"

"Medium rare, please."

"Eggs?"

"Over easy."

"I suspect this mechanical problem's going to cost us an arm and a leg," Christian complained.

"It sure is. A ship in port is not making us any money."

"The idea of having new ships is so incredibly attractive when this kinda crap happens, no?" Christian tried the orange juice. It was sweet and cold.

"Very attractive, indeed. And you know something? We never asked any of these shipbuilders about what kinda warranty they provide with new ships."

"True. But that's because we were never really serious about building new ships before."

"You think it's like with a new car?"

"No, Brad, nothing here works like that. This is the Sea of Cortés. We'll ask, but don't be disappointed with what you hear. I don't know that any of these guys even know what a warranty is."

"Hey, if we're paying them half a million dollars to build us a ship, I expect some sort of warranty."

"Like I said, this is the Sea of Cortés, buddy. What one expects and what one gets are generally two very different things here."

"You mean you'd buy ships that don't have any warranty?"

"I'd prefer not to; however, we have to find out what the local custom is. I guess we can always throw that in as a condition."

"You're damn right we can!"

"How do you see the odds of the San Diego pension people investing with us?"

"They seem to be enthusiastic about our plan."

"Who's the guy, your contact over there?"

"Fred. He and his wife Tonya run the show. But remember, they told me what they'll do is find some venture capitalist or some random bank willing to invest in our nine new ships. They can't invest the money from the pensions they manage."

"Yeah, I remember now. I don't care where the money comes from. If they can get it, and the terms are acceptable, we'll build us the nine ships. You did tell them that this entire plan revolves around the answer García gives us about the fishing permits, yes?"

"They know that."

"Good."

They were devouring the last of the food from their plates when the cellphone rang.

"It's Curtis." Christian answered the call.

"Hey. Curtis. We're finishing breakfast here by the *malecón*. What'd you find?"

Brad Murray signaled the waitress for the check. He thought again one thing he loved about Mexico, the same way he loved it about Europe, was that no waiter in his right mind would produce the check unless he was asked for it. Brad detested the ridiculous vulgar custom of dropping the check on the table while one was still merely half way through dinner, 'I'll take that whenever you're ready,' was the *sottovoce* explanation used by waiters back home. As if that excused it.

Christian completed the call, putting the cellphone away in his pants' pocket. "We got damaged heads on the engine. Curtis said the heads have been barbecued."

"Oh, crap."

"Blanco must've run the engine in the red for a long time."

"Why in the hell would he do that?"

"I don't know. But we're gonna ask him when he gets back here. In the meantime, let's go get Curtis and the burned-out parts and drive back to Phoenix to buy replacements."

"Now?"

"Now."

The waitress brought the check. Christian left a twenty-dollar bill on the table, following Brad out of the place.

The drive back to Phoenix took the same four hours. Only this time they followed a detour after reaching the town of Gila Bend, so they could drive straight north to the Caterpillar dealer near downtown Phoenix.

"Curtis seemed happy to be left behind," Brad Murray was driving.

"Yeah. No reason for him to sit in the back another eight hours. We'll let him relax back there and enjoy the pool." Christian also realized the back seat of the little Bronco II was very confining for anyone taller than a kid. "He's a good sport. I'm glad he's there to back us up. We just can't trust the mechanics there."

"I agree," Murray added. "And with me not knowing a bolt from a testicle far as engines are concerned, Curtis is worth his weight in gold."

They parked at the Caterpillar dealer near downtown. Christian had already called ahead and the parts clerk confirmed they had the heads for a Caterpillar 3208 marine engine.

The two men walked inside the door marked 'Parts.'

"Afternoon gent'men!" the man behind the counter greeted.

"Hi, there. Name's Christian. I called about the heads for a marine Cat engine."

"Yes. You spoke with me."

"Fantastic. You have the parts?"

"I do. You got the damaged ones?"

"Out in the truck. Can you round up a coupla guys to get them?"

"Sure." The clerk called on the intercom, paging someone to help.

"Here's the paperwork," the clerk announced somewhat proudly, offering some forms across the counter. I took the liberty of filling them out before you all got here."

Christian accepted the invoice. "For the love of God, almost twelve thousand bucks?"

"Yep. That's what they cost. Notice I haven't closed it yet. I need to know how much I'm gonna give you back on your old heads first."

Christian produced the company's American Express card, handing it to the man. "Here, use this one. Are your boys bringing the heads in?"

"Already got them! They're in the back examining them as we speak."

Christian checked out the place, it was cold and dark. Good for Arizona, with no windows other than the light coming through the front glass door.

The intercom rang. The clerk behind the counter listened to someone at the other end, thanked him and hung up. "Bad news."

Now what?

"It appears that them heads you boys brought in are fried. Totally fried. Of no use to us at all."

Christian was surprised. Usually any parts exchanged at the Caterpillar or Cummins dealers generated at least a few hundred bucks for the company. "Barbecued beyond all possible recognition?"

"That, they are!"

"All right, just bill that card and we'll get out of your hair."

"Right away."

"No residual value left in the heads?"

"None, Brad. Blanco did a good job frying them."

"Can we get a couple of your boys to help us load the new parts into the Bronco outside?"

"Already done!" the clerk informed them.

The dude was efficient, no question about it. Christian toyed with giving him an 'attaboy'."

"The new parts are already in our truck?"

"They sure are."

"Damn, you're efficient!"

The clerk beamed, handing back the American Express card. "Thank you! I try."

Outside, a man in a bright orange Caterpillar shirt was closing the rear hatch on the Bronco II. "You guys are all set," he assured them.

Christian walked to the back of the Bronco II, lifting the rear hatch open again. Two long boxes occupied most of the area behind the driver's seat. The boxes had 'Caterpillar' stenciled on them. He thanked the man, shutting the hatch again.

"Let's get some food before we head out," Brad Murray suggested.

"Sounds good. I know an exquisite BBQ joint on Central."

"Mind if I drive?"

"Go ahead, Brad. I'll take over if you get tired."

"Twelve thousand bucks later."

"Yes, highly pissing. Now we gotta get back and give these parts to Curtis and the mechanic so they can install them."

"What're we gonna do? Send the ship back out with Blanco?"

"I don't know. Need to talk with him first. The only way anyone could deep-fry the heads on that big

CAT is by running the engine at redline for a long time. If he did that, I want to know why. Was he running away from pirates, or what?"

They drove to the BBQ restaurant before departing Phoenix, passing Gila Bend, then onto Lukeville, otherwise known as 'Gringo Pass,' at the border between the US and Mexico. From there, they traversed the empty highway down to Rock Port. The Bronco II pulled up in front of the office in Rock Port at a quarter to seven that evening. The sun was on its way down but the heat was still serious business.

The two men entered the office. Christian was not in a good mood. What a day: twelve hours driving, twelve thousand bucks poorer, at least two days of fishing lost, equivalent to about another thirty thousand dollars. Overall, not a good day.

Javier Arenas and Juan Blanco were waiting for them. They both stood.

"*Capitán*," Javier greeted.

"Javier, we have the new heads in the back of the Bronco. Here's the keys, please take the parts to the mechanic so he can start working on that engine right away."

"Perfect." Arenas accepted the keys.

"Juan, thank you for coming back so soon," Christian offered with as much sarcasm as he could muster.

"I'm here."

"What the hell happened to the engine?"

Blanco already appeared intimidated. "It overheated."

No shit. "And why did it overheat? Where were you fishing?"

"North."

"North where? North from here?"

"Yes. Up by the delta of the Colorado river."

"And who told you to fish there?"

"God."

"God told you to fish there?"

"Yes."

"And you don't remember how I told you in this very same office that I didn't want you to go fishing anywhere north of Rock Port?"

Juan Blanco appeared baffled. Somehow, he failed to see how the gringo could have the audacity to question the will of God.

"You're fired. Gone. History. Take your crew and get them off my ship. Your stupidity just cost us thousands of dollars, and believe me, my choice would be to withhold the pay I owe you and slam your ass in jail, but since Mexican law forces me to pay you, you will be getting a check from your *coperativa*, but you will never work for me again."

The man became outraged. "You can't fire me!"

"Really? I just did."

"You can't fire me, where am I gonna find another job this late in the season?"

Incredible. Astounding logic.

Brad Murray didn't follow what was going on because of his lack of Spanish, but he could read body language. This idiot had blown it somehow.

"Juan, I really couldn't care less if you ever get another job again anywhere, let alone this season. Now get the hell out of my office before I call the police and have you arrested."

"You will pay for this. I'll put a knife in you."

"Don't start that, or I'll have you put in jail. Get out!"

"I will get a lawyer!"

"Out!"

Brad Murray reached out for the man's arm, ready to intervene, but it was not necessary. *Capitán* Juan Blanco retreated from the small office cursing and muttering.

One hour later, the three Americans sat at a table in the balcony of the *Casa del Pescador* restaurant, trying to enjoy an evening breeze and some Pacifico beers.

"I still can't get over the nerve of the little sonofabitch," Brad Murray had developed an intimate love affair with Pacifico beer. "Telling you he can't be fired because he wouldn't be able to get another job this late in the season. That's just incredible. The gall he had. He screws us and then he wants us to feel sorry for him."

"Yeah, like you're going to be concerned with his welfare after he just cost us forty-two thousand dollars. Sure, let us help you, Mister Juan Blanco. Anything else we can do for you? As a good Christian? From one Christian to another?"

"So why the heck was he fishing up north?" Curtis questioned.

"The delta of the Colorado river up there is full of blue shrimp," Christian explained. "The fresh river water there mixes with the super-salty water from the Sea of Cortés, creating an electrolytic blend that the shrimp just find irresistible. The problem is the silt brought down by the Colorado river makes the bottom of the delta very muddy. Trawling for shrimp in the mud is bad for us."

"How come?"

"We fish by dragging our nets along the floor of the sea. The two huge otter doors holding each net open are very heavy, and the bottom part of our nets have metal chains to keep the nets from floating. The combination becomes very difficult to pull in mud. For us to catch shrimp, the boat has to be moving through the water at least three knots. Anything slower than that, and we won't catch any shrimp because the little critters will just jump out of the way. If you are trawling in mud, it becomes necessary to open up the engine with all she's got in order to make three knots, which is not a good idea. This redlines the engine and if done long enough, it'll burn the heads."

"So that's what our esteemed captain did," Curtis stated, sipping from a beer bottle.

"That's what our esteemed captain did," Christian agreed.

"Bastard," Brad Murray pointed out.

"So, what're we doing for a crew?" Curtis sipped his sixth beer.

"Javier's taking care of that. He'll get us another captain and we'll interview him in the morning."

"This is starting to feel like that movie 'Groundhog Day,'" Curtis stated. "Based on what you've told me, we're really setting the bar for turnover rate!"

20

It's Only Business

The two *pangas* sped across a calm blue sea, northbound on the Sea of Cortés eighty miles from the delta of the Colorado river. The day was clear but horribly hot, with 120 degrees rendering it difficult to breathe. Juan Carlos, the man in charge, sat in the front of the leading *panga*, enjoying the refreshing coolness generated by the sixty-knot breeze resulting from the two powerful 300 hp Mercury Verado outboards propelling them.

The young Mexican man lazily scanned the horizon ahead of them. He was not really concerned about actually seeing anybody out there. Even if they saw any ships of the Mexican Navy, they could outrun any of them, so in his mind the military were not an issue.

Juan Carlos had been running pangas with 'product' to *El Golfo de Santa Clara* and San Felipe for a year now, and he loved his job. And what a job! Two terrific days at sea and ten thousand dollars cash deposited right onto his hands each trip. Where could a man find a better job? He wondered if one day he'd be able to visit the Universal Studios in Los Angeles. He'd never been to America, but he'd heard so much about the studios that he really wanted to visit them soon.

He was an avid movie-goer, and consequently one of his dreams was visiting the place where he was sure most movies were made. He had no passport; in fact, he couldn't even read or write. But that didn't matter. He was well-acquainted with several coyotes who could drive him across the border and drop him off in Anaheim for three or four thousand dollars. If he took his girlfriend with him, they could visit the studios for a couple of days. After all, California was half Mexican now. They had retaken it from the gringos.

Something shined momentarily up ahead. He squinted, trying to reduce the glare. Yes, something up ahead had given a reflection from the sun at high noon. Juan Carlos traveled during the day because his safety was in his speed and nobody could catch up with his *pangas*, and also because running at night in the dark at these speeds was too reckless. In the past some poor bastard or two doing this same job had flown smack into sleeping shrimp boats at sixty knots in the dark, resulting in a very bad day for everyone involved.

The object ahead was definitely something of interest. Juan Carlos sat up and waited patiently. He was not really overly concerned. There was no ship in the entire Mexican Navy he could not outrun. Funny thing about that object, however, it seemed to be getting closer. How could that be? His interest increased. After a few more minutes of watching the approaching object he realized it was not a ship, it was an airplane!

Oh, shit! Well, one thing was for sure, he could not outrun an airplane!

The airplane approached at considerable speed, eventually getting close enough where Juan Carlos could see it was not an airplane at all, it was a helicopter. A friggin' helicopter!

His men all carried AK-47 assault rifles onboard, so he gave orders to the men to ready their weapons. Who flew a helicopter this far out at sea?

The sound of the helicopter engines and rotors grew more intrusive as the big Russian-made craft with Mexican Navy markings approached the pangas. Juan Carlos observed the helicopter maneuvering to fly parallel to the *pangas*, at nearly their same speed.

A very loud cracking noise startled him out of his reverie, as water spouts marched across his bow.

"For the Virgin Mary! They were taking shots at them!"

Juan Carlos saw the Mexican Marine manning a heavy caliber machine gun shooting from the open side door of the helicopter. He immediately yelled orders to his men to throw the AK-47s in the sea, pitching his into the water as well, hoping fervently that the Mexican Marine didn't decide to open fire on them directly.

That sounded like a fifty-caliber, he thought. Not a fair fight. He signaled his assistant at the control of the outboards to reduce power, running the palm of his hand across the front his neck in the classic gesture indicating a command to cut the power.

The two *pangas* reduced their speed until they had no more forward motion. The helicopter flew around the pangas at a slow pace, with the muzzle of its deadly machine gun pointed at the two craft.

Half an hour later, a fast boat of the Mexican Navy appeared on the horizon. Juan Carlos was furious and frustrated, knowing what was coming, but there was nothing he could do. There was no way he was going to outrun a helicopter, and he was pretty damned sure that if he even tried it, the Mexican Marine standing on the side door would open fire against them.

His trip to Los Angeles would have to be postponed a few weeks.

21

Humble Farmers

The Vega brothers entered the restaurant, two of them wearing straw cowboy hats again. All three had on cowboy boots. They saw Christian and Curtis and Brad Murray.

"*Buenas noches*!" Rodolfo greeted. The three men who sold them their three shrimp boats jovially approached their table.

"Gentlemen!" Christian stood. "What a nice surprise, care to join us for a drink?"

"That would be great, thank you," Rodolfo said, pulling a chair from a nearby table, his brothers joining in.

"This is Curtis, my father-in-law. He's an expert with diesel engines and he's now working with us." Christian introduced him.

Handshakes were exchanged all around.

"Pleasure," Curtis repeated three times. His lack of command of the Spanish language put him in the same position as Brad Murray. Observers at the mercy of the interpreter.

"You here for dinner?" Christian asked, noticing the two brothers hadn't removed their hats even while sitting at the table. Interesting.

"Yes, we're here for some food," Rodolfo said. He seemed to be the self-appointed mouthpiece for the group.

"So are we. Want to join us? We haven't ordered yet."

A waiter appeared to take drink orders.

"Bring a bottle of Chivas," Rodolfo instructed the man. "Delighted to join you gents for dinner. How's everything going with your boats?"

"Not too bad, really." Christian wondered if the three brothers had just casually chosen that restaurant for dinner and ran into the Americans or if it was planned.

"Heard you had some issues with the *Orca*," Rodolfo offered.

How the hell did he know that? Christian wondered. "Yes, we had a problem with the engine. The skipper overtempted it."

"That can happen," Rodolfo stated. "Heard you fired the captain."

Was nothing a secret in this god-forsaken village? Christian didn't know whether to be amused or enraged.

"That's right. I fired him. He cost us about forty-thousand bucks."

"I would've fired his ass as well," Rodolfo agreed. "Just be careful with those guys. Keep an eye out."

Christian nodded. Was that Rodolfo's way of telling him to watch out for a knife in his back in a dark alley?

"Rodolfo, you never told me how you guys got involved in the shrimping business," Christian decided to change the subject.

Rodolfo Vega smiled from behind his black mustache. "We weren't born fishermen; our families were in agriculture."

Christian interpreted for his friends.

A waitress brought drinks, pouring a triple Chivas into Rodolfo's glass. Apparently, she knew his preferences. The charismatic rogue took one long swig, downing most of the shot in one gulp.

"Ahh," he was pleased. "We're not from Rock Port, brother, we're from a small town down in Sinaloa. Let me tell you our story. Prior to your last World War our people grew corn and beans, barely making a living. Piss poor, as you would say. When the big war got going, the Japanese controlled all the opium from Asia, so your government got worried about where they were going to get opium for their morphine. Your military needed the morphine for its soldiers and so your Uncle Sam turned to Mexico for help."

Christian asked the waiter for a vodka martini. This was getting interesting.

"So, your government came here and told us they wanted to secure a supply of morphine close to their borders. They provided our grandparents with seeds and knowledge and fertilizer and chemicals and laboratories in which to process opium. The entire state began mass-producing opium and morphine. Everybody was growing it. It became institutional. We even had soldiers up in the hills protecting our plants."

Christian interpreted for Brad Murray and Curtis.

"No shit. So that's how this thing began." Brad Murray couldn't understand a word of Spanish, but he had to admit that these men looked the part.

"Many Sinaloans made their fortune in those years of the war. Your government purchased all the product we could manufacture and paid us top dollar for it. After the war ended, your government no longer needed our opium. They claimed that it was of much lower quality than the Asian stuff. They cut off the subsidies and stopped buying it. Our farmers were told to go back to growing beans and corn. Sure, after all those years of making fortunes they were going to switch back. What is it you Americans say, that after showing the girl Paris, you can't send her back to the farm?"

The waiter returned, taking dinner orders.

Rodolfo poured himself another triple. "For God's sake, what were they thinking in your government? Of course, our farmers continued producing opium and heroin. Operations became clandestine. The product was still being sent to the neighbors in the north, but it had to be done by different methods. A few years later, the farmers turned to marijuana and cocaine. There was a lot more profit in that."

Christian was wondering why Rodolfo was sharing all this with him. The man was throwing caution to the four winds. Or perhaps he should consider it an honor, being brought into the circle of trust. Or something like that.

"My brothers and I didn't really like farming, so we bought sixteen shrimp boats years ago and moved out here to run them." Christian couldn't help smiling. They didn't like being farmers? Well, that was one way to look at it.

That explained a lot. Good God, drug growers and smugglers from Sinaloa. He couldn't help liking the three brothers, but what backgrounds! "You guys no longer participate in the family business, then?"

Rodolfo stared at him. "No, not directly. But of course, we help whenever we can."

"How do your relatives get the drugs, er, product to the States?"

"They use *pangas*. And mules."

"Mules?"

"An Indian peasant. We load him up with a backpack full of stuff and he walks across the desert. Our guys meet him at the other end, pay him, and retrieve our stuff."

"The stuff comes up from Sinaloa in pangas?"

"Yeah. They go up to *El Golfo de Santa Clara* or San Felipe and unload there."

"They go at night?"

Rodolfo inserted a white linen napkin into the top of his shirt in anticipation of dinner. "Used to, but not anymore. Now they go in the daytime."

"Isn't that dangerous?" Christian wondered about the risks involved in smuggling drugs in plain daylight.

"No, it's not dangerous. The pangas have a couple of three-hundred horsepower outboards and they move pretty fast. Pretty goddamn fast. Truth is, nobody can catch them."

Two outboards? Christian whistled. With that much horsepower the pangas must stand on their sterns.

"We had some problems recently. The Navy had a Russian-made helicopter based here in Rock Port and those shitheads intercepted two of our pangas making their way up to the delta of the Colorado river. Our guys were minding their own business, not bothering anybody."

Christian had to control himself from laughing. Rodolfo made it sound like his men were boy scouts on some peace-keeping mission. A few guys just minding their own business, that's all.

"So, what if they intercepted your pangas? A helicopter can't board a panga."

"No, but they *can* carry a fifty-caliber machine gun installed on the side door. They fired some rounds at our guys to make them stop, then the helicopter just hovered there until a Navy ship arrived and arrested them."

"That can't be good for business."

"No, it wasn't," Rodolfo continued. "They stole our pangas and took our merchandise to the military base here by the *Plaza Oceano Azul* hotel. Then they piled all our boxes out in the open and set them on fire."

"What was in them?"

"Marijuana. And some cocaine. They burned really well. The whole town got high." Rodolfo glanced sideways at his brothers, smiling at his own pun.

Christian wasn't sure whether Rodolfo was joking or being serious. What sort of idiots burn marijuana out in the open smack in the center of town in order to destroy it? Right in the middle of a populated area. "Well, I can see how that could be a real problem for you guys." He couldn't believe he was sitting there, enjoying casual drinks and dinner with guys of this caliber.

"Yeah, that was a problem, but we fixed it. We lost the *pangas*, though."

"How'd you fix it?" Now he was more than just curious.

Rodolfo dug into his food, lobster tacos with lots of *poblano* pepper. "We shot down the fucking helicopter, of course."

Christian was shocked by the casual attitude. *What!?*

"You shot down the helicopter? How?"

"Oh, that was easy. We bought some SAM-2 surface-to-air missiles down in Guatemala. They weren't expensive. I think one of your presidents was nice enough to give those to the Contras in Nicaragua years ago. Anyway, they go for about $1,200 apiece. We put some of those in another panga and one of our guys got lucky and took out the helicopter."

Christian translated for his friends.

"You gotta be kidding me!" Brad Murray looked at the brothers in disgust. He was angry and turning red.

"Easy, Brad. Be careful. Be polite. Smile. These aren't the type of guys you want to piss off."

"They shot down the friggin helicopter? I guess it wouldn't be polite to ask what happened to the crew?"

"No, it wouldn't. Now look at these guys and *smile.*"

Brad Murray flashed his best smile. His eyes, however, were not smiling.

"Did the Navy replace the helicopter, then?" Christian asked.

"Hell no," Rodolfo said through a mouthful of tacos. "They don't have the budget for that."

"Interesting story. Thanks for sharing that with us. How about some tequila shots?"

Rodolfo was on his fifth double, yet gave no indication he was slammed. "Did you hear what happened to the *Concepción?*"

Christian had no idea what Rodolfo was talking about.

"The *Concepción* belongs to Carlos Esquivel, out of Guaymas. They were boarded by pirates when the season started. The pirates took about three tons of Blue from them. The crew were locked in the engine room and left to die. And they would've died if some young kid in the crew hadn't found a way to rig an antenna for his cellphone through the engine exhaust funnel. He called for help, saving the lives of the entire crew. Unbelievable. That little punk saved all their lives."

Christian had not heard anything about that incident. "Who was responsible?"

"Pirates," Rodolfo replied.

Christian wondered if Rodolfo was serious. "What kinda pirates?"

"How many kinds are there? The kind that rob you and kill you."

"So, there are pirates in these waters?"

Rodolfo laughed. "Betchar ass there's pirates. Each season they kill a couple of crews just to rob them."

Now, that was disturbing. "Do they take the ships?"

"Naw, those pirates don't want the ships, they just want the shrimp."

"Do you carry piracy insurance?"

Rodolfo laughed heartily. "No such thing, my friend. This is the Sea of Cortés. If the pirates pick your ship, you're shit outta luck. They'll take your shrimp without batting an eye. No insurance company in Mexico will cover you for that."

"So, what if they sink your ship?"

"What about it?"

"Will the insurance company reimburse you for the ship?"

"Oh, ya. If the ship sinks, the insurance company will pay you for the boat." Rodolfo hiccupped. "Some dishonest *armadores* have, in fact, intentionally sank their ships to collect the insurance."

Christian controlled himself not to laugh again. *Dishonest* armadores? This from a guy who just admitted to the production and export of illegal drugs and the shooting down of a helicopter?

"Really?"

"Yes, really." Rodolfo looked at his brothers for approval. "In fact, we recently had to deal with one such dishonest individual."

"What happened?"

"It was sad. This *armador* we knew tried to commit insurance fraud by sinking his own boat. He convinced the captain to sink the boat so the insurance would pay a substantial claim."

"And did he do it?"

"Sure, he did. He sent his shrimp boat down to the bottom of the sea, along with its entire crew. A very bad individual, that captain."

A 'bad individual?' that was the understatement of the century. Christian was no longer amused. He was disgusted. Some ship owner actually killed a crew to collect insurance money?

"Was he caught?"

Rodolfo once again poured himself another triple shot of Chivas. "Was he caught? Ay, yeah. Naw, he wasn't caught, that captain. The owner of the shrimp boat hired a hit man to kill his own captain after he scuttled the ship so he wouldn't have to pay him his blood money."

Christian did not want to interrupt Rodolfo's train of thought, so he refrained from translating the conversation for the benefit of Brad Murray and Curtis. "The owner of the shrimp boat hired a hitman to take out the captain who sank his own ship?"

"Ya, that he did. That was a very bad situation because two of the crewmembers on that boat they sent to the bottom were from here. We know their parents and brothers."

"How'd you find out about this?"

"Because the hitman the armador hired to take out the captain was one our employees."

Christian gasped. Holly mackerel. These dudes didn't joke around. "And what happened to the *armador*? The one who ordered the captain to scuttle the ship with the crew still in it? Did he collect the insurance claim?"

Rodolfo nodded. "Yeah, he collected from the insurance company. But unfortunately for him he wasn't able to enjoy the money. He met with an accident. Yeah, that's what happened, he met with an unfortunate accident. So, he couldn't enjoy the insurance money. Too bad for him."

In the morning, everyone had a mother of a hangover. Somehow, they'd made it back to their hotel without killing themselves descending the unpaved road from the top of the hill where the restaurant was located. The mechanic sent word with Javier Arenas that the two new Caterpillar heads on the engine had been installed.

"Curtis, what do we do next?" Christian was slowly getting dressed in the room of the *Plaza Oceano Azul* hotel.

"I don't know about you, but I gotta have some coffee."

"I mean, what needs to be done next with the engine?"

"We need to take the boat out. Those heads need to get seated, then retorqued."

"How long does the engine have to run?

"Couple of hours. I'd say we should go out there and pull the nets around for a time. Then we can come back here and retorque the heads."

"I'll call Murray. Let's get this show on the road."

The trio drove out to the docks, rounded up the crew and took the *Orca* out to sea. The day was clear and hot. Five miles out, the crew lowered the nets into the water, allowing the ship to drag them along the bottom for twenty minutes.

Christian was impressed with the crews. The men worked together as a team quite seamlessly.

Shrimp slept during the day, so the total production for the morning efforts came down to just one single solitary Blue shrimp.

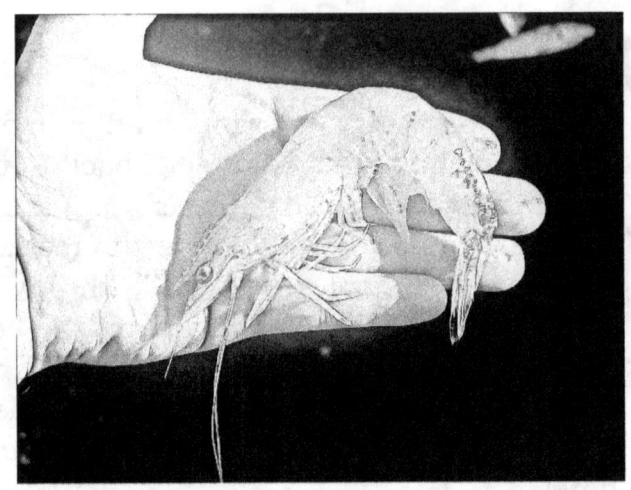

They did catch a sizeable amount of fish considered by the sailors to be of no value. The sailors swept the fish overboard thru the scuppers, much to the delight of the sea lions following the ship. The *Orca* returned to the docks three hours after departing.

Curtis supervised the mechanic while the engine heads were carefully retorqued to Caterpillar specs.

Javier Arenas lined up a new captain and crew for the *Orca,* the third that season. The ship was eventually dispatched, leaving the port before sunset.

Brad Murray was driving again. "I can't believe those guys are for real."

"They're special, aren't they?" Christian was riding shotgun in the Bronco, Curtis sitting in the narrow seat in back.

"Special? I'd say! In my wildest dreams I wouldn't imagine buying shrimp boats from drug dealers!"

"They were there before us, Brad."

"They're still drug dealers. And murderers."

"You mean the helicopter?"

"Yeah. Of course, I mean the helicopter. They killed the crew. And what about that guy who tried to collect insurance by sinking his own ship?"

"The helicopter was bad for business."

"You're kidding, right? Tell me you're kidding."

"No, I'm not kidding. That's what Rodolfo said. They found an obstacle, they got rid of it."

"And that's okay with you?"

"That's none of our business."

"The hell it isn't."

"No, Brad, it is none of our business. Whatever those guys are, or what they do for a living is not our concern. We're here to run a commercial fishing operation. Nothing more. It's not our position to judge anybody."

"They're taking drugs into the States through the delta of the Colorado river. You heard them."

"Yes, and that's none of our business, either. We catch shrimp, nothing else."

"And you don't think we should try to stop them?"

"Tell me you're joking. Are you out of your mind?"

"We could tell the FBI, or the DEA, or somebody."

"Tell them what? That the guys who sold us our boats are members of the Sinaloa cartel? Just share with the feds about our casual dinner last night with some good folks who produce cocaine for a living?"

"Why not? We haven't done anything wrong."

"Brad, perception is ninety-percent of reality. If we went to the authorities back in the States and informed them what you're suggesting, first of all, they would look at us as highly suspicious. Think of it. Why would the Vega brothers confide all this information to us? The feds would immediately assume that we're part of the drug smuggling operation and come after us. And that would be the easy part. The minute the Vega brothers got wind that we're talking to the feds about their business, you and I and our entire families would have to change our names and move to the Outback in Australia forever. And even then, I wouldn't feel safe."

"Oh."

"In case you haven't noticed, these people don't fuck around. I have no idea why they took us into their confidence, but maybe they feel that we've established a friendship. And we're sure as all hell not going to betray that confidence if we know what's good for us. This is not a case of Honest Abe doing the right thing. This is a case of us not wanting to commit suicide."

"You may have a point there." Murray admitted.

"I believe I do."

Brad Murray gritted his teeth. "They're still a bunch of murdering bastards."

"They're pirates, remember?"

"Yeah, no doubt about that. The pirates of the Sea of Cortés."

22

Night Shrimping in The Sea of Cortés

The *San Felipe* crew reeled in the small net known as '*el chango.*' Shrimp boat fishermen referred to this particular net as 'the monkey.' This was a small net that went in the water between the two main big ones. The purpose of this eight-foot net was to sample the catch. Once the two main nets were in the water and the ship was dragging them along the bottom, the crew would recover the small net every ten minutes to determine whether there was shrimp in the area. Retrieving this small net to test the presence of shrimp in the waters was much easier than trying to retrieve one of the two main trawling nets, which were at least thirty times as large.

Capitán Longoria was informed that the '*chango*' had been recovered and it was plumb full of Blue shrimp of the ten count—meaning ten of those would make a pound. He'd been cruising at fifty percent power to save diesel, but he pushed the big Cat engine to ninety percent when he heard the good news. Now his nets would drag across the bottom fast enough to catch as much of the highly-sought Blue shrimp as possible.

The night was hot and the humidity in the ninety-per-cent range. *Capitán* Longoria congratulated himself on his choice of location. His Garmin GPS depth finder showed the seafloor at nine fathoms—54 feet—which was excellent. The tropical storm headed their way from the Pacific Ocean was still three days away, so he'd be able to still catch a couple of tons of shrimp before high-tailing it to port in Guaymas. He punched the soft buttons in his GPS, inserting an electronic marker which stored the Lat and Lon of his current position. He'd use it again once the storm passed to find this same excellent spot. Provided, of course, the storm didn't blow the shrimp away from that area.

His crew sat around trying to keep busy while the *San Felipe* trawled the bottom of the Sea of Cortés. The sailors emptied the shrimp from the *chango*, putting the net back in the water. They would continue sampling the catch for as long as there was shrimp in the area.

The acrid smell of diesel fumes permeated the small wheelhouse. Longoria sipped hot coffee from a ceramic cup with 'Opra' stenciled on it, keeping an eye on the oil temperature gauge on the dashboard. Years of being a shrimp boat captain had taught him to baby his engine. He liked keeping the single light bulb on the bridge turned off so as not to lose his night vision in the moonless night. There was no way for him to estimate how much shrimp was under them. He'd know once the shrimp dried up. When ultimately the *chango* came up empty, then it would be time to stop.

He steamed straight ahead, holding the *San Felipe* at a steady four knots with the engine screaming just below the red line.

Two hours later, one of his sailors reported the *chango* was coming up empty.

Time to recover the main nets.

The crew used the engine-driven winch to reel in the tail-end of each of the two large nets, keeping the main part of the nets in the water. The winch struggled with the weight. The tail end of both nets was lifted over the rear deck of the *San Felipe*, hanging six feet up in the air. That part of the net where the catch was, the very end, was known as "The Sock," because of its resemblance to one.

Both socks were bulging with shrimp.

A sailor reached up, pulling the string under each sock, releasing over one thousand pounds of shrimp and fish onto the deck in an instant.

The men got to work.

The entire crew, with the exception of the captain, sat on small wooden stools in the rear deck among the shrimp, wearing heavy duty leather and rubber gloves. The men removed the heads off the shrimp, dumping the tails into rectangular plastic crates. Once a crate was full, one of the sailors would use a hose connected to a bilge pump, washing the product thoroughly with sea water. The process of removing the heads allowed the intestinal contents of the shrimp to spill, potentially contaminating the tails. This had to be prevented, or the tails would rapidly develop black spots and become worthless. The seawater rinse washed off all of these contaminants.

After washing each crate, the sailors lifted them and dipped them into the *salmuera* precooling tub. This was the brine tub installed on deck containing water and salt, cooled by freon.

That brief dip would remove residual heat from the tails, which were then passed down to the man in charge of stacking the crates in the refrigeration room.

Once all the shrimp had been processed, the heads were pitched overboard and a water hose was used to rinse the deck.

"*Capitán*," the ship's mechanic informed Longoria. "We're done with the shrimp. Twenty-one crates."

Longoria did the math. At fifty pounds per crate, that was over one thousand kilos. Just over a ton. Not bad for the first night of the second trip of the season. It would be dawn soon. Not enough night time left to make another run. "Pull up the nets!"

"Not fishing anymore tonight, *Capitán*?"

"No. Time for everyone to get some rest."

The mechanic left the bridge, shouting commands to the crew to haul in the nets.

Minutes later, *Capitán* Longoria heard a loud scream coming from the aft deck. Now what? His men were a tough bunch and wouldn't scream like that unless something was really wrong.

His first mate appeared at the door. "*Capitán*, Agustin hurt himself!"

Agustin was the youngest member of the crew.

"What happened?"

"Got his big toe and foot cut by the winch."

"How the devil did he manage that?" The winch operated with one-inch thick steel cable.

"He was reeling in the nets. He put his foot up on the winch to balance himself. He's bleeding pretty bad."

"Can you patch him up?"

"We got some rags on him. Francisco got the first aid kit and they're looking at him now."

"All right, let me know." Longoria was not amused. Of all the goddam stupid ideas, putting his foot on the winch.

Minutes later the mechanic returned to the bridge. "It's a pretty bad cut. He's gonna need stitches. Lots of stitches."

Longoria took that in. Oh, crap. Nobody in his crew would be able to stitch up the dumbass. That left one option, head to port. Guaymas was five hours out. He'd no choice. They had to get that sailor to a hospital. That meant they'd be traveling most of the day. He'd have to take turns with his first mate sleeping, so they could fish tomorrow night. That would mean the loss of one day. Just great.

He had no choice.

"Tell the men we're going to Guaymas," he ordered. "We're gonna get that dumbass kid to a hospital."

Longoria plotted a heading from his GPS, turning the helm in that direction. He lifted the satellite phone to inform the gringos back in Phoenix about the event.

23

The $500 checks

"You won't believe what went down yesterday." Christian sat in his studio at home, accepting a cold Guinness from Brad Murray.

"I believe anything with these guys. What happened?"

Night had descended on Phoenix, but the temperatures still hovered above 103 degrees outside. Christian's office was a comfortable 75.

"Captain Longoria called early yesterday to tell me he had an injury aboard."

Murray stared at him, expectantly.

"One of the sailors cut up his foot pretty bad on the winch."

"Ouch!"

"Apparently, the kid needed medical attention, so Longoria headed for Guaymas very early this morning. It took them over twelve hours to reach the port, take the kid to the hospital and finally return to the fishing area."

"Man, that poor bastard. How bad was he hurt?"

"A bunch of stitches on his foot and big toe, according to Longoria. But that's not all."

"What else?"

"Longoria just called me again. Apparently, now the kid's foot is infected and black."

"What? What in heavens name is the kid doing still on the boat? Didn't they let him off?"

"No. Longoria just took him to the hospital to get patched up, then let him back on the ship and they went out fishing again. The deck on the fishing boats is completely contaminated by the contents of the intestines of the shrimp. As you know, with most of the organs of the shrimp being in its head, the lungs, stomach, intestines, once the crews remove the heads then most of that crud ends up on deck."

"Yeah, I remember. So, they didn't leave the kid in the hospital in Guaymas?"

"No. Longoria said the kid needs to make money because he's the only bread winner in his family."

"You gotta be kidding me."

"No, I'm serious. So, the meathead stayed onboard and his foot is now infected so bad that it's black."

"Idiots! Oh my God, *what idiots!*"

"Sounds like gangrene, so I instructed Longoria to head back to Guaymas again, only this time he has to take the kid off the ship and call me from Guaymas before they leave."

"Oh, sweet. That's gonna cost us."

"A bunch of money in lost catch, yes. But not for medical expenses. The *coperativa* provides medical coverage for the kid, so we don't have to cover his medical expenses. I also called Javier and gave him instructions to cut a check for the *coperativa* so they can pay the kid when he comes home. Poor bastard's going to spend a couple of days in the hospital in Guaymas and then we'll buy him a bus ticket back to Rock Port."

"Are we going to pay him for what he's already earned or what he was hoping to earn for the season?"

"We'll pay him for the whole season. It's only around a thousand bucks."

"I remember the last time you were so generous we got sued."

"Yeah, but that was because of the ambulance-chaser lawyer. I don't think we'll get sued again."

"As you wish." Brad Murray was a believer in the basic goodness of mankind, but these good folks down in the Sea of Cortés were working hard every day to change his opinion of humanity.

Four days later, the pair arrived back in Rock Port. Christian parked the Bronco in front of the office, checking out the area. He seldom let Javier Arenas know exactly what day or what time he would be arriving. Just a little touch of extra safety. With these fishermen, one never knew. He'd already made enough enemies to last him a lifetime. Although guns were strictly prohibited in Mexico, Christian carried a Walther PPK .380 pistol, the James Bond gun. One could never be too careful. Javier, his manager, had assured him that money could always get him out of any trouble involving a firearm.

They entered the small office, finding Estela, the secretary, at her desk. She was a twenty-year old local girl Javier had insisted on hiring so she could handle the phones five days a week. Christian suspected the real reason Javier had hired the young woman was to get in her pants, because there was no real reason to have a secretary sitting around when the ships were at sea. However, Javier was a very good person to have on one's team, so Christian had decided to allow him the one perk.

"*Capitán!*" she greeted, taken by surprise.

"Hello Estela."

"Does Javier know you're here?"

"No, I don't think so. Do me a favor please. Give him a call and tell him to meet us here."

"Right away," she lifted the phone.

A vehicle pulled up in front, with the corresponding sound of tires on gravel. It was the company's F-150 with Javier at the wheel.

"*How the devil...*" Brad Murray saw Estela returning the phone to its cradle.

"Magic Javier does it again," Christian smiled. It was downright amusing. The man obviously had some sort of jungle telegraph going that was hard to believe. They hadn't been in town ten minutes, and he appears.

Javier Arenas greeted them wearing his white straw hat.

"You didn't tell me you were coming, Boss, I would've gotten a couple of rooms lined up at the Plaza."

"Not an issue. We'll get the rooms; it's always empty in the middle of the week, anyway. Did you know we were coming?"

"No, I just came by to check on Estela."

Christian raised a bullshit flag. Yeah, right. "And we just happened to be here?"

"Well, yeah! How lucky!"

Christian laughed. No way he was ever going to hear the truth from any of these guys. It was just how they were raised. Lying was their culture. Javier had some sort of telepathy that enabled him know anytime the gringos were in town, but he obviously preferred keeping the specifics to himself.

"How long are you staying?"

"Only a couple of days," Christian informed him. If he was going to be lied to, he would play the same game with these people, but he'd be much better at it. They were leaving in the morning but he was not going to share that information with Javier, or anybody else in town. It wasn't unheard of to be robbed on the one-hour drive between Rock Port and the border. There was only the one isolated road leading out of town and it was the ideal place to ambush a couple of gringos carrying money and rob them. Perhaps even shoot them, just for good measure.

"The kid who got his foot hurt?" Javier queried.

"What about him?"

"He's back in town. They had to remove his big toe."

"Oh, man. That's no good. Longoria called me from Guaymas after he dropped the kid off at the hospital. From the sound of it, kid's lucky he didn't lose his entire foot."

"It was gangrene."

"Very stupid decision on the part of Longoria putting him back on the boat. Did the kid get paid?"

"Yes. I took the check to the *coperativa*. A small problem, however."

"What small problem?"

"A lawyer came by yesterday."

"What for?"

"He said he represents the kid who got injured."

"Don't tell me. I don't recall the guy's name, but was he wearing a green suit?"

"Yes."

"And he wants to sue us for fifty-thousand dollars."

"Yes!"

"So it was that same moron who was here when we had the incident with the other sailor who wanted to torch our ships?"

"Yes."

"What'd you tell him?"

"I told him I had no idea when you'd be back in town."

"He leave you his number?"

"He did."

"Give him a call. Tell him to get his ass out here now."

"Of course." Javier grabbed the phone from the secretary's desk, dialing the number on a card he pulled out of his wallet.

Twenty minutes later *Licenciado* Jose Iturbide entered the office. He was once again wearing a cheap suit and sweating like a pig. The man was downright disgusting.

"José, what a pleasure meeting you again!" The man was instantly intimidated by the use of his first name, a horrible breach of etiquette in Mexico. "And what can we do for you *this* time, *José*?"

The man took a deep breath, wiping the sweat from his forehead with what had once been a clean cotton handkerchief. "I'm here regarding a client of mine, one Agustin Llamas, who was injured aboard one of your ships and lost his big toe as a result of your orders. Your captain refused to take him to the hospital."

Christian laughed out loud.

These people were just too much. "I know the routine." He walked behind his desk, retrieving a checkbook from one of the drawers. Writing a check, he handed it to the attorney. "So, I understand that, by accepting this check, you'll advise your client to forget about any lawsuit. Correct?"

The attorney lifted the check to read it. "Yes! That is exactly how it is! I'll make sure my client doesn't bother you again!" The man placed the check inside a worn-out vinyl briefcase he was carrying, bowing his head as he departed.

"That little piece of shit!" Brad Murray exclaimed.

"Relax. This is one of those things we can't change in this place. Look at it as part of the cost of doing business."

"Why didn't you just tell him to get lost?"

"Can't do that, Brad. That little piece of human garbage is perfectly capable of finding a judge who is either a relative or a friend, a judge willing to slap an injunction against us and hold one of our ships hostage. Then, the problem would cost us ten thousand dollars, not five hundred."

"Absolutely amazing. We should make the sailors sign a document releasing us from liability. They sign it or we don't employ them."

"Brad, this is the Sea of Cortés. Contracts are not worth the paper they're written on. As you have noticed, corruption is their religion, and without doubt, we're much better off just paying the five hundred bucks to the likes of that attorney and forgetting about it.

"I don't like it."

"Neither do I, but this is how they conduct business here. We have to play by their rules or they won't let us play. Basically, our attorney told me that Mexican law favors labor. This is one of the results of the Mexican revolution."

24

Go Trust a Pirate

"*Capitán?*" Javier Arenas was calling from Rock Port.

"Javier! Good morning. What news do you have for me?" Christian was finishing a breakfast of bacon, *huevos rancheros* and toast at home. The shrimping season was starting in one week, and everything was ready to go.

"Good morning Boss. All's well. Just calling to ask your permission for somethin'. Fernando Varas, one of the local ship owners here in town, the guy who owns one of the other shrimp processing plants, came by the office this morning."

Varas? Christian had met the man before. Not a bad character, although not real polished.

"He wanted to ask us a favor. One of his ships, the *Estela*, was getting ready to sail this morning but they suspected a problem with her rudder. They need to lift the ship outta the water so they can find out what the problem is and repair it but can't do that cause they already refueled it so it's too heavy for the traveling crane at the García shipyard."

"Okay? So, what's that have to do with us?"

"Mr. Varas asked if we could help him. He asked me if we had already refueled all three of our ships, and I told him that the *San Felipe* has not been refueled yet."

"And...?"

"He wants to transfer out his diesel from the *Estela* to our ship. Then they can take the *Estela* out of the water and fix the rudder."

"Okay, if I understand you correctly, he wants to use the *San Felipe* as a temporary storage tank for his diesel?"

"Yes. That's what he wants."

"Can we do that?"

"Yeah, sure we can."

"Fine. Let's do it then. Let me know when you've transferred his diesel back on his ship."

"Yessir."

Giving each other a helping hand was one of the unwritten laws of the sea.

The following day, Christian drove down to Rock Port with Brad Murray. They wanted to make sure everything was ready for the upcoming shrimping season.

Javier Arenas showed up at the office not five minutes after they walked in. Again, the man showed up without having been informed that they were in town. Amazing, really.

"Javier!" Christian greeted his manager with a sly smile. "How the hell did you know we were here already?"

"It's a small town, *Capitán.*"

"So I see. Well, it's good to see you. What do we have left to do before the ships can go out?"

"Not much, Father Damian needs to give his blessing to the ships and we need to get the releases from the harbormaster."

"What happened with the fuel situation with Fernando Varas?"

"All done." Javier smiled.

"You gave him his diesel back?"

"Yes, it's all done. They fixed the rudder on the *Estela* and we transferred the diesel back and all's good. And we came out ahead."

"We came out ahead? How do you mean?"

"We kept a little bit of his diesel."

"You *what?*"

Javier smiled again. He was obviously happy. "We kept some of his diesel."

"What do you mean, 'we kept some of his diesel'?"

"Our ships don't have fuel gauges. You know that. We measure the amount of diesel in the tanks using a long wooden stick with marks on it. We insert the stick into the tank and read how far up the fuel is on it. Very inaccurate."

"So? How did we manage to keep some of his diesel?"

Javier was still smiling like a kid presenting a good report card to his parents. "When we transferred the diesel back to his ship, I gave orders for us to keep the tail end of his diesel."

"The tail end. And exactly how much was this tail end?"

"Oh, about four thousand liters."

Christian did the math in his head. "Javier, that's about a thousand dollars' worth of diesel."

"Yes! Isn't that great?" Javier beamed.

Christian had to resist the urge to strangle him. Obviously, Javier Arenas saw this as a masterpiece of deception, a highly-valued quality in Mexico.

"Goddammit Javier! Don't you ever do anything like that again without consulting with me first!"

Javier looked as if he'd been slapped.

"We don't do shit like that!"

Javier's mouth had dropped open.

"What the hell are you doing stealing from the man?"

"We, er, we didn't steal. We did the man a favor."

"You did him a favor by stealing his diesel?"

"Yes, no. I mean, we helped him when he had a need."

"And in exchange for helping him you steal his diesel."

Javier Arenas was stunned. Any other ship owner in the Sea of Cortés would've praised him for his initiative. Perhaps even given him a gift or a bonus for the free diesel. "No, I mean, it was kinda like a commission for helping him out."

"Without him knowing, of course."

Javier Arenas was still perplexed. He thought he was going to be getting an 'attaboy' but, instead, he was being keel-hauled.

"All right, get the Jeep. We have to go talk to Fernando Varas."

Javier Arenas followed the two men out while Christian explained the events to Brad Murray.

The trio parked outside the shrimp processing plant owned by Fernando Varas. Owning a processing plant was a good deal in Mexico. In addition to processing the shrimp captured by his own ships, Fernando Varas processed shrimp for others, something which gave him the opportunity to steal all he could. He would simply replace big Blues with small shrimp brought in by others and hey, *presto*, he had some juicy profits in his wallet.

Everyone was essentially a pirate in that business.

"Good afternoon," the secretary chirped.

"We're here to see Mr. Varas."

She led the way to the back office, where Varas was sitting behind a desk, wearing a white apron and head cover, much like a butcher of old times.

"Fernando!" Christian greeted.

The man stood up, offering his hand.

"What can I do for you gentlemen?"

"It's more what we can do for you."

"Oh?" Fernando Varas had met the gringo twice before. Didn't particularly like him. The gringo appeared to understand the local culture a little bit too well. That made everyone uncomfortable in town, giving the locals the feeling of being judged by the men from the Other Side.

"I understand we helped you out with a diesel situation."

Fernando Varas smiled, wondering. Were they coming to ask for some sort of payment in exchange for having helped? "Yes, thank you very much. We had an issue with the rudder on one of our ships."

"I know. I'm here because when my men returned your diesel to your ship, they erroneously failed to transfer all of it back. They thought we had more diesel on our ship than we did."

Fernando Varas appeared somewhat confused.

"So, it seems we kept about four thousand liters that belong to you."

Christian pulled out a pen and his checkbook; he filled in the latter. "Here's a thousand dollars to pay for the diesel we kept. You may want to top off your own ship before you send it out on the first trip of the season." Christian extended the check to the man, who took it, eyeing it suspiciously.

Javier Arenas stood behind Christian, trying to blend with the furniture.

"Well, thank you." Varas offered. He was not effusive nor overly gracious.

"That's all I wanted to talk to you about," Christian explained, extending his hand again. "We'll get out of your hair now."

Varas shook hands with all three men, still looking confused.

They left the processing plant.

"Chap didn't appear too pleased, did he?" Murray noted.

"No, he didn't. See, I think we induced a major meltdown in his mind by giving him the check."

"Why?"

"Because in this country nobody in his right mind would do what we just did."

"You mean give the man his money back?"

"Correct. In this country, what I've learned is that if someone finds a wallet full of cash in the middle of the street, they will thank their favorite saint before proceeding to the nearest bar to buy rounds for all present. If you even for one second contemplated returning the wallet to its rightful owner, people would think you had taken complete leave of your senses. If you take the wallet to the police, the cops will thank you, then hasten to the nearest bar to buy rounds for everyone."

"Cow's shit!"

"Yep, right now that guy back there is wondering why the hell we gave him a thousand-dollar check. He's going to think we actually ripped him off for three thousand dollars, but only admitted to a grand. He's going to hate us and be pissed, thinking that we actually screwed him."

"So why give him anything at all then?"

"Because, even though we're operating in this country, we're still American and have certain principles."

"Can't he just send one of his men to check the fuel load on his ship and see how much he's missing?"

"No, he couldn't do that. First of all, the damned dipsticks we use to measure the fuel in the tanks are inaccurate as all hell. And, if he told his foreman the story, the foreman would go to the ship and claim that the missing diesel was five thousand bucks, not one thousand. Then Varas would come to us demanding he be paid the difference. If we paid it, then Varas would give the money to his foreman, with instructions to fill up the tanks. The foreman would simply state that he did it, while pocketing the money."

"You gotta be kidding me."

"I wish I was."

"So, even though we gave the guy his money, he still thinks we're thieves."

"Yeah, that's exactly how it goes."

"Javier!"

"Yes, *Capitán*?"

"Don't do anything like that again without checking with me first."

"Yessir." Javier would never understand these gringos. But he loved his job and the perks and the salary they paid him, and if that was how they wanted it, that's how he would do it. Next time, he would just keep his mouth shut. And sell the diesel on his own.

25

Damned If You Do and Damned If You Don't

"So, we're going to have all three ships out of the water day after tomorrow?"

"That's what the shipyard's telling us."

"But how reliable is that?"

"Hopefully, García will do as he says." The shipyard owner had been educated in America, and was considered a man of integrity in the village. If he claimed the maintenance would be done by a specific date, one could generally rely on him. At least that's what Christian was hoping.

Christian was in the kitchen of his home in Phoenix, trying to coordinate the maintenance the ships required before the start of the season in three weeks. Hanging up on Javier Arenas he looked at his 'To do' list.

"So, you think this guy García will be true to his word?" Brad Murray asked.

"You mean, is he gonna take our ships out of the water as scheduled?"

"Yes."

"I don't know. Our experience with the shipyards in that town has not been the best so far."

They'd already had two other shipyards setup appointments to take the ships out of the water for the pre-season maintenance, only to have them cancel at the last minute. Other shrimp boat operators who were related to the men who owned the shipyards managed to slip their ships ahead of the ones owned by the Americans.

"I've already had to yell at two shipyard owners this week. Their word is worth absolutely nothing."

The phone rang.

"*Capitán?*" Javier Arenas calling from Mexico again.

"What now?"

"The ships will need to be painted. The owner of the one paint shop here in town just dropped by asking me if we're going to place an order for marine paint with him."

"What kind of paint does he carry?"

"The good stuff. Copper-based. And he has all that we need."

"What's his price?"

"He's not cheap. One hundred dollars per gallon."

Christian rapidly calculated each ship would require thirty gallons of paint. Three thousand bucks a ship. "The paint for the ships is going to cost us nine thousand dollars."

Brad Murray nodded. "Why don't we buy the paint here, instead? It's got to be cheaper."

"Can't find marine copper-based paint in the States. It's been outlawed."

"Why do we need copper-based?"

"Copper and lead-based paints are the best for our hulls. As the season progresses, barnacles stick to the hulls, and these damned mollusks generate drag, which requires more power to overcome. Consequently, in the long run, the barnacles cost us extra fuel. If we use lead or copper-based paint, however, the minute the barnacles attach themselves to the hulls they will begin to die of lead or copper poisoning. That is a good thing because we don't want the extra drag."

"I see. So, let me guess, in Mexico lead and copper-based paints are not illegal."

"Bingo."

"And why can't we try to buy some of that paint here in America? We're not going to be using it in this country, so we wouldn't be breaking the law."

"I don't think we'll find any of that paint anywhere."

"Nonsense. Let me try."

Christian was delighted having Brad on his side. The man was such a positive influence.

Brad spent most of the morning on the phone and Internet trying to locate copper or lead-based paint, finally succeeding.

"If I understand you correctly, you have black copper-based paint?"

"Yessir." The man at the other end was sitting at his desk in a military depot in San Diego.

"And I can buy it from you."

"Yessir."

"And there are no restrictions, as long as I take it to Mexico."

"That's correct."

Brad wondered if the guy had an IQ much over 60. "Can you deliver it to Phoenix?"

"No, sir."

"We need to pick it up?"

"Yessir."

Maybe even an IQ of forty, he reassessed. "All right. If you give me your information, I'll have one of our men drive there to pick it up. One hundred gallons you said?"

"Yessir."

"And the price is thirty dollars per gallon?"

The man at the other end acknowledged again. Brad Murray shared the good news with Christian. With this purchase of one hundred gallons of copper-based paint from the United States Navy warehouse, they would be able to paint the hulls of their ships at one-third the cost.

Christian called his manager back. "Javier, we found some paint at a Navy warehouse in San Diego. I need you to drive out there tomorrow to pick it up."

Javier Arenas was delighted to hear the news. He absolutely loved going out of town on assignments. He usually had his girlfriend traveling with him whenever he was sent on a mission. "I'll let the local paint shop know that we're not going to be needing their paint, then."

"You do that."

A few minutes later the phone rang.

"Javier, what's up?"

"I called the local paint shop to let him know we're not going to be needing his expensive paint. He said he just happened to fall upon a good deal and he can sell us some copper-based paint for twenty dollars a gallon."

"No shit." Christian was not surprised. In fact, he was slightly annoyed. Everything in the Sea of Cortés was a haggling game. It appeared that the paint shop owner was no different. But he was able to drop his price from one hundred dollars per gallon to twenty? Christian was pretty darned sure it was the same paint the owner had tried to peddle at a hundred bucks a can that now he agreed to sell for twenty.

"What do you want me to do, Boss?"

Christian reflected on this. If he could get the paint cheaper in Rock Port, and without having to send the pickup truck with Arenas all the way to San Diego, he would surely save a little money. He made up his mind. "All right, tell the paint guy in town we'll buy his paint. Cancel the San Diego pickup."

Javier informed that all three ships were already out of the water in the shipyard, and the men were just starting on the preparation of the hulls for painting. This would accelerate things. The shipyard owner was anxious to get the three ships painted and back in the water so they would free up some space on the shipyard for others needing seasonal maintenance.

"So, that takes care of the maintenance?" Brad Murray asked.

"Partly, yes. After they paint the hulls then they have to weld the zinc bricks to each hull."

"Refresh my memory about those, would you?"

"Didn't I tell you? We need to weld a couple of dozen zinc bricks to the hulls to protect them against corrosion."

"No, I don't recall, but go ahead."

"The Sea of Cortés is extremely salty. More so than any other body of water in the western hemisphere. That corrodes metal really fast. In simple terms, the electrons in the metal are stolen by the sea water, which results in rust forming in our hulls. If we didn't take steps to prevent this, our hulls would turn into corn flakes in two seasons. So, what we do is we weld these huge zinc bricks to the hull. Zinc is rich in electrons, so each time an electron is stolen by the sea water, another electron from the zinc brick takes its place, protecting our hulls against corrosion. They call this cathodic protection and the bricks are known as 'sacrificial metal.'"

"No shit?"

"Nope. The sacrificial zinc bricks eventually dissolve, sort of like an Alka-Seltzer in water. That's why they have to be replaced before the start of each season."

"Didn't know that."

"Let's head down there, I want to see that the painting is done right."

Five hours later, the two men checked in at the local hotel where they now kept a suite. The small colorful fishing village by the sea offered some very interesting places to eat, where they could relax until the following morning when the shipyard once again opened for business. Before going to their hotel, they had driven past the shipyard to check on their trawlers.

All three were out of the water, carefully balanced and kept straight with the use of two-by-fours, their hulls carefully sanded of old paint from the previous season.

It was obvious the crews had already been working long hours preparing those hulls for the fresh paint. The crews for each fishing boat had already been lined up for the start of the season, each captain selecting his eight-man crew. Since the crews didn't get paid until the ship returned to port with its cargo holds full of shrimp, the men were anxious to earn some additional money, early in the season, by lending a hand in the preparation of the ships. Using the crews to prepare the ships was considerably less expensive than employing the shipyard labor.

In the morning, Javier Arenas met them on the patio of their hotel, where they were preparing for the day with a succulent Mexican breakfast of thin steaks, fried eggs on tortillas, beans and rice. All of it followed by orange juice and plenty of black coffee.

"Boss, we have a problem."

Typical morning in the shrimping business, Christian mused. Why was he not surprised?

"What is it this time?"

"The shipyard owner told me our ships have to be back in the water by tomorrow morning, the latest."

"Okay. Is that enough time to paint the hulls and let them dry?"

"Yes."

"So, what's the problem?"

"Do we still have that paint available in San Diego?"

"What?"

Javier Arenas was always uncomfortable about reporting fuck ups to *El Jefe*. "See, Toño, the owner of the local paint shop, I just saw him at the shipyard."

"And...?"

Arenas was obviously uncomfortable.

"Just come out and say it. What about the owner of the paint shop?"

"He apologizes, but the paint he offered us is no longer available."

"Oh, shit." Christian quickly calculated. It would take most of the day to retrieve the paint from San Diego, even if it was still available. No way in hell they would be able to paint the ships today. "Can we ask the shipyard owner for more time?"

"No, he won't do that."

"We'll pay him more."

Javier Arenas shook his head. "It's not the money, Boss. With the shrimping season upon us, he still needs to provide maintenance to quite a few boats here in town. Those people are his *paisanos*, he won't leave them hanging. He has to live here."

Christian explained the situation to Brad Murray.

"Oh, crap, now what?"

"However," Arenas added. "The owner of the paint shop said he has plenty of the other paint that he can sell us if we are in a jam."

"What other paint?"

"The paint he'd offered us initially."

"You mean the hundred-dollar a gallon paint?"

"Yes."

"Sonofabitch." So that was the game. Brad Murray had the same impression once Christian translated for him.

"Of all the dirty tricks..."

"This is Mexico," Christian sighed. What were their options? Arranging for the shipyard to get their ships out of the water had been an ordeal but, now they had them out of the water and that window was closing. He suspected the shipyard owner would have absolutely no second thoughts dumping his ships back in the sea without batting an eye if the paint didn't show up. San Diego was out of the question. That would take too long.

"Tell the little shit we'll go ahead and buy the paint from him."

Arenas exhaled. He had been dreading telling the gringos that this was going on. The owner of the paint shop had manipulated the situation to his advantage by lying and cheating.

Javier Arenas left and the men finished breakfast.

"Good God, man, is this the way they do everything here?" Murray was disgusted. "We got setup."

"Looks that way, doesn't it?" Christian shook his head. "Unfortunately, we got painted into a corner, no pun intended."

"So, we're buying the paint from that lying, cheating crook?"

"We have no choice."

"I should call the Navy guy in San Diego, see if he can still sell us the paint for the next season."

"Great idea. But wait until we're back in Arizona. Remember, the hotel here will charge us five dollars a minute for calls back to the States."

Brad Murray cracked a smile. "You know, Christian, sometimes I get the feeling that doing business in this country is a little like falling in a tributary of the Amazon river full of piranhas. Everyone rushes in, breaking their necks to take a bite out of our asses."

Christian smiled at his friend. "Like I said, this is Mexico."

26

Japanese fishing vessel pirating in the Sea of Cortés

Captain Haruto scanned the seas ahead as well as the radar screen mounted on the dash of his 455-ton shrimp trawler, the *Asako*. The weather was clear, at the end of this beautiful day in the south Sea of Cortés. The sun would be setting in the west in another ten minutes. Captain Haruto had been on the bridge for almost ten hours, carefully watching out for vessels of the Mexican Navy. He and his twenty-eight-man crew had entered Mexican territorial waters illegally twenty hours earlier. At this point, they were committed. They had to sail another five hundred miles north deep into Mexico, roughly fifty hours at their current ten knots. The *Asako* was a shrimp trawler, an oceanic shrimp trawler. The ship had crossed the entire Pacific Ocean, over six thousand miles of open water, refueling along the way with the help of three Japanese factory ships strategically positioned along their route.

Their mission consisted of sailing to the Sea of Cortés, in Mexico, and filling their cargo hold with one hundred tons of fabulous Mexican Blue worth at least two million dollars at the Tokyo fish market. The Japanese crew intended to capture the shrimp half-way up the Baja peninsula, where the bottom of the Sea of Cortés became very shallow. Once their cargo hold was filled, they would steam south, departing the Sea of Cortés, afterward steaming two hundred miles from the west coast of Mexico to rendezvous with one of the enormous Japanese factory ships awaiting them just outside the territorial waters of Mexico. The factory ship would subsequently take on their shrimp and the *Asako* would eventually head back into Mexican territorial waters for another incursion. The Japanese fishing fleets, having already fished out the waters around their country had become bolder by the day. Because a great part of the food consumed in Japan came from the sea, Japanese fishing vessels fished illegally in practically every area in the world for fish and shrimp. Territorial waters and fishing permits were but a technicality they didn't feel the need to observe.

Captain Haruto knew the Mexican Navy had limited resources, and even those limited resources hardly ever left port because the men in charge of coast guard operations generally pocketed the diesel money which should be used to patrol the territorial waters. This was his fifth trip into the Sea of Cortés in his career as a shrimp boat captain, and he felt confident that he would be able to fill his hold with tons of Blue shrimp in a matter of just a couple of days. The Japanese embassy in Mexico City supplied discrete intel for their fishing fleets, confirming the location of the Mexican surveillance ships and the fact that they seldom left port. Of course, the diplomatic mission would never acknowledge this fact. This type of intel was not hard to obtain, though. A few drinks with a Harbormaster and a well-placed spy could extract all sorts of good information from the unsuspecting Mexicans.

The *Asako* entered the Sea of Cortés, turning north fifty miles from the city of Los Cabos, in its mission to harvest Blue shrimp off the coastal waters of Mexico.

27

A Pilot's View

Mayor Alejandro Tuero sipped black Guatemalan coffee from the Styrofoam cup. He scanned the sea ahead. He and his crew were at twenty-two thousand feet, descending on autopilot northwest-bound towards the city of La Paz, in Baja California. His

CASA 235 surveillance aircraft had been assigned temporary duty patrolling the Sea of Cortés and the Mexican territorial waters west of the Baja peninsula beginning on the following month. The twin's General Electric CT7-9C3 turboprops hummed in synch, propelling the aircraft towards La Paz at better than two hundred-twenty knots. The aircraft was brand-new, having been delivered to the Mexican Navy merely days before. It still smelled of fresh paint and leather. Mayor Tuero and his crew had been assigned the task of repositioning the aircraft to its new temporary base. They were going to arrive in forty-five minutes, hit the hotel, and hopefully be at the local bar for some adult beverages in no time after that. They didn't have to deadhead back to Mexico City on the airlines for another two days, so Mayor Tuero was delighted with this mini-vacation. Not to mention the pleasure of flying the Navy's newest aircraft.

"That a ship over there?" His copilot inquired, pointing with his index finger against the windshield.

"Where?"

"About eleven o'clock."

Mayor Tuero glanced in the general direction his copilot was pointing. He didn't see anything. The setting sun made visibility somewhat difficult.

"Yeah, may be a ship. I saw the reflection a moment ago," the copilot added.

The silver expanse of sea ahead of them appeared totally empty.

"Nah, don't see anything."

"There! Look!"

Mayor Tuero adjusted his Ray-Ban green aviator sunglasses closer to his eyes, returning his attention outside.

"There! I saw it that time. Yep, definitely a ship of some sort. Probably a ferry doing the mainland run from La Paz."

"Let's go look at it," the copilot suggested. It's practically on our course."

"Sure," Mayor Tuero agreed, disconnecting the autopilot by pushing the red button on his yoke. Anything to break the monotony. The wail of the autopilot disconnect alarm rang for a couple of chimes before being silenced by a second push of the same red button. Mayor Tuero welcomed the opportunity to hand-fly the brand-new surveillance aircraft. He banked the airplane lightly to the left, directing it toward the spot where he could now see a tiny white speck. "Let Mazatlán Center know we're descending and cancel the flight plan once we're below eighteen."

"Sure thing." The copilot began talking into his noise-attenuating mike.

The sun was setting over the horizon, turning the sky a beautiful crimson red. It was a clear sky, with no cloud formations in any direction.

"Wanna go down to a thousand feet and just stay there until La Paz?" Mayor Tuero was enjoying the solid, firm feel of the flight controls. The airplane was very responsive. He imagined a Rolls-Royce automobile would handle the same way—a thirty-four million dollar automobile, in this case.

"That sounds great!" His copilot voiced. By cancelling their instrument flight plan they were free to fly any altitude and course they chose.

At well over two hundred knots the CASA 235 was rapidly closing on the ship ahead.

"Sure looks beautiful from here, no?" The copilot reached for his iPhone, intending to capture a couple of snapshots of the beautiful sunset with the lonely ship.

"Yeah, it does."

"Can you swing to the left a little so I can get a better angle?"

"No sweat," Mayor Tuero responded, banking the turboprop further south. They were almost at a thousand feet about the water.

The Mexican Navy surveillance airplane shot past the vessel half mile south of it."

"Did you take the picture?"

"Yeah," the copilot said, looking at his iPhone. "That's not a ferry, it's a fishing boat. A trawler."

"Really?"

"Yeah," the copilot continued, carefully studying the iPhone screen, "It's a trawler, all right. A big one." The ship had two enormous twin booms spread out to either side of the hull for stability. Those booms were used to drag the nets.

As part of their surveillance training, both pilots had been briefed by Mexican naval intelligence about the types of vessels used by the Mexican fishing fleets in the Sea of Cortés. Mostly smaller trawlers, nothing bigger than perhaps 150 tons. Nothing as big as this.

"A big trawler, you say?"

"Yeah, look." The copilot held up his iPhone, displaying the zoomed-in image to the Mayor, showing what appeared to be a large white trawler, immaculately clean.

"That's no ferry boat!"

"No, it's not. It's definitely a trawler. A big one. And look how clean it is." Both pilots were very aware that Mexican fishing trawlers only looked this good the very first few days of the fishing season. After that, they quickly became rusty and dirty. Continuous maintenance during the fishing season was not a luxury ship owners in that part of the world contemplated. Dirt and rust didn't hurt anything, so might as well let the ships continue fishing like that.

But the photo of the ship they had just passed showed an immaculate hull. And the twin booms definitely suggested a trawler.

"What're you thinking?" Mayor Tuero felt the excitement of the hunt.

"I don't think that's one of hours. It's too big and too clean."

"Wanna go back take another look at it?"

"You bet!"

"Let's do it," Mayor Tuero banked the airplane into a sixty-degree two-g turn to the right.

Following the second low level pass at three hundred feet, the trawler did something unexpected.

"Hey! Those boys are turning!" The copilot pointed out.

"Sure, as all hell they are," Mayor Tuero concurred. "I think you're right, that's not one of hours!"

"Who do you think they are?"

"I have no idea, but from the quick turn they're executing, I would say they know they've been had and sure as shit they have no business being in these waters."

"What do we do?"

"See if you can reach La Paz or Mazatlán center. We may be too low to talk to either of them. If they answer tell them to inform the Navy that an unidentified fishing trawler is just east of Los Cabos and when he saw us, he's trying to make a run for it. We have enough fuel to stay out here another five hours, so we'll just tag along. I'm going to go back upstairs so you can reach Mazatlán."

The CASA 235 began climbing while executing a racetrack pattern around the fishing vessel.

Mayor Tuero was terribly excited. In his four years as a naval aviator he had never spotted a foe in any of the seas he had patrolled.

Capitan Torres, a Mexican Naval officer in his mid-forties assigned to the port of La Paz, in Baja California Sur, received the call from the *Comandancia*. Capitan Torres listened on his cellphone as he jumped in his Jeep, driving towards the military installations of the Mexican Navy. The voice at the other end informed him that a Naval surveillance aircraft inbound over the Gulf ten minutes earlier had spotted a foreign trawler well inside territorial waters. The report indicated the trawler had since turned southwest and was apparently trying to make a run for the limit of the territorial waters. The surveillance aircraft was holding station over the vessel, and would continue to do so, fuel permitting.

Mexico City had been notified and the Department of Defense had issued orders for the Sierra-class Corvette *Adelita* to put out to sea immediately with instructions to pursue and intercept the intruder.

Capitan Torres, the skipper on the *Adelita*, drove to the docks, parking his Jeep alongside the corvette the Mexican Navy had assigned him. He barked orders to his subordinates to prepare the ship while climbing the plank, heading for the bridge. He glanced at the printout of a report handed to him by one of the sailors. The intruder's position was reported as approximately forty nautical miles from the *Adelita*. The intruder was being reported by the surveillance aircraft as steaming at approximately ten knots. Capitan Torres entered the bridge of his corvette, mentally calculating whether catching the intruder was even possible. The *Adelita* could make eighteen knots, which would give him an edge of eight knots. At that speed, It would take him five hours to cover the forty miles currently separating him from the intruder. Say another thirty minutes to make up for the time it would take the *Adelita* to get going. That would allow him to intercept the intruder well inside of Mexico's unofficial 200-mile territorial waters.

Capitan Torres felt the rumble under his boots of the 24,000-horsepower produced by the twin diesel Caterpillars coming alive. By the time they caught up with the intruder it would be very dark. No moon out tonight. That intruder had planned it well. They would have to acquire the intruder with radar, then fire a couple of rounds in front of it to make him stop. That would be tricky. Boarding at night wouldn't be good either, better keep everybody in one place, just wait for the sun to come up while tagging the intruder. He decided that would be the course of action to follow, catch up with the vessel, force him to stop by taking shots and then guarding him until daylight. Once the sun was up, they would board it and take charge. Escorting the intruder all the way back to La Paz would be fun. He would be a triumphant hero returning home with a captured prize. He had no idea of the nationality of the intruder but suspected it must be from one of the Asian countries. Those people were famous for insolently trespassing in other countries' waters.

The *Adelita* began to move under its own power, headed for the Lat Lon position the surveillance aircraft had last transmitted as the current whereabouts of the intruder.

28

R & R The Pirate Way

Capitán Jesus Hidalgo dropped anchor five miles from Kino Bay. His trawler, the *San Felipe*, had fished every night the past two days, then steamed three hours back to port at ten knots. His men were exhausted from two long and busy nights spent catching shrimp, but they'd been able to put in three-hour power naps on the way back and should be somewhat refreshed and ready to party. The weather was clear and the seas calm, so the return voyage to the port had been a pleasure.

Capitán Jesus Hidalgo instructed his men to lower the six-man dingy from the roof of the bridge into the waters of the Sea of Cortés. Three sailors also lifted a voluminous burlap bag up from the cargo hold onto the deck. The bag was the size of a thirty-gallon oil drum, and contained nearly two hundred pounds of large Blue shrimp. The fishing activities the previous two nights had produced nearly three tons of shrimp for the crew, and now it was time for fun.

"Get that shrimp on the dingy and make sure you don't rip the bag!" Capt. Hidalgo bellowed. He intended to go ashore with three of his men and sell the shrimp to the black-market buyers waiting on the beach. The buyers were enterprising young men using a tractor trailer pulling a refrigerated container, buying stolen shrimp from the trawlers and selling it in Mexico City and Guadalajara at substantial profits. These black-market buyers paid the crews roughly half the market price for their product. *Capitán* Jesus Hidalgo and his crew would sell enough shrimp to put one thousand dollars in their pockets. Enough money to finance a visit to one of the local houses of ill-repute and buy many shots of tequila.

Some the men would go ashore first and party, followed by others sometime later in the day. That way, someone would always remain with the ship and the precious shrimp in the cargo hold. The fishing trawler was not equipped with an auxiliary engine, therefore the main CAT had to remain at idle the entire time, driving the refrigeration compressor.

The fishermen manned the oars and directed the dingy towards the beach. The sun was just starting to appear over the mountains. *Capitán* Jesus Hidalgo did not help with the oars. He was the Boss, and as such, he was not expected to help. Instead, he stood near the bow, looking forward to having a good time at *La Gruta Azul,* his favorite bordello. The ladies at that place of business would keep the place open all morning in anticipation of the sailors arriving with pockets full of cash.

The small dingy made it to the beach. Ahead of them was the open end of a semi, backed up on the sand to facilitate loading. Three men stood around a commercial scale resting on the sand next to the trailer.

"Good morning!" *Capitán* Jesus Hidalgo greeted, approaching the men.

"Yeah. Good morning to you!" the men by the scale chanted back. "You got shrimp to sell?"

"Sure do!" *Capitán* Jesus Hidalgo pointed to his three men following close behind, struggling with the bag full of shrimp. He took in the AR-15 semi-automatic rifles being held by two of the buyers. All three buyers had pistol holsters attached to their belts.

"Put it over here!" one of the buyers ordered, a man with a yellow *Caterpillar* baseball cap and his two front teeth missing, pointing at the commercial scale.

The three sailors from the *San Felipe* covered the last few feet to the scale, carefully lowering the bag full of frozen shrimp onto the metal plate.

"What do we have here?" the buyer reached for the string holding the bag closed.

"Blue shrimp!" *Capitán* Jesus Hidalgo offered. "Big ones too, tens!"

The buyer opened the burlap sack, reaching inside and pulling out a fistful of frozen shrimp. The shrimp were huge and they were frozen solid white. They looked as if they were made of white chocolate. The buyer reached behind his pants, producing a powerful three-cell flashlight. The white beam illuminated the handful of shrimp. "Looks like good stuff!" the buyer announced. "I can give you six dollars a pound."

Capitán Jesus Hidalgo was delighted. He had expected five dollars a pound. He did the math. Twelve hundred dollars. Life was sweet. "Six-fifty!" He responded. He came from a culture where haggling was *de rigor*.

"That works."

That same shrimp sold for thirty dollars a pound at the fish market in Arizona.

The buyers adjusted the weights on the commercial scale, finally satisfied with the results. "Two-hundred eleven pounds." Missing-teeth produced a hand-held calculator, the kind that was used in the 1980s, with red LED. He quickly punched some figures into the device, then turning it around, he showed the display to *Capitán* Jesus Hidalgo.

"Looks good to me."

Missing-teeth received a wad of cash from one of his two helpers. He counted out a number of U.S. dollars, offering the bills to the captain. "It's all there."

Capitán Jesus Hidalgo accepted the money, then slowly began counting it. Not trusting each other was the norm in those circles. Not trusting someone was one thing; calling someone a 'thief' was absolutely out of the question. At the very least, such an insult could result in a sharp knife penetrating one's soft midsection. But if done with some diplomacy, nobody took offense if some counting was done provided, of course, it was undertaken with the appropriate respect.

"It's all here," the old sea dog announced, turning around and walking away from the location. His three men followed. Each one of his men was armed with an ultra-sharp knife, which they carried on their belts. The men headed away from the beach toward a couple of waiting taxis. The operation was routine night after night, and everyone in Bahia de Kino was eager to make a buck or two off the back of the ship owners.

The taxi dropped the crew off at the door of the *Gruta Azul* bar. *Capitán* Jesus Hidalgo slipped the driver a twenty-dollar bill and they went inside. The place was still active after an entire night of catering to thirsty patrons with overactive hormones. The group picked a table in the center of a large room with dim light, finally ordering drinks for everyone. The men had not taken baths for over a week, and the beards and moustaches announced to anyone interested that these men were fishermen. Regardless, several girls immediately joined the men at their table. Cash was a powerful motivator.

"Men," *Capitán* Jesus Hidalgo announced, "one hundred twenty dollars for each of you. No more."

The men nodded agreement. This was more money that they would have available for their own private pleasures the entire year. The men considered themselves religious and proper and their pay went to their families, but this was not their pay. This was a bonus, a fringe benefit, and this money belonged to *them*.

Two hours later the satisfied men caught another taxi in front of the bar. They were tired and more than a little intoxicated. Now it was time to return to the ship and allow the rest of the guys to visit the *Gruta Azul* and have their chance at some fun. The sun was already high and daylight was there to stay.

Capitán Jesus Hidalgo was slightly intoxicated. He'd had four tequila shots before cavorting with Lucia, one of his favorites. He was hungry and looking forward to some sleep. He remembered that the ship's cook was going ashore with the next group, so there would be no food prepared by the cook until later that night.

"Driver!" he ordered. "Pull over by that food stand over there!"

The taxi driver obeyed, stopping the vehicle in front of a food stand from which emanated delicious aromas of fried food and lemons. The food stand was nothing more than a wooden cart parked on the sidewalk with its owner cooking on a gas stove.

Capitán Jesus Hidalgo and his men bought food to go and started eating it in the cab on their way to the beach. They had left their dingy on the beach, and they knew it would still be there when they returned. Nobody in his right mind in Kino Bay would consider stealing a dingy from men who carried knives sharp enough to shave with them, and knew how to use them.

The cab dropped them off and *Capitán* Jesus Hidalgo paid the driver with another twenty-dollar bill, which was the going rate. They staggered towards the beach, satisfied and half-drunk.

"*Capitán!*" One of the men called, pointing out seaward.

"What?" *Capitán* Jesus Hidalgo looked up.

Oh, shit.

The imposing grey and black shape of a Mexican Navy frigate was anchored right next to a group of fishing trawlers. Nothing good ever came out of a

Mexican Navy frigate anchored next to one's ship. Where in the hell had they come from?

Capitán Jesus Hidalgo squinted his eyes in the sunlight, trying to clear his head. Where was the *San Felipe*? Shit. The frigate was at anchor right behind his ship. But there were other trawlers all around, so there really was no reason why he should panic. Or was there?

Then he remembered. The turtle excluders!

Oh, shit. He was dead.

The turtle excluder device, or TED, was the specialized device allowing a captured sea turtle to escape when caught in a fisherman's net. Sea turtles could be caught accidentally when bottom trawling was used by the commercial shrimp fishing industry. In order to catch shrimp, a fine meshed trawl net was needed. This resulted in large amounts of other marine organisms also being caught as bycatch. When a turtle got caught or entangled in a trawl net, it became trapped and unable to return to the surface. Since sea turtles are air-breathing creatures with lungs, they eventually drowned.

Hence the TED.

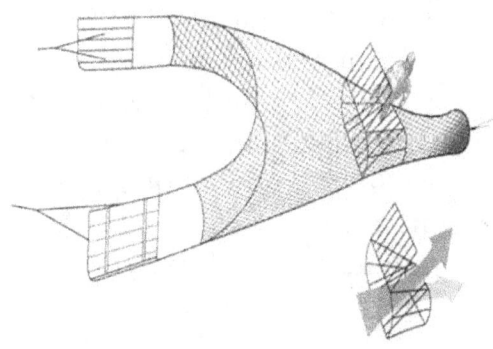

The TED provided a door on the net which allowed the turtle to escape before it was trapped and drowned. This, however, also allowed some of the captured shrimp to escape, which didn't really amount to much, though many captains erroneously believed that the TEDs resulted in a substantial loss of product. Accordingly, they removed the TEDs while they were out fishing.

Turtle Excluders were sewn onto the fishing nets, a time-consuming process that could not be carried out in a hurry. The Mexican Navy patrolling the seas performed random checks on fishing vessels to ensure the TEDs were being used. The penalty for not having the TEDs installed was basically the permanent loss of the boat.

Historically, shrimp fishermen in the Sea of Cortés never used the device, but that all came to an end a few years back when environmentalists in the United States raised a stink about the turtles drowning. Subsequently, the Americans announced that unless all shrimp boats fished with the TEDs, no Mexican shrimp would be imported into the US.

Capitán Jesus Hidalgo was one of those skippers who did not believe in TEDs. He'd had them removed the minute he left port on the first trip of the season.

Of course, the gringo owners of the boat had tried to explain that only a small percentage of the shrimp would be lost through the use of the TEDs, but what the hell did those guys know about fishing? They had not convinced him at all.

If the Navy frigate at anchor next to his ship had already sent a boarding party, they would immediately realize that his nets did not have the TEDs installed. Then he would be in a world of shit.

He began to sober up.

Capitán Jesus Hidalgo and his men reached the *San Felipe*. Soon as he climbed onboard, the skipper felt his stomach doing summersaults. The frigate boarding boat was alongside his ship and several uniformed Navy sailors with rifles stood around on his deck.

Not good.

"*Capitán* Hidalgo?"

"Yes. That's me."

A Mexican Naval officer in a beige uniform approached him. "Are you the captain of this fishing vessel?"

"Yes."

The officer turned to address the sailors under his command. "Arrest this man and take him aboard our ship."

Capitán Jesus Hidalgo took a deep breath. He knew he was no sight to be respected. He hadn't shaved in over a week, or taken a bath, and his breath reeked of tequila and women. Yet, he had to plead with this man. Arrest? No way, this could not be happening. "Why?"

"You know why. You've been fishing without the use of turtle excluder devices, in violation of Navy regulations and Ministry of Fisheries regulations. I am hereby placing you under arrest and your ship is being impounded by the Navy of Mexico."

"Please don't do this. We only did it for one night. One of our nets got caught in a reef and we had to release it and use our backup net. Our backup didn't have the TEDs yet, but we were going to install them today..."

"Yeah, right. Your mother can believe you. Arrest him!"

Two sailors grabbed *Capitán* Jesus Hidalgo by the arms, forcing his hands behind his back. A third sailor approached with a set of plastic handcuffs.

The Naval officer reached in the pockets of *Capitán* Jesus Hidalgo, finding and removing a wad of hundred dollar bills. He glanced at them, putting them in his own pocket. "You're not gonna be needing these."

29

To the Rescue

Christian answered his cellphone. So far it had been a good morning in Phoenix.

"Boss, it's Javier."

"Morning, Javier."

"We have a situation, Boss."

The good morning in Phoenix was probably about to end.

Christian cringed. Nothing good ever came when Javier uttered those words. "What's going on?"

"We lost the *San Felipe*."

"What do you mean we lost it?"

"I mean, we didn't lose it. The Navy has it."

"The Navy has the *San Felipe*? Why?"

Javier hated calling Phoenix with bad news. "From what I've heard, they were fishing without the turtle excluders."

"Who told you this?"

"The Harbormaster here in town."

Christian took a deep breath. His blood pressure shot up. "Who is the captain on that ship?"

"Jesus Hidalgo, Boss."

"And why was that idiot fishing without the excluders?"

"I don't know Boss."

"What did the Harbormaster tell you?"

"Only that the ship has been placed under the authority of the Navy because the captain was fishing without the TEDs."

"Did he tell you where the ship is now?"

"No, Boss. Sorry. I can call him back."

"No, I will call him myself. What I want you to do is notify the *coperativa* that Jesus Hidalgo has been relieved of his command, along with his crew, and that we're going to be needing an entire new crew within the next day or so."

Javier Arenas had heard accounts of the Mexican Navy impounding fishing boats, and they were not pretty stories. Generally, common knowledge was that the ship owner would lose the boat without appeal. So, he was more than a little dubious a new crew would be needed anytime soon. "Yes, Boss. I will do all that."

Christian dialed Brad Murray. He was already wondering how much this was going to cost them. He had no doubt he was going to get the ship back...this was Mexico, after all, and like everything else in that place, it was just a matter of price.

"Hi, Christian!"

Brad's was always a wonderful positive voice.

"Brad, we got a problem."

Thirty minutes later Christian got off the phone with the Harbormaster. The man was an officer of the Mexican Navy and had received several gifts from Christian over the past couple of seasons, ranging from big screen TVs to quad motorcycles. *Quid Pro Quo* being the main religion in that part of the world, the man regularly provided Christian with useful information.

The Harbormaster explained the *San Felipe* was currently steaming south towards the port of La Paz, in Baja California, with a Navy crew in place. Jesus Hidalgo and his crew were in irons in the brig of the frigate, also steaming towards La Paz. The penalty for fishing without TEDs installed was the loss of the ship, its cargo, and all the equipment onboard. The crew of the offending vessel were facing five years in jail, although that usually got reduced to a few weeks, since the jails in La Paz did not have the budget to house and feed nine men for five years.

The top Navy officer in La Paz was a retired Admiral, who word had it, was open to negotiations. The man was retired from the service but still ran the port from his studio at home. It was also rumored that he favored Johnny Walker, preferably Black Label, and that a few cases of that liquor, along with appropriating all of the shrimp onboard a captured trawler, would satisfy his need for justice.

Christian booked two seats on the late afternoon flight out of Phoenix Sky Harbor to La Paz, and he and Brad Murray headed south, intent on recovering their boat.

The following morning, they found themselves waiting for *Almirante* Gutierrez at a small restaurant near the modest hotel where they had spent the night. They would have preferred a four-star hotel, but showing money around those parts was not a good way to start pleading their case.

"How was the guy on the phone?" Brad Murray sipped from a large glass of sweet orange juice.

"Friendly, I guess. How else would he sound, really? The sonofabitch has our radish by the leaves."

"What?"

"An old Central American saying. In other words, he has us where he wants us. He knows he has the top hand here and he's going to attempt extortion at its best."

"In other words, he has us by the ass."

"Quite poetically put, yes. That's exactly how he has us."

The waiter had been around asking for their orders, but they had merely ordered drinks. Expected Latin American protocol and courtesy dictated that they wait to order food until after their guest arrived.

"Explain to me how this works," Murry placed his white linen napkin on his lap. "This guy is retired but yet he runs the port?"

"Yeah, that's what I was able to find out. I called Rodolfo Vega to get some intel, as you know, and he explained that *Almirante* Gutierrez was the commander-in-chief for the Mexican Navy on this side of the world for over twenty years. When he retired the Navy did not replace him; they basically elected to give the old boy retirement pay and keep him in charge until some future time when they found a replacement. It's cheaper keeping him around than nominating a new admiral, I guess."

"What did Rodolfo think about our odds for recovering the *San Felipe*?"

"Oh, Rodolfo was pretty confident about it. He just said it was going to cost us some money. He's always enthusiastic when it's someone else's money."

Brad Murray chuckled. "The man is a pirate."

"Yep, that he is."

The small restaurant they found near the hotel had an open patio surrounded by bougainvillea and Christian noticed the place was getting crowded. He'd spoken with the admiral earlier, and the man had suggested they meet for breakfast. A very clever move, meeting somewhere neutral instead of going to the local harbormaster's offices. And that was certainly a good thing for them. The fewer people involved in this mess, the less money it would cost them. That was a well-known fact around these parts.

The air was already getting hot in the patio.

"That must be him," Brad Murray exclaimed, nodding towards a distinguished-looking older gentleman who had just entered the patio dressed in a white double-breasted tropical suit, linen or lightweight cotton, probably. Oh, and the hat. A white Panama hat with a beige trim. A perfectly-starched white shirt adorned with a white tie completed the image of a well-to-do gentleman living in the tropics. The man had the distinguished look of an old Spaniard *hacienda* owner.

Christian and Brad Murray exchanged glances. Wow. What a character.

They stood, meeting the man, who gave them a big smile from behind a white mustache.

"*Almirante* Gutierrez?"

"Yes, very happy to make your acquaintance, gentlemen," the man offered—in excellent English—extending his hand.

Christian noticed the old timer was wearing a beautiful gold class ring of some sort in his right middle finger.

"Please join us."

"Don't mind if I do," the man pulled a chair, removing his white hat, carefully placing it on the chair next to him.

Old school Spaniard heritage, no doubt.

"Sir, we didn't know what was your preference, so we took the liberty of ordering you a few juices so you'd have one when you arrived." Christian pointed to the four glasses in front of the admiral. Freshly squeezed orange juice, apple juice, guava juice and tomato juice."

The admiral smiled again. He appeared to have jumped out of a travel poster from the 1930s, Christian thought.

"Thank you," the man reached for the tomato juice. "This is very nice. Most considerate of you."

Christian and Brad Murray wore Polo shirts with Dockers, feeling slightly underdressed for the meeting. On second thought, they were not underdressed, the admiral was just big-time eccentric.

The waiter materialized almost immediately, distributing menus to the three men before vaporizing.

"Ah, I've heard this place has excellent breakfast crepes," the admiral announced, scanning his menu.

Christian had no idea what the house specialty was, but he suspected the old coot had been there many times before. He and Brad Murray joined the admiral reading their menus.

The waiter returned, took their orders, and dematerialized again.

"Thank you for meeting with us, *Almirante*," Christian started.

"My pleasure," the old timer responded. "It's always rather pleasant, meeting new people."

I bet it is, Christian thought. Especially when they are bringing you money.

Brad Murray was thrilled at being able to understand the conversation. He studied the old man.

"We're sorry to have caused problems with our fishing boat."

"Gentlemen, gentlemen. Please, let's not talk business before breakfast. There'll be plenty of time for business afterwards."

Christian was instantly annoyed. The old sea-parrot was playing with them. So, the game was, eat first, talk money later. How irritating.

"Tell me, what made the two of you gentlemen partake in the shrimping industry?"

"Same as everybody else: the sweet smell of money and a love of the sea. Oh, yeah, and also a passion for ships."

"That's quite honest," the admiral pointed out.

"Admiral, perhaps you can shed some light on something that still puzzles us."

"Delighted to do so, if I can be of help."

"We are somewhat familiar with the history of the shrimping industry, how it was nationalized by the government. What we still don't understand is why the government of Mexico would hand over an entire industry to the fishermen. Those poor, uneducated men were not prepared to run an industry of that caliber."

The admiral sipped his tomato juice again. "That, my dear sir, has a very plausible explanation. You see, prior to the days of the *coperativas*, the fishing boats were owned and operated by private individuals, who did a good job producing shrimp for Mexico. However, in those days our Minister of Agriculture, Livestock and Fisheries, a very distinguished gentleman, also happened to be the proud owner of fifty shrimp trawlers operating in the Gulf of Mexico."

The admiral took another sip of his tomato juice, dabbing his lips with a white napkin. "This individual, who shall remain unnamed, was running a rather poor shrimping operation with his ships. His fleet of fifty trawlers produced a respectable amount of shrimp, but his ships received no maintenance whatsoever, because that cost money, and the old rascal preferred stuffing his pockets with cash rather than paying for maintenance. Not very uncommon around these parts, as I'm sure you've already observed. Consequently, and as you can imagine, his fleet began deteriorating to the point where it was no longer able to produce what was expected of it. His ships were breaking down all over the place and because of these mechanical problems they were unable to catch much shrimp."

The waiter dropped some hot tortillas wrapped in a cloth napkin in the center of the table and asked the men if they wanted refills on the juices.

The old-timer didn't even look at the waiter, he just waved his hand in a gesture of dismissal.

"As I was saying, this illustrious Minister came up with an absolutely brilliant idea. He decided to nationalize the shrimp fishing industry in Mexico, claiming that the current structure was unjust because the ship owners were taking advantage of the poor fishermen. Those were the days when the Mexican government enjoyed thumbing its nose at Uncle Sam to the north, and anything they could do even remotely resembling leftist tendencies was something they embraced with great enthusiasm."

Christian finished his orange juice then looked at Brad Murray. The big Irishman didn't say anything.

"This particular Minister, however, had his own agenda," the admiral continued. "He didn't give a hoot about the 'poor fishermen,' as he claimed, but was intent on finding some way to get rid of his own decrepit fleet. He therefore announced that all fishing vessels engaged in the capture of shrimp in the entire Republic of Mexico would be taken over by the government and the owners of each trawler would be paid a fair amount of money to compensate them for their loss."

Christian understood. "And I assume the amount of money paid to each ship owner for the loss of their trawlers was a respectable amount."

"But of course. The government had deep coffers."

"Brilliant."

"Absolutely. The Minister then nationalized his own fleet, paying himself a decent amount of money for each of his fifty trawlers. The old rust buckets were not worth a tenth of what he paid himself, but since he paid the same generous amount to all the other owners, nobody objected."

"I see."

"The nationalized fishing fleet was then made available to the *coperativas*, and the government banks provided loans to purchase the ships."

"Now it makes sense," Christian said.

Two waiters brought breakfast, placing dishes with mouth-watering smells in front of the three men.

"But that nationalization of the fishing fleet didn't work out too well in the long run, did it?"

The admiral removed his utensils from a white linen napkin, slowly and methodically using them to cut a small slice of caramel crepe, elegantly placing it in his mouth. He chewed slowly, swallowing before answering. "No, that experiment did not work out too well. As you already know. Those poor fishermen were not equipped to manage an industry of such magnitude. Poor uneducated sailors never had a chance. In fact, I was very surprised they lasted all these years. A little over twenty years. I had thought they would have imploded long before now."

After breakfast, three coffees were ordered. Christian decided it was time to get down to business. "*Almirante*, we are here because we want our ship back."

The old gentleman wiped his lips with his napkin, taking his time before answering. He slowly placed the linen napkin on the side of his plate. "Yes, I realize this."

"So, what are we gonna have to do in order to get our ship back, sir?"

The admiral acquired a look of distant sorrow, slowly shaking his head. "Your captain is guilty of a very serious violation. And by extension, I'm afraid, so are you."

"Yes, we're well aware of that. We have relieved the captain of his command and he's never going to work for us again."

"You understand he was fishing without the turtle excluders. That carries very severe penalties. Our distinguished neighbors of the north have us under constant threat to stop importing our shrimp if we operate without those turtle devices."

Christian was itching to just say to the old salt, 'let's cut through the bullshit and just tell us how much?' but refrained. "Yes, we realize he was doing that. Completely inexcusable."

"Do you instruct your captains to fish without the excluders?"

"Certainly not. We're very conscious of the environment and have always instructed our captains to respect the sea turtles and use the devices at all times."

"In other words, this captain was doing it without your consent?"

No, you old bastard, he was doing it under our direct orders to fish without the turtle excluders, so we could have our ship impounded by you and enjoy breakfast at this table.

"Absolutely. Totally without our consent."

The admiral reached for the glass or orange juice in front of him. "The rules are very clear. The penalty for fishing without the excluders in place is the loss of the ship. Were you aware of this?"

"We know. Yes, we are aware of this."

"However, I have considered the situation here, and it is out of the ordinary. The way I hear it, you gentlemen have invested a considerable amount of money in Mexico, which is a definite benefit for our country and for the town of Rock Port, and I, in particular can appreciate the prosperity you are bringing to the area with your investments."

Christian prepared himself for the closing arguments of the sale.

"And in view of your much-appreciated contribution to the economy of Mexico, I have decided to issue orders for the release of your trawler."

The old sailor took on an air of unmeasured generosity. Caesar, giving the Thumbs Up to the masses, sparing the life of the fallen gladiator.

Christian wondered if he was expected to kiss the man's ring. He waited for the other shoe to drop. How much?

The admiral awaited magnanimously for the gratitude *de rigor*.

"Sir, we don't know how to thank you for your generosity."

The admiral smiled. He liked that.

"And the crew?" Christian asked.

"Ah, yes, the crew. We will release them as well. Those men are facing five years in jail, but I'm going to allow them to head back to their families. In this country, we have a heart."

Christian cracked a smile. Yeah, sure you do. The fact that you don't have the budget to house them and feed them for five years has nothing to do with your decision not to hold them.

"*Almirante*, we are extremely grateful for your decision in this matter. We have a new crew with a captain heading down here by bus to take the *San Felipe* back to the northern waters of the Sea of Cortés. By the way, we'd like to show you our gratitude in the form of a few cases of Johnny Walker, Black Label. We understand you appreciate good Scotch."

The admiral eyebrows raised, as if pleased, yet somewhat surprised that his favorite brand was such common knowledge.

"Would you like us to send these bottles to the Harbormaster's office?"

"No, no. It might be preferable if you could just send them to my residence. I'll give you my address." He paused, reaching inside his jacket for a Mount Blanc pen and a business card. "We don't allow liquor in the office. Regulations, you know?"

"I understand," Christian did his best to keep a straight face. The nerve. No liquor in the office because then he would have to share. Not to mention he was taking a bribe to turn a blind eye to his precious regulations.

"Have your men stop by the office to obtain a release. Your ship is tied up in front of the Harbormaster's office."

"Thank you, *Almirante*. When the crew of our ship are released from prison, we'd like them informed that they're on their own and they should ride a bus back home. Who should we talk to in order to arrange for this?"

"I'll take care of it. Do you wish to leave money to purchase bus fares for the crew?"

"No, thank you. Those boys are on their own. Let them find the money to buy their own fares. After they get home, the *coperativa* will take care of their wages." Yeah, Christian mused, like if he left cash behind it would be used for bus fares. Any cash left behind in the hands of this impeccable gentleman of distinction would rapidly find its way into his own, very deep pockets. "What the members of the crew ultimately get paid for this trip will depend on the catch they had onboard. By the way, do you know if the engine on the *San Felipe* is still running? Or did the Navy run the auxiliary Lister engine?"

"No, nothing's running. Everything's been shut down."

Christian thought of the three tons of shrimp *Capitán* Jesus Hidalgo had reported to him on his last satellite call to Phoenix right before being nailed by the Navy. If these idiots shut down the engines on the *San Felipe*, that could jeopardize the product in the cargo hold. He calculated that the shrimp in the hold could probably last three or four days without the engines supplying refrigeration. So far it had been less than two days since the ship was detained. One day since it had arrived in La Paz, so the catch should still be okay.

"I'm just concerned about the shrimp in the cargo hold."

"Oh, my dear boy, but you need not concern yourself with that at all. That shrimp is no longer on the *San Felipe*."

Christian felt his stomach tighten. Oh, shit. "What do you mean? Where's our shrimp?"

"Unfortunately, your shrimp is no longer your shrimp. It has been impounded by officials of the Mexican government. As I mentioned to you earlier, the penalties for fishing without the turtle excluders are rather Napoleonic. But you are very lucky, because your ship is being returned to you no fault, no blame."

Christian quickly did the math. This early in the season the shrimp were still not fully grown, so one ton could bring in about $15,000. Three tons represented a loss of $45,000. Oh, crap. The ship had been fishing for ten days, so that was another four thousand dollars in diesel lost. This sonofabitch had stolen almost fifty thousand dollars from the company. Just like that. Christian was realistic enough to know that there was no way under God's earth they were going to get that shrimp back. Ever. The old sea-parrot had probably already ordered another dozen white linen suits from his tailor in Hong Kong via the Internet with that money. He probably had to share a little of the cash with the Harbormaster and with the captain on the frigate. Impounded by officials of the Mexican government? *Sure!*

The admiral had his eyes on Christian, obviously waiting to see the reaction of the gringos at the news that they'd just been robbed.

"I see," Christian said, simply. Fighting with this asshole was not a good idea. The gentleman in the white suit had all the advantage, he held all the cards. If Christian offended him, he strongly suspected that the *San Felipe* would be kept by the 'Mexican authorities,' never to be seen again. At least not under that name.

"Here's my address," the admiral extended the piece of paper across the table, still carefully holding his gaze on Christian, waiting for a negative reaction.

"Thanks," Christian accepted the piece of paper, slipping it in his chest pocket. The nerve of the sonofabitch. He steals fifty-thousand dollars and also expects the Scotch delivered to his home.

"*Almirante*, we're in agreement then. We'll send the new captain with his crew to the ship and they'll be able to secure the dispatch release from your Harbormaster?"

"Yes, yes. That is the agreement."

No one mentioned the shrimp.

"Consider yourselves lucky," the old man said. "Just last week, we captured a Japanese fishing boat that had been catching shrimp in our waters. Aah, yes, that was a magnificent operation. And that boat, we did not return."

"A Japanese boat?"

"Yes, a shrimp trawler. A large one.

"How did a Japanese shrimp boat get all the way out here on the other side of the world?" Christian asked.

"Very determined, those sons of the raising sun." The old man sighed. "It was a shrimp trawler. They steamed all the way from Japan, refueling in the high seas from Japanese factory ships at anchor in the Pacific. One of our surveillance aircraft spotted them trying to sneak into the Gulf under the cover of darkness." The old man smiled. "Didn't work. Soon as our patrol aircraft spotted them, we sent the *Adelita* after them."

"What's the *Adelita*?"

"Oh, the *Adelita* is a corvette we keep in La Paz for situations such as these. Our glorious Navy caught up with the Asians, forced them to stop and kept them under guard until the sun came up the next day. Then they boarded the invaders and brought them back to La Paz in irons. The crew were then shipped to Mexico City on Mexicana airlines and delivered to the Japanese embassy."

"What happened to the ship?"

"Oh, the ship is still here. Under guard. They didn't have any product onboard, but they did have thousands of liters of diesel fuel, which our Navy rapidly impounded. Along with all their fishing gear, supplies and electronics. I hear the crew was ultimately flown back to Japan at considerable expense to their embassy, and that their embassy is screaming and demanding the return of their ship, which according to them had been captured in the high seas in an act of total piracy."

Christian almost broke out laughing. The old timer appeared insulted by the insinuation that his Navy could even consider acting with such abuse. "So, are you going to let them have their ship back?"

He old salt smiled. "But of course—eventually. We're not pirates. We'll return their ship. The Japanese are just going to have to compensate us for the considerable expenses we've already incurred."

"What expenses?"

"Oh, the operation did cost us a considerable sum. We had an airplane involved, and the frigate. Very expensive."

"*Almirante*, it's been a pleasure meeting you." Christian stood, extending his hand. Normally he would not terminate the meeting until the old-timer decided it was over, but the circumstances were such that he was pissed. They better cut it short before he considered stabbing the sonofabitch between the eyes with a fork.

Brad Murray also stood. Finally, the Spanish old boy stood as well, realizing that he was being dismissed.

The waiter dropped off the bill, while the admiral reached for his white hat, carefully placing it on his white hair.

"Gentlemen!" He offered, bowing his hat to them.

Christian bowed his head in return, then concentrated on paying the bill with his visa card. By the time he covered the bill, the admiral was gone.

"I will instruct Javier Arenas never to hire *Capitán* Jesus Hidalgo again."

"What are we gonna do about these guys?" Brad Murray asked.

"What guys?"

"*Capitán* Jesus Hidalgo and his crew, the *Orca* gang."

"To hell with them."

"No, I mean, are we going to pay them anything? Are we gonna have to pay them anything for the days they worked?"

"Absolutely not. Remember, we pay these boys a percentage of the catch. In this case, the Mexican government has helped itself to our catch, so we get no revenues from this trip. The crew get a percentage of zero."

"You think the *coperativa* will go for that?"

"The *coperativa* doesn't have a choice. The crew landed zero shrimp. Their pay is zero. If they want a percentage of the catch, they can take it up with the Mexican Navy."

"What next?" Brad Murray asked.

"Let's catch a taxi and head over to the docks. I want to meet the new crew Javier is bringing and make sure the *San Felipe* leaves port without any additional unpleasantness."

"What about the booze for the old gizzard?"

"We'll stop by a liquor store on our way to the airport, get four cases and drop them off at his house."

"We're really going to give him the Johnny Walker?"

"Much as I'd love to stiff the bastard, defaulting on the whisky would be a real dumb move. That old boy has total control of the port here, and even if we managed to sneak out our ship without donating the Johnny Walker, he would make us pay for it tenfold the next time we had a mishap with one of our ships."

"I see. Everyone in this friggin place is a pirate, my friend."

30

Time Is Irrelevant

"Longoria just called me an hour ago," Christian explained. "He said the windshield on the company truck broke when a rock hit it yesterday."

"Gemini!" Brad Murray cried.

"He said he can have it repaired there at a cost of nearly $1,700."

"Jeesus."

"Yeah, that's what I thought too. Instead, I investigated and there are several auto glass shops here in Phoenix who will do it for about three hundred dollars."

"Good job. So, you're gonna have the windshield replaced here?"

"Yes. I gave Longoria explicit instructions to cross the border at six tomorrow morning so he can be here a little after ten. He'll drive the truck and we'll have the windshield replaced here in front of the house. The *San Felipe* is being taken out of the water today for repairs so Longoria has time to drive up here."

"How much is that going to cost us?" Brad Murray inquired.

"A little over $300. Plus, another $70 for gas and lunch for Longoria."

"Still well worth it, I should say."

"Yeah, that's what I thought."

The following morning Christian met the auto glass tech at eleven a.m. in front of his house.

A typical clear skies hot-as-an-oven Arizona day.

"Thanks for showing up," he greeted the tech. "My man should be here shortly with the F-150."

"An F-150, that right?" the man confirmed.

"Yes, an older one."

"No sweat, I'll be here waiting."

By noon the glass installer was getting restless.

"I don't know what the devil happened," Christian explained to the man. "I know my guy should be here by now. I've tried calling him on his cell but he's not responding. How late can you still wait?"

"Another ten minutes, then I have go. I have other jobs waiting."

Christian was concerned and angry. Where the heck was Longoria?

Ten minutes later Christian paid for the windshield and instructed the installer to leave it in the garage. The installer did as asked, then apologized and left.

"Goddammit," he cursed. "Where the hell is Longoria?" He dialed Javier Arenas.

"Morning Boss!"

"Good morning, Javier. Hey, I was expecting Longoria to show up here with our truck over two hours ago, and there's still no sign of the guy. Do you know if he's headed out this way?"

"No, I don't, Boss. I gave him the truck last night when he came by to pick it up, saying that you had asked him to drive up to Phoenix, but I didn't hear anything more."

"Great. Thanks, Javier. Please call me at once if you hear from him."

"Sure thing, Boss."

Christian wondered if the man had been involved in an accident. Maybe he should call the highway patrol.

His cellphone rang.

"Hello?"

"Boss, it's Javier again. I called Longoria's home and his daughter told me that he left at five this morning, and that he was traveling with his wife and his sister-in-law. Longoria left word with his daughter they were driving to Phoenix and that they planned on shopping at the factory outlet shops by Casa Grande."

"Really? Damn. Thanks, Javier, as always, good job!!"

"So, what's up?" Brad Murray was never going to get used to the random behavior of their employees but was learning to expect just about anything.

"Javier said Longoria left this morning but that he brought his wife and sister-in-law with him, and that they were planning on doing some shopping at Casa Grande on their way here."

"Did he say anything to you about this?"

"Certainly not."

'But he knew the windshield installer was going to be here at eleven, awaiting his arrival?"

"Yes. I told him that."

"Jesus Christ, I can't understand these people."

"Don't try it. Basically, they do what they damn well please and damn the consequences."

"I'm beginning to see that. So, he went shopping with the wife. Incredible. And he doesn't feel the need to call us at all."

At four o'clock that afternoon, finally, the navy-blue Ford F-150 parked in front of the house.

Capitán Longoria slowly got out of the driver's side, slowly and methodically opening the passenger's door for his wife and sister-in-law to exit. Then they casually strolled to the front door.

"*Capitán*," Christian greeted them at the door, not inviting them in.

"*Jefe*," the man replied. He was perspiring and appeared somewhat defensive.

"Where were you? We were expecting you hours ago."

"Oh, the women wanted to do some shopping at the factory outlet. They don't get many opportunities do go there." Longoria stared at the ground and his feet, clearly uncomfortable he was being reprimanded in front of his women.

"We had the glass installer here waiting for you for over an hour."

Longoria didn't offer any explanation.

"He couldn't wait for you any longer so he had to leave." Christian was disgusted. This type of behavior was so typical in Mexico, following the predominant belief that it was always better asking for forgiveness rather than asking for permission.

"We're here," Longoria offered, as if that made everything all right.

"Yeah, I see that. The windshield for the truck is in my garage. Follow me and you can get it loaded on the truck so you can head back to Rock Port now. Christian made no effort to invite the man or the women inside the house. Even under normal circumstances it would have been awkward for a man of Longoria's position in life to enter the house of the *Patrón*. And these were not normal circumstances. Christian was upset with the man. No pleasantries were going to be extended in his direction.

The Genie garage door opener lifted the door and Brad Murray helped Longoria load the brand-new windshield into the back of the truck. Several blankets and a long piece of Styrofoam were used to protect the glass during the four-hour drive back to Mexico.

Christian and Murray stood outside, observing the company pickup truck driving away with the new windshield, Longoria and the two women.

"We must be nuts," Brad Murray stated. "How can we put that character in charge of our fleet? Between the cost of the boats, diesel and supplies, we are putting him in charge of nearly one million dollars of our money."

"I've thought of that," Christian reflected. "And yes, we must be insane. The sad part is, I don't think we can do any better than him down there. I have the feeling that no matter who we hire down there in the Sea of Cortés, we're not going to see any better quality than this."

"We're in a business that is based on trust. We need to trust these guys to take our ships out of our sight and produce shrimp for us. How can we possibly trust them when they pull this sort of crap?"

"I know."

31

More Windshield?

Three days later, Christian and Brad Murray arrived back at their office in Rock Port. As was customary, Javier Arenas appeared not two minutes after they entered the office and greeted the secretary.

"Good morning Javier!" Christian had given up trying to find out how the hell Javier knew they were in town. The man was incredible. Either he had lookouts on the outskirts of town armed with cellphones ready to inform of any sightings of the Boss arriving, or he had extra-sensory perception.

Again, Christian and Brad Murray never informed Javier of their intentions to come to town, just in case the information leaked and made them vulnerable to interception out in the desert. Anything was possible in that country.

"Any news from the ships?" Two of the ships were out fishing, two hundred miles to the south, the third one was in town, out of the water at the shipyard, getting its power steering fixed.

"Yes, they checked in with me yesterday, Cruz and Vega are doing well. They reported catching lots of shrimp. The power steering on the *San Felipe* should be fixed later today and then we'll refuel and send them off on their way."

"Longoria got back all right from his trip to Phoenix?"

Javier Arenas looked uncomfortable. "Yes, he did."

"We sent the windshield back with him. Did he get it installed?"

"Yeah," Javier appeared doubtful.

"All right, out with it. What is it?"

"The windshield..."

"What about it?"

"He brought it back."

"Okay? So, did he get it installed?"

"He did, yes, but the mechanic here had some difficulties installing it."

Christian smelled a rat coming. "What sort of difficulties?"

Javier Arenas appeared very uncomfortable. "The new windshield was hard to fit. He put a lot of force on it. He cracked the glass."

"*What?*"

"The molding was too tight, or something like that."

"The installer here cracked the new windshield? You have got to be fucking kidding me!"

"No, I'm not kidding. It was just bad luck."

"Who the hell did Longoria use to install the glass?"

"I'm not sure, some mechanic he knew."

"Some mechanic? Why didn't he use a glass installer?"

"I don't know."

"Do you have the truck here?"

"Yes."

"Outside?"

"Yes."

"Let's go look at it."

The men walked out into the searing heat. The company's blue F-150 was parked in front.

Christian tasted vomit in his mouth when he saw the truck. The windshield was cracked all the way around its edges. Over half the area of the glass was broken and shattered. The shape of the glass was no longer smooth and flat, but wavy.

"What the hell!?"

Javier Arenas looked as if he would like to crawl under a rock and hide.

"The installer did that?"

"Yes, Boss. But he wasn't an installer, he was a mechanic. He couldn't remove the metal frame holding the old glass down, so instead he forced the new windshield in place without removing the frame first."

"What sort of an imbecile did Longoria hire to install that glass? No. Don't tell me. I already know."

They walked back inside where the air conditioning unit had the room at a very comfortable 76 degrees.

Christian went and sat behind his desk, signaling for Javier Arenas to take a seat as well.

"Javier, is there a professional auto glass installer in this town?" He thought of replacing the word 'town' with 'dump,' but thought better of it. Offending his right-hand-man would be counter-productive.

"Yes."

"Good. Then, I want you to go find this glass guy right now and hire him to replace that windshield on the truck. Make sure he does a good job, and for goodness' sake, don't pay him a goddamned cent until you're satisfied that he's done a good job. And by a good job, I mean, no cracks, no chips, no damage to the windshield. Got me?"

"Sure, Boss."

"Go!"

Javier Arenas exited the office at a double pace, happy to be out of there.

"Just another day in paradise," Brad Murray smiled. "Bloody incredible. These folks defy the logic of any sane man."

32

Ali Baba and The Forty Thieves

"Brad, we just got a call from the captain on the *San Felipe*. He told me the generator on the *Orca* failed, which left them without radios."

"What, they're down to battery power only?"

"Yes."

"How can that be? Didn't our electrician check the ships before they went out on the trip?"

"Yeah, in theory at least."

The weather in Phoenix was a searing 115 degrees. Christian had been working on the expense reports for the fishing fleet when the phone rang, with the captain on the *San Felipe* using the satellite phone to call in the news that the generator had failed on the *Orca*.

"We can't allow the *Orca* to remain without radios. That hurricane headed their way in the Pacific

Ocean could become a factor, and without a radio we can't warn the crew to take shelter."

Brad Murray opened a Pacifico beer, relaxing on a rocking chair. "What do we do?"

"I'm going to call Javier Arenas and have him buy a new generator and make arrangements to deliver it to the *Orca*."

"Sounds good. Any idea why the old generator crapped out?"

"No. Not a clue."

Christian reached Javier Arenas in Mexico, issuing him instructions to purchase a new generator and deliver it to the fishing boat four hundred miles south of Rock Port.

"Done," Christian stated. "Javier is going to find the owner of the supply store in Rock Port and buy a generator for us. It's Sunday, but Javier knows where the guy lives, so he's going to go find him at home and ask him to open the store to sell us the generator. That's gonna cost us about six hundred dollars."

"The owner will open the store for us? That's decent."

"Yep. Small town courtesy. Then, Javier is sending a kid on a bus down to the area where the ships are fishing. That bus ride's gonna take a couple of days, I figure. The kid will rent a panga and go out to find the ships and deliver the new generator."

"Holly shit. That's convoluted. A couple of days? Isn't that hurricane headed in their direction?"

"Yeah, but it won't reach the area where the ships are fishing for another four days or so. Well, unless we owned a floatplane, there's no other way to get the generator all the way down there."

"How the hell's the kid going to know where the ships are?"

"I'm not sure. Javier said he'd take care of that. Maybe Javier will talk to one of the captains using the cellphone. Who knows?"

"What's going on with the ships?" Brad Murray sat down in Christian's tiny studio in his home in Phoenix. They had cold shrimp, Swiss cheese and saltine crackers on the desk. Brad didn't eat shrimp but he enjoyed cheese. And beer.

"They've been fishing three nights, as I told you earlier, but now the hurricane's starting to make them really nervous."

"Nervous, why?" Brad Murray helped himself to a recliner. Now that the three shrimp boats were out fishing in the Sea of Cortés, he and Christian didn't have much to do other than follow the ships through the satellite phone and stay in touch with Javier in Mexico by cell phone.

"That hurricane forming southwest of Baja has them worried."

"How far is it?"

"About four more days before it reaches the same latitude where our boys are fishing."

"Four days? So, what are they worried about?"

"Brad, recall what we're dealing with here. Those guys can't read and write, remember?"

"Yeah, I remember. But they trust you, no? Aren't you giving them the daily weather?"

"That I am, but that doesn't mean anything. I can do the math and determine that they can remain on site and keep fishing another day before heading for the safety of the port of Guaymas, but that doesn't mean anything to them."

"Why not?"

"Many of the other ships in the area are already spooked and hightailing it for Guaymas. They're scared to death."

"Of what? Didn't you tell Longoria that the bloody hurricane won't be there for another four days?"

"I did, yes, but they don't buy it. They've been eyeballing the storm for a couple of days, and now that it's been upgraded to a hurricane, they want no part of it. Two years ago, the fishermen in the Sea of Cortés suffered a terrible tragedy when hurricane Ismael was going to bypass Baja and stay in the Pacific Ocean heading northwest, but then at the last minute it hooked inland and headed east, hitting the shrimp fleet dead on. Fifty-seven shrimp boats damaged, twenty sunk, dozens of sailors drowned."

"I understand what happened then, but you're following the progress of the hurricane on the Internet. You know exactly where it is."

"Brad, those guys don't trust anybody about anything. And they sure as hell don't trust me. The Internet's still magic to them. They are illiterate and can't read the weather reports the Mexican Navy puts out, so all they have is information from their families when one of them gets in cellphone range. The families watch TV and become afraid for their loved ones.

Mexican television starts broadcasting that a hurricane is coming and everyone freaks."

"You're telling me the information you're getting online from the weather websites doesn't help?"

Christian pointed to the 27-inch Samsung computer screen. "Look here, this is the hurricane. See the distance between it and our ships? The speed of the cyclone is known. From this screen I can tell you that the hurricane is not going to reach the latitude where our ships are for another ninety hours. And odds are the hurricane won't even enter the Sea of Cortés. It'll probably keep heading northwest bound over the Pacific, but we won't take any chances. Before it reaches our latitude, we will have the ships in port just in case the storm decides to hook, as Ismael did two years ago. I conveyed this to Longoria, but he told me that dozens of shrimp boats have been passing him on their way to the safety of the port and he's feeling very alarmed by this. His crew is freaking out. He wants permission to retreat, as well."

"In other words, he doesn't trust you."

"He *wants* to trust me, but he sees others passing him and prefers to trust his eyes."

"So, we're gonna let them go to port?"

"We don't have a choice. If I tell him to remain on site and continue fishing while all those other boats are zipping by, he'll have a mutiny. Before that happens, he'll head for port with or without our consent. I suggested he take shelter in the port of Yavaros, which is the closest, but he declined because that is a small harbor and it doesn't offer much protection. He prefers to head for the port of Guaymas."

Brad Murray smiled. "Incredible."

"Yep, it is, but we're dealing with a very primitive bunch of people here. It'll take time to educate them and make them trust us. It's not just Longoria. I provide him with a weather update twice a day, which I get from the weather sources online. He shares the information we send him with many of the other shrimp boats within radio range of him, and those other sailors relay the information to everyone they can. Everyone knows the hurricane is four days away, but they couldn't care less. They are ignorant, and when they hear the word 'hurricane' they run, and damned what the gringos have to say about that."

The telephone on Christian's desk rang.

"Christian speaking."

Murray walked out of the small studio to the little bar where the whisky was stored. It was past noon, so it was time for a drink. A beer had to be followed by a shot of Irish whisky. He returned to the studio with a bottle of Tulamore Dew and two Tiffany crystal glasses, placing them on the desk in front of Christian.

"It's Longoria," Christian said, covering the mouthpiece.

Brad Murray nodded, pouring some of the amber liquid for them.

Two minutes later the conversation was over.

"All right. They're going to Guaymas. Longoria got word from his son on the *Orca* that the refrigeration on that ship is not working properly and they have to head to port and unload the shrimp before the catch has a chance to thaw out."

"Oh, crud. Will the shrimp survive the trip?"

"Yes, that won't be an issue. The cargo hold is still cold enough and they won't open the hatch at all until they get to port. But they do have to land the shrimp soon because, with 122 degrees outside air temperature, our product is in danger."

"How much shrimp do they have on board?"

"Longoria said the *Orca* has nearly four tons."

"As of now, then, all three ships are heading for Guaymas?"

"Yes. I gave Longoria orders to steam for port. They were going to be doing it anyway, regardless of our orders, so I guess the *Orca* just gave them the excuse they needed."

"Are we going to have Javier travel down there to unload the shrimp?"

"Yeah, I'll call him. We should head down there as well. I want to know why the refrigeration on the *Orca* is not holding, since I know we paid someone in port to provide that ship's refrigeration system with maintenance before the start of the season. We need to make sure that cargo hold remains cold before we send that ship out fishing again."

"I'll book us on the next flight. When will the ships arrive in port?"

"Longoria said sometime very early tomorrow morning."

"Good. I'll book us on a flight later today. Think that'll work?"

"Yes. I definitely want to be in Guaymas before those boys arrive in port."

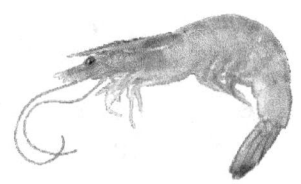

Christian parked the rented Chevy minivan in front of the processing plant. The ninety-minute flight down to Guaymas the previous night was uneventful. Javier Arenas had joined them for dinner in the hotel and had been on the radio with the ships, providing updates as to their location.

All three ships had reached port before dawn and were tied up across from the processing plant. With the arrival of daylight, Javier Arenas instructed the three captains to move their ships and secure them to the docks belonging to the processing plant. The weather was overcast with drizzle and as hot as a baker's oven.

The plant belonged to a Spaniard by the name of Villanueva, who Javier Arenas claimed was a 'real gentleman.' The building was an old warehouse right on the water.

Javier drove up in the company's F-150 blue pickup truck almost simultaneously. They'd agreed to meet at eight am and proceed with the unloading of the shrimp.

"Are they going to be able to process our shrimp here?" Brad Murray asked. So far, they had not unloaded any product anywhere else except at their home port.

"Yeah, according to Javier this should not be an issue. He called Ocean Fruit here in town earlier today and was told they'd be more than happy to buy our shrimp."

"That's good, then."

"Yep. All's we have to do is unload the catch, have Javier supervise the processing at the plant and then we can take the paperwork to Ocean Fruit and get paid."

"That part sounds easy enough. What about the issue with the refrigeration?"

"I asked Javier to find us a refrigeration guy here in town."

Javier walked up in his cowboy hat and boots. "Good morning Boss!"

"Morning, Javier. The ships on their way here?"

"They're already here."

"No shit?" Christian scanned the waterline, but wasn't able to see their ships among the dozen others tied to the docks at the processing plant waterline.

"Yeah, they're down there at the end."

"Great. Did you find a refrigeration man?"

"I did, yes. He's an old-timer who works in town with the local fleet and he's on his way here."

"Good job. Any idea what happened to the refrigeration on the *Orca*? Our guy in Rock Port supposedly checked out the cooling systems on all three ships prior to the start of the season and gave them his blessing."

"No, not a clue. The captain on the *San Felipe* called home last night and relayed to our refrigeration tech in Rock Port that we were having refrigeration problems, and our guy there got on a bus and should be here later this morning."

"What? We don't need two refrigeration guys. And besides, that tech already had his chance to provide us with maintenance and it appears that he blew it. Let the Guaymas guy take a look at the *Orca* and tell us what he finds."

"Yessir. I will do as you say. I'm going to find our captains to arrange for the landing of the shrimp."

Christian and Brad Murray followed Javier down a long walkway to the docks. The processing plant had room in its docks to tie well over two dozen shrimp boats, which was required in order to unload the shrimp.

Processing plants received the frozen shrimp from the boats and placed it on conveyors where the catch was sprayed with water in order to thaw it out and rehydrate it. When shrimp froze it lost some weight. After it was thawed out and rehydrated, it regained the lost weight. Since the shrimp was sold by weight, this was important. Once it was thawed out it continued on conveyors to be sorted by women dressed like nurses in an operating room, with headgear and protective aprons and gloves. These women would then sort out the shrimp by type, such as Brown or Blue, then by quality, looking for possible spots caused by diesel contamination or intestinal juices, and finally by looks. Any shrimp with visible damage such as broken legs would be separated.

Once all the shrimp was classified, then the women separated it and packed it into five-pound Styrofoam boxes, to be frozen again. Blue shrimp was the highest paid. Depending on how many shrimp it took to make a pound, the shrimp were classified by that number, so if it took ten shrimp to make one pound, those would be catalogued as 'tens.' If it took thirty shrimp to make one pound, they would be catalogued as 'thirties.'

The bigger the shrimp, the more money they generated.

If there was spoilage, as evidenced by bad odor or black spots, that shrimp was discarded and considered a loss.

Damaged shrimp was paid considerably less, regardless of what type it was, so broken legs, broken tails and such were not paid top dollar.

Shrimp smaller than thirties was considered 'junk,' and rejected by the plant because those sizes were not considered worthy of export. Ship owners sold this 'junk' shrimp at the docks to local buyers who didn't have a problem with size. Most of that shrimp ended up in restaurants in Mexico as shrimp cocktails. Ocean Fruit exported all the shrimp it purchased from the Mexican fleets.

Processing plants charged boat owners a fee for the processing of the product, and this fee was automatically deducted from the payment Ocean Fruit issued the owner. Once the shrimp was processed, a list of results was printed out in a report, including how much of each species was accepted, what quality and what sizes. The processing plant would issue the report to the ship owner, who would immediately take it to Ocean Fruit for payment.

The prices paid by Ocean Fruit varied daily, based on the world market price for shrimp. Once the processing report was received by Ocean Fruit, a tally was conducted indicating how much would be paid for the product. Ocean Fruit would then cut a cashier's check in U.S. dollars on the spot. The ship owner could then take this check to the local bank and cash it.

The processing plant would then act as escrow agent and hold the shrimp for Ocean Fruit. A rather simple operation but, as Christian and Brad Murray had discovered, there were plenty of sneaky loopholes to benefit the plant owner.

When a load of shrimp arrived at the plant, Javier Arenas had to follow the shrimp all the way through sorting and packing, watching it like a hawk. Otherwise, the people in the plant would quickly replace the largest and finest of the catch with smaller shrimp of cheaper species, thereby reducing the total revenue to the ship owner by a considerable amount. This was an accepted practice in the plants along the Sea of Cortés and if a ship owner let his shrimp out of his sight for any length of time, it could cost him thousands of dollars.

The sorting plants tried their best to separate the shrimp from its owner so they could swap high quality product with low quality product. The standard line was to tell the men bringing the shrimp that the plant was 'terribly busy' and that the recently arrived shrimp could not be processed until the following day.

Sure.

Anyone stupid enough to accept the delaying tactic would lose thousands of dollars due to the clandestine substitution that was certain to occur. Javier Arenas was an expert at arguing with the plant people. Either they processed the shrimp immediately or he would take it back on the ships and go elsewhere. There were *de rigor* shouting matches, with the plant owners routinely alleging to have been deeply offended by the insinuation that anything dishonest was taking place in their plants. They were the most honest people in the Sea of Cortés, they would claim. They went to mass every Sunday. They would never, ever dream of stealing a single solitary shrimp from anybody. Their plants were as transparent as Tiffany crystal.

Ultimately, Javier Arenas would prevail and his product would be processed within an hour or two, under his watchful eye. As a final stratagem, of course, the plant owners would ultimately attempt to bribe Arenas directly with a seductive amount of cash, if he only looked the other way while the plant swapped the product.

Javier loved his job with the gringos, so he would not accept any such offers. He knew that if he ever accepted such a bribe and his Boss found out, he would be fired on the spot and perhaps even thrown in jail. That would not be a good thing.

Christian and Brad Murray observed the unloading operation while standing on the dock. Crate after crate of frozen shrimp along with burlap sacks full of frozen shrimp resembling white-chocolate candies were loaded onto a truck belonging to the processing plant and driven to the receiving bay. Each plastic crate represented roughly seven hundred dollars in revenues to the company.

Later that morning an older Spaniard introduced himself to Christian and Brad as Gustavo, the local refrigeration man. He reminded Christian of Anthony Quinn, the old actor. Christian greeted the man, asking him to go aboard the *Orca* and inform them about the condition of its refrigeration system. The man had an honest face, a rather unusual commodity in that part of the world, Christian mused.

"Boss, that was the last load. It looks like we landed about nine tons of shrimp."

"Great. You're gonna go stay with the shrimp?"

"Yes. Absolutely. On my way now. Let Gustavo work on the *Orca*, I've heard some good references about him."

"Will do. Don't worry about it. You go make sure these good boys don't rob us blind substituting our shrimp with their crap.

The weather was steaming hot and humid.

Ten minutes later Gustavo rejoined them on the dock.

"Your refrigeration system is dry. You leaked all the Freon."

"Oh, crap. That explains it."

"Yes, it does."

"Can you fix it?"

"Yes, but that ship's cooling system is leaking like a sieve, and you're using Freon-502, which is five hundred dollars a can. I can convert the system to Freon-22, which is about twenty bucks a can if you want."

"No shit? Fantastic. How long will it take you and—more important—how much is it going to cost me?"

"It'll take me two or three days. The cost will depend on how much of the system I have to replace. For starters, I need to replace all the valves and the seals. About five hundred dollars, I would say. There are also oil deposits inside the lines. I'll have to burn those off with a torch because those deposits are restricting the flow of Freon."

"Two or three days? Damn! Can't you do it in one? Having this ship parked here is costing me a fortune."

"I can try. But I'll tell ya, if you go out like this all your Freon's gonna leak out and you'll lose your shrimp."

"How long would it take you to convert all three of our ships?"

The old man didn't reply right away. "You want all three done now?"

"Yes, if possible."

"It's a holiday weekend, you know that."

"I'm aware of that, and I want to tell you how grateful we are that you could come down to help us with this, under the circumstances."

Christian shared the news with Brad Murray.

"Bloody hell. Let's get it done, then."

Christian gave Gustavo three hundred dollars in cash to purchase the parts he needed to convert the first ship, then *Capitán* Longoria appeared. Christian informed him of the problem.

"Yeah," Longoria commented, "those slow leaks sometimes happen."

"No," Christian interjected, "Not on our ships, they don't. When we pay for something, we expect to get it. We paid for maintenance and it does not seem that we received it."

Capitán Longoria didn't say anything. The man was perspiring copiously. He had some sort of heart condition and had quickly left his ship the previous night and gone to rent a room in a local hotel where he could sleep in air-conditioning comfort. He claimed he was on some medication called *Metildopa* and, from the looks of him, he appeared to be suffering from high blood pressure.

"I thought we'd paid a technician in Rock Port to provide our refrigeration systems with some maintenance before we left port," Christian said to Longoria. It was a statement, not a question.

"We did, yes. Julio Morales did it for us. He gave all three ships a checkout." The old salt looked uncomfortable.

"What the hell is a checkout?"

"That's when he checks out the refrigeration systems," Longoria offered, giving the impression that he was stating the obvious.

"I seem to remember your guy was very expensive."

Apparently, Longoria didn't know how to respond. The company hired the refrigeration tech in Rock Port at his suggestion, and now he was being put under scrutiny. He did not like the reference to the refrigeration guy being 'his' guy. "Yes, he checked out all the systems, recharged them and gave us a couple of Freon cans to take on each ship."

"He put two cans of Freon on each ship?

"Yes, these systems are old, and they leak, so we carry a little extra with us." Longoria was now on the defensive.

"Wait, he put two cans of Freon-502 on each ship in addition to recharging each system?"

"Yes, we always do it that way."

Christian was not amused. "*Capitán*, those cans of Freon-502 cost five hundred dollars apiece!"

Longoria was at a loss. His previous boss did it that way. Everyone did it that way. Carrying spare Freon was par for the course.

Christian held his temper. The poor bastard was either stupid and didn't know a damned thing about business or he was in cahoots with the refrigeration man to charge the company for Freon that was never delivered. "Ask the men to bring the six Freon-502 bottles here now. We're going to return them. We're going to modify the refrigeration systems on all three ships here in Guaymas today. That man who just left is an expert and he's going to change the systems over to the cheaper Freon-22."

Longoria paled. "We already used the cans," he mumbled.

"What? You already used all six cans of Freon?"

"Yes, we had to keep the cargo holds cold. It's the beginning of the season, we put a lot of shrimp in there."

Christian smelled a rat. He shared the news with Brad Murray.

"You're not serious!" the big Irishman replied.

"Oh, but I think he's dead serious. He used all that Freon just these past few days, he claims."

"That's bullshit!"

"My feelings precisely." Christian asked Longoria to produce the empty Freon containers.

Longoria's facial expression was similar to a kid caught stealing the cookie jar from the kitchen. "We can't produce 'em, we don't have 'em. We threw them overboard after using them," he concluded, visibly satisfied that this could be a reasonable explanation acceptable to the gringos.

"You threw the empty Freon cans in the sea."

"Yes. We did."

"Who is your *motorista*?" Christian asked. The *motorista* was the man in charge of the engine.

"My *motorista* is Eduardo, over there."

"Ask him to come here."

Longoria waved at the man visible on the bridge of the *San Felipe*. The sailor saw the command and walked over.

"*Capitán?*"

Before Longoria could say anything, Christian interjected. "How many bottles of Freon did you add to the refrigeration system over the past few days?"

The man's expression became one of concern. He quickly glanced at his boss, *Capitán* Longoria, as if questioning him or expecting instructions on what to say.

"Two cans," Longoria said before the *motorista* had a chance to open his mouth. "He added two cans of Freon, ain't that right, Eduardo?"

The *motorista* stared at his boss, then at the gringo, before replying. "Yeah, that's right. Two cans, I added two cans to the ship's system."

"And what did you do with the empty cans?" Christian demanded.

The *motorista* glanced at his boss again.

"Don't look at him! Look at me. What did you do with the empty cans?"

"I don't know. I don't remember." The man was obviously uncomfortable as all hell.

"Did you throw them overboard?"

"I don't remember. Maybe. Yes! I threw them overboard."

Christian turned to *Capitán* Longoria. "And I assume the other two *motoristas* also pitched their empty cans overboard?"

Longoria was perspiring more than before. "Ah, yes. They probably did, as well."

"How much was our bill with your refrigeration man in Rock Port?"

"Our bill?"

"Yes, how much did he charge us for the maintenance he didn't do and for the bottles of Freon he claims he gave you?"

"I don't remember exactly."

"You don't need to remember exactly. Just ballpark. How much did he charge us?"

"I'm not sure...about four thousand dollars, I believe."

"Four thousand dollars. That's three thousand just for the Freon he gave you to carry on the ships. So, I guess the other thousand bucks covered his labor and the additional refrigerant he used on all three ships to get them ready for the first trip of the season?"

"Yeah, I'm guessing that must be right."

"How much Freon can we put in one of these ships?"

"What do you mean?"

"How much Freon fits into one of these refrigeration systems?"

"I don't know, I'm not sure."

"Eduardo?" Christian turned to the *motorista*. You must know this. How many of those cans can the refrigeration system on the *San Felipe* hold?"

The man looked at the ground, then at his boss, then replied. "I think the system can hold three of these cans."

Christian stared at Longoria. "So, lesee if I got this right. Our three ships sat for five months during the off-season without being serviced, so it seems to me that all the Freon must've leaked out of their systems during that time, no? I mean, if the refrigerant leaked out two cans' worth just the past few days, sitting there idle in the water five months must surely have emptied all three systems."

Longoria suspected he'd been caught red handed, that much was obvious from his face.

"Hence, if your refrigeration man in Rock Port serviced our ships prior to this first trip of the season, he must've surely had to add Freon to each ship. We're talking nine additional cans of Freon 502 here. That's four-thousand five hundred dollars on top of his labor. But he's only charging us one thousand for everything."

Longoria tried to find his tongue. "Ah, he must've had some leftover Freon that he used."

"Leftover Freon? What do you mean?"

"Our refrig guy in Rock Port must've had some spare Freon in his shop. You know, surplus from other jobs. I'm sure that's what he used to fill our three ships."

"You mean he generously gifted us with some of his own five-hundred-dollars-a-can refrigerant? *And* didn't charge us for it?"

"Yes, he's a good guy. That's it, he gave us some of his Freon."

"And how did we pay this guy? Did you give him a check?"

"No, he hasn't been paid yet, he just submitted his invoice to the company a couple of days ago."

"All right. Good! And we're not paying him one god damned cent, either. If he wants to see any money, he's going to have to produce receipts for the purchase of the Freon he claims he gave to you. And we intend to conduct an investigation with whoever supplied him the Freon all the way back to the factory. We will match batch numbers and confirm beyond any suspicion that he actually bought that Freon from somebody legit."

Longoria was visibly nervous. "If he used some of his own stock, he won't be able to produce a receipt."

"That will be a problem for him, then. According to the refrigeration man who just left here, the air conditioning system on your ship has not been serviced for *years*. How do you explain that?"

Longoria was like a five-year-old caught stealing, being questioned by the teacher. "I don't know. Julio said he serviced it."

"Did you see your guy servicing the *San Felipe* or any of the other ships?"

"No."

"Sounds to me like we're dealing with a crook here. Don't you think so?"

Longoria was not sure whether he was going to be accused of being co-participant in a scam. He appeared visibly relieved that the boss was asking his opinion. "Yes, it would seem so, perhaps."

"Okay. We'll deal with this. Your ship will be the first to be converted to Freon-22. You should be able to set sail sometime tomorrow. In the meantime, let Javier know if you need any supplies."

Christian and Brad Murray entered the processing plant, finding Javier Arenas dressed up in scrubs with head cover and shoe covers. He looked like a doctor in an operating room. He was monitoring the processing of the shrimp recently unloaded from the ships, a wooden clipboard in hand.

"How's it going here?" Christian probed.

Javier smiled big. "Very good, Boss!" The boys brought some good stuff! Lots of Blue and very good quality."

"Happy to hear that. I see they started processing our shrimp right away. We're going back to the hotel for some breakfast. Meet us there after you're done here. We need to bring you up to speed on the repairs that I just contracted."

"Yes, Boss!"

The men left the plant, returning to the hotel for some Mexican breakfast.

"So, what do you think happened with the Freon scam?"

"I'm not sure," Christian replied. He and Brad had just finished another delicious tropical breakfast, complete with scrambled eggs generously covered with red salsa, avocados, bacon, toast and freshly squeezed sweet orange juice. Hot coffee and sweet bread had finished the banquet.

"Looks to me like these guys have a system going back from the days of the *coperativas*, and they haven't changed their ways at all. It appears that the refrigeration man Longoria hired in Rock Port didn't even bother checking our ships. I suspect he and Longoria are probably old buddies, and the extent of the maintenance this guy performed was maybe providing Longoria with some cans of refrigerant to take along in case the system didn't cool the cargo hold. And even *that* sounds highly unlikely. Think of it, where the hell is a piss-poor mechanic in Rock Port going to find six cans of super expensive Freon-502 without paying for them up front? No way. And nobody in Mexico is going to give these guys credit."

"Yes, I agree," Brad Murray expressed. "Seems like they just claimed they provided us with the Freon, at a cost of three thousand dollars, and eventually the refrigeration man and Longoria would have split the three thousand."

"That sounds more like it." Christian was amazed at the level of dishonesty. It seemed they couldn't take one step without someone trying to take a bite out of their asses.

"Jeesus Christ, these guys are all thieves and pirates. So, what's the plan?"

"Hurricane Linda is a real bitch. She's still heading in this direction, and since we don't know if she's going to enter the Sea of Cortés and hit us, we have to keep the ships in port, anyway, and that old gentleman we met, Gustavo, will be modifying the refrigeration systems on all three ships so that we can use the cheap Freon from now on."

"That's a good plan. Expensive?" Brad Murray finished off some of the sweet bread still visible in the basket.

"Not too bad. And the savings are going to be substantial. Think of it: if we leak a single can of Freon-502 into the atmosphere, we just pissed off five hundred bucks. This other type of Freon we're going to be using is a hell of a lot cheaper. About a tenth as much, from what I hear."

"How could these idiots operate all these years with the expensive stuff while leaking it all over the Sea of Cortés?"

"They're not businessmen." Christian reiterated. "Longoria wants to go fishing to the north of here now. He said he's nervous about rumors of pirates operating just south of here. Apparently, there was a shrimp boat, the *Concepción,* attacked by pirates a couple of days ago, not too far south of here. Longoria said the pirates took the shrimp and locked the crew in the engine room."

"Locked them in the engine room? How did they get out?"

Christian waved at the waiter signaling for the check. "They almost didn't."

"What? How so?"

"The crew was going to die. They were going to suffocate in the engine room. Men don't last too long locked up in the engine room in these temperatures. Seems one of its crew rigged some cellphone antenna and was able to call and ask for help."

"You're joking."

"No, according to Longoria, the Harbormaster's fast boat found the *Concepción* after receiving a call from one of the crew."

"Holly crap! How come that didn't make the papers?" Brad Murray was flabbergasted.

"Oh, I'm sure it made the papers around here."

"I didn't read anything about this back home."

"In Arizona? Naw, I don't think that would make the front page of the Arizona Republic. Remember, Arizona and the state of Sonora are not only neighbors, they're business partners. Lots of tourism flowing south looking for beaches, sun and margaritas. It wouldn't do to scare the dollar-bearing gringos with tales of pirates killing innocent sailors."

"This is terrible. What kind of people are these?"

"Brad, we may be just a few hours driving south of the Paradise Valley Mall in Scottsdale, and civilization as we know it, but we really are in a different dimension here. This is another world altogether. Most people back home have absolutely no friggin idea what the hell goes on down here. No, this is not Idaho or Montana. Folks here are not going to give you a hand if they find you stranded on some remote back road. If they *do* find you stranded on some remote back road, you'll probably get your throat cut and your car stolen. Oh yeah, along with your clothes, your watch, and your wallet. And the sandwiches you had brought along for the drive. And far as I'm concerned, this entire country is to be considered a remote back road. When the State Department advises tourists not to drive anywhere in Mexico at night, they're dead serious."

Javier Arenas appeared from the lobby, walking briskly accompanied by another man in his mid-fifties. Arenas had on his ever-present white straw cowboy hat. He handed some papers to Christian.

"The report, Boss!" His infectious smile and his unusual green eyes lit up with the news of a good unloading report.

Christian received the stack of forms, going directly to the summary section for each ship. Together they had landed a little over ten tons of export-quality shrimp.

Sweet.

The total sale to Ocean Fruit amounted to $161,343 and forty-two cents. Not bad for the first few days of the season. The estimated total production for the fleet this season had been calculated at forty-eight tons. The cost to operate the three ships during the months of September through early December had been estimated at thirty tons of shrimp. Considering the estimate for production, the fleet should produce earnings by early December in the neighborhood of eighteen tons. That should translate into roughly

$324,000 in earnings between the three ships, or about $108,000 per trawler.

That, of course, if they didn't rob them blind first.

The following morning Javier Arenas met them at the hotel as they were having breakfast to inform them that the refrigeration man had finished converting two of the ships to the cheaper Freon refrigerant and that only one ship was left to convert. He also informed Christian and Brad Murray that the generator on the *Orca* had been fried and was going to need replacing.

"What?" Christian had just finished another delicious Mexican breakfast, hoping for a day of relative peace. Apparently, no such thing was possible in the shrimping business in the Sea of Cortés.

Javier Arenas sheepishly sat on a chair, removing his white cowboy hat. "The ship needed some welding. The metal floor in the bathroom wore through."

"What the devil are you talking about?" Christian was getting very annoyed.

"The lav. The bathroom on the ship. The plumbing is just a straight tube connecting the toilet to the outside. The men use a bucket to retrieve sea water and flush the toilet after each use. The sea water rusted the metal floor of the bathroom. It rusted completely and broke through so we had to replace the floor with another piece of metal plate. It had to be welded in place."

"And what exactly, does any of this have to do with the generator?"

Javier Arenas hated giving bad news to his boss. "The welder who fixed the floor had to use electric welding equipment."

"So?"

"He sorta forgot to disconnect the ship's generator before he did the welding. He shorted the generator."

"Oh, crap. You have gotta be kidding."

"No. He fried it."

"Are these people just plain stupid? The guy's a welder?"

"Yes. He's a welder."

"And he doesn't know enough to protect the generator?"

"He says he forgot."

"Did we already pay him?"

"No."

"Good! Don't pay him for his work. I'll talk to him. The sonofabitch is going to cost us another generator. That's over six hundred dollars. More than his welding is worth. The *Orca*, you say. Didn't we put a brand-new generator in her just a few days ago?"

"Yes, that's the generator we sent down with a kid, remember? He had to take a bus and then hire a panga."

"How could I forget? Yes, of course I remember. Can you find us another generator out here?"

"Yes. There's a big equipment supplier here in port."

"All right then. Buy another generator and have it installed. Make sure that welder is nowhere near our ship when you do that. I sure as all hell don't want him to fry another one of our generators."

"All right."

"And Javier?"

"Yes, Boss?"

"Bring me back the generator that fried on the *Orca*, will you? I want to see if it can be rebuilt."

Later that morning Javier returned. They met in Christian's hotel room, which had a table and chairs. Javier was carrying a cardboard box with parts in it.

"I bought a new generator at the supply store, here's the receipt. Also, I hired an electrician to install it on the *Orca* and she's now good to go."

"The refrigeration has been converted to the other freon?"

"Yes. Everything's done and she's ready to sail."

"That sounds like a winner. Finally." Christian reached into the cardboard box. A generator and some cables and loose bolts filled the box. "What's this?"

Javier still had his cowboy hat on. "That's the generator from the *Orca*."

"Is this the one that fried?"

"Yes. The *motorista* on the *Orca* gave it to me."

Christian reached inside the box, removing an old, dirty generator. "This generator is a relic. This is not the new generator we sent down to be installed on the *Orca*."

Javier Arenas seemed at a loss for words. "That's the one that was installed."

"Javier, look at this piece of crap. This isn't the new generator we sent down last week. What the hell's the matter with you?"

"Yeah, that's obviously not the new one."

"But this is what they gave you telling you it came from the *Orca*?"

"Yes, I was there when the electrician removed it and then the *motorista* handed it to me."

Christian was furious again. This business was not doing his blood pressure much good. "Someone's playing games with us. Javier. This is not the generator we paid six hundred dollars for in Rock Port."

"Umm, yeah, I can see that."

"We need to find out what the hell's going on. Is the *Orca* still in port?"

"Yes. But I gave its captain the go-ahead to sail about thirty minutes ago. They might be under way now."

Christian took a deep breath. "Okay, next time the ships hit port to unload I want you to fire the *motorista* on that ship. And then have the captain talk to me. Someone is playing games with us and I'm not gonna let them get away with this. I need to know who installed the new generator on the *Orca* when your boy took it down. From the looks of this, I would say someone on the crew lied to us about needing a new generator so they could get their hands on a brand-new one. Then, they probably sold our new generator to someone else, walking away with some good cash."

"Boss?"

"What?"

"We really should pay the welder."

"You mean the idiot who just fried our generator?"

"Yes. Not paying him is not a good idea. He's a local, and we're bound to run into problems if we don't pay him."

"You're serious?"

"Yea. I know he shorted the generator, but even so we should still pay him. These guys are all related and who knows what they could do to our ships if we screw the welder. It's not that much money."

"How much?"

"About fifty dollars."

Christian sighed. This was the never-ending story of *Ali Baba and the Forty Thieves*. "All right. Pay him." It seemed that this here fishing business was like being caught in an ant hill. You're gonna get bitten no matter what.

"You get the impression these people will steal anything that isn't attached to the ships?" Brad Murray asked.

"Yeah, and also many things that are attached to the ships. Remember the very expensive all-weather jackets we bought so the men working down in the cargo hold at thirty below zero would not freeze their asses off?"

Brad Murray nodded. "How much did those cost us? Like four hundred bucks apiece?"

"Yep, and we bought two per ship, remember?"

"I remember. And they ripped them off at the beginning of our first season. Same thing happened to the tool boxes we bought for the engine rooms. Three of those at twelve hundred dollars each. Gone, disappeared the first season."

"How about the crew we fired for stealing shrimp and they walked away with the porcelain toilet bowl from the *San Felipe*?"

Brad Murray laughed. "Absolutely amazing! Who would think there's a marked out here for stolen pre-owned toilets?"

"We didn't replace the stolen winter jackets. Let them freeze their asses off."

"Agreed," Brad Murray voiced.

"And what about the curtains Elaine sewed for each ship? She took days making those so the galley in each ship would look nice."

"They took those as well."

"It makes you wonder what the hell they could do with those curtains."

"Remember the hundreds of bucks Elaine spent buying dishes and cups and silverware and pots and pans for each ship?"

"Oh, yeah. All gone by now, I'm sure."

"Yep, they are, Javier confirmed it. The crews exchanged their old junk from home with our new stuff."

"Hey Christian?"

"What?"

"What the hell are we doing in this business?"

"We're just plain crazy."

33

Midnight Theft

Christian and Brad Murray sipped on ice-cold Guinness beers, sitting in the small studio in Phoenix. It was after midnight.

"Aah," Brad Murray smiled, foam sticking to his lips. "This is true Irish milk."

"I don't know what Irish milk tastes like, but this beer is delicious."

"This beer is thick. Kinda like drinking a loaf of bread."

Christian laughed.

"In Ireland doctors tell pregnant women to drink one of these a day."

"So, is that why you Irish are all alcoholics?"

"We're not alcoholics, we're *connoisseurs*. We appreciate the good things in life."

The phone rang.

"Hello?"

"Sorry to be calling this late at night," the man began. It was Balboa, the owner of a marine supplies store in Rock Port, one of the stores where they purchased most of their fishing gear.

"Are you aware that one of your ships, the *Orca*, is unloading shrimp at the docks?"

Christian stood. "What? Unloading shrimp? Where? Are you sure of this? Our ships are all fishing six hundred miles south of Rock Port, how can that be?"

"Well, this one is not fishing, it's in port, and they are unloading shrimp as we speak."

Balboa had no reason to lie about something like this. The only advantage for him calling was establishing some loyalty with Christian, possibly in hopes of selling him more supplies.

Christian had spoken with *Capitán* Longoria earlier that day on the satellite phone. Longoria had reported their position as being six hundred miles south of Rock Port in the Sea of Cortés. The man had positively stated that all three ships were fishing within sight of each other.

And now this.

"Thank you very much, *señor* Balboa. I really appreciate the call. I will be there in the morning to take care of this."

"You're welcome. Very glad to be of help. Anything I can do. Good night."

"What's going on?" Brad Murray still had beer foam framing his mouth.

"The sonsobitches!"

"I'll take that as it's not good news?"

"No, it's not good news. Balboa just told me the *Orca* is in port, unloading shrimp!"

"You mean in Rock Port?"

"Yes. In Rock Port. Unloading our shrimp in the dark."

"Bastards! But weren't they supposed to be fishing way south of there?"

"Yes, that was the report I got from *Capitán* Longoria earlier this afternoon when I got a hold of him on the sat radio."

"And he didn't say anything about the *Orca* returning to port?"

"No. of course he didn't. Even if that had been the case, that they needed to return to Rock Port for some reason, it would've taken that ship sixty hours to make port."

"Lying bastard." Brad Murray wiped his mouth with a white paper napkin. "So, he told you all three ships were fishing together six hundred miles south of Rock Port, and now it turns out one of the three is in port, stealing our shrimp under the cover of darkness."

"Yes, that's exactly how it sounds."

"So, what do we do?"

The tan Bronco II parked in front of the *Comandancia de Puerto*, the Harbormaster, in Rock Port. It was eight o'clock in the morning the next day.

"Think this guy's in yet?" Brad Murray asked. The four AM departure from Phoenix had been brutal. Not enough sleep.

Christian locked the Bronco. "Don't know, but we're gonna find out."

They entered the small stand-alone one-level concrete building the Mexican Navy called the *Comandancia*. The building sat in front of the small harbor. There was a man behind the counter, dressed in a uniform.

"*Buenos dias*," the man greeted, studying the two gringos.

"We're here to see the *Comandante*," Christian informed the man.

"*Comandante* Apellanis is not here yet," the man explained. "He arrives around nine or so."

"Figures," Christian translated for Brad Murray. "Thank you. We'll return after nine then."

They left the Harbormaster's office and drove to their office by the docks.

Javier Arenas was already there.

"Morning Javier."

"Good morning Boss." Javier smiled and waved at Brad Murray, but didn't say anything to the big Irishman. The men working for the company knew that Mr. Murray did not speak or understand Spanish, so they seldom addressed him directly, although he was generally very well liked. The big man had good Karma.

"Did you go to the *Comandancia*?" Arenas had very light eyes. Sometimes they appeared to be blue, other times they seemed green.

"Yes, but Apellanis is not there yet. Were you able to line up a new crew for the *Orca*?"

"Yes, Boss. I spoke with the *coperativa* very early this morning and they have a crew for us. I found a new captain for the *Orca*, his name is Francisco Bolaños."

"Excellent. Do you have any references on this guy Bolaños?"

"Aah, yes. He's the brother-in-law of Father Mario, one of our local priests."

As if that was going to be any sort of guarantee, Christian reflected. "Have him come here to talk to us before you hire him."

"Yessir."

"Don't allow the new crew anywhere near the docks until we've dealt with the crew that's still on the *Orca*. Were you able to confirm that the ship is here?"

"Yes, Boss, she's here. And my sister has a friend from school who now works at the processing plant by the highway. She confirmed that the *Orca* unloaded shrimp last night. The shrimp crates are sitting at the plant, waiting to be processed later this morning. My sister's friend already marked the crates so we'll know which ones are ours, and she's going to delay the processing of that shrimp until we give her the go-ahead."

"Good job. How much shrimp was unloaded?"

"A little over one ton."

One ton. Probably Blue shrimp. A little over fifteen thousand dollars' worth. The very opportune call from the Balboa dude had saved them quite a bit of money. "All right, we're gonna go talk to the Harbormaster and get some soldiers. Then we're going on the *Orca* and we're getting every one of those thieves off the ship in irons. We're going to put those guys in jail and we're gonna press charges."

Javier Arenas appeared concerned.

"You don't agree?"

"Yes, I mean. I agree. It's just that nobody has done that here before."

"Nobody has put thieves in jail before?"

"Not really. They normally just get fired and that's all."

"Well, we're not going to just fire them. We trusted them and they tried to screw us. We're putting them in jail."

"It's just that they all have families and friends here." Javier Arenas appeared unsettled.

"And what does that have to do with anything?"

"Nothing, it's just that people are going to get mad."

"People? What people? The relatives of the crew? Those men are thieves, they have no business taking our shrimp. If the relatives get mad, so be it. They brought it upon themselves." Christian thought about it more. "What do you think? The buddies of the crew could become a threat to us?"

"No, not a threat. But you know, everyone's related in this town. If you put nine guys in jail, that's going to affect a lot of people."

"How?"

"Well, they all have relatives and friends. All those people will look at us as their enemies."

"I don't care. This mentality is insane. They keep doing this sort of crap because there are never any consequences. That is not gonna be the case with this company. These guys will learn not to steal from us."

An hour later they sat in front of *Comandante* Apellanis, the local *de jour* Harbormaster appointed by the Mexican Navy. The man was in his mid-thirties, dressed in starched whites, trim and fit. "So, you have no doubt these men were stealing from you?"

"None whatsoever. What would you think? They report their position six hundred miles south of here, and then they get caught unloading our shrimp in the middle of the night."

"But you haven't talked to them directly?"

"No. As I told you, there's nothing to talk about. They were supposed to be six hundred miles south of here, and instead they were caught unloading our product last night after midnight. We have information that the shrimp unloaded from our boat is sitting at the plant by the highway, awaiting processing. We have taken steps to secure our product at the plant. These thieves will not benefit from their behavior. We have lined up a new crew that will take our boat back out to sea. We need to get the old crew off the boat and I want to press charges for theft."

"This is very serious," the Navy officer had a serious look of concern. He was obviously not amused at a couple of gringos about to raise all sorts of hell in his little village.

"Yeah, you bet it's very serious. Those good old boys were planning on getting away with a little over fifteen thousand dollars of our product, not to say anything of the diesel they wasted steaming back here sixty hours. I intend to file charges against the captain and his crew as soon as you and I finish our little conversation. Soon as we file the charges, the police *Comandante* is going to issue arrest warrants for the crew. However, I don't want our ship damaged if the crew hears of our plans, so I'm asking you to please send some of your soldiers to remove the crew from the ship before we proceed."

"You want me to send some of my Marines to your ship to remove the crew?"

"Yes, remove the crew and guard the ship so we don't allow any of those rascals to inflict damage on the ship."

The Harbormaster appeared uncertain. Christian wondered if the man was going to act as requested. By sending Marines to remove the crew from the *Orca* at the request of the gringos, the Harbormaster would be exposing himself to the wrath of the locals.

"It's fine. I will send four Marines with you. But they will not arrest the crew, they will simply protect you and the ship when you ask them to get off the ship. If the police *Comandante* later wants our assistance to arrest those men, then we will provide it. But we cannot do that until formal charges have been filed. We are not the police."

Christian stood, extending his hand to the man. "Thank you, *Comandante*. We're very grateful for your help. If it's acceptable, we'd like to head out to the docks immediately to secure our ship with the help of your Marines."

"That's acceptable." The Harbormaster issued instructions to his assistant, and four Mexican Marines appeared from the side of the building, dressed in blue naval uniforms, wearing white helmets and carrying automatic weapons.

Christian and Brad Murray left the *Comandancia*, driving to the docks. Parking in front of the ships they walked up to the *Orca*. She was tied against the concrete docks. The air smelled of salt and dozens of sea gulls and dumb ducks crisscrossed over the ship, screeching for attention.

A crew member saw them approaching from his position inside the bridge. The look of surprise in his face was quite evident. Four Mexican Marines accompanied the owners of the ship.

The sailor disappeared from view, going down to the crew quarters to fetch his captain.

Capitán Longoria appeared through the side door of the *Orca*. He was obviously taken by surprise, and his eyes showed it. He was dressed in a simple pair of cotton pants and was shirtless. He'd been caught with his hand in the cookie jar. A one-thousand-pound cookie jar full of shrimp.

He made a brief attempt at a feeblish smile.

Christian spoke out loud, with the required authority needed when a man speaks in Mexico. "*Capitán* Longoria, I want you and your entire crew off this ship immediately. You are not allowed to carry anything with you and you have exactly five minutes to clear off or these Naval Marines will see to it that all of you go straight to jail."

The old sailor, realizing that he'd been made, nodded, looking down away from his boss. He slowly re-entered the ship.

Christian and Brad Murray exchanged glances. Better to wait on the dock. Never knew when one of the sailors might just get a wild hair up his ass and stick them both with a knife.

"Didn't defend himself, did he?" Brad Murray was disgusted.

"No, how could he? He lied to me on the satellite phone, and now he has our shrimp waiting to be processed at the plant, without any authorization from us to do so. I'm going to wait until the crew is off the ship and we'll leave two of these Marines here to prevent anyone from reboarding. Javier is already working on getting us a new crew lined up with the *coperativa*, and soon as the new captain talks to us, we'll give him control of the *Orca* and release the Marines."

"What about the old crew?"

"Javier is at the police station at this very moment with our company attorney, filing charges against these thieves. These sorts of charges are very serious in this country. The police are going to have to arrest each and every one of these bastards. I gave Javier instructions to arrange for the charges to become effective late tomorrow night."

"Tomorrow night? Why then?"

"Tell you in a minute."

"What's going to happen to the old crew?"

"Not sure. Whatever the law offers is what we're gonna do. These people don't respect anything, they're so used to abusing everything without consequences. But this time I'm not gonna let them go."

"Blows my mind," Brad Murray pointed out, "we pay them more than anybody else in the Sea of Cortés and this is the kinda loyalty we get. Stealing our shrimp right in front of us."

"Yea. They definitely think we're stupid."

The fishermen began to disembark, one by one, carrying their simple belongings in old stained school backpacks. In passing, each sailor looked at the gringos standing alongside their ship, not with hostility, but with mild curiosity.

Capitán Longoria was the last one to leave the ship. He didn't stop to offer any sort of explanation, just walked away without looking back.

"We have another problem, "Christian said.

"What's that?"

"Our other two ships. One of their captains is Longoria's brother, the other captain is Longoria's son."

"Oh, shit. I'd forgotten about that. Now what?"

"Well, word's gonna reach them about this situation. Our other two ships will hear about this in a day or two, and then we could have problems. Those boys could sell our shrimp and pocket the money or damage the engines, or sabotage the refrigeration systems. Who knows? They're capable of just about any kind of chicanery I can think of. I directed Javier to call the captains on our other two ships and order them to head for the port of Guaymas immediately. They will be told that we need cash and that we want to unload our product at once. They might suspect that we're proceeding in this manner because we caught Longoria stealing from us, but they won't take any direct action against us as long as we don't involve the police just yet."

"You're saying we're going to unload in Guaymas?"

"Yes. And then I'm going to fire those two crews and Javier will replace them with two fresh ones. There's no way in hell we can keep operating with those two captains after we put Longoria in jail. We will commission the new crews to guard the ships while they're in port so the thieves can't inflict any damage."

"Damn. Nothing's ever easy here, is it?"

"No. When you're dealing with pirates you have to keep an open mind and expect just about anything."

"So, after we remove the other two crews, then we will proceed with the charges against the thieving mackerels?"

"Precisely."

"Sounds like a plan."

"I also had Javier suspend cellphone service to the company telephones the captains are using, so they won't call their wives ahead and hear about the situation here in Rock Port just yet."

"It's like we're at war with these guys," Brad Murray exclaimed.

"That's exactly what we have here. These guys are at war with us. Think Tortuga Island in the Caribbean. Populated by pirates, buccaneers and privateers. That's what we're dealing with in this business."

The *San Felipe* dropped anchor two hundred yards from the beach in front of Kino Bay.

"Esteban!" *Capitán* Elizondo barked, "I'm gonna sleep for a few hours. You're in charge while I'm resting."

Esteban, the first mate, a skinny local with long black hair and shifty eyes acknowledged the voice of the Master. "For sure, *Capitán*. Are we allowing the men to have entertainment?"

Capitán Elizondo briefly pondered the request. The men had been looking forward to some women and tequila after working four nights. It wouldn't hurt any letting them have some fun. Delaying their much-anticipated entertainment could cause malcontent. "Sure. Let them have some fun."

The first mate stared at his captain, not saying anything.

"Oh, yeah. Right. Have them pull two crates from the hold. Two crates, that's all."

"Sure thing, *Capitán*."

The two plastic crates containing top-quality Blue shrimp of assorted sizes represented roughly fourteen-hundred dollars of revenue for the company. The men would use the shrimp as payment for four bottles of cheap *Alacrán* tequila and the services of a couple of prostitutes.

The *San Felipe* had accumulated nearly three tons of shrimp in its hold over the past four days, roughly $45,000 worth of revenue, so 'shrinking' the catch by a couple of crates was no big deal in anybody's view. No one in the crew was going to lose any sleep over it.

Capitán Elizondo retired into his minuscule cabin to catch some well-deserved sleep. The weather had cooled off significantly towards the end of November and most of the unshaven members of the crew reeked from lack of baths and were sick from bronchitis.

The first mate retrieved his own personal cellphone from a pocket and pushed a quick dial number.

"Yes?" the voice at the other end was deep and masculine.

"Mama Rumba's?" the first mate inquired.

"Yea. How can I help you?"

"This is Esteban, the first mate on the *San Felipe*."

The deep masculine voice couldn't care less. "So? What do you want?"

The skinny first mate with shifty eyes took a deep breath. "Ah, we're out here at anchor. Can you send us a panga with four bottles of tequila and a couple of broads?"

"But of course. The *San Felipe* you say?" The voice softened in anticipation of some business.

"That is correct."

"And what color's your ship?"

"What?"

"What color is your ship? The panga driver needs to know in order to find you."

"Blue. White and blue."

"You want two ladies? And four bottles of *Alacrán* tequila?"

"Yes, that's what we want."

"They'll be there in thirty minutes. It'll be eighty pounds of Blue."

Eighty pounds? The first mate rapidly did the math. The two crates *Capitán* Elizondo had authorized contained at least one hundred pounds. "Wait."

"What?"

"Can you also send some *mota*?" Mota was Mexican slang for marihuana.

"How much do you want?"

"Ten *calillas*?"

"All right. I'll send them with the ladies. That'll cost you another five pounds."

The first mate with the shifty eyes ended the call. He informed the rest of the crew that entertainment was on the way. He would, of course, take first bids on the women. His position as the first mate provided him with that privilege. Seven crewmembers minus the cook, who was gay, that would leave two hookers for six guys.

The men lifted two red plastic crates full of shrimp from the frozen cargo hold of the *San Felipe*, depositing them on the aft deck in anticipation of the arrival of the goodies.

34

Fringe Benefits for Pirates

"You ain't gonna believe this one, Brad."

"Oh, don't be so sure. Dealing with these good folks down there I've learned anything is possible. What now?"

Christian sat down in the patio chairs overlooking his swimming pool in his house in Phoenix.

"Javier Arenas just got off the phone. He found out when the *San Felipe* was seized by the Mexican navy in Bahia de Kino, it was because the skipper was out at the local cat house getting drunk and getting laid on our money."

"What?"

"It seems the sailors who catch shrimp in the Sea of Cortés feel they're entitled to certain fringe benefits. After a few nights of good fishing, the crews head to port and swap some of our shrimp for prostitutes, tequila and drugs."

"Javier told you this?"

"Yea. Just now."

"They steal our shrimp to buy those things?"

"Yes, but they don't feel they're stealing. It's kinda of a fringe benefit, you see. Seems all the fishing boats in that part of the world follow such a time-honored tradition."

"Bastards! How much of our shrimp did they steal?"

"Sounds like three or four crates. Each time they go in, that is."

Brad Murray did the math. "That's about three thousand bucks! Right off the top!"

"That is correct."

"And I assume the other ship owners are aware of this?"

"According to Javier Arenas, this has been going on since forever."

I don't suppose talking to the captains would make any difference?"

"None whatsoever. The captains are the ones who authorize this in the first place. Arenas claims there are bootleggers buying shrimp from the crews on the beach. They pay cash, in dollars, greenbacks which the crew then gladly spend at the local house of ill repute. Women and whisky, my friend."

"There goes part of our profit—again." Brad Murray was disgusted. "Dammit, man. This business really is like falling into a marabunta-infested jungle in the Amazon. Every one of these guys is trying to take a bite out of our asses."

"How did Javier find out the *San Felipe* crew was doing some R&R when the Navy appeared?"

"Javier has a snitch on each one of our ships."

"A snitch? No shit? You mean, a spy?"

Christian nodded. "Seems the only way to really know what's going on onboard our ships is to pay a mole. Javier pays him a retainer and a nice bonus if something juicy pops up."

"How long has he been doin' this?"

"Since we hired him to help us."

"I guess that's the only way to get some real intel around those parts. I got an idea."

Christian shook his head. Brad Murray was right; this was a never-ending battle against pirates of the worst kind. "Let's hear it."

"How about we install closed-circuit security cameras on the boats? We can record everything that goes on and if they steal our shrimp to buy girls or booze, it will be recorded."

Christian smiled. "Already talked that over with Javier Arenas months ago. No cigar. The cameras would be damaged or just plain thrown overboard."

"We could warn the captains that if the equipment is damaged, they would be responsible."

"Won't work. They would still destroy the cameras and face the consequences. Heck, they'd just quit working for us after they steal our shrimp and the diesel."

"Could we hire Javier's spies to protect the equipment?"

"Won't work either. The minute the crew finds out who the snitch is, they would cut him up and thrown him to the sharks."

"How about some of the new tiny cameras one can buy on Amazon?"

Christian hated being the devil's advocate, but he knew cameras just wouldn't work. Those sailors knew every inch of their boat, and they would find any camera, no matter how well camouflaged. "We just have to accept the loss as part of the cost of doing business."

35

Banana Republic

Brad Murray ordered some beef fajitas from the Mexican waiter. The restaurant was located next to a golf course, in the prestigious neighborhood of Ahwatukee, in Phoenix,

"I'm still furious about the situation with the *San Felipe*," Christian began. He ordered some *carnitas* tacos and a couple of Corona beers. *Carnitas* were pork bits fried in oil and presented crispy in a corn tortilla.

"Aah, far as I can see, we handled it as best we could," the eternally-positive Irishman pointed out.

"I know that. It just burns me that they can steal from us so blatantly and with total impunity."

"Hey, at least we got the *San Felipe* back."

"Yeah, that's true, but they still cost us fifty-thousand dollars. That's nearly half of the profits that ship was going to generate for us this season."

"That's a bitch, but like I said, at least we have our ship back. Look what happened to those Japs they caught fishing near Los Cabos."

"Yeah, those boys have bigger problems. They got balls, coming all the way up the Sea of Cortés to steal shrimp."

"What do you think is going to happen to the crew on that Japanese trawler?"

The waiter appeared with two ice-cold Coronas with a lemon wedge stuck in each.

"What's gonna happen to the Japs? Nothing much, I hear they're already in Mexico City. From what I read, they were picked up in Baja and dropped off at the Japanese embassy. I guess it'll be up to the embassy to buy them airfares and ship their asses back to the illustrious Empire of Japan."

"What do you think will happen to their boat?"

"Since they didn't have any catch onboard yet, I guess our friend, the eminent admiral there in La Paz will have to come up with some other way to see some money out of this. I'm sure they'll release the shrimp ship back to the Japanese after all the appropriate fines have been paid."

"And a few cases of Johnny Walker, of course."

"Of course. Considering the size of the captured trawler, I would guess the old admiral may become the owner of an entire liquor store out of this one."

"But you're thinking the Mexicans will return the boat to the Japanese?" Brad Murray downed his beer in two long gulps.

"Absolutely. I really have a hard time believing the Mexican government is willing to start a dogfight with the Japs over one lousy ship. Particularly since the Mexicans have been guilty of going into other countries' territorial waters to steal shrimp themselves."

"No shit? Where did you hear that?"

Christian paused, allowing the waiter to drop off some tortilla chips and salsa on their table. "Years ago, I believe it was in the late fifties, Mexican shrimp boats routinely entered the territorial waters of Guatemala illegally, grabbing some good shrimp in those waters. The Guatemalans were furious and complained to the Mexican government about the intrusions but were told so sorry, Jose, ain't nuthin we can do 'bout it. The Mexicans claimed they had no way of knowing which shrimp boats actually entered Guatemala's territorial waters. Just another Mexican copout, of course."

"So, what happened?"

"Kinda tragic and funny at the same time. The next time those Mexican fishermen felt the desire for some Guatemalan shrimp, the Guatemalans scrambled their P-51 Mustangs, intercepting the Mexican shrimp boats. The fighters attacked the shrimp boats with their fifty-caliber machine guns, killing three fishermen and injuring a bunch more. Some of the fishermen jumped in the ocean, and were rescued hours later by Guatemalan coast guard boats."

"No shit."

"No shit. The Mexican government severed diplomatic relations with Guatemala, closing their embassy in that country and destroying a bridge over a river that separates the two countries, and also sending a bunch of airplanes with bombs to take out the Guatemala City airport La Aurora. The president of Mexico, however, recalled the airplanes before they crossed the border into Guatemala. The man decided to pursue a diplomatic settlement with Guatemala, instead of going to war. It worked, since the two countries were able to resume diplomatic relations shortly afterwards. The government of Guatemala did end up paying compensation to the victims."

"Jeesus Christ. These guys have some history."

"They sure as hell do. They don't call them 'Banana republics' for nothin'."

"I see that. So, we're just going to eat the fifty thou from the *San Felipe?* The old dog admiral ripped us off stealing our shrimp and the diesel from the ship."

"Afraid so. Very pissing, but there's not much else we can do about it. That's the breaks when one operates in Mexico."

"Why don't we ask for some help from the Vega brothers?" Brad Murray suggested.

"Help with what? Getting our money back from the thieving admiral?"

"Yeah. Those boys seem to have ways of achieving miracles down there."

"Naw, that money's probably all gone by now. I'm sure the admiral and his cronies have spent most of it already. And I don't know the Vega brothers would want to go up against the admiral anyhow. That could disrupt their own business."

"Are you kidding?" Brad Murray finished a Corona. "Those are the guys who shot down a fucking helicopter of the Mexican Navy, remember? I don't think an old coot dressed in white linen would intimidate them."

Christian pondered this. "Nah, the way those guys solve problems, they'd probably just shoot the old bastard, and we don't wanna be responsible for that. Not at all."

"He took our money. He robbed us."

"And that justifies killing him?"

Brad Murray stared at his friend. "I don't know. Does it?"

"Brad, our manager Javier shared a Mexican saying with me. 'When one sleeps with dogs, one wakes up with fleas.'"

"So?"

"So maybe we've been doing business in Mexico too long, if we're starting to think killing some old bastard is acceptable."

Brad Murray raised his hand catching the waiter's eye, signaling for another round. "You're right. *Whattahell* am I saying? Of course, we don't want to take out the old bastard. Although he may be well-deserving because of the shit he pulled on us."

36

Situation Normal
SNAFU

"I cannot believe this people can be so stupid!" Christian expressed.

Elaine sipped from a glass of Pinot Griggio, listening to Christian vent.

"This is the third time the so-called electrician we use on the boats has cut through the satellite telephone cord. The guy must be brain-dead. I have told him multiple times not to cut that cable, since each costs us four hundred dollars, but the man just can't learn. The cable has to pass through a hole in the metal bulkhead of the bridge, but instead of making the hole bigger, the guy just cuts the cable with a wire cutter, and then tries to use electrician tape to splice it back together. Well, this is a highly specialized coax cable, made of multiple layers of different materials, it cannot be reconnected after being cut."

"This is really upsetting you?"

"Of course, it's really pissing me off. I lined up the entire crew on the docks and yelled at them warning them that the next time one of them cut through the satellite telephone wire I was personally going to shoot the sonofabitch who did it. That was not something I would ever say to anyone, but I lost it. It's just that dealing with these people is wearing me out. It's one thing after another. Brad Murray said it right, it's like sleeping in the jungle and getting your ass stung by a million ants.

Elaine became serious. "Was it Nietzsche who said 'if you stare into the abyss, the abyss stares back at you?'"

"What do you mean?"

"Dealing with that flavor of humanity down in Mexico might be starting to affect you."

"You mean I'm becoming like them?"

"Perhaps."

"You may be right. When threatening to shoot some poor bastard because he cut through a cable becomes acceptable, maybe it's time to rethink this."

"Assuming we decided to abandon our shrimping company, how would we go about doing it?"

Christian pondered this. Although he'd grown tired of the multiple challenges he faced everyday dealing with *Ali Baba and the Forty Thieves*, he had not considered getting out of the business. But Elaine did have a point, his relationship with the pirates of the Sea of Cortés was definitely affecting his personality. Maybe she was right suggesting it may be time to end the adventure.

37

The Investor

"Mike Dugan wants to come down to Rock Port with his wife and kids to check out the operation," Christian shared with Brad Murray over a couple of beers at the Cantina restaurant in Ahwatukee, Arizona.

"Remind me, which one is Dugan?"

"He's the widebody captain living in Elvistown. I thing he invested about fifty thousand with us. I don't recall the exact amount, guess I'll have to ask our accountant."

"Elvistown?"

"Memphis. That was Elvis Presley's hometown."

"Oh." Brad Murray's familiarity with American Rock and Roll idols of the past did not include in-depth knowledge of Elvis, much less his hometown.

"He's one of our venture capitalists?"

"Yeah. A nice guy, really. However, his wife is a little bit of a bitch, I've heard from other pilots. They want to come down to see the shrimp boats and have his kids play on the beach and enjoy some margaritas."

"Gee, sounds like fun, especially if the word is his wife's a bitch." Brad Murray hadn't met all of their venture capital investors who contributed capital to start the business, so he guessed this was a good opportunity to meet another one.

Christian remembered the man. The guy had been invited to join the shrimping adventure by a mutual friend, a United captain. Too bad his wife was coming along, if it was already a known fact she was unpleasant.

'I'm thinking we can rent a boat and take him out fishing for some fresh catch. And beer, of course."

"I'm in."

38

Ten miles off the coast in the Sea of Cortés.

"This is the life!" Mike Dugan loudly announced, after downing half his Corona in one big gulp. He was already two sheets to the wind.

The trio were ten miles out in the Sea of Cortés onboard a very old twenty-five-footer Bayliner. They had been fishing and drinking all afternoon in the 110-degree desert heat.

The men had bagged several bonitos and a couple of huge yellowfin tunas. The three Mexican locals operating the fishing boat had found a good spot and for the four-hundred dollars Christian had paid them the men helped bait the hooks and clean and filet the catch. They had also provided an apparently never-ending supply of Corona beer.

"You two assholes are lucky!" Dugan continued. He was already more than just a little intoxicated, having polished off two six-packs of Corona by himself. "You get to come down here anytime you want with the excuse of running the shrimping business. Admit it, what you guys are really doing is coming out here fishing every chance you get."

Christian decided not to explain the shrimping season to Dugan again. Dugan was drunk anyway, so any attempt to converse with the man logically was not going to lead anywhere. Christian was routinely amused by the fact most of his friends and investors from the States were apparently oblivious to the high alcohol content of Mexican beer.

The previous day they'd driven down from Phoenix in a full-sized rental van with Dugan and his family. His kids were well-behaved, a boy and two girls, but his wife was not pleasant. Since arriving, she was one continuous nag constantly reminding Dugan he drank too much and he should put that beer down and she hated Mexican food and she hated the heat, and why were there so many Mexicans out here? *Ad nauseam.* A bit of a bitch? Christian thought. No, she was not a bit of one. She was a full-fledged cast-iron bitch.

Unpleasant as all hell.

No wonder Dugan had been in such a hurry to leave the family on the beach and escape to the holy solitude of the small fishing boat. But perhaps his wife did have somewhat of a point. Dugan had been gulping down beer at an amazing rate. He was out-drinking even the Irishman Brad Murray, which by anybody's standards was no easy feat.

"This place is paradise!" Dugan blurted, gazing at the white sandy beach in the distance. He was in his early forties and made better than a good living flying widebody airplanes for the overnight package delivery company.

"I could live here full time," the pilot voiced.

"Naw, you don't wanna do that," Brad Murray put in. "The schools here suck. Your kids wouldn't have a good school to attend." The big Irishman had already put away a fair amount of beer as well.

Christian suspected there was little substance to the possibility of Dugan moving to the fishing village in the Sea of Cortés. It was just the beer talking. His wife clearly hated it there, and the commute from Rock Port to Memphis would not be realistic. Anyone crazy enough to consider commuting from Mexico would first have a four-hour drive just to get to Phoenix, followed by a three-and-a-half-hour flight to Memphis before he could even start flying the big jets.

Opium dreams, nothing else. Or Corona dreams, as was this case.

"You wouldn't want to live here with your family anyway," Brad Murray ranted. "Too many assholes living here."

"Uh? How's that?" Dugan inquired.

"These are not all nice people, you so much as look at someone cross-eyed, and they kill you."

Christian paid attention. He was not comfortable with the direction of the Irishman's rambling.

"What' ya mean?" Dugan replied.

"These good folks don't mess around, Mike. Like I said, you so much as eyeball one of their girlfriends, and they will hunt you down and kill you. Shoot you dead."

"Ya, right," Dugan laughed.

"Don't laugh, it's true. They shot down a military helicopter with a missile, killing the entire crew, without batting an eye."

Oh, crap. Christian discreetly looked at the three locals manning the boat. Did they understand the conversation? Brad was throwing caution to the wind.

Dugan frowned from behind his beer stupor. "Who shot down a military helicopter?"

Christian rapidly considered the best way to terminate the conversation, but Brad Murray was not going to take any hints in his present intoxicated condition. Dugan didn't really need to know anything about the pirate events going on in this area of the world, and Christian was also leery of the three Mexican men crewing the fishing boat. One never knew exactly how much English those boys understood. It was not uncommon for the locals to fake ignorance of the English language in order to eavesdrop on the conversations between the gringos. The information Brad Murray was sharing with Dugan was confidential, entrusted to them by the Vega brothers, whom Christian suspected would not be amused to hear that a drunken Irishman was divulging family secrets—so to speak—to the four winds.

"The drug guys, the narcos," Brad Murray continued. "Mexican Navy pukes here were interfering with their drug operations and they blasted their asses out of the sky."

"No shit?" Dugan looked at Christian for confirmation.

"I don't know that's exactly what happened, but why don't we have these guys bait us three more lines and try to catch something else before we head back?"

Dugan was not having it.

"Wait, hold on a sec! The narcos shot down a helicopter here? What narcos?"

Brad Murray reached for another beer. "The ones who sold us the boats, that's who."

Dugan looked confused. "We bought our boats from the narcos?"

Christian stepped in, laughing. "Naw. Brad's just pulling your leg. He does that to everyone. This area of the world is remote and mysterious, so Brad enjoys weaving a yarn to add some spice to the situation. He's a writer at heart."

Christian gave Brad Murray a vitriolic look.

And if you say another fucking word about narcos or dead helicopters, I'll throw you overboard myself so you can go get up close and personal with the multiple shark species living here, you kucklehead!

Something got through the thick haze in the big Irishman's drunken brain, because he desisted on his attempt to stay on the topic.

Dugan, however, was another story.

"Christian, we bought our boats from narcos?"

'Not exactly. But let's not talk about it here now in front of these guys," he nodded towards the deck hands.

Dugan would not drop it. "Wait! You guys know these dipshits are narcos? Have you told the FBI? Or the DEA?"

"That's not how it works here, Mike."

"The hell it isn't! We should go to the local authorities and turn them in. Shit, let's go talk to the immigration dudes at the border crossing point. They'll know who to call."

"Mike," Christian said in a more menacing tone. "Back off. We're not gonna do any such thing. Now, just enjoy the beer and let's change the topic."

Dugan nodded in tacit acknowledgement, apparently intrigued to find himself in the middle of some sort of mysterious conspiracy.

The topic soured the mood. Time for them to head back.

By that evening, Dugan had sobered up. Christian and Brad Murray together with the wives joined Dugan and his family for dinner at the Casa del Pescador restaurant on top of the cliff.

"So, what was all this bullshit about shooting down a helicopter and us buying the boats from the narcos?" Dugan asked, as they followed the women up the path towards the restaurant after parking the vehicles in a sandy parking lot.

Christian had an earlier conversation with Brad Murray, reading him the riot act for sharing confidential information with the drunk aviator. Brad Murray—as was to be expected—had been mortified.

I'm so sorry I stepped on it," Brad Murry expressed. "What're we gonna do about it?"

"We have no choice. We have to bring Dugan into the Circle of Trust. Otherwise, the dude's capable of asking embarrassing questions in town. That sort of crap can only cause problems for us. If we're straight with him and tell him what we know, hopefully, he will understand and drop the subject."

"Think that's a good idea?"

"No, it probably isn't but at this point we have to give him something, or he'll start digging."

"Hey, we really haven't done anything wrong. We had no idea the Vega brothers were running a *pharmaceutical* wholesale business here, and we sure as all hell didn't have anything to do with the shooting down of that Mexican Navy helicopter."

"Remember what Benjamin Franklin once said, 'giving the appearance of being honest is just as important as being honest?' If it comes right down to it, we would not be able to disassociate ourselves from all the bullshit going on in this place."

"I see. You may be right"

"So, we'll give Dugan some information while at the same time appealing to his sense of discretion. He will learn some of what's going on here, but not everything."

The three men lagged behind the women and the kids on their way to the restaurant.

"So, you guys are going to let me in on whatever is going on around here?" Dugan insisted.

Christian stopped. "Mike, there are some things you need to know." He then proceeded to give Dugan a quick synopsis of their situation in Rock Port and their relationship with the Vega brothers.

"Holy shit. You guys are in on some serious crap here," Dugan finally pointed out.

"No, not really. We're aware of some serious crap going on, but we're not in it."

"Have you thought of going to the authorities with this?"

Christian gave Brad Murray a resigned look.

'Stupid' can't be taught, he surmised, looking at Dugan.

"And which authorities would those be, Mike? The Mexican authorities? Or did you have someone else in mind?"

Dugan seemed confused. "Who cares? Any authorities. You can't let this sorta crap go on like this. Those guys who sold you the boats are murderers. Murderers and drug cartel operators. We can't just let them go on with their business."

Christian noticed Dugan had automatically included himself on the side of the Crusaders, the good guys, with the use of the Royal 'we.'

"Mike, Brad and I have gone over this before. We came to the Sea of Cortés to run a shrimping operation. None of what goes on outside the business of fishing is of any concern to us. In other words—it's none of our business. These people have been operating the same way for the past sixty years. They were doing it before we showed up here and they will continue operating like this long after we're gone. Far as we're concerned, we have not directly participated in any of their activities. For some reason they took us in their trust, and now we're compromised. We cannot betray their trust or there could be some very serious consequences for all of us."

"Serious consequences?" Dugan replied. "Like what?"

"What do you think?" Brad Murray put in. He was getting tired of this idiot. "Serious consequences as in they could take you and your wife and kids and feed you to the sharks. After they chop you all into little pieces—that is."

Dugan stared at the two men. "You're fuckin kidding me!"

"No," Brad Murray smiled. "We're NOT fuckin kidding you."

"Well, shit. That's all the more reason why we should go the police—to get some protection from these assholes."

Christian shook his head. Jeesus, he was dealing with a six-year-old. This sort of behavior was not unexpected in people who'd never traveled outside of their county, but an international pilot like Mike should have more street smarts.

"Mike, trust me. We're not in Kansas anymore. We need to focus on our own business and ignore everything else going on around us. These people allow us to come here and participate in the shrimping business because for whatever reason they seem to like us. We are making some good money here, but don't doubt for one second, the folks involved in shrimping and other—shall we say—more colorful activities, could chase us out of here in two minutes. Not to mention, if we pissed them off, they'd have no problem coming after us in Phoenix or even Nashville."

Dugan was not giving in. "These assholes don't intimidate me. In America we have laws, and we have the police and the FBI. And I have guns. Just let them try."

Christian and Brad Murray exchanged glances. It was painfully evident bringing this moron to see the operation had not been a good idea. He had guns? What a laugh. Dugan had obviously no idea the kind of firepower these 'farmer' Mexicans could bring to a fight.

"Look," Christian decided to diffuse the situation. "Why don't we go join our women and have a great dinner and a few drinks and we can talk about this later."

"I can't have a fucking drink, Lydia's up there."

Christian nodded. He'd forgot the continuous bickering going on with Dugan's wife about his drinking. "All right, let's just go get some good food then. Far as this issue is concerned, both Brad and I believe we're better off just keeping things as they are. Make no waves, make money instead."

Christian hoped mentioning money would appeal to Dugan's greed. If the pilot made a stink, it could affect his investment.

Dugan nodded in apparent agreement. "Fine, let's go have some dinner."

39

The Vega brothers

"You're sure that's what you heard?" Rodolfo Vega surveyed the three young fishermen with a look of concern.

"Yea, Don Rodolfo, that's what the gringos were discussing."

The other two local fishermen nodded in agreement. All four men were standing by the docks, in front of several shrimp boats unloading their catch. Rodolfo Vega was both feared and respected among the population of the small fishing village, and few of the locals would pass up an opportunity to do the man a favor, with eyes towards potential gratitude from the powerful narco.

The three local fishermen had contacted the woman owner of the local tortilla factory immediately after returning from their fishing expedition with the three gringos. The woman, Doña Lupe, was the local contact to get in touch with the powerful Vega brothers. Rodolfo Vega, the sharpest and meanest of the three brothers had driven out to the docks upon receiving a call from Doña Lupe.

Rodolfo Vega drove his brand-new black pickup truck away from the docks after his conversation with the three fishermen. He was experiencing mixed emotions. On the one hand, he liked Christian and Brad, found them fun and enjoyed socializing with them, but on the other hand, their conversation with the third gringo was most disturbing. The three fishermen had done well reporting to him. All three understood English very well, having been on the other side working the fields in California.

The gringos were obviously not aware of this fact, that all their conversations were being monitored.

The little guy, the new gringo visiting with his wife and children was a little too curious about stuff that did not concern him, asking Brad Murray if he'd bought shrimp boats from narcos. That angered Rodolfo Vega. He did not think of himself as a narco. He hated the term. He liked thinking of himself as a businessman, and anything other than that was just plain insulting. He reached for the flask of whisky from his glove compartment, enjoying a much-needed drink.

He dialed his brother Ramiro.

"Rodolfo? What's up?" His older brother answered.

"Sorry to bug you before lunch. We may have a small problem."

"I'm listening."

"It seems that Christian and Brad Murray brought a visitor to Rock Port, some acquaintance of theirs from the other side. They went out fishing with

Rodolfo Salcedo on his Bayliner and after they had some drinks the conversation turned to us."

"Continue." The older Vega was a man of few words.

"Salcedo reported to me the little gringo was insisting on a visit to the FBI or the DEA to inform them of our activities here."

"Is that so?"

"All three fishermen confirmed this."

"Did Christian and Brad Murray agree with their guest?"

"No, it seems they were troubled by the conversation and tried to stop it."

"And this little sonofawhore specifically mentioned the FBI and the DEA."

"Yes, he did."

"And where are they staying?"

"At the Plaza."

"Very well. Thank you for letting me know."

"Keep in mind," Rodolfo added, "it doesn't look like Christian and Brad Murray had anything to do with this."

"I'll keep that in mind. Say, Rodolfo, why don't you have a talk with Christian and kindly let him know—in the future—we would prefer if he kept our business out of his conversations."

"I will do that." Rodolfo Vega took another generous gulp from the whisky which he consumed at the rate of a fifth per day.

Christian and Brad Murray were eating lunch at a restaurant by the beach when Rodolfo Vega appeared. Christian noted the man was again dressed in black and wearing his customary white cowboy hat. A bad choice of colors, considering the sizzling temperatures in the village.

"Rodolfo, what a pleasure running into you," Christian stood, extending his hand.

The Vega brother shook hands with a firm squeeze.

"Care to join us for some breaded tilapia?"

Rodolfo pulled up a chair, shaking hands with Brad Murray.

"Naw, thanks, I'll just have a drink."

"What brings you around?"

Rodolfo Vega hesitated just long enough to set off several alarms in Christian's head. The hesitation was not characteristic of the lovable scoundrel.

"I got word that your guest from the other side has been somewhat impolite."

Christian translated for Brad Murray, who sat up straighter.

"Who?"

"The guy you took fishing."

"You mean Mike Dugan?"

"I don't know what his name is, but yeah, the guy you took fishing was being very indecorous making threats, and around these parts that's not a very good idea."

Christian was very surprised. Making threats? Dugan? Who the hell would he be threatening?

Then it came to him.

Oh, shit.

"What kinda threats did you hear he's been making?"

Rodolfo became serious, but with a veil of sadness across his face. "According to what they tell me, this guy with you threatened to take our business to the FBI or the DEA."

Christian briefly considered a bluff, immediately dismissing the idea. Rodolfo Vega was anything but stupid, this guy could smell horseshit a mile away. Trying to lie to the man would cause nothing but trouble and lose his trust.

"I wouldn't say Dugan intentionally threatened you or your brothers, he was drunk and has probably seen too many Hollywood movies about drugs and this sorta thing."

"Ramiro asked me to talk to you. We want to ask you, please keep our business affairs away from strangers. If you could do this, we would be most grateful."

Christian could feel his heartrate accelerating. *Jesus Christ goddamned Mike Dugan,* coming here making trouble. Christian valued his relationship with the Vega brothers because they were obviously the big boys in town, and could help him out if he ever needed it. But now this imbecile Dugan appeared to have damaged that relationship. How bad it had been damaged still remained to be seen. Not to mention the fact that these good people could very easily have him and Brad Murray killed, fileted and thrown to the fish at the bat of an eye.

Christian translated for Brad Murray.

Brad was shaken. "Tell Rodolfo," he stared at the man. "That I am the one who touched on the subject with Dugan. I was drunk, but didn't mean anything by it. I consider Rodolfo and his brothers friends and I apologize if I created a problem."

Christian switched back to Spanish, explaining to Rodolfo what Brad Murray said.

"There's no problem," the Vega brother reassured them. "Just one of those things, you know?"

The waiter arrived, delivering drinks and some exquisite tilapia baked with bread crumbs and salsa.

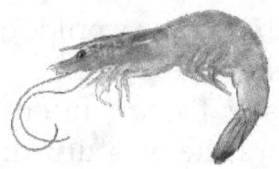

"What the hell are we gonna do?" Brad Murray asked.

"Not sure yet, but one thing comes to mind. Mike Dugan and his family have to get the hell away from this town. It's no longer safe for that idiot here."

The couple were driving their Ford Bronco headed for the Plaza hotel.

Christian had been stunned by the jungle telegraph these people had. The Vegas had learned about their conversation on the fishing boat at lightning speed. No doubt the three locals who took them fishing understood English and had reported to Rodolfo the theme of their conversation when Dugan insisted they go to the authorities.

Christian was unsure about how much he could trust Rodolfo Vega. Human life wasn't worth a tortilla around these parts. Rodolfo could very well be putting on a show feigning friendship right before he sent a couple of his thugs to assassinate them all.

Farfetched? Not in Mexico.

If that was the case, their adventure into shrimping was over. It was hard getting a handle on just how pissed Rodolfo was. And even if they managed to survive this incident, and Rodolfo actually forgot about the whole thing, how safe were Mike Dugan and his family?

"Ya think Rodolfo will take action against us?" Brad Murray asked.

Christian didn't take long to respond. "No, I believe if he was going to do anything against us, he would've done it without bothering to warn us or ask us to be more discrete."

"What about Dugan then? You think they will try to hurt him?"

"I don't know, Brad. That has occurred to me. I really feel we should drive him back to Phoenix with his family. He's a dumbshit, but I really don't want anything happening to him, or—God forbid—his family."

"He's not gonna wanna leave. He's got two more days here."

"That may be a problem. We need to talk with him, although we cannot disclose our conversation with Rodolfo."

"So, you're thinking of jumping on the van and taking the whole gang back to Arizona? When, today?"

"I believe that would be best, however, I am also concerned because the Vegas could interpret our mass exodus as an escape. And if they did, then things could get sticky."

"Sticky like how?"

"Like how? As in a couple of pickups with eight guys and automatic weapons intercepting us on the way to the border."

"Bastards! You don't really think they would do that?"

"What do you think, Brad? Lessee, they took out a helicopter without batting an eye. You think they'd have any acid indigestion taking out a van full of gringos? Especially if said gringos are beelining it for the nearest DEA office?"

"I see your point."

"This is Mexico, remember? Corruption is their religion and human life is not worth a taco. I think I'm gonna come clean with Rodolfo and tell him we're driving Mike Dugan and his family back to Phoenix later today so he can't cause any more trouble. Better be up front with Rodolfo."

40

FBI Office, Phoenix Arizona

Agent Henderson at the local FBI Phoenix office hung up the phone, walking over to agent Espinoza sitting at his desk. "Hey, Luis, I just got a rather unusual call."

Agent Espinoza put down the fish and chips lunch he'd just started enjoying. "And I guess I'm gonna hear all about it, eh?"

Agent Henderson decided to ignore the sarcasm. "That call was from some guy claiming he's a freight pilot down in Rock Port, on vacation with his family. He called to blow the whistle on drug operations he believes are going on down there, as well as—get this— the shooting down of a Mexican Navy helicopter, in which three Mexican soldiers apparently died. This guy claims to know how the Sinaloa boys are bringing drugs into the US by using skiffs loaded with cocaine and marijuana."

Agent Espinoza did not appear too excited by the news. The Phoenix FBI office was no stranger to these types of calls. "And what makes you think he knows what he's talking about?"

"He said he had the names of three big drug guys operating from that fishing village."

"He give you those names?" Agent Espinoza put a hot, fried potato wedge in his mouth.

"No, he told me he wants to come by our office in two days' time to give us more details. The man said he's flying back to his home in Memphis but wants to talk to us before he flies out."

"All right. I say we wait and if he shows up, we can listen to what he has to say and go from there. You good with that?"

Agent Henderson nodded. "Ya, I'm good with that."

"Fact is—" Agent Espinoza added—"How would some dude on vacation down in Mexico with his family come across this type of intel? The guy must be watching a lot of *Criminal Investigation* episodes on TV. He probably had a drink or two at the hotel bar and the bartender must've filled his ears with all sorts of bullshit in exchange for a large tip." Like I said, if he shows up, we'll talk to him. But don't hold your breath. This sorta loonies pop up quite often."

Agent Luis Espinoza finished his lunch, excusing himself announcing he needed to walk down to the local Seven Eleven to buy some cigs.

The agent walked a block to the convenience store, cringing at the 110-degree weather. It was hot enough to cook eggs on the pavement. Some people were fond of saying yeah, but it's *dry* heat! As if that made a difference. Just ask your average Thanksgiving turkey how he liked the *dry* heat in your oven.

Agent Espinoza bought some cigarettes and a burner cellphone, using a fake Arizona driver's license he carried for this very purpose. He stepped back out in the heat, pulling out of his wallet an international long-distance calling card he'd purchased online.

The number he called in Rock Port rang twice before being picked up by a young man's voice.

"This is Luis Espinoza in Phoenix," the agent spoke in fluent Spanish. "I have some information for Don Rodolfo..."

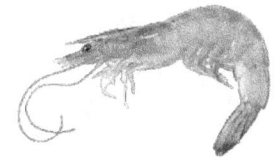

Mike Dugan sat on the bed in the hotel room at the Hacienda hotel next to Sky Harbor International airport in Phoenix. His wife Lydia and their kids were dropped off there an hour ago by Brad Murray and Christian. Mike was not happy; Christian had insisted they cut their vacation short by two days because he claimed transportation back to Phoenix would become a problem if they stayed two more days.

Mike Dugan's wife Lydia had jumped at the news. She hated Mexico, disliked Mexican food, thought the village was too damn hot and was generally annoyed at her husband's continuous drinking. She wanted nothing more than to get on an airplane and fly back home to Nashville. Mike had been looking forward to another fishing expedition on the little Bayliner, away from his wife where he could enjoy some brewskies together with the boys.

But his plans had been cut short.

Now the kids were down in the hotel pool and Lydia was arranging their clothes on the hangers.

"I gotta make a quick call to the FBI," he announced, regretting it the moment it came out of his lips.

Lydia looked at him. "The FBI? What the heck are you talking about?"

"I called them from Mexico to tip them off about the drug dealers who sold us our boats. I told them I would go by to see them when we came through Phoenix."

Lydia stopped what she was doing. "Are you out of your goddamned mind?"

"Why?"

"You called the goddamn FBI from Mexico? Are you nuts?"

"No, I'm not nuts. I have to report those guys. They are bringing drugs into our country!"

"And who told you this exactly?"

"Brad Murray did."

"He told you they bought the boats from drug people?"

"Yes!"

"And exactly when did he tell you this?"

"When we were out fishing."

Lydia looked disgusted. "When you were out fishing. You mean, when the three of you were shitfaced drunk while you were out on that boat?"

Mike Dugan did not like her insinuation that he had imagined the conversation because he was drunk. "I did not imagine this. Murray told me."

"I'm sure he did. One drunken buddy to another. And you called the FBI over this?"

Dugan began doubting his own story.

When he didn't respond, Lydia took it as a tacit admission. "I don't know what the hell you were thinking calling the feds on some idiotic product of your intoxicated mind, but you sure as peaches are *not* calling them back again. We're catching that morning flight back home tomorrow, and you're not going to go visit any FBI office between now and then, do I make myself perfectly clear?"

Dugan evaluated the situation. Clearly, Lydia was in no mood to discuss the topic any further. If he insisted, he would have to deal with her horrible personality that evening and the next day. Definitely not worth a call to the FBI, much less a visit. And besides, she was right, he would not have time to visit the feds if they were going to catch that morning flight. Aw, crap. He'd just wait and call the feds from home once they got back to Nashville.

41

The Troublemaker

Rodolfo Vega ordered a double Chivas and a beer chaser. The three Vega brothers gathered at the *El Catalán* seafood restaurant overlooking the turquoise Sea of Cortés.

"It appears the situation has turned ugly," Ramiro stated. Being the oldest of the three, he got to speak first.

"It seems that way," Rodolfo agreed. "We knew this was always a possibility."

The men ordered fish and shrimp tacos.

"I see that gringo Christian brought is still making trouble," the youngest brother added.

"Espinoza, our guy at the FBI office in Phoenix told us he had a call from some gringo who was here in Mexico vacationing, and allegedly, the gringo mentioned to Espinoza he had the names of three reputed drug dealers moving drugs to the United States."

The brothers stopped the conversation long enough to distribute the drinks brought by the waiter.

"You think that *pendejo* gringo was the same one who was out fishing with Christian?"

"Who else would it be? Yeah, I think we're talking about the same guy," Rodolfo expressed, downing his Chivas.

"Did the caller provide our names to Espinoza?"

"No, it appears the caller refused to divulge any information by phone. He indicated to Espinoza his intention to visit the Phoenix FBI office in person, but he never showed up."

"He never went to the FBI in person?"

"No."

"What do you think, he changed his mind?"

"We have no way of knowing. Apparently, the gringo flew back home with his family."

"But the possibility exists he could start singing to the FBI office back in his hometown, no?"

"That is a fact."

"Looks like we need to take care of him."

"If we take care of him Christian and the Irishman are not gonna like it."

"Then maybe it's time the Americans return to America."

"What do you mean?"

"We allowed Christian to own a few boats and fish in our waters. Now, he's becoming a problem with these idiots he's bringing from the other side. Allowing those guys to fish was not a threat to us, but now their presence is endangering the family business. We can't let that happen."

Christian sat across from Brad Murray at the kitchen table in Phoenix.

"We may have a serious problem."

"Dugan?"

"Yes. I think the sonofabitch could cause problems for all of us."

"You think he's going to open his big fat mouth with the cops about what he learned in Mexico?"

"Can't be sure, but if he does, we're all up a shit creek."

"Rodolfo was pretty clear, the Vegas know Dugan was blabbing about going to the cops."

"I'm very sorry I caused this," Brad Murray was sincerely distraught.

"Shit happens. You had no way of knowing Dugan was going to react the way he did."

"But if I hadn't said anything he would have come and gone and everything would be just fine."

"Brad, you had some beer and fucked up. It's done. Now, what I'm worried about are the Vegas. Are they going to go after Dugan in his home town?"

"You think they'd do that?"

"What do you think? Those guys don't seem to have a problem taking out anyone who crosses them. Remember what they did to the ship owner who sank his ship for the insurance claim?"

"What'd they do?"

"They killed him, that's what. Did you by any chance detect any sort of regret on the part of those three brothers when they told us about the helicopter they blew out of the sky?"

Brad Murray had no choice but agree with his friend. "So, you think Dugan's done?"

"I don't know, but honestly, who gives a damn about Dugan. Has it occurred to you the Vega could erroneously assume we are a threat and come after us?"

"Oh, for Chrissakes. Are you serious?"

"You're goddamned right, I'm serious. We can be guilty by association. We took Dugan down there, they're not gonna let us forget that."

"Oh, shit. What do we do?"

"We can't just run. Those guys would come find us. We need to face them."

"Face them? How so?"

"We drive down there and we talk to them. We don't run. We tell them we want to keep fishing. If they see we're willing to continue being involved with the people in the fishing village, they might allow us another chance."

"Naw, that's crazy. Those guys are perfectly capable of pretending to let us fish, only to have us shot on the road or stabbed in the office."

Christian considered this. Brad was right. Shrimping was already stressful enough having to deal with the day to day operation without having to keep looking over one's shoulder. "If we sell the ships and abandon the business, they will surely smell a rat. They will conclude we're running because the DEA is on its way."

"I agree. How about this, how about we ask the Vegas to manage our ships for us. They know our ships represent a big investment and we're not gonna just leave them and run."

"That could be an idea, but to be honest, I don't trust anything those good old boys say down there. It's their culture. Those guys just don't understand how we value the truth in our own culture. They'll tell you one thing and do something entirely different."

"Okay, so what do we do?"

"Not sure. But if Dugan goes to the cops in Nashville and the Vegas find out, we're gonna be in a world of hurt. Dugan might be an idiot, and he probably deserves whatever the Vega want to dish out, but we can't allow this to happen."

"What do you mean?"

"Brad, we know if Dugan goes to the feds, eventually the Vegas and all their cronies in Rock Port are going to learn the Yankees are on the warpath. The next thing they're gonna do is send somebody to take out Dugan and his family. And maybe us, for all I know."

"Not a good prospect. Definitely not a good prospect. I really blew it, didn't I?"

"Brad, things happen. Now we have to fix them. I think we need to convince Dugan that if he opens his mouth to anybody about what you told him in Mexico, he and his entire family could easily become targets for some very bad people."

"Yeah, that might be tougher than it sounds. Remember how the idiot reacted when we told him they could come after him? What was it he said, he has guns?"

"I remember," Christian recalled the bravado of the dumbass. Those 'agricultural' people down in Sinaloa could show up at your house in the middle of the night with a team of heavily armed men, sporting the latest fully automatic assault rifles available on the market. Try fighting that with a handgun.

"We need to talk to Dugan and his wife. She can control him," Christian suggested. "She needs to know the sort of trouble Dugan could bring down upon them. Then, after Dugan assures us he's going to keep his mouth shut, we go talk to the Vegas and tell them Dugan is going to behave."

"Wait a minute. You're saying we're gonna vouch for Dugan? Make it our responsibility to assure the Vegas he's gonna keep his mouth shut?"

Christian thought about it. Brad was right, that would be a totally asinine thing to do. "No, you're right, we can't do that."

"What we can do, is have a talk with Dugan and his wife, then tell the Vegas about it. That way, we are not assuming any responsibility for Dugan's behavior. And we tell the Vegas that. We give Dugan and his wife a heads up and if they decide to ignore it, and go to the authorities, then good luck to them dealing with the Vegas."

"So, we're pretty much authorizing the Vegas to do as they please with Dugan and his family."

"Not exactly. We need to think of our families as well. The safety of all of us cannot depend on whether Dugan keeps his mouth shut. His actions should only affect him and his wife. He's an adult. We will explain the situation and it will be up to him whether he takes it seriously or not."

"What about the Vegas?"

"Don't know. We're taking a risk, here but I think we should talk to Dugan first and then drive down and talk to Rodolfo."

"Sounds risky."

"Brad, we can't just disappear. If those guys want to come after us, we'd have to move to friggin New Zealand, change our names and our identities, and even then, if they wanted to find us, they probably could."

"So, what you're saying is we must convince them they can continue trusting us."

"I think that's our only choice here. We gotta tell them we are not responsible for Dugan. If that idiot creates a problem, he'll have to slug it out with the Vegas. And we must tell Rodolfo if that happens, we're all right with it."

"So, if they go after Dugan, we become accomplices?"

"That's pretty much it. If we don't play it this way, we run the risk of having a bunch of pissed off cartel pukes coming by to pay us a visit."

"We have no other choice?"

"I don't see one. Dugan left us no choice."

"Let's do it then."

42

Casa del Pescador Restaurant

The three brothers appeared at the door sporting cowboy hats, silver belt buckles and black boots. They scanned the dining area, smiling when they saw the two Americans.

Brad Murray and Christian stood, shaking hands all around like old friends. The restaurant was only half full, since the sun had not gone down yet. No civilized Mexican would dare enjoy dinner before dark, but Christian had invited the Vegas for a drink, not dinner.

"*Amigos*, how've you been?" Rodolfo greeted.

"Not bad, now that the season is finally over," Christian replied.

Rodolfo ordered drinks all around. "And how was your season?"

Christian was fully aware Rodolfo had access to the Ocean Fruit books and the processing plant records, so the man probably knew—to the pound—how their season had been. "Not a bad season, really."

"Are we going to eat, or just enjoy some drinks?" Ramiro asked.

"Whatever you gentlemen prefer," Christian offered. The men were already scanning their menus.

"Let's get some food," Ramiro stated.

The waiter came and took five orders for carne asada. Not very imaginative, but it seemed everyone fancied that dish once one of the brothers ordered it.

"You wanted to talk to us, you said," Ramiro asked.

Christian glanced at Brad Murray, then Ramiro.

"Yes, if you gentlemen don't mind, we wanted to talk about that investor of ours who was here and said some very indiscrete things."

"Go ahead," Rodolfo offered.

"This guy, his name is Dugan, is not a very bright man. He doesn't understand how things work down here, so Brad and I spoke with him and pointed out what he did wrong, asking him at the same time to keep his mouth shut from now on about any of our business."

"Yeah, not a very smart guy, that one," Rodolfo added.

"So, like I said, we talked with him and he seems to have understood he made a mistake. He promised us he's going to keep his mouth shut from now on. However, Brad and I are not going to be responsible for Dugan's actions. If he changes his mind and decides to become a pain for any of us sitting here tonight, then Brad and I agree that you can deal with Dugan in any way you see fit. Basically, we enjoy your friendship and would like to continue fishing as we've been doing these two years."

The Vega brothers exchanged glances.

"We understand," Rodolfo finally replied.

"Something you should know," Ramiro offered. "As you know, the government subsidy of our diesel is what allows us to make money fishing. Without it, our costs would go up about one hundred thousand dollars per boat. That would neutralize our profits."

Christian wondered how this was relevant to the conversation.

"Anyway, as you know, the government of Mexico will have a new president later this year. Whenever there is a change like this, most government employees lose their jobs. They know this, so before they get fired, they lay their hands on anything of value they can find. One of these things of value is our diesel subsidy." Rodolfo paused to take a shot of Chivas.

"We heard from our people in Mexico City, the diesel subsidy won't be here in September, when the new fishing season starts."

Christian nodded, then interpreted for Brad Murray.

"This is official?" Christian asked.

Rodolfo shook his head. "Of course not. But it will happen. Once the government starts charging three dollars per gallon, that's the end of it."

Christian wasn't too convinced what Rodolfo was saying was necessarily true. It could very well be a subterfuge to convince the gringos to abandon the business. "What's everyone else going to do? There's over three hundred shrimp boats out here."

Rodolfo appeared serious. "The subsidy's not gonna go away forever. It'll be a couple of years and then the government may start subsidizing us again, but not all at once. What we've learned is they will make us pay for the diesel up front at three bucks a gallon, and come the end of the season they will give us back a dollar per gallon. The second year it will be two dollars per gallon, and so on."

"That means no profits for us one entire year, then half the second year, and so on."

"Yeah, that sounds about right," Rodolfo agreed.

"And you're sure this is gonna happen."

"Pretty sure."

"What're you guys gonna do?" Christian asked.

"We have eleven boats left. We're just gonna park them for three years."

Christian pondered this. "You're going to take them out of the water?"

"Yes, we are planning on paying a shipyard to do that for us."

Christian suspected the Vegas had plenty of cash to survive for three years without fishing. But what about the rest of the fishermen in the village?

He asked Rodolfo this.

"Most of these folks will probably take out equity from their homes to keep fishing these next three years. It's sad, but history repeats itself. Their boats are just not going to be maintained."

Christian brought Brad Murray up to speed.

"Oh, shit," the big Irishman scoffed. "What are we going to do?"

"Assuming everything goes as advertised, we have a problem. We haven't finished paying for the boats yet. We could sell them, but in view of the circumstances with the diesel subsidy, I don't think we'd get our money back. These guys are just going to take their boats out of the water and park them in a shipyard. They have plenty of experience in this business, I'd say we do the same thing."

"So, we just stop fishing?"

"I'd say that's a good alternative. We can't operate our boats if we're just breaking even. One big mechanical failure and we're in the hole for a bunch of money. And also, this takes care of the Dugan issue."

"We just park them for three years and go home?"

"Unless you got any better ideas."

Brad Murray shook his head.

"Thank you for tipping us off on this," Christian expressed to Rodolfo. "Looks like you guys have the right idea. Any chance you could give us some advice on how we can follow your example and park our boats for the next three years?

Rodolfo Vega stared at his gringo friend long and hard. "You're telling us you want to stay in the business?"

Christian stared back at the man he considered a loveable scoundrel. "Yes, that's what I'm telling you. We want to stay in the business."

The two men looked at each other, analyzing their antagonist. DEA was not mentioned. FBI was not mentioned.

"No more monkeys?" Rodolfo asked.

"What monkeys?"

Rodolfo Vega smiled from behind his moustache. "The monkeys in the business, you know."

Christian understood. "You mean no more monkey business?"

A big smile materialized. "Aah, yes, most definitely! No more business of monkeys. I understand." The fisherman farmer stood, walking around the table to face Christian. "We shake on it."

Christian took the hand being offered. Rodolfo Vega had an iron grip. A reminder these men were for real.

Christian suspected at that moment the Vega brothers had just pulled him into their Circle of Trust. Perhaps in Mexico these good ole boys didn't call it *Omertá*, but whatever they called it, Christian was now a part of it.

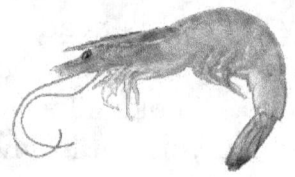

The two American couples and their kids had just arrived after a four-hour drive from Scottsdale, Arizona and all were hungry. They settled themselves around two large plastic tables on the patio of the Playa Encanto Hotel. The patio was partially protected from the scalding Sonoran Desert heat by dozens of blue umbrellas.

Dr. Alexiadis, a neurosurgeon, had organized the trip down to the colorful fishing village inviting his colleague Dr. Della Croce and his family. They were enthusiastically looking forward to a weekend of beach and water and fun.

Dr. Alexiadis admired the turquoise waters of the Sea of Cortés, the white sandy beaches, and the incredible blue skies without a single cloud. He was perspiring heavily, desperately yearning for a cold beer. The multitude of fishing boats at anchor in the harbor caught his attention.

A young waiter greeted them with a friendly smile. He introduced himself as Ramón, while distributing paper menus to the newly arrived Americans.

"Before you do anything else," Dr. Alexiadis addressed the waiter, please bring Cokes for all the kids and beers for the rest of us. Pacificos, please."

The waiter nodded with a smile, rapidly relaying the orders for drinks to another waiter standing by.

Once the drinks arrived, accompanied by multiple ice-filled glasses, Dr. Alexiadis gulped down half a Pacifico beer. "What kind of boats are those?"

Ramón, the waiter flashed a bright smile, leaning on the back of one of the chairs with both hands. "Those are shrimp boats, *señor.*"

"Shrimp boats? Who owns them?"

"They're owned by the *coperativas, señor.*"

"The what?"

"The *coperativas, señor.*"

"And what are those?"

Ramón looked at the American, smiling. "They are the owners of the boats."

"Well, that was clear as mud," Dr. Alexiadis remarked.

43

Angel the Shrimp
Sea of Cortés

Angel the shrimp swam with the cloud late at night, at last entering the deeper southern waters of the Sea of Cortés. The water temperature getting colder was the only indication Angel had that something was changing. They were diving. The cloud of shrimp descended into the deeper waters of the sea, distancing itself from its multitude of enemies swimming closer to the surface.

Millions of shrimp would have felt happiness, if they had been able to feel. Happiness at having escaped the mouths of predators on their five-hundred-mile voyage starting at the delta of the

Colorado river. The relatively lucky few still forming the cloud would now settle in deeper waters, their collective instinct telling them there was nothing more to fear. The remaining of their two years of life on this blue planet would be spent in the peaceful pursuit of plankton and enjoying the company of others of their species.

Angel finally gave himself the luxury of swimming away from the cloud. He tentatively drifted away from the millions of traveling companions he'd cherished for over one month, adapting to the cooler temperatures of the water two thousand feet below the surface. The million-year old program guiding his actions directed him to concentrate on two things, finding food and finding a mate. During his young life, on his southbound journey Angel had managed to avoid being eaten by numerous marine predators and captured by the tentacles of the surface monsters.

Finally, Angel, the Blue shrimp, was able to swim without peril in the deep waters of the Sea of Cortés.

Life was good.

The End

TERMS OF USE

The author gratefully acknowledges the copyrighted or trademarked status and trademark owners of the following mentioned in this work of fiction:

Aeromexico, American Express, Arizona Republic, ASU, Bayliner, Boeing, Caterpillar, Chardonnay, Chevy, Corona, Crown Royal, Cummins, Dos Equis, Ford Bronco II, Forrest Gump, Genie, Jeep Cherokee, Johnny Walker, Mercury Verado, Metildopa, Misty, Modelo, Mustang, Outback Restaurant, Pacifico, Patron Tequila, Samsung Galaxy. Suburban, Tecate, Tiffany, Tullamore Dew, United, Yale.

Other novels on Amazon by Maurice Azurdia

THE FOURTH STRIPE

Captain Valerie Wall is a pilot for a major international airline. She knows that being in command of a commercial airliner is one of the most stressful professions, yet all her training has not prepared her for the dangerous intrigue she accidentally encounters when flying based out of Berlin on a temporary assignment.

The Fourth Stripe allows a rare and candid behind-the-scenes glimpse into the exclusive and sometimes glamorous world of international airline pilots, taking the reader from the shady streets of Istanbul to some of the world's greatest cities, Mexico City, Berlin, New York.

Available as an eBook at Amazon and other bookstores.

e - A novel

The Ebola epidemic in west Africa continues to explode, as the world watches. America is not invulnerable to the virus. As the first suspected cases of hemorrhagic fever begin to appear outside of Africa, strange events surround them. Dr. Ariel Chevalier, an emergency medicine resident at a prestigious medical center in Phoenix, Arizona, finds herself in the middle of the newly developing crisis. But Africa is not the problem. The problem is something else. Something unreal. And the creepiest part is its inherent plausibility.

Available as an eBook at Amazon and other bookstores.

About the Author

Maurice Azurdia is a pilot instructor for a major airline and has seen his writings published in FLYING Magazine and his cartoons published in the magazine of ALPA, the Air Line Pilots Association. He is a cartoonist, artist and novelist.

Maurice flew as an international airline pilot for one of America's legendary airlines, is an aerospace engineer and found himself Romancing the Stone in Guatemala, going after a green marble quarry.

He currently resides in The Great American Southwest with his wife Cheryl, where he is writing his next novel.